Friction | 7

Friction 7

Best Gay Erotic Fiction

Edited by
Jesse Grant

alyson books
los angeles

© 2004 BY ALYSON PUBLICATIONS. AUTHORS RETAIN COPYRIGHT TO THEIR INDIVIDUAL
PIECES OF WORK. ALL RIGHTS RESERVED.

MANUFACTURED IN THE UNITED STATES OF AMERICA.

THIS TRADE PAPERBACK ORIGINAL IS PUBLISHED BY ALYSON PUBLICATIONS,
P.O. BOX 4371, LOS ANGELES, CALIFORNIA 90078-4371.
DISTRIBUTION IN THE UNITED KINGDOM BY TURNAROUND PUBLISHER SERVICES LTD.,
UNIT 3, OLYMPIA TRADING ESTATE, COBURG ROAD, WOOD GREEN,
LONDON N22 6TZ ENGLAND.

FIRST EDITION: FEBRUARY 2004

04 05 06 07 08 **a** 10 9 8 7 6 5 4 3 2 1

ISBN 1-55583-827-8

LIBRARY OF CONGRESS CATALOGING-IN-PUBLICATION DATA
    FRICTION 7 : BEST GAY EROTIC FICTION / EDITED BY JESSE GRANT.—1ST ED.
      ISBN 1-55583-827-8
      1. GAY MEN—FICTION. 2. GAY MEN'S WRITINGS, AMERICAN. 3. EROTIC
    STORIES, AMERICAN. I. TITLE: FRICTION SEVEN. II. GRANT, JESSE.
    PS648.H57F757 2004
    813'.01083538'0866420951 1—DC22   2003063000

COVER PHOTOGRAPHY BY BODI BROWN.

Contents

Preface

I couldn't be more pleased with this collection. Well, I suppose if John Ashcroft had come through with that foot-slave story he promised me, I'd be a *little* more pleased. That John—he's such a tease!

Boys, what you have in your sweaty mitts is the raunchiest, edgiest, most wank-a-licious collection of erotica I've assembled to date. And as you know, I've assembled quite a few collections, and I've done a lot of wanking. What wouldn't I do for my art?

In "Tail Spin" newcomer J.D. Roman spins a slick and steamy aquatic tale that makes most of my three-way experiences look positively tame. (I usually try to perk up a ho-hum three-way by pulling a fourth hottie onto the flesh pile.) Dale Chase comes up with some downright wicked solutions to political hypocrisy and corporate greed in "Politically Incorrect" and "Payback." Jim McDonough continues the up-the-ass-of-the-establishment theme with a scandalous confessional scene in "Act of Contrition." And Jack Whitestone takes us back to those innocent adolescent days of summer love and Vaseline in "Arkansas Heat." Looking for the perfect recipe for a little one-handed late-night delight? Add to the aforementioned naughty mix some piggy sex from Bob Condron, a nice slab of muscle worship from Bearmuffin, a hundred-yard dash of jock action from Kyle Walker, and a heaping helping of raw man-on-man action from a host of your favorite smut scribes. Just like the colonel's chicken, this collection is finger-lickin' good!

—Jesse Grant

Over the Moon
Christopher Pierce

"Hey, this is a 28-year-old Brother, 6 foot 2, 200 pounds of solid muscle, short buzz-cut hair, goatee and mustache, nine-inch cock. I'm looking for another Brother to be my personal bottom boy. I'm gonna send you over the moon, man. Leave me a message. Name's Todd. Peace/out."

I'd never answered an ad on a phone line before, but there was something about this voice that struck me.

Right between my legs, that's where it struck me.

My dick started to get hard at just the sound of it. I wondered what this guy was like in person...whether he could do this to me with just his voice, what might it be like to actually meet him?

But I knew I'd delayed long enough—I had a secret, and I'd kept it long enough. I had to tell it to someone. I had to reveal what I'd been hiding for years, ever since I first came out. And this man sounded like just the stud I could bare my soul to.

Besides baring my hungry butt to, I mean.

I left the guy a message in his "mailbox," my voice probably sounding meek and timid after his full, deep intonations, including my phone number.

To my surprise, he called me within an hour.

"Hello?" I said.

"This Randy?" that unmistakable voice said in my ear, and my

1

cock started to get stiff. I lay down on my bed on my back, staring at the ceiling.

"Yes…Todd, is that you?"

"You got it, man." he said.

"I…thanks for calling me so soon. I figured you must get a ton of messages."

"I do," Todd said, "but yours is the only one I wanted to answer tonight."

"Wow," I said, knowing it sounded stupid even before it was out of my mouth. Todd didn't seem to mind, though. "Thanks for calling."

There was a pause.

"You already said that."

"Did I?" I said, realizing that I was lightly sweating. "Sorry."

"It's OK. So you said in your message to me that you've got a secret. What's up with that?"

"Oh, well, you've gotta meet me to find out." I said, hoping he wouldn't hang up on me. Instead, he laughed.

"All right—a little mystery. I like that." Todd said. "How old are you again?"

"Twenty-six."

"And the rest of your stats—remind me."

My right hand, which had been resting on my chest, slid—as if by its own will—down my abdomen until it was between my legs. I started to rub myself through the denim of my jeans as I obeyed his command.

"5 foot 9, 165 pounds, light-skinned, short hair, kind of slender."

"You sound good enough to eat," Todd said.

"Now you're getting me excited," I said in what I hoped was a seductive voice.

"Randy, you've been excited the whole time we've been talking. Am I right?"

I felt sheepish. Not much slipped past this guy. I figured I might as well be honest with him from here on out. It was obvious he could read me like a book, even though I was a total stranger and we couldn't even see each other.

"Yes, you're right," I answered.

"And how did I know that?"

"Uh…" I said, fumbling for an answer. "You're real smart?"

Todd laughed again. Delicious warmth from my groin was seeping through the rest of my body, making me feel dreamy and horny at the same time.

"Wrong!" he said. "I *am* remarkably intelligent, but that's not why I know you before we've even met."

He paused for so long, I had to ask the obvious question.

"Then why?"

" 'Cause you're the one, Randy."

"The one what?"

"My bottom boy." Todd said. "The guy I'm going to make my little bottom boy."

I couldn't believe what I was hearing.

Reaching down between my legs, I unzipped my jeans and took hold of my cock and started jerking myself off.

"You serious, dude?" I asked.

"I'm always serious," he answered. "You're the one I'm going to send over the moon."

"Cool," I said, hoping he'd explain more. I gently stroked my tool, letting the raw, hot pleasure fill me up. My breathing started to get harder.

"You know what I'd do if I was there?" he asked.

"What?"

"Are you lying on your bed?"

"Yeah," I said.

"I'd come in the room and stand at the edge of your bed."

"And?"

"And I'd just look at you, just stare, without hardly even blinking, just look at you and your body, as if I could see through your clothes."

"Yeah?"

"And you take them off—your shirt, your shorts, everything. I don't have to say anything to you, do anything to you…just by looking at you, I make you strip."

I let go of myself only long enough to set the phone down on the bed and rip my shirt and jeans off. Grabbing the phone in one hand and my dick in the other, I started jacking myself even faster than before, loving the sound of his voice in my ear and the feel of my hard cock in my fist.

"That's hot, man," I said. "I bet I'd stare back at you, waiting for your next move, wondering what was going to happen…"

"Uh huh, you got that right," Todd purred into my ear like a jungle cat. "Then I'd slip my own clothes off and climb into bed with you. I'd take your cock in my mouth and line mine up with your mouth and you'd know what to do."

"Oh, yeah, man, I'd suck you off nice and good."

"So there we'd be, in a perfect sixty-nine, and we'd pleasure each other until we had to pull out…"

"And then?"

I was reaching crisis point. My balls were drawing up inside my body, preparing to release the mounting pressure within them.

"And then," Todd said, "I'd jerk your dick and you'd jerk mine until we both shot our hot loads all over the bed and each other. And while I listened to you groan and cry with passion, I'd know I'd accomplished my goal."

"Which was?" I panted.

"Sending you over the moon, of course."

And I came, squirting my spunk juice like a fountain of milk, and it splattered onto my chest and pecs. I don't know how long I lay there, luxuriating in the orgasm Todd had created in me.

After a while, I heard him talking, as if coming out of a dream.

"Randy?" he said. "You OK, man?"

"Yes," I said. "Oh, yes."

"You ready to meet me?"

"I'm there!" I said, delighted.

Todd gave me his address, and I wrote it down on a piece of paper. We didn't live too far away from each other—we were only about 15 minutes apart.

I trembled the whole time I drove to Todd's place. It was so amazing, what I was doing—I'd never done anything like this before. But here I was, driving to a stranger's apartment in the middle of the night.

It was more than a little strange.

But…

I really wanted to be his bottom boy.

And I really wanted to get sent over the moon.

After five minutes of looking, I finally found a parking space near his building. I walked up to the gate and buzzed for him.

"Randy?" his voice said from the speaker.

"It's me, Todd."

"Come on up. I'll unlock my door."

The gate clicked open and I walked in. I rode the elevator to the top floor and walked out into the hallway. It was very quiet, and I didn't see any other guests or residents. Well, of course I didn't. It was after midnight—most normal people had jobs to go to in the morning and didn't call phone-sex lines when they should be sleeping.

Come to think of it, I had a job to go to in the morning myself.

But that hadn't stopped me from doing this.

It was the voice.

Todd's voice…

Soon enough I found his apartment. The door was slightly open, and all I could see through it was darkness.

"Todd?" I said softly.

There was no answer.

I pushed the door open and walked into his entryway. Once inside, I quietly closed the door behind me.

It was a big place, I could tell that even in the dark. There was a lot of open space, not much furniture. After a moment's hesitation, I slipped out of my shoes and walked into the main room in my socks.

"Todd," I said again, just before my mouth dropped open.

A fantastic view opened out in front of me.

I could see the whole city.

It was incredible—the window I was looking out of seemed to

take up almost the entire wall. Here, from the top level of this tall apartment building, I could see everything.

Thousands of shimmering, sparkling lights defined the shape of the city, blanketing the land like the stars above covered the sky and far above, looking down on everything, was the moon.

It was breathtaking.

I didn't even want to know how much the monthly rent for this apartment was. It was probably more than what I made in a year.

Suddenly there were hands on my shoulders—someone had come up behind me while I stood there staring at the view.

"Randy."

That voice was in my ear again, but this time it was real. He was there with me, right behind me.

"Don't turn around yet," he said. "I want you to see the city while I undress you."

"You're going to un—" I started to say when he gently put a hand over my mouth.

"Shhh…" he whispered, and I shut up. Todd pulled my shirt up and over my head, loosened my jeans and let them fall. I stepped out of them, stripped off my socks, and stood there naked.

Trembling.

And his hands were on me. Everywhere. They caressed me, stroked me, ran over every inch of my body. When his palms lightly passed over my nipples I actually gasped. Todd's hands were cool, smooth, almost delicate as they felt me, yet I could sense the strength that lay behind them.

Then he took hold of my cock and balls, gripping them in one hand, squeezing them gently in his fist.

"Mmm…" I murmured in pleasure.

"Yeah," he said. "My little bottom boy likes his man's hands on him, doesn't he?"

"Oh, yeah…" I whispered.

So far I'd only felt his hands, but then he pressed his body against mine. I felt his enormous penis rub against my ass and I couldn't resist pushing back against him. This seemed to amuse him.

"You want it bad, don't you, bottom boy?" he asked.

"Oh, yes," I said. "Please, Todd, please..."

"Please what?"

"Please...take me! Do whatever it is you're going to do! You've got me so fuckin' hot, I'm going out of my head!"

"Bend over, boy," he said, and I obediently followed his command, bending at the waist and reaching down for the floor with my hands.

Just as I was realizing that my asshole was now totally open and vulnerable, I felt Todd's warm face between my butt-cheeks.

"Mmm..." I moaned as he gently licked and sucked my asshole, breathing in the clean, musky scent of my body.

"Oh yeah," he said between licks of his tongue. "You like me rimming your ass, don't you, boy?"

"Yes..." I whispered.

I could feel the soft hair of his mustache and goatee on my most delicate body part as his mouth did its magic work. My erect cock was jutting out from my body, its length angling up toward the ceiling of the dark room.

"You like your big strong Brother to take care of you."

"You know it, man," I said.

Then he stopped and stood back up, putting his hands on my shoulders again.

"Go where I direct you, Randy," he said into my ear.

"Yes, Todd," I answered, "I'll do anything you say."

With the pressure of his hands on my shoulders he directed me where he wanted me: out of the big main room, down a hallway to a smaller room, this one with the blinds drawn. What little light there was came from under the slats, probably from the moon and stars outside.

It was Todd's bedroom.

He gently pushed me in, toward the bed.

"You can turn around now," he said, and I did. Even in the dark, I could see enough of him to know one thing...

God, was he hot!

Totally naked—big and muscular, very dark skin, handsome facial hair, strong face, nice big half-hard cock swinging between his legs...this guy'd stepped out of a muscleman magazine!

My cock flexed at the sight.

Todd smiled as he saw my reaction to him.

"Now," he said, and I knew just what he meant.

I backed up onto the bed, leaning up against the pile of pillows at the head of it. Todd followed me, crawling onto the bed like a jungle cat, sleek and beautiful and completely seductive. He was big and muscle-bound but somehow graceful at the same time.

He crawled on top of me, resting his weight on me, pinning me down. I couldn't think of anywhere I'd rather be.

He kissed me.

My whole body was infused with warmth and pleasure as his mouth touched mine and gently massaged it with lips and tongue. It was passionate, intense...we'd just met, but somehow it felt romantic and meaningful, as if this was the beginning of something wonderful.

His tongue entered my mouth and I welcomed it, caressing it gently with my own tongue as he explored me.

He wrapped his arms around me and held me tight, his kiss getting more insistent. I hugged him back, loving the feel of his strong body on top of me, and the sensation of his now completely hard cock against my leg.

I don't know how long we kissed, but it seemed both extended and short, as if it lasted forever in the moment but was over too soon.

Todd looked down at me with his stunning eyes.

"Tell me," he said.

"What?" I asked, delirious from his kiss.

"Tell me your secret, Randy."

"Well..."

"Don't close any part of yourself to me," he said as he flexed his fingers, kneading my flesh and muscle between them. "I want to know what you've hidden. Share it with me..."

Now that the moment was here, I felt somehow ashamed, even though I knew that was ridiculous.

"I've never been," I whispered.

"What do you mean?"

"I've never been with a Brother," I said.

"Never?" Todd asked. "You've only had sex with white boys?"

"No Brothers yet."

He didn't say anything, just gently kissed and nibbled my cheeks, my chin, my neck, playfully, affectionately.

"Todd?" I said.

"Yeah?"

"Did you hear me?"

"I heard you," he said.

"Well, what do you think? Are you…mad?" I asked.

"Mad?" he said, his head rising up so his eyes could meet mine again. "Of course not."

"No?"

"No," he said firmly. "If I'm your first Brother, then that means something special."

"What?" I said.

"It means that you're mine," Todd said, grinning.

"Yeah?"

"Yeah."

"Well, if I'm yours…what're you going to do with me?" I asked.

"Send you over the moon, of course," he said.

"How?"

"Turn over on your stomach," he said, getting up on his knees.

I obeyed, and rested my head on my arms against the pillow. I heard Todd open the drawer of his bedside nightstand and take something from it.

The distinctive crackling sound of a plastic condom package being ripped open was loud in the quiet room. The squirt of a lube bottle followed, and then I felt Todd's finger nuzzle in between my butt cheeks and touch my tight brown asshole.

"Mmm…" I moaned, even though he really didn't need any encouragement. He knew what he was doing and wasn't going to stop for anything. He massaged my hole, gently rubbing up and down with his finger. Slowly but surely he started pressing in, and soon I opened to him and he was able to push his finger inside me. Just having that one tiny part of him inside me, his condom-covered finger, was exhilarating.

I pushed my butt back toward him to let him know I was having a good time.

"You like that, don't you?"

"Oh, yeah."

"You'd like it even more if I put more than one finger in, wouldn't you?"

"Yes," I said. "Please, I want more of you inside me."

A second finger joined the first, and soon three of his fingers were in. He pushed smoothly in and out, and my butt hole obediently gripped him, stretching to accommodate the welcome intrusion.

"That's real nice," he whispered, "yeah, it feels so hot, you're one hot boy, my hot boy, yeah…"

"You're making me feel so good, Todd." I answered. "You're so fucking sexy, man."

"I think you're ready for the main course," he said as he pulled his fingers out of me. I felt empty without him and couldn't wait for what was coming next.

I heard Todd open a fresh condom and unroll it onto his tool. After slicking it up with some lube, he lay down on top of me and started sliding it between my ass cheeks. Panting with desire, I groaned beneath him.

"Please fuck me, Todd," I said. "Come on, man, please!"

"I'll fuck you when I'm ready, bottom boy," he said. "First I want you to get all hot and bothered."

"I'm already hot and bothered!" I said, hoping I didn't sound as desperate as I felt. "Plow me, dude!"

I couldn't see him, but I knew he was grinning.

"You want this bad, don't you, Randy?" he said.

"I need it, Todd! More than anything!"

"Now *that's* what I wanted to hear," he whispered.

And he fucked me.

As he entered me from behind, I felt every centimeter of his exquisite cock penetrate through the ring of muscle that was my sphincter and slide inside me. It was an incredible, heart-stopping sensation, and I gripped the pillow beneath my head tightly as the waves of feeling washed over me.

"I'm taking you, Randy," Todd said into my ear, as he started thrusting in and out of me to a hypnotic rhythm only he could hear. But then I heard it too—it was the beat of our hearts, two Brothers together, sharing an exquisite experience, performing a primitive ritual as old as the earth.

I started pushing myself back, to try to get as much of him inside me as possible, throwing my head back in ecstasy.

"I reclaim you," he said above me. And it was true.

Nothing I'd ever felt could compare with this.

It was like my life was starting over—here, and now. I was reborn, pulled from the womb by this powerful man.

I felt Todd explode inside me, filling up every inch of the condom with his hot spunk.

"You're mine," he said.

And it was true. My own orgasm bloomed inside me, and I was hurtling, just as he said I would be, over the moon and into the stars.

It was as if I'd died and gone to heaven—nothing would ever be the same.

I don't know how long we held ourselves there, but it seemed like a single second of time being stretched far beyond its limits, a second of timelessness where nothing existed except us. When every last drop of semen had squirted out of us, and our carnal howls of passion had ceased, we separated, and I collapsed into Todd's welcoming arms. I knew that when I woke up, I would have a new day—and a new life.

Vulnerable Youth

Roddy Martin

Morning washed over the suburbs, making the leaves green and the air delicious. Mr. Wood knotted his tie and grabbed his briefcase. Crisp and blond, he was off for a spot of insider trading, and then luncheon with the board of Vulnerable Youth, an organization that saved 18-year-olds from cigarettes, dope, and pornography.

He heard noise in the bathroom. The shower? How could that be? His wife had left an hour ago. But yes. The shower was running, and someone was in it.

"Hi, Mr. Wood. Remember me?"

Through the glass door, Mr. Wood saw broad shoulders and a slender waist. He saw lower-back dimples. As nonchalantly as he could, Mr. Wood said, "Sorry, your name's not coming up."

Out beamed a face with a Florida tan, a bright smile and bright black eyes. "Joseph, Marta's son."

Marta, the cleaning lady? Mr. Wood said, "Of course."

"And you got me that job through Vulnerable Youth, waxing floors."

"Sure. So, what brings you here?"

"Our shower's out." Turning, the guy scrubbed and hummed.

What to do? Mr. Wood decided to play along, to see the guy out and change the locks. He went to the den and called his assistant, Stanek. "Listen, I'm running late."

"How late? We've got the…"

"I know. I'll be there."

Mr. Wood watched minutes tick by. The sound of the shower grew vexing, aggressive somehow. It crackled through the nerves like static. Mr. Wood felt vague trepidation.

He strode into the bathroom. "We need to put a cap on this."

Joseph was soaping his front. His pecs were hard-edged and beefsteak flat. Suds ran down a canal from breastbone to navel and into side trenches. And lower…

"Did you say something?" Joseph shouted.

"Just checking my tie. You don't mind?"

"It's your place."

Lower, the glass got blurry, and why was Mr. Wood looking anyway? He looked again, though.

Such a vital kid. Surely Mr. Wood would remember helping someone like this, if indeed he had. But then Mr. Wood's involvement with Vulnerable Youth was advisory, more about cachet than social concern.

He found that his tie was crooked and his nipples stiff. "Well," he said, "I've got to get going, so if we could——-"

"Still can't hear you."

The door opened. The soap flew out and skidded across the floor. "Dropped it," Joseph said cheerfully.

"Here."

Handing it in, Mr. Wood determined to keep custody of the eyes. Of course in that context, most guys would take a glance, just to check, and Mr. Wood…wow.

"Gimme the soap," Joseph said.

"You're wearing briefs."

"Yeah. It seemed rude to get naked in someone else's house."

A high-cut, filmy flesh-tone, the briefs etched the elevations on Joseph's very long shaft—the mounds at the bottom, the crown at the top, surface pipe in between. For some reason, all Mr. Wood could see was the Dow shooting up.

The next thing, he was down staring at Joseph's waistband. He would reach for it in a moment—he felt this in his palms. He'd pull it down, get socked and ridiculed, all for an inexplicable whim. But the moment passed.

"How about that soap?" Joseph asked.

"Yes, sure."

"Can you—?" He lifted his foot. Stupid with relief, Mr. Wood was overjoyed to wash it. Who cared about water? Who cared about sleeves?

"Cool. How about the other one now? How about my back?"

The rear panel of Joseph's briefs was an elongated V. It covered only the cleft, and not even all of that. Mr. Wood worked around it. Far around it, using the length of the soap bar.

"What a great day," Joseph remarked.

"It is."

"Move in more. Yeah, great day to hang without a shirt, check out beautiful women. Move the soap in more. Don't be shy."

Joseph hooked his thumbs under his waistband and snapped it down. His butt was a cinnamon peach.

"Is that how you'll spend the day?" Mr. Wood asked.

"Maybe."

I'm having a homosexual response, thought Mr. Wood. His tongue tasted scary. Thank God this was an aberration and would soon pass. In an hour, he'd stride into his office, still a semiyoung Turk.

"Deeper," Joseph said.

Bending split the peach in two. Mr. Wood's pulse went fizzy.

"Deeper."

Squatting split the peach all the way. Mr. Wood beheld a hard, round perineum lined with fluff. He beheld a slit the size of a sideways dime. He lathered and scrubbed them with his bare hands.

"Great, rinse."

Ass water splashed back on Mr. Wood's front, and in his face. He knelt, buoyed by adrenaline bubbles, while Joseph pulled on his briefs.

"Thanks, man," Joseph smirked, as if that was that.

Mr. Wood couldn't form a response. The shower beat in his ears like stripper music. He watched Joseph's shaft glide counterclockwise. The tip emerged, with its V-groove and foreskin tether. Mr. Wood dove for it.

"What are you doing?" Joseph asked blandly. "Stop. Don't. Oh hell, if you gotta." He shoved his cock down Mr. Wood's throat.

"Umgh, umgh, umgh." Now Mr. Wood had what he wanted, thighs, flanks, pecs—youth! Youth was hard. Youth was salty. It didn't give a crap. It jerked in your mouth.

"Suck my balls," Joseph growled.

"Umgh."

"Lick my hole."

"Umgh, umgh."

"Oh. Oh yeah. Ooh!"

Everything south of Mr. Wood's tailbone clenched. Orgasm…when he came to, his hair and shorts were full of sperm. He sat in the water, gulping.

Joseph said, "Sir, you're a mess."

Meanwhile in the city, Mr. Wood's assistant ran his fingers through his expensive haircut. Stanek was perspiring. If he didn't hear from Wood, he'd soon be perspiring a lot more. He took off his tie, opened his collar.

There was a knock on the door. "Enter," he barked.

"Hey, Mr. Stanek. Need your signature."

Looking up, Stanek saw a shiny, brown-eyed brunet, one of Wood's Vulnerable Youth gofers. He said, "Brian? Run and get me an iced latte."

"Love to, but can't."

"I beg your pardon?"

"I brought a package," Brian replied. "I'm not an intern here anymore."

"No? What are you?"

"Self-employed."

Stanek took in the courier's cap and the clipboard. He said, "Terrific, but can't you run and get a—" The phone rang. "Excuse me. Hello."

"Dave, it's me," said Mr. Wood. "I'll be later than I thought."

"No way," Stanek hissed, carrying the phone toward the window. "No dice. Listen, the SEC—"

"Something's up."

"What's up? Sir, your voice is funny. Are you all right?"

The line went dead.

Brian said, "Mr. Stanek, the package." Turning, Stanek saw washboard abs and a swimmer's chest, a cock like plumbing fixtures.

"What are you doing?" Stanek sputtered. "Pull up your shorts."

"Make me."

Lunging for the shorts, Stanek caught the inside of Brian's thigh. The flesh was solid and cool. Soothing. Stanek lingered. Rolling the skin over Brian's cock muscle, he felt his energy rebound.

Brian said, "I could make jokes about latte."

"Save them."

"I still need for you to sign."

Stanek signed and sucked. He didn't notice the credit card authorization.

"Dave, it's me. I'll be later than I thought."

Mr. Wood was flat on the bed. His legs were open. Joseph was fingering his butt.

"No way, no dice," said Stanek.

In went a finger. It felt inconvenient, neither good nor bad. Mr. Wood said, "Something's up."

"What's up?"

The finger hit a wall. It prodded, started to buff. All at once, glitter swirled in Mr. Wood's testicles.

Joseph parted Wood's legs. Pumping his cock, he rubbed the head on Mr. Wood's asshole. "Want it?"

"Sir, are you all right?" Stanek asked.

"Oh, God, yes!"

The journey up the canal was searing. It seemed longer than Joseph's eight or so inches. Once Joseph was docked, once his balls bumped butt, Mr. Wood's sphincter went wild.

Joseph gasped, "Holy crap fuck!"

"What's wrong. Are you stuck?"

"No."

But Joseph's tugging and toiling threatened to drag along Mr. Wood's entrails. "You are stuck," he said.

"I'm not stuck." Joseph threw his head back. He screwed up his features, turned red with concentration. Mr. Wood felt three hot shots deep inside, and Joseph's cock began to move.

"Now." Joseph hoisted Mr. Wood's ankles ceilingward. "Payback time."

Mr. Wood watched Joseph's abdomen grind and flex. It looked the way it felt—painful, gorgeous.

"Great mattress," Joseph said through his teeth.

His bush had been trimmed to a two-inch crescent. Every time it lurched forward, fluid forced its way through Mr. Wood's cock slit.

Joseph nodded at a picture on the bed stand. "That your wife? She's hot."

Sinews, protein, butt-crack hair...

Mr. Wood's ankles were at his ears. Joseph had pivoted around. He was bouncing, fucking backward. He threw his feet onto the wall.

The kid was a derrick. Aah...

So much come. Coating Mr. Wood's chest. Flowing from his ass. Drying in his ear. Mr. Wood rolled over.

There was Joseph rifling through his wallet. "I don't want you to change the sheet," he said.

Midnight enveloped the suburbs. Stars glowed. Fireflies flickered. Joseph climbed through Mr. Wood's kitchen window, wearing his designer briefs and nothing else. He examined Mr. Wood's collectibles. He raided his refrigerator.

There was a sound. In wafted a *Playboy* babe, trailing a diaphanous peignoir. *Hola,* the wife! Joseph plumped his basket.

But with a furtive glance, Mrs. Wood opened a cupboard under the sink. She fished out a vodka bottle and a cookie jar, from which she pulled a brownie. She sat at the table and proceeded to get fucked-up.

The phone rang. "Dave Stanek again," rasped a voice. If you're there, pick up. We're under siege in many respects. Pick up, damn it."

Joseph shook his head. These people were unbelievable.

Upstairs, Mr. Wood was out at last, when his wife, back from her midnight snack, collapsed on top of him.

"Honey, are you all right?"

"Bitchin'," she murmured, rolling over.

Mr. Wood's spine felt like wood and his eyelids like sandpaper. The corners of his mouth were chapped, his ass felt sore, and his cock slit blasted. Somehow, all this gave him a hard-on. He'd go deal with it in the guest room if he didn't have to lie atop the come spot, lest his wife find it. Why, oh why hadn't he changed the sheet?

The door opened. In strolled two figures in moon-white briefs. "There he is," said one of them, Joseph. Mr. Wood's heart raced.

"He wears pajamas?"

"Looks like it."

Mr. Wood recognized the companion. It was that Vulnerable Youth intern, Brian. He'd been such a success story—why was he here? Why was he tossing aside the coverlet, ripping open Mr. Wood's pajamas? Why was his mouth sliding down Mr. Wood's cock?

"God," Brian said, between strokes. "These sheets are a mess."

"I know."

"Shhh," said Mr. Wood. "My wife—" Joseph's balls plopped in his mouth.

"Fucker's a mouthful," Brian muttered.

"Fucker needs a shave." Joseph rubbed his wet balls all over Mr. Wood's face. "I kind of like it."

"Hmm."

"Beats waxing floors."

Joseph turned Mr. Wood's cheek to the pillow. He started to fuck his mouth. Now the world felt right. Mr. Wood stopped listening for his wife's breath.

"Coming," Joseph huffed.

"Fuck, me too."

"Oh, yeah."

"Oh, yeah!"

"Oh...yeah."

Once again, Mr. Wood found himself soaked in sperm. Joseph clapped Brian on the back. "What now, pizza?"

"No, Chinese."

Their bare butts drifted out the door, leaving Mr. Wood alone with his future. Before he could contemplate it, he sank into sweet sleep.

Quads of Death

Greg Herren

His head is trapped between my thighs. My legs are crossed at the ankles and I am squeezing them together. His face is turning red. With his free hands he is trying to pull my legs apart to relieve the pressure on his head. Like he could pry my legs apart. Like anyone could. I squeeze tighter. He slaps my leg. "OK, OK, OK!"

I let go.

"Goddamn." He sits up, shaking his head. His reddish-blond hair is drenched in sweat. Beads of sweat roll down the deep valley between his pecs. "You weren't kidding when you said you had the quads of death."

I laugh. "I get a lot of submissions that way."

"I bet." He grins back at me. He's a good-looking guy. He's wearing a pair of baggy basketball shorts.

I'd seen him at the gym a few times. He had a great body, about 6-4 and all muscle. Great legs. Hard, round ass. Beautiful chest and arms. The first time I saw him he was wearing a skintight orange tank top and baggy shorts. My first thought was, *I've got to wrestle that dude.* Over the next few weeks I kept checking him out. He checked me out too—always a good sign. One day he came over and asked me to spot him on the bench. One thing led to another, and here he is, in my wrestling room. He'd never wrestled before, but he was definitely interested in it. He had the right look and body to be a major video star. When I felt he was ready, I'd introduce him to the right people. His debut match would be against me, most likely; that was how it usually worked.

In the meantime, I get to train him in the sport.

He stands up and stretches. All the walls in the wrestling room are covered in mirrors. The floor is covered with wrestling mats. I watch him, watch as the muscles in his back flex and contract. Damn if he isn't the sexiest guy I've had in here in a long while.

"You want to give it a try?" I ask. I've wanted to feel his legs around my head since I first saw him.

He turns back and grins at me. "Sure." He walks back over. "How should we do this?"

I get on my hands and knees. "Straddle my head." A standing head scissors is a great way to give him a feel for it. I feel his legs going on either side of my head. "Cross your ankles." He does. "Now squeeze." I feel some pressure, very slight. "Harder." He squeezes tighter. "Harder, Jamie. Put everything you've got into it."

"Are you sure?"

"Trust me."

Fuck me! I knew he had strong legs, but Jesus. He lets up for a minute and I gasp in some air. He squeezed again. I smack his leg. "OK, dude, OK!"

He lets up and I slip my head out. "Are you OK?" he asks.

"Fine." I grin up at him. "Great legs, man."

"I was worried I'd hurt you."

"Dude," I shake my head. "In wrestling you can't worry about that. Believe me, when you're fighting someone they will submit before you hurt 'em. If you start worrying, you'll get beat."

"How many times have you lost?"

"On video? Never." I grin at him. "I've lost private matches before."

"Wow. Cool." His face colors slightly. "Can I ask you an embarrassing question?"

I shrug. "Sure."

"Is it weird to get a hard-on when you're wrestling?"

"Dude," I laugh and pull my shorts tight across the crotch. "I got one right now."

He smiles. "Me too." He shrugs. "I mean, your head was right there between my legs, and I was squeezing, and it felt good, you know? I mean, like I had complete control over you. If I wanted to hurt you, I could. And I just started getting hard." He looks at me. "I mean, I even liked it when you were doing it to me."

"Head scissors is a pretty hot hold," I say. "It's my favorite—to put on or to be in. It always gets me hard."

"Cool."

"You wanna try to go a round?" I say. He isn't really ready. I've taught him some holds, but not how to counter anything. Then again, it's the best way to find out about his instincts, how quick he can think and move.

"Can't hurt, I guess."

I walk over to the closet and open the doors. I dig through a box and find a pair of bright red Speedos. I toss them to him. "Put these on."

He looks at them then at me. "Really?"

"Gotta get used to fighting in Speedos, Jamie."

"But…"

"Don't worry about getting a hard-on. Guys don't buy the videos to watch—they buy 'em to jack off to. You get a hard-on, that'll sell more videos. Don't be shy."

He hesitates for just a moment, then drops his shorts and jock. He kicks them off to a corner. His pubic hair is trimmed, and he does have a monster boner. He pulls up the suit. It barely covers his cock.

I drop my shorts. I've got my black one on already. My cock is hard and the head is peeking out of the top. I rearrange myself so it's covered. He's looking at it. I smile as I walk toward him. "Ready to get your ass kicked?" I growl.

He grins. "Bring it on."

We circle each other. I lunge at his legs and take him down. He falls back onto the mat with me on top. Before he can do anything I snake my legs around his and stretch his apart. I lock my arm around his head. My cock is pressed against his ripped abs as he struggles. I can feel the tip of his cock against my balls. I stretch his legs farther apart.

"Ouch! OK! I give!"

I let go but stay on top of him. He grins up at me. "Not much of a fight, huh?"

"You'll get better."

He reaches up and pulls my face down to his. Our lips meet. His are full and thick, and his tongue darts out into my mouth. His hands drift down to my ass and squeeze. I start to grind against his stomach. He shifts his weight and we roll until he is on top of me. Our crotches are together. He rubs his cock against mine. Damn, but it feels good.

His legs snake around mine and pull them apart. My eyes open. "Hey—"

His mouth closes down on mine again. His tongue is in my mouth as his legs pull mine farther apart. It hurts, but I can't speak as his tongue explores the inside of my mouth. He yanks again, and I moan. He lifts his head and smiles down at me. "Had enough, big guy?"

"You don't fight fair!" The sentence dies in a scream as he pulls my legs farther apart. "I give, you bastard! I give!"

He lets go and swings his legs around so that he is sitting on my stomach. His Speedo has come down a bit so that the head of his cock is pressing out.

"That was a dirty trick," I say.

"Never let your guard down—didn't you tell me that?" He is smiling. He lightly punches my pecs.

"You're learning." I reach up with both hands and put my thumbs underneath his chin. I shove back. As his head goes back I bring my legs up and wrap them around his head. The momentum flips him back, and I roll him over onto his side. His head is now trapped between my legs. I squeeze. His beautiful ass, encased in red Lycra, is right there in front of me. I smack it with one hand.

"Fuck!" he shouts.

I squeeze harder. I smack his ass again. His head feels great between my thighs. He is completely at my mercy. I yank at his trunks and pull them down. I smack his bare ass again. "Whaddaya say, boy?" *Smack*.

"No way!"

Squeeze. Smack. "OK, OK! I give I give I give!"

I let his head go and grab his Speedo with both hands and yank it all the way down to his ankles and off. He is naked, lying on his back on the mat.

"Oh, man." He shakes his head.

I stand up and slip off my Speedo. I stand looking down on him. I put one foot up on his chest and flex my upper torso. "Yeah," I say. "Still the man." He lies there, beaten. I'm not done.

I sit on his chest, my legs on either side of his head. I grab him by the hair and pull his head up. "Come on, pretty boy. Suck my dick."

He tries to twist his head away. "No way."

"Suck it or I'll hurt you some more."

I grab my cock with my free hand and use it to slap his face. "You know you want to."

"No."

Slap. Slap. Slap. "We're gonna stay here all day until you do."

He looks up at me, and a smile starts to form. He opens his mouth, and I slip my cock into it. He sucks on it, his tongue licking its underside. A low moan escapes my lips. "Yeah, that's it. Suck my cock." I reach over to the side of the mat where my bag sits. I pull out the bottle of poppers and uncork it. I take a deep whiff up one nostril and then the other. "Oh, fuck yeah." More blood rushes to my cock, making it stiffer and bigger. I bring the bottle down to his right nostril. He stops sucking for a moment while he inhales, then I put it under the other. His head drops back for a minute, and then his mouth is back on my cock again, bobbing on it, licking it. He grabs both of my nipples with his hands and pinches them both. Hard.

His head falls back. He smiles up at me. "I want you to fuck me."

"How bad do you want it?"

"I said fuck me!"

I slowly stand up. "Get up." He stands, his big hard cock swinging. I press the bottle of poppers to my nose and inhale again. I pass it back to him and he takes two big hits. I put the top back on and put it back in the bag. "You want me to fuck you, you gotta earn it." I smile at him as I walk toward. I make fists with both hands and punch him hard in the pecs. He staggers back a few steps and then jumps on me. I fall back on the mat, and before I know it his legs are around my head and he is squeezing the fuck out of it. His cock and balls are right in my face. "Come on, tough guy!" he shouts down at me. "Ain't so tough now, huh?"

My head is pounding. The fucker, the sneaky little shit, I'm not going to give in, I won't, I won't...

"Aargh! OK, OK, OK, I give I give I give."

He lets go of my head. He stands up. "Did I earn it?"

"Oh, you earned it all right." I stand up, still a little woozy. My cock and balls are aching. He's gotten the bottle of poppers and takes a couple of hits. I get out a condom and slip it over my cock. I get the bottle of lube out. "Down on all fours."

He smiles at me and gets down on his hands and knees and lifts that beautiful, so sweet, white ass up in the air. He wiggles it a little at me. *Oh, yeah, you're going to get fucked, boy,* I say to myself. I take the bottle away from him and took a hit. He spreads his cheeks wide. I slip the head of my cock into his ass.

He moans.

I slap both ass cheeks with my hands. Hard.

He moans louder.

I slap them again.

He tries to move back toward me to get my cock to go in. I move back. "Oh, no, bitch, I told you to work for it."

"I said fuck me!" he roars.

"Demanding little bottom whore, ain't ya?" I start to slowly slide my cock into his tight hole. It starts to open for me, willingly taking it in. He moans. I slowly start to slide it back out, but he tries to move back so it won't come out. I smack his ass again. "Hold still, bitch, or you won't get nothin'." He obliges. I keep sliding back, bit by bit. He is moaning. When it's almost all the way out I slam it back in as hard as I can, clenching my ass to shove it even farther. He screams.

"Yeah, you like that, don't you?" I start moving back slowly. I reach for a sock and dump the bottle of poppers into it. When the head of my dick is all that's left inside, I lean forward and tie the sock around his nose so that he can't help but breathe it in. He starts writhing. I slam it in again and start moving faster.

His ass feels good, moist, and tight enough. He is breathing hard, faster. "Oh God oh God oh God oh God——"

I feel it. "I'm gonna come."

"Go ahead, I already have twice," he moans out.

I keep pounding, harder and faster. I explode with such force that I swear, if it weren't for the condom, I'd blow his head off.

I stay inside as my cock finishes dumping its loads. Then I pull back out and sit back on the mat. He stands up. There is a puddle of come on the mat. He unties the sock and throws it aside and sits down next to me. A string of come is hanging from his big dick. He leans over and kisses my neck.

"Damn," he says. "That was hot."

"Yeah."

"Is this how all of our sessions are gonna end?"

I grin at him. "I'm game."

He smiles. "Count me in, coach."

We kiss.

Act of Contrition
Jim McDonough

The smell of stale incense and burning candles set off a flood of memories as I entered the church. The sounds of the priest's footsteps echoed throughout the sanctuary as he walked down the marble aisle. I followed slowly behind him, not wanting him to see me, although my sneakers squeaked as I did so. Kneeling at the altar railing, he made the sign of the cross and then walked toward the confessional booths, stepping inside one at the front of the church— the same booth where I was forced to confess my many sins, once a week, by the nuns at school.

Sitting at a pew in the back, I stared up at the altar. The church still looked the same, even after 10 years. Light streamed inside, colored by the stained glass windows, and danced across the nave. I fully expected to be struck down by lightning for all the impure thoughts that were racing through my mind—my heart pounding as I got up and headed toward the chancel.

I stepped up to the altar where I had once served as altar boy and grasped one of the long, tapered beeswax candles off the altar and blew out the flame. I would need this later, I thought as I sauntered toward the confessional. Luckily, nobody else was in the church. My footsteps, like the priest's, echoed through the chamber. I paused at the confessional booth, and my heart raced. What if it wasn't him? What if I was wrong? I gulped and drew back the dark

27

green velvet curtain and stepped inside the booth. The curtain fell back, enveloping the small vestibule in darkness. I dropped to my knees. Moments later, the priest slid open the panel that separated us.

I began, making the sign of the cross. "Bless me, father, for I have sinned. It has been 10 years since my last confession."

I could just barely make out the priest's features through the screen, but I knew it was him—Father Blackwood. A guy doesn't forget the first man to suck his cock.

I wasn't sure why I had followed him inside. Maybe it was morbid curiosity; I certainly had no reason to be in the church or even in the neighborhood. After eight years at St. Paul's elementary school, four years at the high school, and the decade since, I was hardly a devout Catholic anymore.

He was a little older, but then again, so was I. From what I could tell, he had aged well. I noticed the graying around his temples. He was probably in his early 40s now. I was now in my late 20s. It had been 10 years since I had seen Father Blackwood—for that matter, 10 years since I had been inside the church—the last time being the summer after I graduated from St. Paul's. That was the summer Father Blackwood taught me all about cock sucking on a CYO trip to the Cape.

"It's been a long time, my son."

My cock grew stiff in my jeans as I thought back to that morning. His voice sent cold shivers down my spine. It was him—it was the same voice that had encouraged me to suck his cock in that motel room. I felt slightly panicked, wondering whether he recognized my voice.

Father Blackwood had led the weekend retreat of about 20 young people—all seniors in high school. He was always involved with the youth group. I wondered how many others knew why. I got stuck sharing a motel room with him and two other guys. I had just come out of the shower, my other roommates having already taken off for the day, when Father Blackwood returned from saying Mass. Standing with a white towel wrapped around my waist, I was still damp from the shower when he entered the room. The priest startled me at first. It's mostly a blur now, but I do remember his hand on my shoulder, the towel dropping to the floor, and Father Blackwood on his knees, worshiping my teenage dick with his mouth.

After he sucked me off, he pushed me to my knees and undid the zipper of his black pants. He forced me down on his hard flesh and I sucked him until he filled me, not with the word of God but with a mouthful of hot come. He made me swear on the Bible that was in the nightstand that I would never say anything to anybody about what had happened. The next morning after Mass, he did it again. I was racked with guilt for years afterward.

I gulped and tried to speak, trying to remember the words before they all came back to me. "These are my sins." I confessed to a few minor infractions—lying and taking God's name in vain.

"Are those all your sins?"

"No, Father. I have committed sodomy."

"Sodomy?"

"Yes, Father. Sodomy."

"Just one time?"

"No, Father. Hundreds of times. With hundreds of men." My cock was aching so…reaching down in the darkness, I gave in to sin. Undoing my fly, I pulled out my cock, slowly stroking it to its full glory.

"I've had sex with strange men at rest stops along the highway. I've participated in orgies and had my dick sucked at glory holes in rest rooms at the university."

I heard the priest gasp.

"Father, I don't feel complete unless I have a guy's cock in my mouth. I love the feel of a man's hot flesh sliding down my throat until he shoots a creamy load."

As I continued, the priest's breath became shallow and labored.

"And there's nothing I like more than having a guy ram his pounding cock up my tight asshole."

In the darkness, coming from the other side of the partition, I thought I heard the familiar sound of a zipper being pulled down, but I wasn't quite sure.

"You see, Father, an older man took advantage of me when I was in high school—in fact, here at St. Paul's. I've been hooked ever since."

"Did this man take you against your will?" he asked.

"At first, but then I realized that I liked it. Loved it, in fact."

"You didn't come here to confess your sins. Did you?"

"No. I came here to commit some more. I want to suck your cock, Father. I want to shove my big fat dick up your asshole."

The priest fell silent—most likely contemplating my generous offering.

"My son, this is the house of the Lord."

I snarled. "So what? I've done it just about everywhere else. Why not a church?"

"This is blasphemy."

"Oh, please, Father. I know you want it. The tone of your voice betrays you. You want me on my knees with your cock rammed down my throat. You've got a nice big one. Don't you, Father? Think how good it will feel having my mouth wrapped around your nice hard cock. I'll bet you're hard—aren't you?"

The priest didn't answer.

"What's the matter, Father? You only get off by fucking pimply-faced altar boys? How about trying it with a grown man?"

I didn't wait for a response. Getting up off my knees, it was time to set the rest of my plan into action.

Stuffing my hard-on back into my zipper, I yanked up my jeans. Drawing back the velvet curtain, I stepped back outside, reached for the handle to the cubicle that Father Blackwood occupied, and opened the door. The priest was shocked. From his expression I knew he recognized me. Stepping quickly inside the cubicle, I slammed the door. Enveloped in darkness again, I knelt on the floor in front of him.

There wasn't very much room to navigate, but I reached out and grabbed his crotch before the priest had time to act. He had already pulled out his cock, which was hard, just as I had suspected. No doubt Father Blackwood had been jerking off while I confessed my sins. I grinned, certain this wasn't his first time.

My fingers remembered his dick as if it had been the day before.

His skin was smooth, warm. I fondled his cock, coating it with his flowing precome. Unzipping my own pants, I hauled out my throbbing dick and slowly began to jack off.

In no time the confessional began to steam up from our hot breath. Father Blackwood surrendered to my lust, groaning as I manipulated his tool, which continued to ooze a heavy flow of precome. Flicking my tongue across his spongy cock head, I lapped up his nectar as if it were the sweetest wine. The taste of his dripping desire took me back to the first time I had sucked his prick in that motel room—my first taste of another man. I pressed forward, taking his entire length into my mouth. The priest groaned softly as I buried my nose in his pubic hair.

Forced to breathe through my nose as the priest's cock head slipped deeper into my throat, I became intoxicated by the different smells: the musky scent of his crotch, the faint odor of incense, the smoke from burning candles, which lingered in the background.

I pulled back and swirled my tongue around his cock head and into his piss slit, lapping up more of his flowing juices.

Knowing I would have to work fast, before another repentant sinner came to cleanse their soul, I reached behind the priest and slowly inched his pants down past his ass. He bolted upright, but I forced him against the wall of the confessional, which gave me more room to maneuver.

We grappled in mutual desire, a burning lust filling both our souls. I pulled my T-shirt over my head and, dropping it to the floor, then pulled at the buttons on his shirt, ripping off his clerical collar.

I fumbled in the darkness for the candle that I had removed from the altar earlier, pulled my lighter out of my pants pocket, and quickly lit the taper.

"It's time to do your penance now, Father. To make amends."

"No, Jacob."

He did remember. His eyes were wide pools, reflecting the flickering candlelight. Our shadows danced on the walls of the small enclosure. As I moved the flame closer to the priest's chest, he watched my every move.

Father Blackwood was in pretty decent shape for a man his age, for a man of any age, truth be known. His chest was well-defined and covered with a dense mat of dark fur. Watching him, I wondered whether he still coached the boys' softball team, wondered if he still hung out in the locker room after the softball games, checking out all the teenage boys before going back to the rectory to jerk off.

Hot wax dripped down the candle and burned my hand. I quickly repositioned the taper at an angle over the priest's chest and watched as drops of scalding paraffin hit his skin and drizzled down his chest, running down and through his chest hair like ropes of white-hot spunk. The priest grimaced every time the hot wax scalded his flesh. As he struggled to get free, I grabbed one of his nipples and twisted it hard. I then moved the flickering flame closer, singeing his chest hair.

Tempted to bring the flame closer to his nice round nipples and give Father Blackwood a true taste of hell, I said, "Don't cross me, Father. Do you know how long I felt guilty for what you did to me?" True, the memory of the pleasure remained, but so did the shame.

Holding the candle closer to his face, my hands were shaking, though my body was on fire. The priest trembled with fear but remained silent and finally stopped struggling, seemingly accepting his fate, his destiny.

"I felt guilty for years," I continued, ripping off the priest's shirt and dropping it to the floor. He stood nearly naked before me.

"Turn around, you motherfucker."

It was strange, as if Father Blackwood had taken a vow of silence. His pants draped around his knees, he slowly turned, exposing his pale white ass cheeks.

"Bend over." I said, pressing the palm of my hand to his back and pushing him.

The priest obeyed. I blew out the candle, and we were shrouded in darkness again. Taking a few moments for my eyes to adjust to the darkness, I groped blindly for his ass, the cheeks of which were covered with a fine coat of down. Probing his crack with my finger, I searched for his asshole. Finding it, I then replaced my probing finger with the blunt end of the candle. The priest groaned as I pushed the taper through his tight sphincter.

"Come on, Father…take it."

I shoved the candle deep inside his bowels before quickly pulling it right back out. Father Blackwood was moaning in pleasure—the pleasure no man of the cloth should ever know.

"Oh, Jesus," cried the priest. "Oh, Christ."

I fucked the priest with the candle until the heat of his bowels softened the once-rigid wax. He continued taking the Lord's name in vain as I plunged the taper in and out his gripping chute.

Leaving the candle buried deep inside his bowels, I forced the priest to turn around once more. Although it was difficult to see his throbbing member in the dim light in the confessional, he was stiff as a board, and a long string of precome dangled off the end of his tool, glistening in the hot shadows.

I had to have him.

I knelt down in front of the priest, my head slightly bowed. Ready to take his communion again, I looked up at him, waiting impatiently for him to give me his body and soul. Light, seeping in the cracks of the door of the confessional formed a halo around his head, making it seem as if I were kneeling before a vision.

Without warning, Father Blackwood leaned forward, forcing the entire length of his priesthood back into my throat. Uttering the same words of encouragement he had shared with me 10 years earlier, he said, "Take my cock, you little cocksucker."

I sucked the priest's cock as if it were my religious duty. He grabbed my hair, held me down, and furiously fucked my face, his cock plunging in and out of my warm, wet mouth. Even as I gasped for breath and started to choke, the priest continued to slam his shaft down my throat. He simply wouldn't let up.

I grabbed his nut sac and squeezed Father Blackwood's balls as hard as I could. The priest's cock slipped out of my mouth.

"You little bastard. You fucking shit," he sneered.

"I told you, Father. Don't fuck with me."

I grasped his ball sac again, rolling his nuts around in my right hand, kneading them in my fingers. Running my hands over his hallowed ground, I then grabbed the rosary beads that were dangling out of his pants pocket and wrapped them around his balls, pulling them tight. Taking his constricted nuts in my mouth, I rolled them around on my tongue, anointing them in my saliva. I lapped underneath his sweaty ball sac, in the hairy crevice between his scrotum and his legs. I took in a deep breath of his sweaty, funky odor—the scent you only come across when you're down between another man's legs. A shiver ran down my spine when I realized that this was not my imagination or a dream.

Father Blackwood moaned with every swipe of my tongue between his legs. Grabbing him around the waist, I motioned for the priest to turn around again so I could have better access to his ass. The priest let out a sharp groan as I yanked the taper from his rectum.

I was so far removed from what I was doing that it seemed my tongue had a mind of its own. I licked a path up his ass crack. He opened the interior of his body to my tongue, and as if I had died and gone to heaven, I felt myself open up to a new world. Only, my heaven was within the man who stood before me in the darkness. He clenched as I darted my tongue inside his hole, prompting me to respond by tugging hard on the rosary beads that were still cinched around his ball sac.

Father Blackwood's sphincter contracted with every twist of the rosary beads. I snaked my tongue deeper and deeper into his bowels, fucking him senseless with my tongue as the priest groaned loudly.

"I'm going to fuck you, Father. I'm going to take you to the promised land."

"For whatever you ask in my name, I will do it."

Oh, fuck, I thought. He was quoting Scripture.

Backing off, I pulled a Gold Coin condom out of my pocket. "Father, how many of these did Judas betray Jesus for?"

The priest looked over his shoulder with the smoldering look of lust in his eyes. I laughed and twisted the foil packet to free the rubber and quickly rolled the condom down my stiff staff. Pressing my cock head against his twitching orifice, I said "Bless me, Father. For I have sinned."

My cock slid deep inside the priest.

"It's been 10 years since my last confession."

His bowels were burning like the flames of hell.

"These are my sins."

I pulled out my cock and immediately nailed him again, pistoning his ass as the priest's moans and groans echoed throughout the marble sanctuary. I grabbed the priest's collar from the pile of discarded clothing that lay at my feet and stuffed it into his mouth.

I slowly inched my shaft back into his hot chute. The priest was tight, so fucking tight. Sweat dripped off my forehead, stinging my eyes. The lingering smell of incense had been overpowered by that of hot, steamy sex. My dick felt like a pipe that was about to burst.

I gave one quick push and I felt my pubic bush scratching the priest's ass cheeks. Quickening my tempo, I pulled my cock almost all the way out of the priest and then shoved it right back in. Father Blackwood thrust his ass backward to meet every one of my movements. After a few more jabs, I quickened the pace even more. My ball sac slapped against his ass cheeks, sounding like the crack of a whip across a man's back.

I listened to the priest's muffled grunts and groans while pounding his ass. I couldn't see much of what was going on, but my other senses were overwhelmed as a tingling sensation rose from my arms and then spread down my legs. Fucking incredible…

Continuing to pound the priest's butt hole, once again I pulled my shaft completely out of it and plugged it right back in. I lapped at his back, which was drenched with sweat, and then pushed my cock into his bowels one more time. Father Blackwood let out a groan of passion.

My climax continued building in my loins. My come was churning inside me, waiting to erupt. I allowed my cock head to pop out of his hole and then pounded him again. That was it; I had never before experienced such a feeling of perfection. I had never realized how divinely intense it was to be with another man. Overwhelmed,

I felt as if time and the universe had stood still. What seemed like a swift oncoming tidal wave of splendor overcame me. I began to spurt ropes of hot goo, yelling, "Oh, fuck. Oh, fuck. I'm coming," and filled the rubber with my seed.

Standing motionless behind the priest, my body covered in a fine sheen of sweat, I tried to catch my breath. I pulled my dick out of the priest's chute and rolled the rubber off my softening cock, spilling my come on the floor of the confessional.

Father Blackwood turned around and faced me, furiously jerking his cock. Moments later, he erupted in three quick blasts, spraying his hot come over my heaving chest.

Father Blackwood pulled the collar out of his mouth as I stood silently there staring at him.

I scooped up large dollop of his freshly spent sperm off my chest, raised my fingers to his lips and offered the priest a taste of his seed like it was the holiest of Communions. Father Blackwood licked his come off my fingers.

I yanked up my shorts and jeans and pulled on my T-shirt. Cupping my hands around the priest's face, I plunged my tongue into his warm, moist mouth.

"I absolve you of all your sins: in the name of the Father, the Son and the Holy Spirit."

I unlatched the door to the confessional and walked out into the light.

Politically Incorrect

Dale Chase

When he told me he was an attorney, there was no reason not to believe him. He had that air of authority common to the breed, confidence bordering on arrogance, the world owing him an undefined something the rest of us would never see. I accepted what he said because his energy was nearly palpable and because I kept picturing him with his cock up my ass.

We met in a Washington, D.C., bar that was off the politicos' path, so there was no inkling he might be one of them. Small talk, a drink, his hand on my ass. I was drawn to what appeared a powerful physique, dark good looks, and a masculine aura that I knew would mean a hard ride. And that was what I wanted. Always wanted.

He wore a business suit, but not an expensive one, and I liked that. He'd moved up in the world but not too far and now, coming down here, was looking for something less, somebody more down-to-earth. I could see he liked my scruffiness, jeans and faded sweatshirt, hint of beard. I explained that I was an artist just surfaced after two days completing a painting. His response was a look that said he'd like to submerge along with me.

His apartment was plain, more like a hotel room than a permanent address, but I had no time to comment. Once inside, he threw off his jacket, unzipped his pants, and fished out his dick. Shiny wet,

37

half-hard, it drooled precome and he took it in hand, squeezed out more. "Suck it," he said.

I thrilled to the command, catching a slight military bearing now. Ex-marine, maybe? One whose barracks buddies had serviced him?

I didn't give him a "Yes,sir!"—I'm not into the power scene—but I did savor his assertiveness as I knelt. When I closed my mouth around the now-stiff prick, a substantial, cut piece of meat, he let out a long moan. I ran my tongue along his shaft, licking, sucking, as I buried my face in his crotch.

He didn't last long. Obviously pent-up from his lawyering, he grabbed me at the ears and fucked a load of cream down my throat, grunting as he emptied. When he quieted, I pulled off and he stared down at me, eyes wide, his expression not that of a satisfied man. "Lick it," he said, and when I looked up he added, "The rest of my come. I want you to lick it off."

Always appreciative of each man's quirks, I did as asked, making a show for him, sticking my tongue out and tickling his piss slit, gathering the last of his residue. I took my time and found that instead of softening, he grew hard again. His breathing grew raspy, as if he hadn't just climaxed. I knew I was headed for a good, long fucking.

He didn't take me to bed. He undressed me there in the living room and stripped away the rest of his clothes to reveal a wonderfully furry body, with a dark pelt that spread across well-developed pecs, down onto his stomach, and ran rampant around his cock. His balls were big, low in the sac by sheer virtue of their weight. I envisioned pints of jizz.

When we were naked, he pushed me to the floor and proceeded to examine me with near-clinical care, as if he'd never taken time with the male body. He ran his hands over my face, forehead, cheeks, lips, and when I opened my mouth, he stuck in a finger. I sucked it for a moment, which he seemed to enjoy. From there he worked down to my chest, playing with my nipples so long I began to wonder whether maybe his history was with another kind of tit.

I began to grind my hips because he was driving me crazy. After the two-day lockdown in my studio, I needed a good come, preferably followed by several more. That first one, though, was most important. I'd been building up to it the entire time I worked and dedicated artist that I am, I'd refrained from handling myself. Everything dammed up as part of the process, and now, released from self-imposed isolation, I was beyond ready.

He slid down beside my swollen dick, ran a finger into my pubes, and lingered there until I started squirming, giving off little moans, trying not to tell him to get the fuck to it.

Finally he closed his hand around my cock, which did it. I started bucking and he held on, watching intently as I bounced my way to a massive come shot. I kept my eyes on him the whole time because part of what made it so intense was his reaction. Jaw clenched, face darkened to a grimace, he fixed on the sight of juice squirting out of me, and when I was done he held on, then ran his thumb through the residue on my knob. As my breathing steadied, I saw his had not, saw his hand on his own cock. "How about you fuck me?" I suggested, and he looked at me with pure panic. "Isn't that what you want?" I added.

He shut his eyes, turned away. I should have known then he was trouble. Reluctance with a hard-on is always bad news, but I didn't entertain such thoughts. I just thought about how his big dick would feel driving up my rectum, how it would make me come again—and coming with a cock up my ass was the ultimate. "You can," I told him. "It's what I want."

He was lying beside me, wet cock against my thigh. I rolled onto my stomach, presented my ass with a slow grind. I felt him shift, knew he was considering, felt his hands on my cheeks, then his thumbs in my crack, then the spreading. He was looking at my hole, which I keep shaved for moments like these. I clenched my muscle, heard a low moan, then felt his hand release the cheek.

"Wet your finger," I told him. A couple more seconds and he was poking my rim. "Stick it in," I said. "All the way."

He went in slowly, and I tried not to squirm too much, lest I scare him. I let him feel around in there and when he did nothing more, told him, "In and out. Finger-fuck."

He was tentative and I was getting dry. "There's lube in my jeans," I said. "We're going to need some."

He pulled out, sat up as if he had no idea what to do with this information. I retrieved the lube, tore open the packet.

"Give me your finger," I said and he held out the digit that had been up me. I slathered it, then took another gob, rolled back over, and shoved it up my hole.

"Oh, God," he said as he watched.

"Now you," I told him. "Work me like it's a cock."

He went back in, felt around, then started to stroke. I was slippery now, nice and juicy, and I told him to add a second finger. That was better. "Now fuck me."

I knew his dick was dripping, that what he really wanted was to climb on and ride my ass, but he held himself in check, gave me a digital number until he finally couldn't stand it. When he pulled out, I rolled over. "Good, huh," I said. Sweat was all across his forehead, he was so worked up, and he had a fist around his prick, holding on for dear life.

"Why don't you give me the real thing," I suggested. "I'd love your cock up my ass."

He sat back on his haunches, cock aimed like a gun ready to fire. I watched him do his battle, my concern as to what lay behind it gone. "Fuck me," I said. "There's a condom in my jeans."

"You guys always carry supplies?" he asked.

"Yes."

He thought about this, then got up, retrieved the rubber, struggled with the wrapper, finally got it out. He stood while he rolled it on and I told him to get another lube packet, grease himself. He did as asked, taking surprising care with himself. When he was ready, he got back down onto the floor and I rolled onto my stomach, stuck my ass up at him. Again hesitation. Again "Fuck me."

While he worked his way to what he wanted, I thought about his initial air of authority, how it was now nowhere to be found. But I knew it would be recovered, that once he had his cock in me, the man would reemerge and do me like nobody ever had. I envisioned a marathon, if only I could get him started.

I wiggled my ass. "Stick it in," I said, deciding I'd talk him into it. "Fuck my hole, shove it up me because I need it in there, need your big dick!"

He rammed into me with such a massive thrust that it reduced me to nothing but a grunt because it was like having a horse or a bear or a bull, something beyond human, up me. And it wasn't gonna be gentle, this creature, it was gonna fuck out its load, get itself off in this hole it had found. He slammed into me, long moans in accompaniment, and I reveled in the feel of him finally doing it. His big balls swung forward, slapped me as his stroke went full-out, buried to the root each time he drove into me. And then he began to growl and I was loving it—this animal fucking me, this bear of a man, digging his fingers into my ass as he rode.

He wasn't quick this time, but I was. I didn't last long at all, spewing cream onto his rug because I was gone with the feel of that big sausage up my chute and the creature behind it. I let out a yell as I came, but he didn't stop to consider what I was doing; he just kept on pumping. It was after I'd quieted, after I'd settled into taking what he was giving, that he began to call out. "Mother of God, oh Mother of God, oh shit, oh fuck." He kept up his litany as he shot his wad, his wet slap continuing until he'd finally finished. And even then he simply eased his stroke, as if reluctant to stop, slowing gradually, then settling atop me, pressing me flat on the floor. He didn't move for a few seconds and at first I thought he was resting, then realized he was enjoying the feel of his dick up me. He also wasn't going soft.

"Am I too heavy?" he finally asked, and I had to be honest.

"A little."

He pulled out, rolled off. "Sorry."

I turned over, watched him look down at the rubber as if he'd just discovered it. And then he fled. I remained on the floor while he spent time in the bathroom. When he didn't return right away, I got up, positioned myself on the sofa, lying back, one leg up, cock lolling across a thigh.

"John, wasn't it?" he said when he came out, towel around his waist.

"Johnny. And you're—no, let me guess—Cameron, wasn't it? Or no, Carlton. Or was it Fred?"

He laughed, and I felt him relax clear across the room.

"Ted," he said.

"Hey, I was close."

"I don't usually do this," he offered when he came over to me.

"Not bad for a beginner," I assured him.

He looked at me with what seemed pure affection, and I leaned forward, started to kiss him. He pulled back. "I'm, uh, I'm not ready for that."

Another red flag—how many did I need to not see? "Then how about this?" I said, pulling at my dick. "You ready for this?"

He looked down at my soft prick, paused, then moved down for a look. "No hands this time," I said, and he looked at me as if I'd just challenged him to climb Everest. "Suck on it. I guarantee you'll like it."

The final frontier: another guy's dick in your mouth. Once you've done that, you're gonna do it all, you're gonna get so far down the road that before long you'll have your mouth plastered on an ass, your tongue scouring out a bunghole. He leaned in, stuck out his tongue, played around the knob. "It's like a tit," I coaxed. "Just start sucking on it."

He gave me a long look, then opened his mouth, scooped me in, and closed his lips. I felt him acclimating, then the start of a tentative suck. "Do it," I said, "suck my dick, c'mon, suck it," and that got him going. Seconds later, he was frantically trying to devour my knob and I was trying to get my whole dick into his mouth. Hard now, of course, and too much for an untried mouth, but he gave it a good try. As he pulled on me, his hand dropped to his crotch and he started in on himself, fisting his meat until it was up. He then drew back in what seemed a near-panic, shoved me off the sofa and onto the floor where he flailed about until I got us into a sixty-nine, got my mouth on his dick and shoved mine back into him. He quieted immediately and we lay suckling each other in silence.

I, of course, gave him what can be called a blow job, but he wasn't good in this department, content, it seemed, to simply pull on my knob. I tried to push into his mouth, to get him to take more, but he wouldn't go farther, never mind that he was ramming his big thing into my throat. When he came this time, I pulled out of his mouth, jerked my cock until I erupted onto him.

"Jesus!" I heard him cry mid climax. I wasn't certain if it was a response to coming or to being come upon. And who cared at that moment? I just needed more than he could do.

After this round, he lay still for a moment, then got up. "I'd really like to see you again," he said, which meant it was time to leave. He dressed and I did likewise. He didn't give me a business card but asked for my number, which I gave him. "I'm in town for another couple weeks, working on a case," he said, "then will be back home awhile."

"Where's that?" I asked.

"The Midwest. Can I see you tomorrow night? I'm not sure when we wrap up, so I'll give you a call in the afternoon. OK?"

He didn't put an arm around me, didn't shake my hand or pat my back, and God forbid, didn't kiss me. "I had a great time," I offered as he opened the door.

"Me too," he said. He suddenly seemed vulnerable, and after the door had closed I pictured him opening his briefcase, reviewing documents to reconnect himself to the man he presented to the world.

He called the next afternoon and I again went to his apartment. He met me in just a robe, and as soon as I stepped inside, he tore at me. He was already hard.

This time he couldn't wait to get at my ass. On the floor again, he flipped me over and stuck in a finger, then let out an appreciative groan. Home at last. Had he drifted off in court, I wondered, testimony unheard as he recalled what it is to fuck a guy? Did he sit there with a hard-on?

"Two fingers," I told him when he seemed content with a simple digital probe. "Either that or your cock."

He added more lube and the second finger. I could hear his breathing, heavy, tinged with grunts. Finally he withdrew, sat back, and pulled open my cheeks. But he didn't go in.

Apparently he wanted to look at the forbidden place where he'd had his finger and his dick, where he was about to go again. I squeezed my muscle, wiggled my ass, and then he got a condom from my pocket, pulled it on, added lube, and eased himself into me.

"Oh, yeah," I said when he was all the way in. I gave him a few squeezes, which set him off. He began to ride me like I was some bucking bronc and he was trying to stay in the saddle.

Slapping against my ass, he pumped and pushed, his moan taking on a pleasurable tone, like he was finally allowing the whole of himself into the act. I didn't handle my dick but let it hang stiffly between my legs, knowing that if he kept on like this, I'd probably shoot unaided.

"I'm going to..." he said, and then he gripped me tightly at the waist and pounded out his climax, slamming into me so hard my knees burned on the carpet. God, how I wanted to get this guy to a bed.

He took time to empty and again lingered, cock as hard as when he began. I was amazed at his staying power. He flattened me to the floor and began to grind against me. "I want to keep it in you," he said in a hoarse whisper. "My cock up your ass."

I squeezed in reply and he moaned. My dick, meanwhile, trapped beneath us and stimulated by his slow grind, hit the limit and fired. "I'm coming," I yelled as cream spewed out of me, his big prick still working my rectum.

When I was done I told him he needed to get off me. He was too big to tolerate for long. He pulled out and I rolled over. He discarded the rubber, then took his prick in hand and began to stroke. "I want to fuck you in the mouth," he said, and before I could respond, he pulled me over to him, got me down to his crotch, and shoved his cock into my mouth. As I closed my lips and tongue around him, he let out one of his now-familiar groans.

You wouldn't have thought this guy had just come.

He ran his hands through my hair as I did him and I knew he was watching me bob on his cock, that he was savoring the sight, creating a mental image he could draw on later. "There are so many things I want," he said and he pulled out of my mouth. "Would you sit on me?"

"My pleasure."

He lay back and let me apply rubber and grease. I stood over him. "Any preference? Front or back?"

"Front. I want to see your dick."

I descended to a squat, positioned myself over him, then sank onto his prong, thrilling to the feel of it going up my rectum. His arms were at his sides. He was going to watch me fuck myself with his cock.

He smiled when I began an easy bounce, a grateful kind of expression that told me he'd been imagining this. *How much more?* I wondered. I decided to take things up a notch. "Big dick up my ass," I began. "Cock up me, fucking myself with your dick, sitting on your fat prong, feeling it shove up me. God, you are so big. You're up in my bowels and I'm gonna fuck a load out of you because I want your juice in me, want you to blow a gusher inside me."

My prick was stiff, flapping at him. He looked at it but didn't take hold. I didn't either because I didn't want to come just yet. I knew he was working up to something more and I wanted to wait for it.

Finally he began to issue little cries, then grabbed me and pushed up. "Come for me, baby," I coached, "shoot your load up my ass. Oh, yeah, fuck my ass."

I kept bouncing and he kept thrusting, which made for collision-force fucking as he shot his load. As before, he wasn't quick, and I wondered if those big balls ever went dry.

Finally he quieted and I relaxed. He began to soften and I slid off.

When he just lay there, I pulled off his rubber, tossed it aside. I was still hard, and as much as I would have liked to jerk off onto his furry chest, I held back. He turned his head to one side, and after a long silence and with obvious difficulty, he told me the rest of it. "I want you to do it to me."

Holy shit, I almost said, but I managed to remain relatively composed and keep it at, "Do what?"

"You know."

"You have to say it before I'll do it."

"I want you to fuck me."

"I'd love to."

"You understand," he began, then grew hesitant. "I haven't ever...not with...a dick."

I said nothing, knew he would continue.

"I've had a finger in me, my own actually." He swallowed with some difficulty. He was breathing hard now, confession laced with anticipation. "Sometimes I stick it up there when I jerk off."

"Feels good, doesn't it."

"Oh, yes. I thought about getting a dildo but..."

"The real thing is so much better."

"I'd like to find out."

"Say it again."

"What?"

"You know."

He turned to me, face flushed. "Fuck me."

"How about we get into bed."

"No, I can't do that."

"Why not?"

"I just can't. Bear with me, please. Here is fine."

"Except for the knee burns."

"Please."

"Whatever."

I got another condom, put it on, greased myself. He got over onto all fours, stuck his ass up at me. I could tell by the way he moved that the position thrilled him, that he'd wanted to get his ass up for a good fucking for a long time. His crack was hairy, and as I parted his cheeks, looking for the dark center, he let out a long groan.

"We need to loosen you up," I said, and I lubed a finger and ran it into him. He wriggled and squirmed, then clamped down onto me. I worked him a little, then added a second finger. This was too easy. He'd had more up there than his finger.

"You're easier than I thought you'd be," I told him. "What else you been sticking up there besides your finger?"

"Please, I don't want to talk about that."

"Hey, I'm the guy with his fingers up your ass. It's not like we can get embarrassed here."

He shook his head, so I prodded his prostate. He let out a yelp. "In a few minutes I'm going to fuck you," I told him. "My dick will be up your ass. That probably outdistances any object you've played around with. So what's been in there?"

He blew out a big sigh. "An enema nozzle. And one time a banana. I came like hell with that in me."

"Now you know what we're all smiling about."

I withdrew my fingers. "You don't need anything but a cock in you." And I shoved my dick into his hole without regard for ease or acclimation or anything else beyond fucking him blind. "The real thing," I said as I began a steady thrust.

All our talk about what he'd been doing to himself had gotten me royally primed. I thought about him doing what he'd said, high-powered attorney shoving a banana up his ass as he jerked his prick. "Feels good in there," I told him. "Steamy hole, dirty little rectum that needs things shoved up it. I know you're loving the feel of me inside you. You're gonna want cock up you all the time now, you're gonna want to sit on dicks every minute of the day, keep that hole occupied." I rode steadily as I spoke, and he gave off little cries that I knew were a mix of pleasure and pain because this was far more than a nozzle or fruit of the day. This was a guy plowing him, picking up speed as the load began to rise.

"I'd love to keep fucking your ass, but I'm headed for a come shot. Oh, man, I'm doing it. You're taking come up the ass. Fuck, yeah. Oh, fuck." I finally couldn't speak. All I had left was a long moan as jizz shot out of me in great long pulses that sent waves through my entire body. I pumped until I was dry, then pulled out and stared at the wet furry hole, lube running down onto his balls. He rolled over, grabbed his prick, and began to stroke. Eyes shut, he unleashed yet another climax, this one, I was certain, powered by the tingle in his just-fucked ass.

When he was done, I reached over and played in his spunk and he watched me scoop up a fingerful and put it into my mouth. "Oh, Christ," he said, eyes wide. "We have to stop. I need some rest."

"Want me to come over tomorrow?" I asked as I dressed.

He slipped into a robe, tied it securely, but didn't immediately reply. Finally he said, "We shouldn't."

"Why? I'll fuck you again."

He shook his head. "You know you want it," I added.

"Yes, OK, but I'll call you and tell you when. My days are unpredictable."

"So are your nights."

For the next week Ted and I carried on like rutting pigs. He had me arrive earlier and earlier, naked when he opened the door, already hard. Our sessions lasted longer and longer, incredible wallows full of tongues and fingers and cocks. Now that Ted had allowed himself the pleasure of a man, he couldn't seem to get enough. He also overcame any and all barriers, his tongue finally and quite eagerly going into my bunghole. He came when he did it, mouth plastered against my ass, tongue fucking me as he pulled on his prick. He had me bring over a dildo one night and he stuck it up his ass while he fucked me, then stuck it up me while he sat on my cock and jerked off. I loved every second with him even though I knew there was something underneath his relentlessness, something beyond mere release. What we did felt like a descent, sinking down toward the really dirty part of sex and not knowing how far he'd want to go.

When he asked if I'd give him an enema I had to say no. He accepted this, then wanted to masturbate each other while sitting on dildos.

We didn't quite get to that scenario, however, because one morning I opened the door to my building and looked out onto a sea of reporters who began to shout.

"Is it true Congressman Evans has a sexual relationship with you?"

"How long have you and the congressman been involved?"

"Did you know he's married, father of three?"

"Are you aware he's a staunch conservative?"

I said nothing, slammed the door, ran upstairs to my apartment, bolted the lock. Sank to the floor. It was then I recalled the warning signs: the reluctance to do what he wanted—sure sign of married guy; the bare apartment, life in the Midwest; the pent-up quality he continually exhibited; the descent. He was unlike anyone I'd ever been with, and I'd had a couple married guys, but they were waiters and insurance men. As with so many conservatives, Ted's political agenda was in opposition to his sexual orientation.

I seldom turned on the TV, but I did now and discovered my driver's license photo on the screen. I also learned all this had come about because Ted Evans, critic of the gay movement and the man behind the current attempt at crushing a new rights bill, had been seen receiving a gay man at his apartment. "The freshmen congressman who has allied himself with the far right on matters pertinent to gay rights now stands revealed as allegedly homosexual."

There were photos of the wife and children and one of Ted avoiding the camera, hurrying into the congressional office building.

I didn't work that day, nor did I leave the apartment. After more than 20 calls from reporters but none from Ted, I unplugged the phone. The day was spent with the wrenching task of moving from surprise to hurt to outrage and finally to action. I weighed the man's career and family life against the people he'd trampled with his political agenda. I thought about him with his butt thrust up at me. Then late in the afternoon I called his office. "Tell him it's Johnny Randall."

There was a long pause, and I was put on hold. When the secretary came back on she said, "Congressman Evans asked me to thank you for your inquiry, but said he has nothing to say to you."

"Fine," I said. "Tell him it's his call." And I hung up.

I sat for a long time after that occupying that blank space between cause and effect. I would do what I saw as right, speak out with the truth. And then I would forget Ted Evans, though I doubted he'd ever forget me.

Man Amplified, Man Squared

Michael Huxley

Rich kid, spoiled punk, goddamned little hunk, born with a silver cock in your mouth: You even 20 yet?

My crew and I were working a residential job this past summer, laying a half-circular driveway. It was a sizable, labor-intensive effort: setting individual pavers into a meticulously graded sand bed that curved a 400-foot span before one of those immense, Italianate, stuccoed monstrosities popping up these days like toadstools after a suburban rainstorm. The entryway into that pastel mausoleum was so grandiose, so fucking pretentious, that I felt embarrassed for the owners. New money, without a doubt.

But who am I to cast aspersions? I'm no exception to obsession.

Cock: When not asleep, dreaming of it, I'm busy thinking about, scoping for, or engaging it. Otherwise, I can be found on the work site or at the gym—both being excellent places to lure it.

Cock... At the gym I can parlay a sidelong glance from a hot-looking satyr into a quick blow job in the steam room without having to articulate a word. And how many times has a minimum of verbal communication resulted in a fiery late-afternoon fuck at my place or his hotel? That's right, never with a gym regular, for surely by now my skill at sniffing out a randy tourist or a dude in town on business has come to rival that of a police dog's exposing a hidden stash of heroin. It's a big city, a popular destination, where I live.

My looks, my body, my cock, the way I exude sexuality—these are my prized possessions. That I come across as straight is no affectation; there is nothing false about my masculinity—or subtle. I am Man Amplified/Man Squared. Cabrini's my surname, for what it's worth. I was given the name Adam. I am 33 years old. At 17 I murdered my father. How do you like me so far?

But back to the rich kid.

I'd just reached into my truck for my smokes when I noticed him emerge from that vulgar entryway and cast his gaze my way. How could he not? I was, after all, me—stripped to the waist, firing up a Camel. I laughed to myself when he yanked off his T-shirt in response and sauntered to his Jeep so nonchalantly, reaching into the depths of his cargo shorts for his keys. Those shorts, I might add, reposed a good five or six inches below his navel. I saw evidence of neither boxers nor briefs.

Oh, yeah, he was the complete package: pumped up, shaved head, ears and nipples pierced, scarcely discernable goatee, multitattooed arms and shoulders, with another piece on his chest. You get the picture: a careful study in someone attempting to disguise his aristocratic bearing, if not genealogy. That notwithstanding, he was a knockout. I'd seen him coming and going since taking on the job several days earlier, and he'd noticed me, but his parents were always hovering.

Where are your folks today, spoiled punk? I thought, taking a deep drag. *Off being cosmetic surgeons?* As if his parents hadn't informed me they'd be attending a medical conference. *Where you off to now, brat hunk, some designer gym?* As if his Nike bag in tow wasn't evidence enough. *You wanna fuck, poser?* As if his driving slowly across the lawn toward the street, his stopping not 10 yards from where I stood and waving me over wasn't the answer in and of itself.

"Hey, man, can you spare a smoke?"

"No problem," I replied, handing him my half-empty pack and

lighter. Our both wearing dark shades did not obfuscate the eye contact we shared.

"Thanks, dude," he said, inhaling profoundly, returning my nicotine works. He surveyed our progress, feigning interest. "You're making headway. Fuckin' hot morning already, though. How can you stand it?"

"I dig the heat," I said, "enjoy working shirtless."

"No doubt," he observed wryly. "I like your body art, by the way," he continued. "Where'd you get it done?"

"In the pen," I smiled, thinking, *Suck on that info, fucker.*

He paused briefly, exhaled a tiny snicker through his nose, and shifting into first, said, "Cool."

"Y'think?" I goaded.

"Sure. Why the fuck not?" Releasing the clutch and pulling away, he added, "Thanks for the smoke, dude. Later..." He glanced over his shoulder, lusting back at me as he eased the Jeep carefully over the curb, having locked the bummed cigarette between his sculpted, smirking lips.

Hot little only-child smart-ass, summer-jobless university punk, home alone Richie Rich fag magnet... I ground my smoke into the dirt under boot. Once I was bolted in the Porta-John, I began playing with myself, in no time jerking off like a simian, thinking about the kid's pecs, his nipple rings, his facial bone structure, his fucking *ass* in those shorts, man. About *Arcangelo...*

Considering the ins and outs of ass penetration, what wouldn't I have given to explore your interior just once with my hard-on, Arcangelo? But that was off-limits, wasn't it, you hot-looking sleaze/you shit-hole tease? You sure knew how to blow a load, though; we had that in common, didn't we, you gorgeous no-account bum/you bursting sack of come? I think I loved jerking you off/you jerking me off more than anything else we did together when alone. I'd sell my soul right now if I had one/if there were such a thing, to watch you fucking that rich kid behind those bars, you insatiable closet case. Watch me jerk off, man; I'll fucking come in your face...

I dropped my bitter load of disdain on the sticky floor and, leaving it there, headed back to work.

On the inside we had nothing but time, so we spent our many "free" hours engaged in erotic pursuit. In retrospect, I view my incarceration as a fascinating dichotomy of doing time/making time, working out/making out, sucking up for advantageous measure/sucking cock for pleasure, with bunkmates who masturbate—cellmates crying/sperm cells flying. And oh, yes, the drugs: I never shot them up, but popping, snorting, and huffing? Absolutely. Getting fucked up/getting fucked up the ass, condoms packed with powder/condoms crammed with cock. Oh, lucky me, I successfully dodged HIV. I recall Junior, coked up, playing with his monster dick, myself coked up, so easily enticed to take a lick.

Junior fisted me, more than once—and guess what? I liked it.

Getting raped—it's a good thing I was no stranger to rape—and having tender love made by and/or with Albert in the shower, Tim, the daytime C.O., perched in his tower, Jean Michel that one time on the bench press, Sean in nooks and crannies, but most notably Arcangelo, my cellmate for the final, 18-month stretch. I think of Arcangelo oftentimes while masturbating and always will. At such times, I can feel his 98.6-degree flow of come spilling over my hand, see his exquisite face twisted in ecstasy. How many times did he blast his wad up my rectum or down my gullet? Those were the only moments, afterward, that he would allow himself to say, "I love you, Adam," or kiss me. With one exception…

Where are you now, my doomed, breathtaking Arcangelo? If you still exist, I'm sure you fondly remember those lavish lip-lockdowns.

Straight guys and bi guys: Of all the damning lies, the latter of the two surely takes the bigger prize. Junior, the two Mikes, Pico, and Eric: The list goes on; they came and went. But oh, Arcangelo…

I won my parole after five, leaving Arcangelo forever behind, his crimes against humanity being far more heinous than mine.

Our wrenching, sexless, final embrace, our farewell kiss:

"I loved you, Adam."

I was on lunch break when the kid returned a little past noon, nodding with a thumbs-up as he drove by. He paused briefly before entering the house, cruising me again. His hands buried in his pockets, he lifted his chin as if to say, *Follow...*

I finished my sandwich, downed the last of my brew, and making some lame excuse to the guys, got up, lit a cigarette, and approached the house.

But wait! Making excuses to the guys? Just a formality, I can assure you. They know well enough by now what goes down with me, what *went* down; Paul confirmed that. Funny, though, how it remains unspoken, how they'd never dare to bring it up, like I could give a shit if they did. Beyond that, the guys are fucking oblivious, except for Paul. No, Paul wasn't oblivious at all.

I should never have hired Paul Cass; he was too fucking hot. Married, adored his wife and kids, and straight as the whole nine yards. Working with Paul was disconcerting, to say the least. His smile was such a come-on! His heavy stubble, visible no matter how closely he shaved, *moved* me. Besides being genuinely friendly, he was a hard worker—wouldn't you know it?

Every time he stripped his shirt off, my libido devoured his partial nudity. True, his pecs and nipples were outstanding, but for me it was more the way his soft, dark chest hair converged into a trail above his navel, where it spiraled over his taut belly and continued downward from there, disappearing from view behind his well-packed button fly. That frontal mystery-cargo led my eyes into Levi-temptation every Monday through Friday, but the Porta-John remained my only recourse. *Clearly,* I remember thinking, jerking off, *that furry path leads to a place I would much rather go— down on Paul.*

It was autumn, almost a year ago. I was loading my truck, ready to take off at workday's end, when I noticed him approaching.

"So, Paul, I see you're the last one to leave again."

"I need t'speak t'you in private, Adam. Y'got a minute?"

"Sure, what's up? You're not unhappy working with us, I hope."

"It's nothin' like that, man. I love my job."

"I'm glad to hear that, Paul. You're a good worker."

"Thanks, Adam…"

"So what's the deal?" I inquired, getting comfortable, leaning against my truck.

"It's personal," he said. "It's taken me a few days t'get up the balls t'talk t'you, but now I'm not so sure. I don't wanna lose my job over this, Adam. It has t'do with you."

"Spit it out, then," I said. "If it's personal, about me, you have nothing to worry about. I like you, Paul."

"All right, then," he began cautiously. "OK, look: The guys told me all about you bein' a man's man, if y'get my drift, an'… I just wanna let y'know I'm OK with that. I got a gay brother, an' he's the best, but he's sure not like you… If the guys hadn'ta told me about you, I never woulda guessed it."

"So that's it?" I prodded.

"No. I wanna ask y'somethin', just between us." Pausing again, he looked at the ground.

"What is it, Paul? You can trust me."

"Jeez, this is hard t'say, but what the fuck." He raised his head and looked into my eyes. "You think I'm a good-lookin' guy, Adam?"

I laughed softly then said, "Come on, Paul. You know you're a great-looking man."

"I know, but… Maybe I'm not makin' myself clear. What I wanna know is…if I turn *you* on, y'know? If I don't, it's OK; you can tell me so, an' I'll be on my way."

"What if I said you do, Paul?"

"Then I'd ask if you wanna do me, man, 'cause I want ya to."

"What about your wife, my friend?"

"Let me tell y'somethin' Adam, an' this ain't bullshit: I love bein' inside Rebecca more than bein' alive, man. But ever since the new baby, Beck don't want me anywhere near her like that anymore; an' that just ain't like her. B'fore, she couldn't get enough. I know she can't help it, an' the doctor says it'll pass, but it's been goin' on like this for the longest damn time now. I been jerkin' off like crazy in private, but it's got t'where I feel like I just…gotta get off *inside* somebody so damn bad I can't stand it. I've…always been the real horny type, I guess." He laughed self-deprecatingly before continuing.

"See, I don't wanna cheat on Beck with another woman; I'd feel too damn guilty. But with a guy—with a man like you—I wouldn't. I think you're great, Adam, all the guys do. Y'know, what happened with your father 'n' all… Truth is, I wish I could be more *like* you." Paul cleared his throat after saying that. "So. Whaddya say, man? I figure it'd be like buddies, helpin' each other out."

I recall stretching my hand across the impossible chasm that separates one human being from another and placing it squarely on his shoulder. "I appreciate what you've told me very much, Paul. My answer is yes. I'd be honored to help you out, but it's not just for you that I'm saying that. I've been hot for you since the day you started."

"Yes!" he swore triumphantly. "That makes me fuckin' glad t'hear, Adam, but shit," he paused, anxiously looking around. "Where can we go? Are you cool with me wanting it right now? You got the time? I want it so bad."

Utilizing my smile, I moved closer and discreetly groped his obvious erection through his Levi's. I lowered my voice seductively, "I can see that, man. My truck's roomy. No one can see through the tinted glass. I've nothing but time, Paul; let's climb in."

He took the passenger's side. I instructed him to pull his jeans down and followed suit. His cock—its size, formation, and hardness—exceeded my expectations.

"You have a beautiful cock, Paul."

"Not quite as big as yours, though," he commented.

"Who *gives* a shit, man? Look at you!" I began to rub his belly, first with my hand, saying, "I love this part of your body, Paul," and then with my face. Breathing his scent, I ran my tongue down his fur path, took his cock into my mouth and worked him for about 30 seconds before asking, "You like that, Paul? You feelin' better now?"

"Fuck, yeah. Do it some more."

I then proceeded to nurse that veiny alabaster with my oral fixation in ways he never dreamed possible. And he made no bones (save one) about letting me know, blow by luscious blow, how his carnal fix was making him feel, by punctuating his pleasure with salacious commentary throughout:

"You got it, man," he began. "Yeah, there's a good buddy… Your head's fuckin' *hot*, Adam. You got me feelin' so fuckin' *dirty*.

"*Whew*, Beck could learn a thing from you, buddy. When she's better, you wanna come over and do us both sometime? She'd flip over you, Adam, what chick wouldn't?

"Shit, man, I never felt this dirty before. You got me feelin' like a king, sittin' on a throne in hell—my cock on fire, doin' *bad* shit, doin' *dirty* shit, gettin' my dick blown by another dude. By *you*, man.

"Just keep on doin' what you're doin', bro'. Yeah, just like that…

"I lied, man," he continued, more confidently. "I knew you'd say yes. I seen you starin' at me. I seen you lookin' at my belly an' your eyes goin' down. I read your signals. *Jesus*, that feels so fuckin' *good*."

My time with Paul passed at a leisurely pace. *So leisurely*. Such a turn-on. Inevitably, though, it became more and more apparent that he was beginning to lose control.

"*Fuck*, Adam, my cock's in flames. The fire's *way* down deep! I love you for this, man. You're so fuckin' hot, I'm trippin' out. I'm *inside* out. Don't stop, man; I'm gettin' close… Oh, *fuck*, don't stop for nothin'; I'm gonna blow *big* time… *Yeah*, take it all, Adam."

And then, almost as if possessed, he snarled: "You fuckin' *take it*, stud! *Yeah!*"

I felt his cock expand and contract a dozen times or more in rapid, involuntary succession, suffusing my taste buds. I did not disengage from Paul until he collapsed, sweaty and mute from bestial satisfaction. Savoring the by-product of his rapture before swallowing it, I was surprised when he then offered to jerk me off. Naturally, I was more than happy to accept. The pent-up ferocity of my come-blasting, instigated by his deft hand action, truly astonished him.

"*Whoa*," he startled. "Holy fuckin' *shit*."

Goddamn, I loved blowing that man! *Lucky woman, his wife,* I remember thinking. *Once she gets better, doubtless she'll soar every time he slips her that fierce, stunning probe, thrill with every silken love-thrust, gush with every wad he shoots off inside her.*

Was it a mistake, doing Paul a second time?

The following day, after eight work-hours of acting like nothing had happened between us, I noticed him hanging around again, and sure enough, he approached me after everyone had left, but this time much more assuredly. Back in the cab of my truck, when I started going down on him, he took my head in his hands, raised it from his cock and said, "No, man, I want ya t'do *this* with your mouth first..." at once kissing me with ardent tongue. Within moments Paul was in such an agitated state of arousal that he seemed almost insane. He broke away, practically yelling, "I can't help it, man; I gotta say it! I just *gotta*... I fuckin' love ya, Adam; I swear t'God I do. I felt that way ever since I first laid eyes on you, an' after yesterday I can't think about nothin' else. I ain't afraid t'say it either. Not now. I fuckin' *love ya*, man; I *love* ya, an'... *I wanna fuck ya,* Adam. I wanna fuck ya so bad, I can't *tell* ya how much. C'mon, baby; kiss me some more. Yeah. *Mmm...* "

After several galvanic, mouth-mating moments, he backed off, swooning, "That means 'yes,' don't it Adam? *Don't* it..."

Flabbergasted as I was, I cannot deny that Paul's amorous overture had swept me completely overboard into a warm, acceding sea. I managed to dislodge myself from him, but only for long enough to start up the truck and tear to the rear of the deserted construction site, where I parked behind two huge mounds of sand. With lightning speed, we stripped naked outside the truck, welded our bodies, and resumed our mouth-swirl with out-of-control abandon—our bodies grinding against one another with a groping delirium that after some minutes, became almost intolerable, unsustainable. Much to my continued amazement, sliding down my body, he dropped to a crouch and began fellating me, his subtly nuanced expertise bearing proof that, no fucking *way* was I the first man he'd ever blown. Thereafter we took turns giving head, utilizing the lowered truck-gate, each round more sublime, more elevating than the one preceding it, leaving us breathless for the next, and the next.

When at last we could no longer endure our foreplay, we blindly ejected the tools from the bed of my truck and spread out a dusty insulating blanket. Taking control, I literally picked the man up, sprawled him on his back in the truck's bed, straddled him while facing him, and utilizing a bit of 10-W-30, took his resplendent cock up my ass.

Interesting that he'd come prepared with a condom.

I took my time to hump that beautiful fucker dry, all the while, his repeated mantra, 'I love ya, Adam; God knows I do. I fuckin' *love ya,* man,' sustaining, transporting me. There could be no doubt; Paul *did* love me. It was palpable, not only in his verbal stream of emotion. I could feel it just as evidently in the nurture of his upthrusting, in his solicitude of my indescribable pleasure, in the way he held my hips. My heart aches to recall the unabashed vulnerability his eyes revealed.

On the cusp of simultaneous orgasm, I took special note of Paul's facial expression, which bordered on the maniacal, before flinging my prodigious overload on that fuzzy belly of his. Crashing to his torso, I found myself encircled in powerful, proletarian arms, clinging to me hopelessly, his thorax heaving, abruptly wracked with sobs. Paul turned his face away from my attempt to mollify him with a kiss, his tortured lament erupting in jagged chunks:

"Oh, *God,* Adam, I dunno what's happening.

"*Now* what the fuck am I gonna do?

"I don't know what t'fuckin' *do,* man.

"God—*help me;* tell me what t'*do.*

"What the fuck happens *now?*"

Come what may, that late afternoon with Paul will rank among the most bizarre, revelatory, and extraordinary events of my entire life, and that's saying more than you—or I—know at this point.

Paul didn't show up for work the next day. Nor the day after. I tried any number of times to contact him by phone, but never made it past his voice mail. *"Hi!"* a perky-sounding female voice would begin. *"You've reached Paul and Beck's madhouse. Sorry we can't come to the phone right now, but if you'll just leave a message…"* Until finally one day, a far different female voice droned: *"I'm sorry, the number you have dialed is no longer in service…"*

I never saw him again.

I rang the inane doorbell, which was mounted on a brass plaque in the shape of Michelangelo's *David*. When the kid opened the door, neither of us spoke for a second, until I broke the charged silence.

"You home alone?"

"You know damn well I am," he scoffed.

"You want some company?"

"And here I thought I'd made that pretty clear."

I just smiled. "You're a smug little fuck, aren't you?"

"Why on earth does that fucking matter?" he responded indifferently. "And I'm not 'little,' by the way," he added, stroking the hefty elongation now quite evident in his shorts. "Or hadn't you noticed?"

"Is my telling you how hot you are the price of admission or what?"

He offered no snappy retort; merely stepped back a pace or two, opened the door wider, and said, "You can't smoke in here, dude."

You can't smoke in here, dude…

I took a prolonged final drag and flicked away the butt. I hadn't even completely shut the door behind me when he pounced, pinning my backside against it with his entire body, task accomplished with a slamming thud. He instantly initiated a heavy make-out scene from which there was no escape, had I any desire just then to do so. No, from the moment our tongues meshed, our naked torsos made contact, I was gripped by an overriding urgency to bleed that virile young organism for every additional moment's pleasure I knew instinctively lay ahead, that I'd derive a hundredfold in continuing. Without question, the brat was *that* fucking good. So it was with unbridled and wanton propriety that I unbuttoned the waistband of his shorts and let them drop to the Saltillo tiles.

He kicked the shorts aside and stood before me, entirely naked, juggling the contents of his scrotum with his right hand, and pinching his right tit-hoop with his left, as I offed my boots and jeans. His Prince Albert, already doused with precome, transcended the cliché of its presence, upheld as it were, so proudly in pierced midair.

Fixating on my erection, he exclaimed, "*Fuck,* man," and dropped to his knees. He sucked my dick for two, maybe three minutes, moaning the entire time, as I occasionally interjected a dusky and cock-felt *yeah.* He backed off, stood up, milked a fresh leak of precome up his many good inches, and spread it tauntingly over his cock head.

"C'mere," he commanded, adding an understated thrust of his pelvis. "Taste it."

More generous with my going-down time than he, I savored every bit of his preseminal production and paid particular tribute to the underside of his slick, immaculate circumcision with every downstroke.

"You gotta stop," he cautioned. "I don't wanna come yet, not this way. Let's go t'my room; all my stuff's up there."

No surprise to me that I ended up fucking the shit out of that gorgeous brat in his king-size bed upstairs, his penchant for getting rimmed being the first clue. Certainly no virgin, the kid proved himself a fucking *ruthless* swine bottom. I must have drilled that gilded lily's star-caliber ass for a full 45 minutes, forestalling shooting off as best I knew how by continuously varying my pace, my backbeat, the intensity of my thrusting. As he writhed beneath me, belly-down in mindless lust-surrender, the kid, his head jammed sideways into a pillow, cried out over and over again, "Oh, *shit...* Don't stop, dude. Just keep *fuckin'* me. Don't you fuckin' *ever* stop, man."

And so it continued. For a time.

I was just beginning to experience the first, out-of-sight glimmers of impending orgasm when he *said* it, whispered it frantically:

"Dude! Tell me you love me. Y'don't have t'mean it. Just *say* it. Tell me you *love* me."

Too caught up in the searing escalation of coming to be daunted by pathos, nearing the point of no return, I blurted, "I dunno about that, but I'm sure lovin' *fucking* you, buddy. I'm *lovin'* it. I'm *gone* in your ass, man; I fuckin' *love* it. You got…maybe the sweet-est…insides I ever felt."

Bye-bye, kiddo.

On regaining consciousness, it actually occurred to me that I might have blown a hole in that condom, the force of my nut-bust having been that fucking intense, that fucking mind-blowing, that overwhelmingly *fine.*

I rolled out of him, threw the spent condom on the carpet, gath-ered him in one arm and jerked the little fuck off. He went berserk, launching his sperm cells: rolling his head, bucking his hips, cursing like a motherfucker, his come spurting up and away from his piss slit like the geyser of youth in repeated arcs.

An uneasy silence set in almost at once.

I have to get back to my crew, I thought, feeling anxious to get out of there, away from him as soon as possible. *This place is all wrong. Where are my fucking jeans? My boots?*

He started in:

"I'm sure you know my parents are out of town until tomorrow. You wanna maybe snag some dinner out somewhere after you knock off? Maybe spend the night here? Dinner'll be my treat, man. I wanna see you again."

No. Absolutely not.

"That's real nice," I said, placing a manly hand on his shoulder and looking into his eyes with the utmost sincerity, "but I don't think my wife would much appreciate that."

Iron bars instantly clanged shut between us. He pulled away from my touch. His eyes narrowed.

"I don't believe you."

"But that's how it is, man," I said, glancing away. "Believe what you will."

"You're *lying;* I can tell. You're not fucking *married.* You're writing me off!"

Struggling with guilt, I said, "C'mon, let's not spoil the pretty fuckin' great time we just had."

"Get the fuck outta here, Mister," he sneered. "Fucking *liar*. *Coward*."

"Hey, I'm sorry if I…"

"Get out!" he exploded viciously. "You got what you wanted, so…*get back to work.*"

That did it. I took a deep breath and set my teeth, stepping closer. "Look here, whatever your fucking name is. If you want me out of this house, that's your prerogative. No sweat. I wanted outta here the second I shot my load. But *no one* tells me how to spend my time on the outside, least of all you. You haven't the *authority*." With "authority," I shoved him, albeit not too roughly, back onto the bed and added, while glaring down at him, "You *got* that, punk?"

He didn't respond right away. Instead, the kid clamped his bent, tattooed arms against the sides of his face and slowly retracted into the fetal position. I stood there, observing with morbid fascination as he settled into a rigor mortis of humiliation, not backing away until he finally broke the spell by uttering a feeble and abject "Please. Just go."

My eyes still riveted to the scene on the bed, I found myself in the room's doorway, heard myself speaking to him, confessing.

"I regret lying to you. That *was* cowardly. And I had no right to shove you. For that, I apologize."

But he remained dumb, dead on the bed, made no attempt to follow me downstairs, where I rapidly dressed and left.

Arcangelo, Paul, the rich kid, the solitary tourists seeking a thrill, the traveling businessmen who fancy my type, all the myriad others and myself: so many cowards, it would seem, so many liars. In seeking our humanity through sensation, have we become less than human? Subhuman? Inhuman? And if so, what is it, if anything, that we have missed in not becoming truly human? What are we afraid of? Is it that in digging to unearth our true natures, we may exhume deeper-still multiplicities of unanswerable questions or, rather, the unutterable answers that belie those questions, that cause us pause?

Many years ago, lying on my belly, pinned against the mattress, my face buried in the pillow, gritting my teeth—not with pain, but with rage at the effort it took to deny pleasure—I could smell the scotch on my father's breath, hear him saying:

"Can you feel the *love,* Adam?

"Can you *feel* it?

"*Can* you?

"I can feel *your* love.

"It's *flowing,* Baby.

"It's *love…*

"*I* can feel it…

"Can *you?*"

Meet in the Middle
Landon Dixon

After several drinks in the hotel bar before dinner, a couple of bottles of wine during dinner, and a liqueur after dinner, I was feeling little or no pain. No pain, but plenty of frustration. Because it looked like a severe hangover and a major dent in my expense account was all I was going to get out of this particular sales call.

I gave it one last try. "So, whaddaya think, Trent? I can ship the equipment to your plant tomorrow. Just gimme the word. Howzaboutit?" I wiped a stray wisp of drool from the corner of my mouth and fixed Trent with a winning smile and a wavery gaze.

He regarded me with all four of his eyes. I wasn't that drunk—he was wearing glasses. "I…don't know, Mark," he said slowly, agonizingly, as I studied his lips for comprehension.

"What's to know?" I said loudly, my dreams of 1979 being a bonus year fading away like my cognition. I tossed back a shot of ice water to steady my nerves and stomach.

He said, "Uh, well, maybe if we went back to my office, crunched some more numbers." He shrugged and smiled; smiled like a tightfisted tightwad, the idea of number-crunching bringing him the only joy in his buttoned-down world.

I frowned and thought, *This guy wouldn't buy a mousetrap during the bubonic plague*. Still, going back to his office was better than calling it quits. "Sure, sure," I said, slurring my words. "Whatever you want. Let's crush some numbers. I mean, crutch some plumbers...well, you know what I mean."

I paid the exorbitant dinner bill, and we walked, more or less straight, to his office a couple of blocks away. His 13th-floor executive digs were a symphony of sophistication and taste. I stumbled over to a blurry map on the wall that highlighted the location of his company's various plants and distribution warehouses. It was a busy map. For a young, short guy, he was one big businessman. Of course, his daddy had helped him out in that regard.

As I blinked at the impressive corporate topography, I suddenly realized that Trent was at my side, his hand resting casually on my shoulder. I guessed that it was to keep me upright. Nevertheless, I turned my head and looked down at the hand. It was smooth and tanned and manicured—a hand that could crush or coddle. I jerked my head back up, let my brain slosh around for a bit, and then looked at him looking at me. His glasses were gone, and I noticed that his eyes were a deep, warm brown color. His face was smooth and tanned like his hands, fine-featured, and his short blond hair was parted on the right.

He was mumbling something or other about him hoping that I didn't think he was being forward with me, or something like that, and then he stood on his tiptoes and kissed me on the mouth!

I went sober as a judge. Then thought, *Who am I to judge?* "That's a new way of closing a deal," I said, chuckling. "I thought you Europeans normally kiss on the cheek."

"Normally," he replied, smiling. His teeth were white and strong and even, and his golden face shone in the muted light. "I am going to sign that contract for your equipment, Mark," he continued, "but I was hoping that we could transact some personal business first."

I grinned crookedly. "You scratch my ass, I poke yours—is that it?"

"Well, I..."

"What are we waiting for?" I grabbed him by the shoulders and planted a wet one on his stunned kisser. It looked good on him.

"Now, Mark," he protested, "if you're uncomfortable at all..."

I snorted in frustration. "Let's can the chatter and get busy." My head was totally clear now—and swelling nicely.

He finally made a quick decision and rapidly stripped off his jacket, shirt, shoes, socks, and pants, like a fireman in reverse.

"Wow," I said, staring at his hairless, sun-kissed body. He was lean and limber, his nipples large and dark. My eyes traveled down to the business end of him, and I noted that his cock was rigidly outlined against the thin white material of his briefs.

I clumsily pulled off my clothes and scattered them about until I was wearing his style of birthday suit. My tall, thin body wasn't quite as well-tuned as his, but it was still highly functional. Light brown fur sprinkled my chest and dove down into my shorts. To reaffirm my commitment to his firm...cock, I pulled my shorts down and kicked them aside, almost taking out a lamp in the process. My eight-inch cock leaped out, eager for action.

He followed my lead and was quickly in the altogether. His cock was pointing at me, hard and uncompromising—not quite as large as mine but still more than adequate for putting out any fires that needed putting out. His balls were shaved clean for maximum pleasure, with only a small triangle of downy blond fur left just above the base of his arrow-straight cock.

"You've got quite an inflated opinion of yourself," I quipped, then dropped to my knees in front of his capitalist tool and got the true measure of the man. I started stroking him with my sweaty hand.

"Yes," he groaned, tilting his head back.

I stroked him up and down and around, pulling him as long as I could. His cock felt great in my hand—hard and thick and alive—but I knew it would feel even better in my mouth.

"Suck my cock, Mark," he said, reading my mind. He fondled his erect, chocolate nipples as I prepped him with my hand job.

I steered his straining cock toward my open mouth, then flicked out my tongue and slapped his swollen head with it. He moaned, urging me on. I licked at his hood, swatted his slit with my tongue, then bathed the entire glorious length of him with hot saliva. I painted his cock with my wet, eager tongue—up and down, up and down, over and over. I flicked my tongue underneath his balls, corralled them in my mouth, and sucked on them.

He gripped my head excitedly. "God, that feels good," he moaned, his fingers riffling through my lustrous brown hair, then tugging it as I bounced his balls around in my mouth, all the while still stroking his slickened cock.

His balls were thick and heavy, and as I played with them I could smell the musky manness of him, the essence of his eroticism. I sucked his pouch, pulled on it, attacked it with my mouth, reveling in the clean-shaven taste of his balls. Then I turned my aroused attention back to his studly cock. I sucked his cock head into my mouth, popped it in and out, smacked my tongue against it, and then, to show him that playtime was truly over and that the serious matter of a cock-and-mouth meeting had begun, I gulped down as much of his cock as I could. And that was the entire length.

"Jesus!" he cried out, shocked, his body jolted with joy. "Deep-throat me, baby!"

Years of practical training in countless glory holes on the road was put to good use, yet again. I squeezed his entire raging cock tightly into my mouth and throat, the suction driving him wild, then snaked out my tongue and lapped at his balls. His body trembled with erotic overload as I clenched his buttocks and drove his cock as deep as I could into my throat.

"I'm going to come, Mark!" he screamed all too soon, tearing at my hair, frantically pulling on his engorged nipples as his passion burst into flame and consumed him.

My oral communication skills had obviously proved extremely persuasive. I quickly disgorged his soaked cock from the warm, wet womb of my mouth and then sucked on it with a frenzied intensity, my head bobbing vigorously up and down, pumping him for the white, hot, liquid protein that I craved.

"Here I come!" he yelled. His hips jerked back and forth, pounding his cock into my mouth like he was pounding an open ass, his balls cracking against my chin with each desperate thrust.

He let out a mighty roar, and sizzling semen sprayed into my grateful mouth, filling me up instantly. His ass and legs started to quake as his torso was jolted over and over again, as he blasted load after load of salty spunk into my mouth and down my throat. I swallowed hard and often, not gagging once. There's no better nightcap, in my opinion, than a good hot semen shake.

His glistening body convulsed one final time, and the last of his thick goo shot out of his fiery cock and into my sucking mouth. I chugged that come as well, then sucked long and hard on his twitching cock, milking every last delightful drop of jism from his spent member.

He finally pulled his dripping cock out of my greedy mouth and collapsed to his knees in front of me. "That was fantastic," he whispered, his eyes half-closed, his body drooping with the exhaustion of ecstasy.

"That was the just the beginning," I replied matter-of-factly. I clasped his head in my hands and planted my come-smeared lips on his. I shoved my tongue inside of his mouth and let him taste the sticky by-product of our mutual lust. Then I pulled back and said, "I'm gonna fuck that tight ass of yours, Trent."

"Please do," he responded wearily, and he dropped down into the mounting position, sticking his taut, rounded ass into my face.

I clambered upright, then lowered my rigid cock down to ass level. I spat into my hand, rubbed the warm spit on my hard cock and his soft asshole, and then pressed my massive purple hood up against his incredibly small pucker. His body jumped, and jumped again when I boldly shoved my bloated cock head into his tight ass. "Here it comes, Trent," I warned him, somewhat belatedly, as I slowly slid my huge cock into his tiny opening.

I had just about a third of my cock buried in his sexy man-catcher when he suddenly pushed backward and swallowed the rest of my cock with his ass, as I had swallowed his cock in my mouth. "Yeah," I moaned, overwhelmed by the incredibly heated hold his ass had on my cock. I was buried to the balls, and the feeling was fantastic. I began gyrating my hips in a rhythm as old as

Grecian commerce, plunging my rock-hard cock in and out of his vise-like ass.

"Fuck me, Mark! Fuck me!" he begged.

I nodded, letting the sensual sensation of fucking his tremulous ass flood my body. It was like someone had plugged my cock into a wall socket and filled me full of electricity. My whole body tightened and tingled. I stared at my cock planted to the hilt in his butt, savoring the moment for only a moment, and then started pounding away with religious fervor, plundering his ass faster and faster and faster.

"That's the way," he grunted, my balls smacking loud and clear against his butt cheeks in the deserted office.

I picked up the pace even more until I was banging that beautiful man like a bongo drum, plowing my cock into his ass with abandon, over and over again. Sweat flew off my superheated body and splashed down onto his glistening bronze rump as I split him in half with my battering ram, smashing into his sphincter recklessly and relentlessly.

I threw back my head and let out a cry for the whole world to hear, semen bubbling to the boiling point and beyond in my balls. I hammered his exquisite ass for all I was worth, gripping his narrow waist and watching through lust-misted eyes as his buttocks rippled with each frenzied thrust of my cock. I held out as long as I could, heating my cock to a molten state in his fiery ass, but all too soon I screamed, "I'm gonna blow my load in your ass, Trent!" Telling him, not asking him.

"Fill me with come!" he screamed back. He desperately tried to flail away at his own restiffened cock, but it was no good—I was pounding him too hard, riding his rump like a hard-nosed boss.

My body tensed, my fingers clawed at his hips, and then my cock detonated inside of him. I saw stars, and I was jerked around like a fish on a line as I blasted load after load of liquid man seed into his sexy ass. "Fuck almighty!" I bellowed, my mind sent reeling by flashes of pure, raw ecstasy, my body spasming uncontrollably, my cock spraying searing semen into my lover's ass. The white-hot sexual joy of it all rocketed me to the very edge of unconsciousness, my mind blanking out, and I clung to his shaking ass like it was my last hold on reality.

Finally, after the longest sustained period of orgasm I had ever experienced, my cock splattered one last gush of come into Trent's sweet ass, and then I collapsed on top of him, my body and mind and soul wasted.

After an eternity of heavy breathing, he grinned and said, "I hope that I didn't pressure you into a sale that you didn't want to make?"

I licked behind his ear, bit into his neck, tongued some sweat off his back, and then uncoupled my cock from his gripping ass and showed him the butt plug I had been wearing all evening long. "I had a feeling that we would be able to close the deal tonight," I told him.

Army Green

Jay Starre

The sun was setting, but the temperature was still sweltering. Kevin trudged toward the sergeant's tent with heavy footsteps. His body dripped sweat and his uniform clung stickily to his large, muscular frame. Kevin was a husky guy, and that fact only added to the discomfort he suffered in the jungle environment. He was sweating from every conceivable body part.

"Sarge, can I speak with you a minute?" Kevin asked as he bent to enter the tent.

"Come on in, Kevin. I'm fucking beat, though. What did you want?" A low drawl greeted the younger soldier from a corner of the tent.

Kevin stared at the prone figure on the small cot. The light was dim, pleasantly so after the brightness of the tropical day outside. But he had no trouble making out the figure of his sergeant sprawled at the other end of the tent on his camp bed. Kevin was momentarily speechless at the hot sight. The sergeant was half-naked, wearing only his black army boots and socks, and a pair of skimpy army-issue shorts that did little to hide his beefy, hairy thighs.

If Kevin was a large man, the sergeant was even larger. Six inches over six feet tall, with powerful shoulders and a wide, hairy chest, Sarge must have weighed a good 280 pounds or more. Kevin stared at the sergeant's hairy torso, his blue eyes wide as they traversed the hirsute territory of the big officer's bulging pecs and downward along the trail of fur that led inevitably to the waistband of his baggy shorts. One of Sarge's hands was down in those shorts, lazily scratching at his cock and balls while Kevin gawked in open-mouthed fascination. Was it the beginning of a hard-on that rose up beneath the thin material of those shorts? Was Kevin's imagination running away with him?

"What was it you wanted, Kevin? Maybe a piece of this?" Sarge murmured quietly. His buried paw moved beneath the shorts, and a moment later a big fat cock appeared as the shorts were shoved down to expose it.

Kevin gasped and stumbled forward on shaky legs. He had been fantasizing about Sarge's hot, hairy body since they had come to that godforsaken jungle nearly a month ago. Was the officer teasing him? Kevin was too hot and too horny to stop himself from dropping to his knees beside the green cot and snorting in the sharp reek of Sarge's sweaty body. Just below him that big cock waved at him, growing fatter and longer with every passing second.

"I'm too fucking tired to beat around the bush. Suck it, soldier, or get the hell out of here."

The burly private heard his own low moan as if it had come from some disembodied source. His mouth was opening and his face was dropping, as if he had no will to stop it. That fat cock rose up to meet his lips as the sergeant lifted his hips lazily and fed Kevin his engorged rod.

"Yeah, that is so sweet. Suck it good before you spread your beefy can and take it up the ass."

Kevin snorted in shock at the sergeant's words. Take it up the ass! His mouth had just tasted the salty-sticky knob when the officer uttered that provocative suggestion. Kevin shuddered at the feel of that shiny pole on his tongue and lips as he imagined the giant thing worming its way up his snapping sphincter. What a thought!

Sarge had the base of his erection gripped in one hand, feeding it upward into Kevin's opening mouth while his other hand moved down to clasp the back of the private's thick neck. "I been hoping you would come around eventually," Sarge muttered between deep sighs. "Seeing a hot blond hunk like you day after godforsaken day makes a guy very horny. My cock's been leaking thinking about your sweet mouth and ass. I bet it's big and hairy, isn't it?"

Kevin couldn't answer with his mouth full of swelling pecker. But he knew what the sergeant was talking about: his big, hard butt. Sarge wanted his ass. Kevin eagerly slurped at the cock being crammed into his mouth as he thought of what was to come. He wrapped his lips around the hard meat and bobbed his head up and down enthusiastically. Leaking precome oozed over his tongue and tonsils. He sucked it in and swallowed it noisily.

Sarge was moaning in a low, guttural drone by then. His speech had degenerated to a series of soft utterances of "yes" and "oh, yeah." Kevin was sucking loudly in the tent's silence and grew bold at Sarge's words of encouragement. He reached up and ran his hands over the sprawled man's hairy torso. The hard flesh was covered in slick fur. Each of the Sarge's big pecs was a mound of taut beef. The long nipples protruded fleshily from the matted hair, swelling under Kevin's tweaking fingers.

"That's nice, so nice," Sarge muttered and lifted his chest to meet the tugging fingers. Then he abruptly lifted Kevin's face off his cock. "Suck my nuts. Lick the sweat off them," he ordered quietly.

Kevin was trembling from head to toe. It was a good thing he was down on his knees, because he could not have stood on his feet. His head was swimming. He was soaked in sweat and gasping for breath. But the sight of those big bull balls rolling around in the sergeant's fingers was too tempting to resist. He buried his face in Sarge's crotch and sucked up the pair of hairy 'nads. He got both between his gaping lips and tickled them with his tongue. He rubbed his face over the base of Sarge's hard cock and sniffed in the stench of his furry crotch. He got his chin up under Sarge's ball sac, stretching the baggy army shorts and nearly tearing them. Sarge chuckled as he shoved them down over his knees and lifted his thighs to pull them over his boots. When his legs rose in the air, he exposed his hairy butt cheeks, and Kevin couldn't help pulling back to get a glimpse of them. Sarge's balls popped out of his mouth.

He was staring at a hair-ringed pucker hole. Sarge had pulled his thighs back and was holding them up against his chest. "Go ahead, soldier boy. Eat some army ass."

Kevin groaned. Without a second's hesitation he burrowed into the open crack, rubbing his nostrils and mouth all around in the hairy cleft. Big, beefy butt cheeks wrapped around his face. A warm, moist crack parted for his exploring mouth and tongue. He swiped at the hairy furrow with his outstretched tongue, tasting sweat and musk. He went deeper, groaning again as he found the crinkled slot, hairlessly slick and quivering. He barely heard Sarge's deep moan as he bathed the little hole with attentive slurps. The butt lips spasmed and gaped apart, allowing Kevin to stuff his tongue into the heated depths beyond. He felt faint as he clamped his mouth over that hole and jabbed it with his tongue, amazed that he was actually tongue-fucking the big, hairy sergeant.

Then he felt strong hands on his back and then his ass. A low command penetrated his focused attention. "Get up on the cot. Sit on my face."

Kevin cooperated with the hands on his back and butt pulling him upward. He kept his mouth locked over Sarge's quivering slot and his tongue digging into the hot butt passage while he crawled up on top of the man. His legs straddled the officer's chest and head and he felt his pants being undone and pulled down, revealing his under-wear-covered butt. A moment later that underwear was being ripped down to his knees. His naked ass was seized by big paws and pulled down over Sarge's face. A wet tongue dived into his parted crack. Kevin shivered all over as that tongue found his hole and went to work on it. He increased his own efforts at tongue-drilling the sweet slot between Sarge's spread thighs as his own hole was getting tongued.

The two men writhed on the cot, each busily eating the other's hairy ass. The sergeant was naked, except for his boots, but the private was still wearing his tight tank top, and his pants and under-wear were tangled around his knees and ankles. Through the intensity of the mutual butt-feast, Kevin felt Sarge slap one of his hairy butt cheeks and push upward on his hips.

"Get naked. All the way, Private."

Kevin instantly obeyed the muttered command. He sat back down over the Sarge's face but raised his upper body to tear off his army-issue tank top. Then he bent back down with his face in the sergeant's crotch and squirmed out of the rest of his uniform. He lapped at the sergeant's big nut sac dangling down between his raised thighs as he did.

"Get back to work on that army asshole, Private!"

Kevin spread the sergeant's ham-huge buttocks and immersed himself in his asshole once again. Groping hands played with his own upended ass, tickling the parted crack and poking at the spit-wet hole. He shuddered as those fingers began to penetrate the moist slot, two of them digging past his gaping butt lips and into the dark furrow beyond. Kevin heard the sergeant's chuckles as the man began to finger-fuck his hole with twisting, intimate probes.

Kevin drove his tongue deep into the sergeant's slackening butt pit as those fingers stretched him wide open. His big thighs were trembling so badly, he wondered whether he was going to tumble from the cot. But Sarge's hands on his butt held him in place as they explored every inch of the big cheeks. One of them slid down and squeezed his nuts, then moved to his cock, squeezing that as well. Kevin groaned around the butt lips he was slurping over.

"Time to fuck this hairy butt! Turn around and sit on my cock, Private!"

Kevin came up for air, licking his lips and tasting the funky sex-smell of the sergeant's crotch on them. He was so hot and sweaty he practically slithered over the officer's naked body as he turned around and faced him. Sarge was lying back with his arms behind his head, lazily staring up at the younger private. The sergeant smirked and licked his own lips, winking brazenly at the same time.

"See if you can take my beer-can bone up that wet slot of yours. Sit on it, Kevin."

"Yes, sir," Kevin murmured in shaky reply. He was straddling the large man beneath him, his hairy butt in the air over the officer's crotch. He could feel the sergeant's monster meat pressing up into his butt crack. He reached behind himself and took hold of it, amazed at the gargantuan proportions of the meaty pecker. It barely fit in his fist. And it seemed to be at least a foot long.

"I know it's a big fucker and fat as hell. But I think you're man enough to take it up your sweet little hole, don't you?"

Kevin breathed deeply as he pointed the blunt head at his spit-wet asshole. His slot quivered with trepidation. He bent over the sergeant and wiggled his big fat ass over the upthrust pole, pressing downward at the same time. Kevin's moist hole spread apart for the blunt head, but it was not enough to get the wide flange past his spasming ass rim. He worked his ass in circles and rubbed his tender slot against the big fucker. That seemed to loosen up his hole, but it still wasn't enough. Sarge lay there passively and grinned up at him, waiting for Kevin to do the job himself.

Kevin gritted his teeth and shoved with his butt. He held Sarge's cock stiff in one hand as he squatted down over it. Something had to give; it was the private's straining butt entrance. The lips parted, and suddenly a fat boner was sliding up into Kevin's convulsing butt oven.

"Shit! That is fucking awesome! Your hole is like an electric eel over my cock! It's flinching and twittering and squeezing my meat something fierce! Good job, Private!"

The sergeant was beaming his approval, while lifting his hips slightly and feeding another inch of fat cock to Kevin's aching asshole. Kevin held the cock in place and sat down on it. Now that it was captured, he took it all. With a grunting effort, the big private swallowed a foot of mammoth poker.

The two men groaned simultaneously. Kevin was sitting right down on the sergeant's lap. Kevin felt stuffed. He was packed with hard, throbbing cock. His ass lips clenched around the giant invader with vise-like intensity. The sergeant's eyes were half-closed with concentration as he lifted his hips and twisted his cock inside Kevin's quivering guts. Kevin rose up and slowly allowed the big bone to slide from his clutching anus. It was painful and incredibly pleasurable at the same time. The private rose up all the way until only the broad head remained inside his stretched butt rim. Then he began the slow descent, eating up that fat cock inch by relentless inch. He gasped and muttered with the effort but managed to swallow it all once more. Although he felt just as stuffed, this time his asshole seemed more open to it. Squatting on the sergeant's waist, with his big cock all the way up his ass, the private felt an odd sense of fulfillment. It seemed right. That big poker crammed up his tight asshole was heaven itself.

Then Kevin rose again. He felt every inch of the thing as it slithered from his spit-slick hole. It rubbed his butt lips with awesome pleasure as it came out of his hot butt hole. When it was nearly out, he felt the slick length with his fist. It was so big! Fat, hard and wet, the pulsing pole still seemed too impossibly large to fit up Kevin's asshole, or anyone's asshole. But he had done it! And he would do it again. With a determined grunt, he impaled himself with the whole shaft again.

"Good effort, Private! Keep it up," Sarge murmured. He moved his hands from behind his head up to Kevin's chest and searched out the taut little nipples poking out from his blond-furred chest. He pinched them, sending electric chills down into Kevin's battered guts.

Kevin arched his chest into the tweaking fingers and wiggled his butt over the fat boner buried up it. He began to squirm over Sarge's cock, feeling the thing pressing way up inside him against his prostate and pulsating anal walls. His ass lips caressed the base of it in little fluttering convulsions as he sat on Sarge's lap. It felt perfect.

But Sarge wanted more. He laughed quietly as he pulled Kevin forward by his nipples. Kevin found himself prone over Sarge's big, slack body. Their sweaty chests mashed together. The sergeant gripped the back of Kevin's head and pulled his face into his own. Sarge's tongue invaded the private's mouth. Then he began to buck up into Kevin's ass.

Kevin grunted with every sharp jab. The fat poker was slamming up into his ass. His own cock was straining against Sarge's hairy belly, swollen and aching for release. The insistent, steady drilling began to work Kevin into a frenzy. He squirmed all over his hairy, muscular mattress, moaning into the officer's mouth and attempting to take all that fat cock as it plundered and plugged his defenseless asshole

It was too much. His body tensed all over and his cock jerked against Sarge's stomach. A river of goo oozed out to coat their bellies. The sergeant had to have noticed, but he kept up his forceful fuck, slamming deep into Kevin's convulsing asshole. Every time the officer jabbed Kevin's butt, the private's cock spurted another gob of spunk. More and more come oozed from Kevin's cock until there seemed to be a quart of the sticky stuff sliding between their mashed bellies.

"I think it's time to really fuck your ass, Private."

Kevin could hardly believe his ears. His asshole felt stretched and bruised and fucked to death already. What did the sergeant have in mind? He found out. With strong hands, the officer maneuvered Kevin around so that suddenly he was on his belly, his hairy thighs spread wide, and the sergeant was lying on top of him. All 280 pounds of him! Kevin felt buried in sweaty male flesh. His fucked ass was only momentarily empty. The sergeant was poking around between Kevin's hairy mounds with rough fingers. Three of them dug into his stretched butt hole. Kevin groaned at the invasion, but then he found himself enjoying it as they expertly twisted and tugged at his already loosened gap. His cock actually began to grow stiff again.

Those fingers slid from his hole and were replaced by that giant cock. The blunt head popped inside his aching rectum effortlessly. The foot of shaft that followed slithered up his guts with unbeliev- able ease. He had become a slack hole. The sergeant's big cock rode up inside him without any trouble. Kevin closed his eyes and sur- rendered to the exquisite sensation of hot, hard meat rubbing his insides. The sergeant fucked him slowly at first, feeding him that fat salami with deep but easy thrusts. Then he began to increase the tempo. Soon he was once more slamming into Kevin's butt.

Kevin lay there and took it. He had become a slack, gibbering mess. All his muscles had gone limp. He spread his legs wide apart and opened entirely to the mammoth piston reaming his insides. Heavy, sweaty weight pressed down on him. Hairy thighs pinned his, and giant palms pressed his chest down into the army cot. The big boner rammed his ass with furious passion.

"I'm shooting jizz up your big fat ass!"

Kevin groaned when he heard the sergeant's declaration. He was getting scummed by the hot officer! Kevin felt entirely open to the pulsing cock up his ass. He took all that jizz without any regret. Then a strange thing occurred. His cock was hard, but his balls were emptied of jizz. Yet he experienced a sudden, flooding orgasm. It was an orgasm of the body. His, slack, pounded body twitched and spasmed beneath the sergeant's weight. His asshole fluttered and caressed the meaty invader rubbing all around inside it. He was coming in his asshole.

The sergeant was dripping sweat as he dropped down over Kevin in a sudden collapse. Kevin was twitching with rapture. He turned his head sideways and opened his mouth to the officer. Their tongues entwined.

They fell into an exhausted sleep that way.

All Soaped Up

Doug Smith

I don't think it would have happened at all that summer if we had not been caught in the rainstorm. Thunder boomed across the Oklahoma cornfields, barely preceding the bank of dark clouds that swooped in from the west. Jerry and I had been out tossing the football around in an abandoned field about a mile from home.

"Shit! We better run for it!" Jerry shouted above the sound of the rushing wind.

Earlier we had walked to the field from our parents' places, which happened to be right next door to each other. Now we had to flee or get drenched in the sudden storm. With the football tucked under my arm, I followed close on Jerry's heels as we ran down the dirt road toward home. It was too late for us to escape, and within moments the deluge fell around us.

Mud splattered up from the pounding rain and our racing feet. I kept my eyes on Jerry's sturdy form ahead of me through the sheets of water. It was only seconds before we were soaked. Jerry's cotton shorts clung to his beefy butt cheeks as they pumped steadily in front of me. I remember that well—my eyes glued to those sexy mounds and my cock growing stiff in my own sodden shorts.

"Let's go to my place!" I shouted ahead to Jerry. "My parents are away for the night."

Whether my parents were home or not shouldn't have mattered. But my mind was already racing ahead, plotting something I had been fantasizing about for the past few months since Jerry and I had graduated from high school. Jerry's rain-soaked ass had a lot to do with that barely formed but devious plot.

We banged past the screen door and into the back porch, laughing with relief and shaking the water from our bodies like dogs. "Let's get in the shower downstairs and clean off this mud. Leave your clothes here," I suggested. Without waiting for Jerry's response, I quickly shed my own soaked shorts, shirt and underwear.

My big boner was suddenly right there in front of Jerry. It was a risk to be so blatant, but I figured Jerry would laugh if off he wasn't interested. But I was hoping like hell he *was* interested.

"Fuck, Doug! You got some stiff rod there! The storm make you horny or what?" Jerry was laughing. But he was stripping too.

I held my breath. Jerry had a great body. He was a tad on the chunky side, with broad shoulders and a thick chest and back. His legs were like big hams, and his butt was big and round, like two basketballs. He had been a football tackle in high school and had the tank body to go with it. I watched as he swiftly revealed that thick body while the storm raged just outside.

"I guess all that thunder made me kinda hot too," Jerry chuckled.

There it was, his big fat poker growing bigger between his hefty thighs. That was a welcome sight. Maybe he would go for my next suggestion. I would have to wait and see. I wanted to get him in the shower and right next to me first.

"Race you to the shower," he was grinning as he bolted down the stairs toward the basement.

I was once more following Jerry's pumping butt. God, it was hot! Two big cheeks, dimpled and jiggling as he banged down the stairs ahead of me. The crack was tight and appeared deep. My frenzied 18-year-old imagination pictured a sweaty, warm hole between those cheeks, tight and hot.

My cock was hard as a rock and twitching by the time we reached the basement bathroom. There was a big shower stall there, used to clean off after dirty farm work. Jerry was already inside and turning on the water when I crowded in after him. My swaying cock bumped against one of his hefty butt cheeks, and I gritted my teeth with stifled lust.

"Yeah, this hot water feels fucking great! Soap me up, Doug. I feel like a mud-soaked hog!" Jerry was giggling as he placed his hands on the wall of the stall in front of him and stood beneath the cascading showerhead. He spread his legs and planted his feet wide apart.

My eyes nearly bugged out of their sockets. Was he asking for it or what? We had talked about sex incessantly all summer, but neither of us had said we were into guys rather than chicks. Of course, I hadn't admitted my own gay fantasies, so I figured he might not have either. Now was the time to find out. I just couldn't hold back any longer.

I took up the bar of soap from the soap dish on the wall and began to rub it with both hands all over his broad back. He had a huge back. The skin was lightly tanned from the few times he would go shirtless, but as my hands descended the flesh, it became markedly less so. By the time I reached his thick waist, there was a definite line where his back ended and his butt began. I held my breath and slid lower. Suddenly both my hands were soaping up his hefty butt cheeks.

"That feels good, Doug. You experienced at butt-soaping?" Jerry giggled from under the spray of the shower.

My hands were working in circles over each of his thick butt mounds. They were incredibly smooth, completely hairless, and although they were big and chunky, they were very hard too. I slid both of them toward the crack and with an abrupt lunge I dug them between the hard cheeks and into that deep crevice.

"Sure, I've soaped up the whole football team already. You're just the last of them," I joked in a quavering stutter. Would he freak out at my brazen move?

Amazingly, Jerry just laughed. Then he bent over and put both hands on his thighs. "Soap me up good, then. It feels great."

My hands were in his butt crack. I was rubbing sudsy foam all up and down the velvety crevice. I could feel the puckered asshole with my fingertips, tight and twitching. We had suddenly gone beyond the point of no return. This was not something mere buddies did. This was gay stuff! And I was in heaven.

"How about this? Do you like this?" I said more boldly. My fingers had strayed downward toward his balls and then suddenly one hand was cupping them and massaging soap into his big pair of 'nads.

"I like that just fine," Jerry murmured just barely loud enough for me to hear. He had dropped his head and actually moved his feet farther apart when my hand surrounded his balls. That was a signal I did not miss. My hand moved higher up between his spread thighs and encountered his stiff boner. I rubbed soap along the twitching shaft slowly and deliberately.

"I like that just fine too. You can play with my butt hole if you want," Jerry muttered in a shaking voice.

Music to my ears! I'd wanted his asshole all summer. I had been dreaming about that tight slot. I had been jerking off to the thought of what it would look like and feel like almost daily. Now it was being offered to me! I stared down at his spread butt cheeks. White foam coated the mounds and the deep crack. Both of my hands were down there, and my hard cock rubbed against one of the soapy cheeks. While one hand continued to stroke his stiff shaft and play with his balls, the other ran up and down his soapy crack, grazing across his puckered butt hole with every pass.

I moved to settle on the wet hole. I stared down at it. His legs were wide apart and I was getting a perfect view. But I wanted more. I knelt down on the wet floor behind him. There it was—his big ass right before my eyes.

"Getting a good look? See something you like?" Jerry managed to tease in a shaky voice. He wiggled his ass suggestively and we both laughed nervously.

"I like your big sexy butt. I want to stick my fingers up your ass," I admitted. My fingers were already tracing the crinkled ring of flesh at the entrance. I wanted to poke inside, but it looked too tight.

"Do it. Shove a finger up there. I want to know what it feels like," Jerry admitted.

I placed a fingertip at the center of the soapy slot and began to press. The flesh was tight but much more pliant than I had expected. The soap helped lubricate the pressing digit and the rim began to open up.

"Relax, shove out with your butt hole muscles," I suggested.

Jerry dropped his ass slightly, so that he was in a partial squat. That did the trick. Suddenly his ass lips bulged outward and my finger slid inside. God, it was hot and tight and throbbing!

"Oh man, that feels incredible! Rub it in and out!" Jerry grunted. His big ass was quivering like a huge bowl of Jell-O. His asshole was pulsing and spasming around my buried finger. I began to slide it out, then shoved it deeper and then pulled it nearly all the way out again.

He groaned and his thighs shook. My other hand was pumping his stiff boner, and he was wiggling his butt around in slow, grinding circles, as if he was fucking himself over my digging finger. It was the hottest moment of my life. I shoved deeper and harder. Then an amazing thing happened. His asshole seemed to blossom open. The tight anal walls just gaped apart. Without thinking, I took advantage of his asshole's yielding and plunged another soapy finger up his soapy hole. I rammed two of them as deep as I could.

"Fuck! That feels so fucking good! So fucking good," Jerry grunted.

I watched as both fingers slid in and out of his sudsy asshole effortlessly and his butt cheeks clenched and squirmed around them. It was fascinating. My other hand kept up a steady jerking of his hard cock. His asshole swelled outward as he squatted down in front of me and groaned. I held my breath and added a third finger. Jerry cried out, and his asshole convulsed over my three fingers twisting around inside him.

"I'm shooting!" he shouted.

I felt his cock lurch under my fingers. Then it began to jerk and spray funky come all over my hand. His asshole clamped like a vice over my fingers and I rammed them deep and twisted them in circles. Jerry fell to his knees and dropped his face to the wet floor of the stall, his ass in the air with my fingers still buried up his spasming butt hole.

It was a very hot sight. His big butt mounds were covered in suds, quivering wildly, while his entire body jerked in the throes of his orgasm. My own cock was drooling and ached so badly I wondered if it would burst apart.

"Fuck me, Doug! Fuck my ass," Jerry groaned.

He wanted me to fuck him! I would have imagined that now that he had shot his load, he would want to call it quits. But he was hotter than ever! I wasted no time in following his request. I slipped my fingers from his swollen asshole and gasped at the sight of his gaping hole oozing suds. I whipped the bar of soap over my stiff cock, which I then pointed toward his upturned ass. I spread his soapy butt cheeks wide and rammed forward with my cock. The stretched hole welcomed my cock like a perfectly fitted glove.

This was back in 1977, before there was even a hint of the AIDS epidemic. We didn't even think of using condoms. So there was nothing between my sensitive cock and the pulsing walls of Jerry's sudsy anus. The fleshy glove wrapped cozily around my cock as I jabbed it in and out like a rabbit. Jerry lay there and took it, moaning and shoving back with his ass to meet every poke. I was enraptured, my mouth open and my tongue out, my eyes glued to the sight of his big can wide open and taking my fat cock so easily.

Then I began to slow down. I wanted to make it last. It was feeling so good—I didn't want it to end before I was able to savor the moment. My first fuck, and his. I lunged forward and buried my cock to the hilt and held it there. Jerry grunted, and his asshole leaped and spasmed around my entire shaft like a nervous puppy. It was amazing. My balls were up against his soapy butt cheeks, the silky flesh smooth and slippery. I used both hands to hold on to his big cheeks and began to pummel him, all the way in and then all the way out.

"Yeah, fuck me good, Doug. Oh, yeah, bang my big butt with your hard cock! Bang my ass good!" Jerry chanted in time to my steady drilling.

I had to slow down, or I would have creamed his ass and it would be all over. I pulled my cock all the way out and stared down at the gaping orifice his formerly tight bunghole had become. I rubbed more soap over the swollen ass lips and then plunged two fingers inside to feel the heated interior. It was so sexy! He grunted when my fingers slid into him. I pulled them out and then stuck my cock back inside, burying it to the balls. He grunted again and wiggled his butt in response. I pulled my cock all the way out and then stuck my fingers back inside to feel his hot innards again. I repeated the action over and over, amazed at how loose and slippery his asshole had become. I could fit three fingers inside with no trouble. He must have been a natural bottom, as his cherry hole had opened up so easily.

Jerry lay there on the tiled floor with the shower pummeling his head and shoulders while his soapy ass got felt and fucked. He seemed to be totally into it. I could not believe my good fortune. I had dreamed of this moment. I took my time and alternated my fingering with a few good pokes before finally abandoning all caution. I crouched over his spread butt, held on to his cheeks with both hands and drilled his squishy, sudsy butt like a madman.

"Oh, fuck, yeah! Fuck! Fuck! Yeah! Do it. Unload those big balls of yours!" Jerry grunted encouragingly.

The friction of his slippery butt hole was taking its toll. The volcanic fuck tunnel was melting my resistance. I grunted along with Jerry and rammed into him faster and faster. I felt the wave of orgasm approaching, then overtaking me. I shoved my cock to the balls and held it tight against his sudsy ass cheeks.

"I'm filling you with jizz!" I cried out. My entire body seemed to be coming inside out. Spewing from my cock head into his hot guts, my energy seemed to be draining out of me in an irresistible river. His hungry ass sucked me dry.

He bucked and his ass shook and he milked me of every drop of come. I fell over top of him and the shower drenched me. We lay on the floor with my cock up his butt for a long time. Finally he came to his knees and dislodged me with a groan.

"You fucked the hell out of me! I think my butt hole is going to be sore for a month," Jerry smirked as he turned and faced me.

We were both sitting on the floor of the shower. Our eyes met. Then he winked at me. "Do you wanna find out what it feels like?"

I blinked. He wanted to fuck my ass? I felt the tight hole twitch in response to the suggestion. What would it feel like? Jerry had apparently loved it.

Then I felt Jerry's hands sliding around behind me, down toward my butt. I didn't move. The bar of soap was in his fingers. Those fingers were in my crack, and then the bar of soap was rubbing over my asshole. I flinched and gasped. The tickling sensation was incredible. Then a finger began to stroke my hole. I gasped again.

"I think you'll like it. Trust me," Jerry grinned as his finger began to press past my spasming butt rim.

I leaned over and spread my legs. "Go for it. Fuck me."

All soaped up! That was the day I got my first piece of ass and the day my ass first got fucked. I will never forget it.

Bitch

M. Christian

There was a used condom in the trash. Just lying there, slightly yellowed, glistening, full at the tip. Next to the rest of the garbage, the bloated white plastic, the dark-stained brown paper bags, it was brilliant and shocking. As Quinn looked down at it, envy raised burning bile in his throat. Finally the weight of his own trash in his arms broke in, and with an unconscious hiss of strain, he lifted it high and slammed it down into the can.

Walking back down the narrow alleyway, retracing his slippered steps to the stairs up to his apartment, he caught sight of one of them, high up on the balcony, leaning flamboyantly back, a half-full glass in his hand glimmering in the dying sunlight. Looking perhaps too long, Quinn summoned him, causing the young man to sip from his glass and look over and down. Eye contact: the lean body, the delicately sculptured hair, perfect porcelain smile, the wicked mocking grin, directed at Quinn. Then a kiss, not blown but rather thrown—like a stone, mocking. At Quinn, at the garbage. Face burning, heart pounding, Quinn walked with heavy steps up to his own place, each tone of his laughter, each bird-chirping sound a cut into his back.

Upstairs (sticky key in gummy lock, stubborn door groaning with age) Mr. Boots was waiting for him. Sometimes, not often, the sight of the skinny little black-and-white cat made Quinn feel that he had, indeed, arrived home. Other times, like evenings discovering the leftovers of someone else's pleasure, the sight of the old, mangy cat just reminded him of Billy. Much had been taken by the Latino hustler—his camera, his stereo, the $2,500 in his bank account—but he'd left at least two things behind. One was a note, the condescending words a bitterness he recalled too often, and the other was the sad little kitten they'd picked out together at the shelter.

"OK, OK," Quinn said, shuffling inside and dead bolting the back porch door, "I'll feed ya." It was a standard, the closest the older man came to a religion, a litany that held his life together. Again, the dark, smelly kitchen, the piles of magazines, newspapers. The Tom of Finland signed print in the dusty frame that Lorenzo had given him—Lorenzo, who had left with not as much money, not as much damage, and so more frequently dropped into Quinn's fantasies.

The living room was as dark, with a bouquet of its own—a musty, lethargic smell. The weight of too many days lived exactly the same way. Walking in, Quinn first thumbed the set on, then the machine. The old television crackled menacingly, humming a firm base, then glowed into a newscaster's head and shoulders. The other machine did a much more clean start, showing the familiar ripped chest backdrop, the same Mapplethorpe pectorals, the intimate parade of icons down one side. Normally, when the litany of his days was more comfortable, he might have wandered down to the Shamrock, watched some game or other with the cronies there. Or he might've sat at the kitchen table with his latest *Honcho, Inches,* or *Torso,* sipping from an amber bottle until the images seemed to swim in a lazy haze of self-imposed steam.

Condoms in the trash. The anger was too present, too acid. The old desk chair creaked under his ass, the mouse skipped across the screen—a half-conscious reminder to clean it—and with a click Quinn opened a door.

It hadn't always been that way. It was a quicksand of life, a slow descent. He hadn't struggled—at least not at first. Birth was in a cool house in Virginia, mother who drank, chief petty officer father, and Benjamin, their "sensitive" son. First memories he painfully recalled as a dull ache when he sat at the kitchen table, of muscle magazines smuggled up into the attic. Thinking of them, of their strong smiles, their marble muscles, made him long for their innocence: children's desires mixed with ancient dust. One summer—the summer he'd first seen another boy's penis at swim camp—he'd stayed there so long the dust had lodged in his throat. Till the day his mother died she expressed concerns over the allergies that had so affected him then.

He used to keep some shutters open, the one to the left in the bay window, looking across the narrow alley at the neighbor's mirror Victorian. Sometimes, sitting in front of one glowing screen or other, he would catch sight of them—the boys with the golden hair, the magical eyes, the so-smooth skin. A picture book he'd seen as a boy, that same year as when the "allergies" had made his eyes water, the artist long since forgotten. But the images—naiads flitting through carbonated pools under an azure sky, clouds like white satin—had remained. An ideal, an absolute. Mythical sprites, with skin like fresh cream. A favorite fantasy from then on, being something other than the old Quinn, the bowed and balding Quinn. Being one of them, diving through the bubbling waters, hips brushing against theirs, mouths fluttering sweet kisses, eyes full of love and sweet desire.

Once the painting had been across that tiny alley, once he'd looked out the frame of that open window and seen them: blue eyes, wheat-field hair, laughter like the chiming of precious bells, chests like marble—stone carved by swimming, running, fucking. Then one of them had looked, had seen Quinn staring back. The stuff of dreams…but then he had laughed, producing the cruel, biting caw that had since begun living in his disturbing half-sleeps, his hollow and lonely nightmares.

Are you horny tonight? The bluntness of the newbie, flashing up on his screen. The skies were phosphors—microscopic dots arranged in a grid, illuminated by a tight spray of electrons. No clouds. No water. But the boys could be as lithe and alluring as in that painting. All it took was a polite deception, a sensual lie. It wasn't idyllic, wasn't perfection, but maybe someone, somewhere, would think that. For old Quinn, in his threadbare slippers, with his old cat, his stacks of yellowing porno magazines, it was still a kind of magic.

Tonight though he didn't feel like being Troy, or Lance, or Julian. Tonight, Quinn was too much…Quinn. He didn't answer the message, and instead just lurked, watching the scrolls of chatter, feeling the anger chew and gnaw.

Empty-headed peacocks. A simple, bold font.

You're insulting peacocks, Quinn clicked/clack back, his hands dancing on the faded letters of the keyboard. *At least peacocks produce something.*

It hadn't always been this way, which made it so much worse. When you fall, however slowly, you know what is possible, what's being denied, been taken away. He'd never been one of the…peacocks, but he hadn't always lurked in the heavy darkness. Some good timing—the death of his father, a heart attack at 55, had left him some real estate. His mother dropping into a sullen old age. The ties cut, severed quick and clean. He'd had money—enough—and a mission. To put flesh to dreams, to make dusty attic fantasies real.

Disgusting. Just disgusting—

Rude, inconsiderate, Quinn typed back, watching the characters appear on his glowing screen. *Parading around, flouncing it up. Rubbing our faces in it. Yeah, fucking disgusting—*

Many years of goodness—a heavenly parade of memories. Boyfriends, money, glitter balls, and beer. Snapshots that flipped through his mind when he didn't want them: the Latin boy, all darkness and smiles, jeans too tight, lips too full. The hot kiss after the parade. Then, there, the world had been wide, open—full of love and the potential for more. The blond treasure who'd served him coffee one day—beaming grin, flirting eyes. "Call me, hon," slender fingers grazing Quinn's palm. The seven digits on the check. He'd been too scared to call, too intimidated by perfection. Now he masturbated in the dark, hating himself for his cowardice.

Hate them. Know how that is. Disgusting peacocks. So pretty, so stupid. Shoving our faces in it.

He felt lied to, the bitterness seeming right, justified. He'd crossed that bridge of knives, lived with the hatred: "Fag! Homo! Fucking queer!" He'd wanted to be welcomed, embraced, brought into the Muscle Academy, whisked away to the dude ranch where cowboys would use him to his utter enjoyment. He'd wanted...to taste it. Now, though...now he knew it for what it was, a rainbow lie. It was there, but only if you had the money, the looks, the courage. If you didn't have any of that, then it was all out of reach or—soiled condoms in the trash—just a bitter reminder of failure.

Just disgusting. Hate looking at them, he typed, feeling a little strong in his hatred, his bitchiness. The other, Rollin58991, was an illusion—but he felt a closeness nevertheless. An illusion because so much was unknown—or just unnecessary to share. Quinn imagined him as a mirror, somewhere in the city, somewhere like where he was: seeing the beauty, having the hunger, but knowing the smiles were mocking, not inviting.

They chatted for a few minutes more, till the anger exhausted Quinn. Slippers on his feet, he shuffled off to bed. He thought about masturbating, but the sourness in his throat made their lithe young bodies hard and cruel, distant and viscous. He let sleep take him.

A day—or it could have been just a bit longer. He did remember the walk back from the bar. Three beers in his pale belly, legs tired from the hill. Disco thumping down the tree-lined street. With the first note he knew it was a party, knew it was next door.

It was. Pretty young things, features cut from tanned stone, brilliant smiles flashing desire. Lithe bodies poised on the balcony, sparkling laughter and gruff desire drifting down, mixing with the sexual bass of the music.

Quinn got older, fatter. He hadn't noticed his reek before, but now it hit him—booze and cigarettes, the perfume of the pathetic.

Key in the lock, gate swung wide. Down the alley, upstairs, the other balcony. Cheap plastic tumblers in thin, strong hands. So easy...so easy he did it without thinking: those hands around his cock, those soft lips on his own. He felt himself stir despite the pain of reality.

One of them turned, looked down. His smile lit up the world, a burst of innocent light. That it could have been pity never entered Quinn's mind—that he had looked and not looked away was enough. It was a kind of touch, a kind of love. Distant, yes; never more than a look, but there was something special in this young statue, this young David's glance: He saw a man, someone like himself. They had something in common—a lust for men's bodies, for men's love.

But then someone took his arm, pulled him back into the tanned and buffed chaos, back into the merciless rhythm of the party. Words, maybe his or maybe someone else's, drifted down, lacerated Quinn, poured alcohol into the cuts: "fucking troll…"

He didn't feel it at first, not as it slipped past his ears and into his mind. But with the first heavy foot on the old wooden steps, it started: the anger, the shame. Upstairs, the dark, smelly apartment, the cat—and the reminder of the acid in the smile, the promises not kept but, rather, taken advantage of. "You just ain't got anything I want," the little Latino had said, almost his last words to Quinn.

Nothing was there—the apartment, as always, was empty. Alone and burning, he walked into the darker front room. He'd left the machine running, a fact that surprised him. A creature of habit, Quinn had rolled his routine around him—a warm blanket, thick armor. The machine had been left on. Unusual.

A screech of mating modems. Chat, at first—pleasantries, but feeling forced, wooden. He was a false Quinn, one following the rules he'd set out for himself.

There's something wrong. "Them" again?

Fingers paused above keys. The anger, the shame, bubbling— making his ears ring, his breath come in ragged gasps.

Fucking hate them, he finally typed, slowly.

I know. I know how they make you feel. I understand.

Disgusting. Stupid, fucking, pretty-boys.

Let it out. All of it. It'll help.

So he did. Fingers, slowly at first, but then faster, spelling out his pain. The hate. Later, looking over his shoulder at that dark room, lit only by bluish technology, he realized just how much hate had poured out of him. He opened a vein and bled on the keys—frustration, bitterness, resentment. The lies of love and happiness. The lies of *Honcho, Torso,* and Tom of Finland. The rainbow lie. It could all be yours if you were anyone but Quinn—fat, ugly, and old.

Mostly, he talked about his anger. The disgust he felt for them—the way they paraded around, showing off their shallowness, their petty, whining voices. Peacocks, empty-headed peacocks. Giggling like girls—nauseating.

Finally he couldn't see anymore. Going into the bright yellow bathroom, he pulled off a long streamer of toilet tissue, blew his nose, gagged, then threw up—something that always happened when he cried.

When he went back, the machine was still on, the screen still glowing.

Can you sleep?

Smiling, Quinn typed an affirmative.

Then sleep. It will all be better in the morning.

No alarm clock. Sirens, instead. A short, sharp whoop. The sound of tires scraping a curb, breaking a bottle. Quinn rolled over and felt sleep tug at him again.

But then—another sound. It wasn't something he was used to hearing, so it pulled him back out of his doze. A basic kind of sound. Getting up, he threw on his threadbare yellow robe and fumbled to the window, the one that looked out onto the narrow alley. When he opened the old window, the sound was louder. For a moment, and just that, he thought that perhaps it was the cat—trapped and maybe dying somewhere. But a glance over his shoulder showed him the small animal, asleep, curled into a ball on the kitchen table.

Crying. No—sobbing. No—screaming. No—a sound he hadn't quite heard before, but still essentially human. It came from within the house next door, in waves.

Quinn went around to the front: blue and red flashes through the thick curtains. Parting them, he saw a police car. No, two. And a white-paneled van.

Quinn watched, not feeling much of anything, as the stretcher was brought out. Long form in a black plastic bag. One of the men, nothing more than a boy, walking alongside, face haunted, drawn.

After a point, the cars and the van left. The neighborhood, after, was soft and quiet. Quinn didn't think that morning—at least he tried not to. He was confused, puzzled, and sad. Instead of thinking, he absently watched television, the sound loud, booming. Finally, as the sun started to set and the night grew cool, he went into his living room and to his computer.

A piece of mail was waiting for him. The words, at first, not making any sense. So he read them again and again.

Disgusting fags, the message said. Then, *I hope that will make you feel better.*

When he did believe it, the tears started again—but not for himself.

The Help

Scott D. Pomfret

The last place I expected to see beautiful, shirtless boys was in the fields near my parents' country place. It's desolate. For hundreds of miles, you won't find a single club, coffeehouse, or chic little storefront crammed with hot, trashy Gucci boys and Banana Republicans.

So when I cruised around the long, slow curve just before my mother's driveway and got a sudden head-on glimpse of rock-hard man flesh, I nearly drove into a tree.

He was shirtless, mounted at the end of a stone wall in the meadow at edge of my parents' farm. He stood like a colossus, one boot on either side of the wall, and hefted a massive boulder. His shoulders bulged with the effort, each muscle defined even at that great distance like an amateur anatomy lesson. A pair of baggy carpenter jeans belted by a loose knot of rope slung low on his waist— low enough so that I could see his butt muscles bulge.

I could almost smell the musty crotch of the man, the fingernails crusted with grease. He was filthy. An animal. A gorgeous animal.

At the meeting of our eyes, I thought my little blue Miata had come to a complete stop. The breeze stopped blowing, the sun stopped beaming, the world stopped turning. It was magnetic. Electric. Hell, it was downright nuclear.

Only when my tires left the pavement did I remember that I was still moving. A quick twitch of the wheel made the tires spin. The Miata shuddered and its bumper passed within inches of the tree. The back end fishtailed and then fell into line, and I slammed the brake and squealed down my mom's long driveway to the house.

"Mom," I yelled. "Mom!"

She was sitting on the back porch drinking a Dirty Jane martini with about 150 of my aunts all around.

"Who's that giant stud down at the end of the driveway?"

Mom hugged me and kissed me and said, "Welcome home."

"Yeah, yeah, yeah," I said, "but who …?"

"You mean Nick? That's the new help I hired."

"Your mother is always *so* good at finding good help," one of my aunts remarked.

"Amen!" I said. "Mom's always looking out for me."

"For you?" My aunt asked. "He's just here to build the wall."

Not if I can help it, I vowed to myself. As soon as I could get away from the relatives, I locked myself in the second-floor bathroom. Nick was now in the back yard, stripped to the waist beneath the hot sun. His skin was bronzed and glistening, the fine hair of his forearms gold as grain. His hair was wet with sweat. He had a shovel in his grimy hands and a big old wrench in his pocket.

I pulled back my mother's lace curtains for a better view. My cock swelled in my trousers, but the movement of lace must somehow have caught Nick's eye. He whirled. I was caught red-handed. And red-faced.

I tried to make myself think about SATs and the troubles in the Middle East, puppy dogs, and little girls.

But that night, as soon as all my relatives had gone to bed and Nick had gone home, I couldn't think of anything but Nick.

Mea culpa, Mom, but what's a boy to do when you won't hire anything but gorgeous studs? College was great for finding the cute boys, but I could always count on Mom's taste in men. She was the best fag hag a boy ever had.

I imagined the firmness of Nick's pecs and flat belly. The

sweaty writhe of his shoulder muscles under my palms. I imagined digging deep into hard flesh with my fingers. Kissing those closed blue eyes with their long lashes. Putting my face in Nick's musky crotch and...

Suddenly the night was jungle-hot and moist, and my hand was in my pants. I touched my cock and imagined it was Nick. I unbuckled my trousers and pulled my cock free, stroking it from the head to the hilt, weighing my balls in my other hand.

I imagined myself astride Nick's chest. Rutting against his firm pecs, between them against the sternum. Imagined sliding upward toward Nick's face. Nick taking me in his mouth.

I imagined my hands at the back of Nick's head, cradling him there. And then, unable to stop myself, unable to control Nick's hungry tongue, I imagined myself fucking Nick's mouth. Fucking it hard, seeing myself, the smaller of the two, fucking that mouth hard, feeling the slight gag of his tonsils, the danger of teeth, the roughness of tongue.

Days' worth of sexlessness swelled inside me. I felt the pressure of my own hand on my cock, the tapping of my hand on the downstroke right on my balls. And then it all surged up and I convulsed in the bed, and bursts of hot come shot in the air, landing hot and wet on my belly, leaking around my hand.

Man, I thought as I cleaned it up, *I've really got to get me some of the real thing. This guy's got to have more talents than lifting rocks and being good with power tools.*

The next day, Mom granted my only wish. She sent me to the cabin on the lake down at the far end of the property, where we had a little fishing shack (in which I used to masturbate as a kid).

"You're in charge," she said. "There's a storm coming."

"In charge of what?"

"Making sure everything's secure." She added, "Take Nick with you. He'll be glad to help, I'm sure."

My heart jumped and I shot a look Nick's way. He was blank and impassive as ever, eight inches taller than me and hard as rock.

"I'm sure he will," I said. "Right, Nick?"

Nick nodded obediently.

We rode down the half-mile of forested road in silence. The tension in the pickup truck was thick. He was amazing. His biceps kept the cuff of his shirt stretched and taut. His Popeye forearms were covered with golden sun-drenched fur. His pecs were like a cleavage. His jaw was set with the ferocious tenacity of a bulldog, which added a brutal strength to his handsome Grecian face.

We got to the cabin all too soon and had to get out and go about our chores, separately and alone. I was wondering whether he was available, if he was gay, whether he would ever make a move.

We let the shutters down over the plate glass windows and stowed the plastic yard furniture underneath the cabin in a crawl space. We pulled the canoe up over the pine needles and tipped it over so that it would not catch rain.

We were nearly finished when the storm hit. The rain came down so hard, it was like being peppered by marbles. The wind upturned everything, shattering the lake's calm surface.

We bolted for the cabin, getting in under the roof in a matter of seconds, and yet still soaked to the bone. The shirt was clinging to Nick's chest, and his nipples had hardened in the chill the storm brought with it.

My mouth went dry. I swallowed hard, trying to choke down the rising desire. The cabin seemed suddenly tiny. Too small for the two of us.

Nick stood behind me, looking out over my shoulder through the storm door. So close I would only have to lean back to feel his frame. Perhaps his cock. I could feel his breath on my neck. He was huge, hot, twice my size. At least 6 foot 3, probably 220 pounds, lean, and hard.

No one would hear me if I screamed, I thought. There was nothing around the cabin for a half a mile. Nothing but forest and heavy rain.

This huge, hulking stud could break me open, I thought. *If that was what he wanted.*

I didn't feel in charge any more. The fear flickered in my belly and made me hot. I imagined Nick's massive hands moving down over my shoulders, frisking me, flattening my belly, skirting the belt loops on my pants. Pinning me.

I pictured the thrust of him from behind, the insistence of that massive frame, the hungry man-smell of him permeating all my pores. Permeating, entering, pleasing, tasting. Consuming me bit by bit.

How can he not feel it? How could he not know what I am thinking? The air was choking; the camp was turning colors around us.

Three times I almost turned and clambered up Nick's body like a kid up a tree, wanting to get a closer view into his eyes.

Come on, I thought. *You only have to ask. That's what servants are for. If it was meant to be, the time is now. The clock has struck midnight.*

As if there were a sign from above, the moment was shattered. The wind howled, and a branch broke and fell against the cabin with a grating, wrenching sound. The concussion made the kitchen cabinets burst open and shattered glass all around us.

In fear, I clutched at Nick, half expecting the cabin walls to come down.

Nick seized me, grip tight, hands shaking, as if torn between the desire to thrust me away and the desire to take me in. There was more fury in his hands than any thunderstorm could ever hope to produce. I forgot entirely about the wind and rain and damage to the cabin. I felt only the grip of Nick's touch everywhere on my body, a hundred firebrands.

Not a word was spoken. Nick shifted slightly, and under his feet the broken glass made a sound like beach sand.

I broke Nick's grip with a quick upward stroke of my arms and proceeded to tear the shirt off his body. It was soaked and fell to the floor with a satisfying thwack. I turned my attention to Nick's trousers, unbuckling the thick leather belt.

"I don't normally do this," Nick tried to explain. He was looking down at his loose belt helplessly.

"I do!" I spouted.

I stepped back, stretched my arms, and revealed a patch of bare hip. It captured Nick's gaze, obliterated his thought. As I had known it would.

I tore off my shirt. His eyes got busy on the angles and fruits of my body. I turned slightly, holding my abs tight. His gaze was powerful. His eyes were like a pair of high-voltage klieg lights, burning, searing my skin. He made me feel as raw and naked as I ever had.

Nick's pants flopped to mid thigh and his cock bulged through his boxers, out through the flap, the tip of it red and swollen, a drip of precome on the end, glistening even in the low and shrouded light.

Nick reached down for me. He was eager and nearly lifted me off my feet. He pulled me against him, his hips thrusting against my frame with bruising impact.

I felt his hardness, that massive, rude organ. Nick took one step forward through the litter of broken dishes. He braced me against the cabin's door frame and again he thrust up against my body, crushing the breath out of me.

Nick's lips closed firmly over mine. His tongue parted my lips, and his hand slipped behind my neck, freezing me, holding me cocked and ready.

I felt like a butterfly in a collection, stuck through with pins. I could not help but respond to the brutal kiss.

Nick's breath was hot and sweet. The lips firm, the tongue animal, raspy, probing. The smell of his skin was masculine and intoxicating, somehow richer than I had even imagined it would be, with the slightest taste of clean over it all.

It was like a tidal wave closing over my head. Fighting for the surface before I drowned.

I wanted nothing more than to feel his large hands descend over my bare torso, brushing my rock-hard nipples. Down along my ribs, to my butt and hip and pelvis. In my crotch. Around my cock, under my balls, weighing, teasing, and fingering my asshole in a slow, agonizing circle.

Nick gripped me, held me, visibly vibrating with some internal conflict I could not fathom. Then he crushed me to the wall a second time and kissed me. Hard. Forcing his body against mine. Rubbing. Crushing me with its size and power.

His lips fit over mine with an airtight seal. I felt his cock. Hard. Insistent. Demanding.

I felt weakness in my belly, a quiver of my sphincter, the *sproinging* of my own member in response.

When he let me go, I slid downward, back to the wall, as if I had no strength in my legs.

And I kept sliding. Sliding until I was on the floor and flat underneath him and the floorboards were cutting into my shoulder blades.

Nick crouched over my face. His powerful haunches were above him.

I ran a finger down the crease in Nick's ass. I pulled aside his muscular cheeks.

Nick lowered his ass over my face as if he would suffocate me with it, his butt inches from my face. I slid my tongue in to the place I had been invited. I worked down the crack, to the round puckered flesh. He worked my tongue in forcefully, so that Nick was driven upward by the surprise or the shock, as if my tongue were a live electric wire.

I am going to reacquaint this guy with his asshole, I vowed. And then I settled into my work, wriggling slightly over the hard floor.

I felt my tongue actually inside Nick, along the walls of flesh. I used my teeth to knead the tiny puckered folds of flesh, to draw them away from one another, stretch them out. I tongued hard at the base of Nick's shaft, used my finger to slick through the wet, up in the ass. I probed and made room for my tongue. I smelled and felt the delicious assy stink on my face. On my cheeks and tongue. I felt the few stray hairs and the weight of Nick balanced on my tongue so that I was like a gay Atlas, holding up the whole world.

Nick began to masturbate himself. I tongued harder, in time with his strokes. I felt Nick's helpless spasmodic jerks, the shaft grow more taut, the butt-wriggle more desperate. The strokes were hard and convulsive. Nick's voice was raspy and low and from another world. "Oh yeah, oh yeah, oh yeah, oh *yeah*!" Nick cried out. And I felt the drops of hot spunk spill on my chest—molten lava, hot solder, fusing us together.

And then, as quickly as he had begun, Nick released me. He

stood, turned away, snatched up his pants and his shirt from the floor in one smooth move. He buckled his trousers and made a beeline for the door.

"I told your mother we would be back soon."

I was too stunned to speak. I felt abused, mussed.

For a moment I did not move. Then I gathered myself up from the floor and leaned back up against the wall, feeling the roughness of the wood grain against my skin. My breath came back to me, but my hard-on would not go away.

Then I heard the truck's engine roar, and the gravel crunch under the tires.

"Hey! Hey!"

I ran outside buck naked, my clothes in my arms, and pounded on the door panel.

The truck skidded to a stop. Nick looked up, startled, as if he had entirely forgotten I was here. As if he did not remember who I was.

I yanked the door open. "You brought me here, remember? You've got to give me a ride back to the house."

"Get in!" Nick ground the truck into first gear. It began moving before I even had a chance to vault myself through the open door. Gravel shot out from the tires.

We bounced and careened over the pitted road.

"Turn here," I said.

Nick didn't hesitate and we shot down a pitted logging road.

"Stop."

He did.

I reached over and dragged that massive head down to my crotch.

"Eat me!" I said.

He did. His warm hot mouth closed over me. His hands slid under my hips. I thrust upward and forced my cock against the back of his mouth. His lips were hot and wet, and I stared at his gorgeous bobbing head, his muscled shoulders, which were straining against the shoulder belt.

The cab of the pickup smelled like sweat and spit and a spilled ashtray.

Without warning, Nick suddenly sat up and savagely ripped off the lap belt. He opened the door and swung his legs into the rain.

Before I could even think he was going to flee a second time, he ripped off his pants. His cock was already stiff again. Riveted, hard as marble, but visibly trembling, vibrating like a tuning fork. That predatory look had again come into his eye.

"Fuck me," I ordered. After all, I was the employer around here. You can't let the servants run the place.

"Oh, I'm going to, rich boy," he said.

And he did.

There was a handy condom in the glove compartment. He lifted me off the seat, banged my head on the roof without apology. He folded me, pressed me down and around until I was crouched on the passenger seat, praying to Mecca, my face pressed fast against the door. The rain beat down on the roof.

I looked back at him. He was magnificent. Chiseled shoulders, body tanned to the waist, bulging pecs, hard nipples, narrow waist, and abs that begged me to run my hand over. The black hair on his chest was tamed but not shaven. His thighs were defined but not too thick, the quad muscles quivering on each side of that pulsing hardness.

He placed his cock against my butt, in the crease. I felt it slide back and forth looking for an opening. There was the sound of a tearing package, a trickle of spit hawked up from his lungs, the stretch of a condom.

I felt his thick fingers moisten my ass, rough calluses on bare skin. My mouth fell open, hungry and panting. His fingers kneaded my ass, opening me up for him. And then the largest finger ever to penetrate me made me cry out. My body rebelled, and yet I wanted it so bad.

He shushed me with a finger to my lips. He was gentle, but insistent. He said "Shhh" and my whole body relaxed and his cock was magically deeper in me, in the core and heart of me.

His hands were steel traps on either side of my body. The gentleness turned into firmness. He opened me wide, until I thought I could go no wider—I was sure something would have to give or tear. Yet I wanted more of him in there, and then more was in—the whole of his member, his scrotum slapping up on my ass, the ring of my rectum stretched in a fire of something that might have been pleasure, might have been pain.

It lasted forever. The murmurs and grunts, the pounding of his weight, the pressing of my face on the vinyl of the passenger seat. I reached for my cock, which was stiff and almost painful.

In rhythm with Nick's strokes I beat myself off. Nick's body quaked and quivered, and when he exploded in me, convulsive and hot, it was as if a stone wall came tumbling down, and I shot my own hot load into the seat in a fiery, convulsive mess.

"What an incredible ass," Nick said in his heavy Greek accent, his huge hand cupping my bum.

And that was not the last he got of it that week. Each night I stayed at my mother's, Nick came to my room, and in the daytime we did it out in the barn. I just had to crook my finger, and Nick would come running obediently. And fuck my brains out.

As I drove back to the city after that vacation, stretched and sore and happy, I sighed and thought, *My aunt is right. It really is hard to get good help like that anymore.*

Shrinks

Christopher Pierce

I swear, fucking one of my therapist's other patients wasn't what I had in mind for that night, but when that hot guy slid a condom down onto my hard cock, wrapping it tight in latex, I couldn't say no.

I'd seen him the last few times I'd gone to therapy, every Monday at 8 p.m. He'd be leaving as I arrived. He was probably my height and weight—six feet tall and 180 pounds—with short dark brown hair and nice blue eyes. He had a handsome mustache and goatee the same color as his hair. He looked to be in his late 20s, like me.

When we passed each other in the parking lot we made eye contact a few times, and once I thought I saw him smile at me. But after we passed and I glanced back, he was facing away. It seemed that he liked me but didn't want to make the first move. I wasn't sure what to do about it until I had a realization—I was there to see my shrink anyway, so I'd talk to him about it.

"What are you thinking about?" my therapist asked me when I sat down on the couch in his office.

"How much I want to have sex with this certain guy," was my answer. The shrink looked at me, beady eyes behind round glasses beneath a rapidly receding hairline. I imagined the other patient, remembering his nice eyes and the way his cheek dimpled when he smiled.

"Who is he?" asked my therapist.

"Just a guy I've seen around. He's really hot," I answered.

"That's interesting," the shrink said. "You're the second patient to bring this up. It might be a pattern."

"Who was the other patient?" I said.

"You know I can't tell you that. I shouldn't have even said that. Let's get back to you. What would you like to happen?"

I hoped the patient who'd also talked about a hot new guy he wanted to get it on with was the same cute one I had been thinking about. But I knew I couldn't ask for any more information from my therapist; he'd already said more than he should have and he knew it.

"What would I like to happen?" I repeated. "I'd like a definite sign from this guy that he's interested in me. I'm tired of quick glances and mysterious smiles."

The shrink adjusted his glasses and looked at me.

"When a patient is frustrated with a situation, I usually tell him to take action—a definite step toward resolving the conflict. That way he's working for a solution, not just complaining that he doesn't like something."

"That's good advice," I said sincerely. "Thank you."

I hardly know what else happened at the session; my mind was a thousand miles away—actually, only a few hundred feet away—in the parking lot that the handsome stranger and I passed every Monday night.

When the session was over I headed out to my car. There was a pleasant surprise waiting for me there—a piece of paper wedged under one windshield wiper. I got it out and read the words written on it: "I see you every Monday when I'm done with therapy. I think you're hot—call me, please." He'd left a phone number.

I liked the "please"; it showed a touch of vulnerability that I found very sexy. Most guys swagger up to you to show how macho and insensitive they are. The fact that this man, obviously very handsome and aware of it, was humble enough to say please made me like him even more.

I got in my car thinking about what the therapist had said about taking decisive actions. I apparently was not the only patient he'd given that advice to tonight.

I dialed the guy's number. He must have been waiting for me to call, because he answered before the first ring was over.

"Hello?" he said.

"Hi," I said. "I'm Chris. You left a note on my car?"

"Yeah!" the voice said excitedly. "Thanks for calling, man!"

"No problem," I answered.

"I see you every Monday night," he said. "You're coming when I'm going." There was a slight pause, and I knew he was realizing what he'd just said. "I mean—" he started. I could practically hear the blush on his cheeks.

"I know what you meant," I said. "What's your name?"

"Jack," he said. "What's yours?"

"Chris," I answered. "I just said that."

"That's a nice name," Jack said. "Short and masculine."

"Kind of like me."

"Yeah. Listen, Chris, here's why I'm calling—I think you're really attractive and I'd love to have sex with you."

"Well, that was honest," I said.

"My therapist told me I should be more honest about what I want," he answered.

"That's good advice," I said. "My therapist told me that I need to take action to resolve situations. So it sounds like what you want—is me."

"Looks that way," Jack said.

"Where do you live?"

Jack gave me his address, and when I asked when I should come over, he said "Now!" He told me he'd leave his front door unlocked and that when I came in I should "follow the trail."

"What trail?" I asked.

"You'll see," he said. "Just follow the trail."

"Tease," I called him.

"Count on it," Jack said, and hung up.

I love a good tease, especially if it was leading up to a big payoff.

It didn't take long to drive to Jack's place, but the whole time I imagined him and what I wanted to do with him. My imagination ran wild—I pictured what might have happened if I had come back to my car earlier that night. What if, instead of the note, Jack himself had been there?

He'd look at me, I'd look at him, and no words would be necessary. Our attraction would be obvious and electric, just like the first night we'd seen each other. Jack would be leaning up against my car's bumper. His arms crossed, he'd hit me with a sexy, cocky grin. I'd walk right up to him and put my arms around his waist, slipping my hands between his butt and my car.

I'd squeeze his ass cheeks, savoring their firm flesh. He'd put his arms around me, then bring his lips to my ear. Just like before, he didn't need to say anything—just hearing and feeling his hot breath against my ear and neck was communication enough.

Jack would take my earlobe between his teeth and bite it gently. In response I'd squeeze his buttocks harder and push him back against the car. He'd exhale deeply, but it would be cut off by my lips as I kissed him hard on the mouth. I'd push my tongue deep between his teeth as if treasure waited within.

And in a way it did.

His passion would rise to match mine, and together we'd explore each other's mouth. I'd raise my hands to his face, holding him gently in place, not that he'd try to get away. He'd arch back on the car, pushing his crotch into mine. I'd respond by matching his pressure until our cocks were rubbing against each other, only the denim of our jeans separating them.

All inhibition would disappear, and together Jack and I would unbutton our pants to reveal the hard cocks inside. We'd stare at each other's organ for a few heartbeats, for the moment the mere sight of them enough to satisfy us.

But not for long.

We'd both reach out at the same time, our eager hands finding each other's dick and taking their full, hard weight between palm and fingers. I'd be able to feel every beat of his heart in his cock. Then we'd put our arms around each other. We'd hug each other tight, pressing our cocks together, starting to move and grind our bodies.

The friction is so electric, I'm sure there must be sparks flying out around us. I'd kiss Jack, my mouth hungrily devouring his. He'd stick out his tongue and I'd gently seize it with my lips and caress it with my own tongue. I'd squeeze him in my arms, trying to show him without words how I excited I am, how joyful I am be to be doing this with him.

His breath would come out in one long sigh, and when our kiss was broken he'd give me a look of such pure pleasure and excitement, it'd make me laugh out loud. Then, right there in the parking lot, we'd take off our clothes and stare at each other's nakedness.

We wouldn't care if people saw us; this would be magical, and nothing, especially mere reality, would be able to spoil this feeling, this passion.

The excitement of our grinding dicks would grow so hot he'd know we couldn't go much longer without shooting our loads. Just in time we'd pull away from each other, crystalline droplets of ecstatic precome oozing from our piss slits. Like before, we'd each take the other's quivering cock in one hand and with a quick jerk release the tension that had been building up.

Our loads of semen would spurt out, sparkling in the moonlight, to land perfectly on each other's chest. We'd stand there, nude and dripping with spunk, looking at each other for a few minutes.

Then finally we'd get cleaned up with some paper towels from the car and head back to my apartment, where the real lovemaking would begin.

A few minutes later I found Jack's place. I parked and headed up to his apartment to find his door slightly open.

"Follow the trail," Jack had said. What did he mean? Then I walked in. I closed the door behind me and turned around. The place was nice, if a little messy, dimly lit, with techno-industrial music on at a low volume from some unseen stereo.

There was also a line of small shiny objects on the floor. I bent down to look at them more closely. They were small foil packets— condom packages. I grinned. *Looks like I won't have to talk to Jack about safety,* I thought. *He's obviously got what it takes in more ways than one.*

As instructed, I followed the trail of condoms, which led through the main room into the kitchen, then down a hallway to what I hoped was his bedroom. Like the front door had been, the door to his room was slightly open. I pushed it open the rest of the way, and was delighted by what I saw in the room.

Jack was sitting on a chair, smiling up at me. He was also naked, with his cock already nice and hard. At the sight of me he flexed it, and I lusted after him as his love muscle did a stretch just for me.

"I like where this trail leads," I said.

"I hoped you would," he answered.

"Can I have some of that?" I asked, gesturing to his erect rod.

"You can have all of it, man," he said. "It's all for you."

I walked into the room, and as I did so I undressed. First my shirt fell to the floor, then off came my shoes, followed by socks and pants. I started to take off my underwear, but Jack stopped me.

"I want to savor this," he said, reaching out to touch my boner through my tented shorts. "This is choice."

His fingers felt fantastic on my cock, even separated as it was from them by the fabric. Jack leaned forward and put his mouth on it, and his hot breath on my rod was wonderful. I hoped I could make him feel at least half as good as he was making me feel.

While Jack was breathing on my cock I noticed a bowl of condoms on the desk beside his chair. He was definitely ready for whatever I could come up with. Then he pulled my underwear down, exposing my dick to the air. I let my shorts drop and I stepped out of them, leaving them in front of the chair right where the trail of condoms ended.

Jack took a condom from the bowl on his desk and tore it open. Then he put it in his mouth and pulled me close. Putting his mouth onto my now-naked cock, he slowly slid the latex sheath down the length of my organ. It felt bizarre and also incredible, unlike anything I'd felt before.

The condom must've been superthin, because I sure didn't lose any sensation having it on. Jack sucked my dick, taking as much into his mouth as he could. It felt wonderful to be sucked that way, but I wanted something even better than Jack's cock sucking. I wanted to taste his mouth—I wanted to kiss him!

I took him by the shoulders and pulled him up into a standing position. My cock slipped out of his mouth, but I didn't care; I wanted his mouth somewhere else just then.

When we were standing face-to-face I brought my lips to his and kissed him, deeply, passionately. His passion rose to meet mine and he kissed me back, hard. We put our arms around each other and squeezed tight—not wanting to let go for any reason, ready to hold on for as long as possible.

There was something magical in that embrace, that moment we shared, something special that belonged to us, only us. No one could ever take this from us—this was our moment, for now and ever. Whatever power joined us in that brilliant moment, that ecstatic embrace, was gone a second later.

But our passion remained.

And the memory of that moment would always stay with us, no matter what else was happening or would happen.

I don't know how long the kiss lasted, whatever the length of time, it was wonderful. I didn't want to break the kiss, but I knew we had to. As much as I needed to kiss him before, now he needed to see me just as badly. And I wanted to see him too, this man I had fantasized about for weeks. He was so handsome—that short brown hair, those blue eyes, and that sexy smile surrounded by his mustache and goatee.

So we broke the kiss and just looked into each other's eyes for a few seconds. Then Jack took my hand and led me to his bed, where he gently sat me down on the edge. Now my cock was standing up between my legs like his had been. He took another condom from the bowl and gave it to me. I opened it and unrolled it down onto Jack's hard cock. Then he pulled a bottle out of a drawer, and squeezed flavored lube on both our dicks.

He climbed into the bed next to me and leaned over to suck me some more. I stopped him and said "I've got a better idea," and I lay down on the bed and guided him until his groin was in my face and mine was in his. This way, in a perfect sixty-nine position, we both had complete access to each other's dick.

I sucked him and he sucked me in beautiful symbiosis. It's almost indescribable how good it felt—the intense pleasure of having my organ loved and caressed by the mouth of a sexy man, plus the fantastic experience of having my own mouth filled with his cock, tasting him like he was tasting me. Add to this the knowledge that I was making him feel just as good as he was making me feel.

We moaned at the same time, and for a moment it was just like my imaginings on the way there. It was as if nothing else existed, like together we'd created a wall around ourselves, an impenetrable bubble that surrounded us, preventing anyone and anything from interrupting us, from bothering us—it was just us, and that was all and that was everything.

In this moment we owned each other, he was mine and I was his, and nothing and no one could come between us or take away what we shared.

Our cocks pulsed and breathed, and I swear I could feel every beat of Jack's heart through his in my mouth. The urge to kiss him again took hold of me, and I moved, trying to reach his mouth with mine. Jack must've felt the same desire because he moved with me, no groan of protest as our cocks slid out of each other's mouths.

We kissed again and it was sublime.

Oh Jack, I thought but did not say, *this is amazing! You're so fucking hot and you're with me, lavishing your pleasure and love on me, no one else, right now, just me!*

I wanted to go further with Jack. I wanted to really make love to him. I wanted to feel him inside of me, to be as intimate as two people can be.

"Jack?" I asked.

"Yeah?" he said.

"I really want you to fuck me," I said.

"You do?" he asked.

"Yes," I answered.

"Awesome! Turn over on your stomach." He said. Seconds later he was on top of me, gently using his fingers to open my asshole so it could take his cock. Soon enough he was satisfied.

"Are you ready?" he asked.

"Go for it!" was my answer.

Jack pushed forward and his dick slid into me nice and smooth. It felt so good—I absolutely loved it! He made love to me then, slow and steady. A few times I pushed my butt up and back to meet him and was rewarded with groans of pleasure from Jack. When I was up like that I could reach under myself and feel my own cock, which was harder than ever and dripping all over the place.

"I'm going to come," I said.

"Yeah?" Jack said, "Me too!"

"Let's shoot together," I said.

"Ready?"

"Go for it!"

And we shouted together as both of us blew our loads. That's my favorite way to come—with a hot guy fucking me. It was fantastic to come with Jack; it was the best orgasm I'd had in months. I know he liked it because he collapsed on top of me, wrapped his arms around me and squeezed me so tight I could hardly breathe for a second.

He was also mumbling in my ear the whole time—just dirty talk, but I loved it. Slowly he pulled out of me and we lay there for a while. When our orgasms abated, we got up for a minute to clean up and throw away the condoms. Then we got back in bed and snuggled close together.

"I think going to therapy was a good idea." I said.

"What we just did was like therapy to me," Jack said.

"Do you still want to keep going?" I asked.

"To therapy? Of course," Jack said, "Look what we've gotten out of it so far—who knows what the future will bring!"

Making the Team

Bearmuffin

Coach Thorman propped his feet on his desk and rolled his jock-strap down to his knees. He turned on the TV. One hand fisted his hot, spasming cock, and the other clicked the VCR remote control.

Stop. Freeze-frame. Two ripped college wrestlers appeared on the screen. The monster-muscled wrestlers boggled the mind with their tree-trunk thighs, hearty bull-necks, and super washboard abs. Their bubble butts were packed in wrestling singlets so transparent one could see the grimy, sweaty jockstraps underneath. Coach licked his lips at the sight of thick cocks trapped inside sweaty jocks.

A new shipment of wrestling videos had just arrived. Taped matches of beefy wrestling studs from all over the USA. The cameraman knew exactly when to zoom in on those hot, muscular bodies. Coach tripped out on the pins and takedowns. He loved to see those crotch holds. Yeah. College wrestlers got him good and fucking hot!

Coach clicked the play button. "Aw, fu-u-uck!" he moaned as the image of blond, blue-eyed, supermuscled Brandon Duke flashed on the screen. Coach's fist whizzed over his cock. Just a few more tugs and he'd shoot!

"Fu-u-uck!" Coach's body rocked with lust. His cock thickened as bolts of ecstasy shot through his granite-hard body. A sputtering, heavy wad shot high into the air. That was followed by three more come spurts that splashed on the monitor. Long, thick dribbles of come dribbled over the screen.

"Yeah!" Coach grunted thickly. "I'm gonna fuck your ass, stud!" Coach's deep-set brown eyes sparkled excitedly. Intense macho desire coursed through the muscle slabs rippling under his sleek, sun-bronzed skin.

"Gonna fuck ya, stud!" Coach panted roughly. "And fuck ya good. Real good!" The coach grabbed his pulsing, vein-etched cock by the root. He gritted his pearly whites and clenched his eyes shut. His sweating body jerked in the chair.

"Aw, fu-u-uck!" he screamed. Another hard shudder of lust bolted through Coach's hot muscles. He leaned back and his cock exploded. "Yaargh!" Another steaming come load splashed against the screen.

Yeah! Brandon Duke would be a hot addition to his wrestling team. Coach loved the wild machismo boldly etched on the young blond's classic all-American features.

Coach scooped up a handful of lube to lather on his hot, pulsating cock. The greasy gobs crackled and sputtered noisily like coals in a fire, melting over his lust-swollen prong.

"Fuck! Fuck! Fuck!" Coach grunted as he whacked off his drooling cock. His sweating, hairy nuts were swimming in a raging sea of pent-up bull jizz. He was about to shoot another load when there was a knock at the door.

It was Assistant Coach Edwards. "The new recruit is here, Coach," he said.

Holy fuck! Coach almost toppled from his chair when the door opened and in walked Brandon Duke. The room echoed with Coach's loud gasps of amazement and admiration. His eyes immediately zeroed in on the prize wrestling stud's awesome, lust-provoking body.

Brandon's crew-cut blond hair sprouted an inch above his bullet-shaped head. Thick, bushy brows joined over the bridge of his squarish nose to shade a set of piercing baby blues that glittered with grit and ambition. The stud's strong cheekbones matched his defiant, jutting jaw. Just the barest hint of a silky blond mustache appeared over full, sensuous lips.

Brandon's thick bull-neck connected solidly to incredible barrel shoulders. His superb arms splayed away from an equally superb upper torso that flared wide like a cobra's hood and tapered dramatically down to his narrow waist. His heart-stopping abs were furrowed and silky smooth.

The stud's spectacular V-shaped torso firmly rested on thick tree-trunk thighs. His humpy bubble butt resembled lush cantaloupe halves tanned to a glimmering gold hue. The stud was naked except for a grimy, threadbare jockstrap hugging his stupendous basket.

The frayed jock was a shredded mass of tangled and tattered elastic revealing his thick, 12-inch cock. Thick, sweaty folds of foreskin hung two inches over the wide tip of his mighty cock head.

Brandon's balls were impressively huge, hanging extra low and heavy like two baseballs inside of his golden-haired nut sac. They swayed lustily between his tree-trunk thighs. Coach's eyes strayed to the golden blond hair swirling over Brandon's brawny legs.

"Turn around," Coach barked. He wanted to get a good, long look at Brandon's ass. As the stud maneuvered his huge, hulking body, his jockstrap fell apart. It slid down his mammoth legs and gathered at his feet. His buttocks rose into view.

"Sorry 'bout that, Coach," a sheepish Brandon said.

"Don't worry about it, Brandon," Coach replied. Coach moaned at the tempting sight of Brandon's glorious buttocks. They were full, ripe, and peach-fuzzed. Coach grabbed his cock and squeezed it. He couldn't wait to stick his lust-hardened meat between Brandon's sweaty cheeks.

"You can turn around now," Coach said. Coach's piss hole seeped juicy strands of precome when he got a gander at Brandon's unbelievably huge cock. Coach's eyes firmly focused on Brandon's cock, which now curved lazily over his mammoth balls. Thick, throbbing, blue veins crisscrossed the shaft. Coach was dazzled by the sight of the most awesome cock he'd ever seen.

Coach's heart flip-flopped while he glared at Brandon's cock head. He did a double take when he saw single thick drop of transparent, glistening liquid slowly ooze from the gaping piss slit.

His quivering tongue slipped between his lips as he imagined the bittersweet taste of that drop that hung precariously for a single second and then dripped to the floor between Brandon's thick toes.

Coach dropped to his knees before the mighty stud. He yawned wide and took Brandon's meat between his lips. His hands feverishly ran up and down over the jock's sweaty muscles until they landed right on his eye-popping pecs. Coach twisted and pulled on Brandon's thick, eraser-like nubs. Brandon responded with moans of pure ecstasy. The stud loved nipple play, and Coach was an expert. His cock coasted down Coach's throat.

Coach bobbed his head over Brandon's cock. Brandon clapped his hands over Coach's ears, drawing him in. Brandon enjoyed the hot sensation of his meat swelling thickly inside Coach's wide-open throat. Coach was an ace cocksucker. Within minutes, Brandon was ready to come.

"Aw, fu-u-uck!" Brandon moaned. A tremor of lust shook the stud's mighty muscles. His mouth yawned open, and he heaved a heavy, lusty groan. "Gonna shoot! Gonna fuckin' shoot!"

Coach cupped his hands around the golden mounds of Brandon's hard bubble butt and forced the young stud's groin against his face. His nose burrowed into Brandon's musky pubes. The odor of young, ripe manhood made Coach's head spin. Coach relaxed his throat to accommodate Brandon's pulsing meat. Within seconds, the wrestler's 12 inches plummeted all the way down Coach's spasming throat.

Brandon shouted. "Aargh! Fu-u-uck!" He slammed his groin against Coach's face. His bloated cock swelled and exploded. Thick jets of sperm blasted from his furry nuts down Coach's gagging throat.

"Ggaargh!" Coach choked on the hot, gushing torrent of scalding stud semen as it flowed down the corners of his gaping mouth and his granite-hard chin.

Sweat poured down Brandon's body. Coach pulled his mouth off Brandon's cock and enthusiastically licked his way from Brandon's come-drenched bull-nuts, over his washboard abs, up to his pecs. Brandon's stud-tits cried out for a supermacho tit workout. So Coach siphoned those huge, rivet-hard nipples between his lips. Brandon moaned, his entire body bristling with macho power.

Coach's feverish lips suctioned hard over Brandon's left pec. He caught one large, sweating nipple between the edges of his teeth and seesawed it. Brandon whipped his head back and forth, rasping huskily, "Aw, fu-u-uck! Aw, gonna come!" Brandon mashed Coach's face against his saliva-soaked pec. "Fu-u-uck!" Brandon bellowed. He gripped Coach in a bone-crushing bear hug. Overwhelmed by lust, they crashed to the floor.

Coach thrust himself between Brandon's legs. Brandon's pulsing cock quickly stiffened and rose full mast to throb against Coach's powerhouse abs. Coach responded with a hearty macho grunt as he plunged a finger up Brandon's butt hole.

"Aw, fuck, yeah!" Brandon howled. Encouraged by Brandon's hearty response, Coach rammed two, then three fingers up the wrestler's slimy hole.

"Yeah, dude! Ream my asshole!"

So Coach jammed his fingers knuckle-deep into Brandon's asshole. Brandon's tight hole sucked around the invading fingers. Then Coach wrenched out his fingers and brushed them against the jock's full sensuous lips. Brandon's feverish tongue eagerly popped out of his mouth. He slid his quivering tongue over the butt funk–drenched finger.

The jock smirked while he lapped at his butt juices coating Coach's fingers. Within seconds he'd licked them as clean as a whistle. He moaned lecherously, drunk with own smell. "Mmm. Fuck, yeah! My ass tastes fuckin' good, don't it?

Coach glowered at Brandon. His eyes were filled with lust. "I wanna fuck you," he growled. "So fuck me," Brandon replied. His pulsing cock bobbed with anticipation. "Yeah! Do me, Coach!"

Brandon shot his legs into the air, resting his calves on Coach's wide shoulders. Brandon choked a hot grunt when Coach slipped his hard, pulsing cock between the wrestler's sweaty cheeks. A lusty shudder rocked Brandon's body when he felt the tip of Coach's cock graze against his pucker. Coach rubbed his cock head all over Brandon's twitching asshole.

"Aw, fuck!" Brandon howled. Overcome with lust, Coach plunged his cock right through Brandon's tightly muscled anus ring. "Fuck, yeah!" Brandon screamed. His lusty cries bounced off the walls. Brandon gritted his teeth and clenched his eyes as he thrashed wildly and dug his burly fingers into Coach's broad, muscled back.

Coach felt Brandon's slick butt hole dilate and suck in his plunging cock. Brandon clamped his butt muscles around Coach's meat, keeping it firmly planted up his stinking, sweating hole.

Coach sucked on Brandon's tongue, and their mouths glued together in hot macho passion. The blond jock wrapped his thick thighs firmly around Coach's waist and held him fast in a bone-crushing bear hug. Coach grabbed Brandon's buttocks and clenched them as he rammed into the stud's tight, spasming butt hole.

Brandon whipped his head back and forth, hot sweat flying off his hair. Paroxysms of lust seized them both. Coach felt the heat knotting up inside his balls while he clapped a steady tempo on Brandon's peach-fuzzed nuts.

The two men were hurtling over the very brink of supermacho lust. Electric bolts of desire shot through their sweating bodies, unleashing the raging torrents of pent-up jizz burning deep within their come-bloated balls.

"Fuck, yeah!" Coach howled. "Take my load, stud!" Take my fuckin' load!" Coach trembled as he pumped thick, scalding jets of sperm up the blond jock's shuddering asshole.

"Aw, fu-u-uck! Brandon howled his pleasure as spasm after spasm rocked through his muscles, making him shoot a geyser of stud semen that blasted between their bodies, drenching them with come.

Coach grabbed a towel and wiped the thick come dribbles from his face. He smiled lewdly. "OK, Brandon," he said. You made the team." Brandon scooped up his come-soaked jockstrap and padded to the locker room. Coach grabbed his cock and worked on getting another hard-on. He couldn't wait for the next recruit to appear.

Where the Buffalo Roam

CB Potts

"**Y**ou have got to be kidding! We're doing *what* for vacation?" I couldn't believe what my sister was telling me. Instead of our long-anticipated trip to Europe, my parents had made other plans.

"We're going to a dude ranch, for a cattle roundup. Mom saw it on *Oprah*—it's supposed to be very bonding." Sarcasm dripped from Katie's tongue. "Now she thinks we'll all get a chance to really know each other."

"So I'm going to not only spend spring break on a horse but having heavy discussions with Mom about the real reason I'm not going to give her any grandchildren? Great." I sighed, flopping down on the lawn chair. "I should have gone to Daytona with the rest of the frat."

"Aah, quit your bitching! Next year, you'll be graduated college and out in the big world—Mommy and Daddy won't be paying for your vacations anymore, and you can go where you want." Katie grinned slyly. "Besides, some of those cowboys might be cute!"

Cute *isn't the word for it,* I thought, looking wide-eyed at the wranglers assigned to take our tour group on this cattle-driving adventure. Talk about stunning—every last one of them could have been a model. Long hours doing ranch work were obviously responsible for the hard, defined muscles they all sported.

I felt strangely inadequate with my gym-earned muscles beside these fine specimens. That didn't stop my cock from stirring to life, and I cursed the tight jeans that had seemed the perfect attire when we'd packed. Confined by the close-fitting denim, my manhood swelled against my thigh. The friction felt good, but the situation was uncomfortable, and I turned against my horse to hide my erection.

"Time to saddle up!" announced Clint, the head wrangler. He stopped by the head of the dappled mare I'd been assigned. "I can give you a hand with that, if you want."

Clint was definitely the alpha male of the wranglers. He was the oldest by at least 15 years, and the sun had etched wrinkles around the corners of his deep brown eyes—eyes that took in my turgid state with just a glint of amusement—or was that interest? My face started to flush, and I managed to stammer, "No, thanks, I can take care of it myself."

"That may be," Clint replied, with a slow drawl that kept me hanging on every syllable. "But some things out here are better with a partner." There was no ambiguity in his smile, and it was clear that he meant more than mounting horses. Awkwardly, I swung into the saddle, my eyes riveted to Clint's ass as he walked away.

Years of experience had taught Clint to dress more practically than me, but his jeans were still tight enough to pique my interest. Long, confident strides brought him quickly to the front of the roundup, and with a grace that belied his considerable height, he mounted a tall black horse.

"Everyone gather around!" Clint commanded, and 12 tenderfeet obeyed. The horses, at least, were used to this routine and ignored the confused commands of their riders. We listened attentively as Clint outlined the rules and routine of a safe adventure—or at least that's what the others were attentive to. I merely watched Clint's lips move, mesmerized by the sound of his voice, the shape of his chin.

Over my college career, there'd been a few professors I'd found interesting, but this was the first time I'd ever been so profoundly attracted to an older man. I couldn't even pretend it was Clint's wealth of knowledge or greater education that was turning me on. How could I, when I hadn't heard a word he'd said since the partner comment? After one glance at me, he knew what I wanted, and more important, let me know what he wanted.

My attention was quickly brought back to the present when Clint began to divvy up duties. My mom and dad seemed grateful to be delegated to "bringing up the rear," and Katie couldn't contain her pleasure at being paired with a big, strapping wrangler. When Clint turned his attention to me, I squirmed in the saddle, uneasy but excited by his scrutiny.

"Mark," he drawled, "You seem to be in pretty good shape. You can ride point up front with me."

And so it was that I spent the next five hours thrust in the midst of 300 head of stubborn cattle. I barely know one end of a horse from another, yet there I was, trying to obey Clint's commands to "bring 'em up." Sweat poured down my face, blurring my vision. Every muscle ached. I was sore in places that I only had the most passing acquaintance with. But when I stopped a straying heifer from forging her own way and Clint granted me a few words of praise, it was all worth it.

The drive stopped for lunch—at least for the tourists. As we huddled around the chuck wagon, ravenously munching down bison burgers, Clint and the other wranglers stayed on horseback, patrolling the edge of the milling herd.

Dad and I grinned, listening to Mom and Katie relay the details of their "cowgirl adventure." It was great to see my family enjoying themselves so much, but I have to admit I was distracted. Constantly, I'd scan the dust cloud around the cows, watching for a glimpse of Clint's tall black steed. It was difficult to find him in the sea of constant motion, but every time I caught sight of Clint, he was staring directly at me.

"Look at Mark!" Mom announced. "He can't wait to get back out there." She beamed, satisfied. "This is the type of thing I'd hoped we'd discover about each other. Who knew my little boy would be an expert cowhand?"

Katie smirked. "Yup, he's Wyatt Earp, all right. Driving them little dogies to the Rio Grande!"

Well, dogies did have to be driven, even if we were running parallel to the Rio Grande rather than toward it. On the way back to my mount, I stopped by the chuck wagon to grab a sandwich.

"If that's for Clint," the attendant told me, a faint smile lingering behind her eyes, "you'll want to bring this—he's a vegetarian." She handed me a saran-wrapped burrito that appeared to be stuffed with two pounds of salad.

"Thanks," I said, blushing.

"Don't worry about it," she replied. "We've all been there—or at least wanted to."

"Here," I told Clint, maneuvering my mare beside him. "I brought you something to eat." Clint took the sandwich, letting his well-callused hands linger just a moment on my own. The horses shifted, and our thighs touched. His brown eyes were inches from mine, and disconcertingly, he grinned.

"Thanks," he said. "I like a man who likes to please me." Clint gestured toward the sandwich. "But this isn't really what I'm in the mood to eat."

He wheeled his horse away, leaving me astonished and horny as hell. Throughout the afternoon, I tried to concentrate on the complicated business of cattle driving. Good thing we had professional wranglers with us, though, because my mind was completely captured by Clint.

He didn't move without me watching him. When he steered the black horse through a thorny knot of brush to retrieve a straying calf, my eyes were glued to every movement. I noted with pleasure how the muscles in his back flexed as he reined in his headstrong steed. And his hands! I loved his hands and the strength so evident in his arms. They were hands I could imagine all too well on my flesh, in my arms, on my neck as I knelt before Clint.

He knew I was watching him, of course. On one occasion when he felt my attention studying his hands, he slid his fingers farther and farther up his thigh until he was brushing against his own denim-clad cock. Then he turned, eyebrow raised just a millimeter, and grinned.

Just when I was thinking, *Damn the family watching, damn all these cows, damn the other wranglers, I'm going to ride over there and grab Clint and make love to him in front of the entire world,* he called a halt.

"It's been a long day," he announced, "and you've all been working hard." Brown eyes turned directly toward me, accompanied by that taunting grin I'd come to know so well. "Some of you harder than others."

We broke for dinner and then lingered around the campfire. City bodies, not used to life on the range, soon gave out. Mom was the first to go to bed, and then Katie. The wranglers lingered around the campfire, trading jokes and stories. Dad and I stayed. Dad was determined to get the most out of his vacation; I was determined to get close to Clint.

The stars seemed bigger out west than at home. They were hanging low in the night sky by the time Clint broke his silence and sang. His song was a sad lament in a language I didn't speak.

"Lakota," he announced, answering my unspoken question. "It is a song of my people."

"It's beautiful." I answered. It was as if we were alone, as if no wranglers were by us, as if my Father wasn't sitting inches from my side.

"You are beautiful." Clint answered, rising to his feet. "Come on."

We left the circle of firelight and walked a good distance from the camp. It was absolutely still. Crickets kept their peace. Night birds had all flown. Only Clint existed, Clint and the great dark silence.

His hand traced my face in the darkness, and I turned my lips toward his palm. My tongue tasted sweat—sweat and old leather. The strength I imagined in his fingers was surely there, and when he pressed his thumb against my lips, I sucked it as fervently as if it were the cock I longed for.

"Hmm." Clint's free hand ran across my chest. "Not bad for a college boy. Bet these muscles are sore."

"The only place I'm sore," I protested, bringing Clint's lips to my own, "is the muscle I haven't gotten to use yet."

Starlight reflected from Clint's grin. "We can't have that, can we?" His fingers worked expertly at my belt. In just a moment my manhood was free in the cool night air. The pads of his callused fingers brushed against my balls, stroking not quite gently.

"Are you sore here?" he asked, then slid his hand forward to encircle my shaft. "Or is the ache more in this direction?"

I'm not sure my answer was exactly coherent as I groaned aloud. Clint's strokes were steady and sure. Once again his lips claimed mine, demanding all of my attention, all of my breath. As my knees buckled, I felt my scrotum tighten and the first hot jets of my orgasm shot into the night.

"Well," Clint chuckled. "Your pain might be gone, but I find I'm in a little discomfort of my own." My hand brushed the front of Clint's jeans to find him rock-hard.

I sank to my knees in the dirt and fumbled with Clint's belt. In my experience, I had never encountered a belt buckle quite that large, and it took a few precious seconds to undo. His jeans fell freely from slender hips, briefs quickly following. All of this fabric bunched atop his boots, which I had to stop and admire. First with my eyes, then with my tongue.

"Good boy—I like that." Clint's fingers twined in my hair. "But there are other, more important things to be doing." The pressure he exerted had my cock quickly stirring to life again. My lips brushed against his cock head, and I began to set to work.

"Hold on a moment, cowboy," Clint breathed. He bent over, rummaging in his jeans pocket. Only after he'd sheathed himself in a condom did he let me continue.

Clint's cock head was apparently very sensitive, as he moaned loudly when I applied my tongue to it. I focused there for a few delightful moments, enjoying how the wrangler lost control under my onslaught. Then I slid my lips forward and began the long process of swallowing his shaft.

Clint's cock was not particularly thick, but it was the longest I'd ever encountered. When his head hit the back of my throat, I thought I'd gag, but Clint's fingers on my neck prevented me from pulling off. I breathed deeply and relaxed enough to let the tip of his shaft into my throat.

"Jesus!" Clint groaned, thrusting his hips forward. I moved as much as I could, applying suction to the throbbing shaft. My hands wrapped around Clint's muscular thighs, and I pushed my nose to the base of his prick. Usually I revel in the feeling of pubic hair against my chin, but Clint was nearly hairless. Only a few strands clung to his balls, too wispy for any tactile effect.

Sliding my hands farther up, I encountered the most muscular ass of my life. Saddle-hardened cheeks warmed under my palms. Clint didn't even resist as I sneaked a finger against his sphincter. Only his quick intake of breath and flexing of his cock let me know I had made any impact at all.

"You want?" I hissed, wiggling my fingertip. Clint didn't reply but pushed his hips backward against my questing hand. First the tip, then my knuckle, sank inside his hungry anus. At the same time, I increased the speed of my oral activity, lashing the underside of his shaft with my tongue.

"God," Clint groaned, and forced my nose into his stomach. I could feel the condom grow taut within my mouth as he exploded into orgasm.

Afterward, we walked back to the campfire. No one commented on our absence or our unkempt appearance upon our return. Only Dad, as he was about to head in for the night, grinned and said, "You know, I think you only get one midnight ride with this package, son. You better make the most of it."

"What do you mean by that?" I asked. Clint was a few feet away, and I couldn't tell if he was listening or not.

"I mean," Dad said, "that chances are your mother and sister won't notice a thing if you spend the night with your cowboy. Tomorrow's another day, and who knows what will happen."

"Really?"

"Really. Go sleep under the stars." Dad left the campfire, where Clint and I stood grinning at each other. He'd definitely been listening, and was obviously happy about what he'd heard. In more ways than one, I noticed with some delight. He wasn't the only one, though, and my jeans were growing uncomfortably tight.

"I don't know about the under the stars bit," Clint said, reaching forward to grab my hand, "but I have a very roomy sleeping bag."

Maybe it's the absolute darkness of the countryside that seems to stop time. Clint and I moved in slow motion, removing garment after garment from each other, pausing after each piece to taste the newly exposed flesh.

His arms, his neck, his chest, all ridged with muscle, were my delights. His pecs were pronounced enough to form a hollow over the sternum, and I rested my nose there, reveling in the scent of him, a scent of horses and honest sweat. When I brushed his nipples with my fingertips, Clint drew in a sharp breath. So of course I returned to that spot again and again, trading fingers for tongue, pleasuring the sexy wrangler.

Rough-skinned hands pushed me downward. This time his belt was no obstacle, and soon Clint was naked before me. I wished for a moon so I could see him in all his glory. Instead, I had to see with my hands, with my fingers, with my lips.

"Sweet Jesus," Clint groaned. " I may not let you go home." He pulled me up into his arms, kissing me deeply. "I've never been so fucking turned on in my entire life as I am right now." His shaft jutted against mine, and we crossed swords for a moment. The head of his cock butted against my balls, causing an electric shock to jet through my entire body. I knew what I wanted.

"Please, Clint," I breathed, kissing his neck. "I want you to fuck me."

"Mmm," he agreed, tumbling me onto his bedroll. "I want me

to fuck you too." He positioned me on all fours, looking out into the deep prairie darkness. I shuddered with anticipation as he ran his hands over my exposed ass, dallying for a few moments in the sensitive spot behind my balls.

"This is cowboy-style," he announced, pressing his latex-clad sheath against my anus. "Don't want to worry about you rolling around on any scorpions."

Every scorpion in the world could have been directly in front of me, marching in formation and singing show tunes, and I wouldn't have noticed. Clint's cock slowly slid into me, widening my sphincter millimeter by millimeter. Those rough hands I'd admired, those callused fingers I'd sucked, now kept an iron grip on my hips. As much as I wanted to fling my ass backward, forcing all of Clint's considerable length into me, I could only kneel, trembling, and Clint doled out the pleasure a fraction at a time.

"Please, Clint, give me all of it," I panted My own cock jerked with need, my need to be shoved full of Clint's hot prick.

"Easy, easy," Clint replied, using the same tone I'd heard him use to settle a jumpy mount earlier in the day. He fed me another few inches, and then began to slowly saw his hips back and forth.

"Christ, you're so fucking hot!" Clint moaned. He brought his hand around to stroke my trembling shaft, and I used that moment to push my hips backward on him. A deep moan of pure pleasure escaped me once I was impaled on Clint's prick, his balls bouncing gently against my own.

My knees started to give way under the sensation of it all. Somehow Clint anticipated my collapse and positioned us so that I was sitting astride him, my cock slapping at his washboard stomach.

"What about the scorpions?" I asked, not wanting to give up the pleasure of having Clint's shaft deep inside me.

"Fuck the scorpions!" Clint replied. "I want to see you ride my cock, Mark." He bucked his hips a little, setting my prostate aflame with sensation.

I slid up and down on Clint's prick, reveling in the absolute darkness, the stars hung mere inches from my head, the glorious feeling of being buggered by the sexiest cowboy ever to walk the face of the earth. My own cock was going crazy from the merest touch of Clint's skin, and when I felt Clint's cock twitch deep in my bowels, I knew my own orgasm wasn't far off.

"I'm gonna come," I growled. "Gonna shoot my load all over you."

"Yeah," Clint replied, latching on to my hips with his iron grip once again. "I want to drink your come, suck you down." His pace increased with his words until we were slamming together harder than any bucking bronco could imagine. "Love fucking your ass, Mark." He grunted. "Here it comes!"

My cock exploded in jets of hot come. I couldn't see them, but I imagined them landing, sizzling, on Clint's tanned skin and well-defined muscles. The first splash had just hit when Clint groaned and let loose with his own flood. The condom grew very hot and full inside me, proof of a job well done.

Afterward we lay in Clint's sleeping bag, my head resting comfortably in the crook of his arm. I looked up at the stars and smiled.

"I could do this every day," I said. I felt Clint turn his head to look at me.

"Is that true?" he asked.

"Sure," I replied, turning in his arms to face my new lover. I kissed his chin. "Wouldn't you want to do this every day?"

"Don't fuck with my head, Mark." Clint ran his fingers over my face. "I'm into you way too much as it is."

"And what's wrong with that?" I asked.

"Because this week is going to be over, and you're going back to college. I'll still be out here with 300 cows and a herd of nitwits." Clint paused for a moment. "What do you do over the summer?"

I thought briefly of the plum internship I'd lined up. I'd be assisting at one of Chicago's premier insurance companies, learning all about the finance industry I'd been studying. It would be a jewel in my résumé, practically a guaranteed job-getter no matter how bad the economy got.

"Nothing," I said, running my hand slowly over Clint's nipples. I could feel his cock stirring slowly to life again. "Why?"

"Maybe you could work with me one summer. Spend some time out here. We could get to be together, and uh," Clint paused, at a loss for words when my hand encircled his shaft.

"And then we'll see what happens," I finished for him.

Mom won't be too happy about the change in summer plans, I thought, wrapping a condom on Clint so I could enjoy a late-night snack, *but Dad will understand.* One midnight ride just wasn't enough.

Lucky Night

Simon Sheppard

A piece of ass. Warm piece of ass in the bitter cold. I'd just killed somebody—maybe two hours before, maybe less—when I saw the guy in the alley's shrouded darkness, big, vacant eyes catching green/white/green neon. "You a Mullah Assassin?" he asked, and grabbed his crotch.

"Yeah, me," I said. Even through the gloom, he'd been able to recognize my uniform.

"Fuck. Killer. Turns me on." He walked closer, hand on hardening dick. "You want?"

I pulled down my night visor for a better look, everything clearer now, though tinged with lurid dark red. Short, Jesus, maybe only 5 foot 2, but handsome, a shock of dark hair, scraggly beard, little punk. From what I could see, his compact body would be worth a fucking. He took his jack-off hand from his dick; meat pleasingly small, even on a man as short as he was.

"You one of the Benway Gang?" I asked, walking right up, grabbing his shaft in my gloved hand.

"Hell, no. Lousy junkies." When I squeezed down hard, he squirmed.

"You fucking piece of lying shit," I said. He spit in my face, a big gob. The back of my leather-clad hand across his face lifted him damn near off his feet, only my grip on his dick anchoring him to Earth.

"Suck your cock. I want," he said, blood trickling. "You want?" Somewhere there were sirens, far enough away.

"Your ass instead." I took my hand off his cock, curving upward through the dark. Hungry little snake. "Drop your pants."

"Make me."

I made him. The trickle became a little red river. He had nice, meaty thighs, powerful. But he'd shaved his pubes. I hated that.

"I hate that, shaving. You want to look like a little boy?"

"Why care what you think?" Taunting, asking for trouble. He'd reached down, started stroking himself, foreskin darting back and forth over shiny infidel head.

"I kill people. You forget that?"

As if to say no, he turned around. Nice ass, really nice ass, smooth, sculptured, though with a telltale red rash on one cheek. Not that I wouldn't fuck him regardless. I grabbed hold of his shirt with both hands and ripped at the cheesy nylon.

"Hands on the wall."

He just stood there.

"Hands on the fucking wall, cunt." I was getting angry.

His smooth, muscled arms stretched up to rough brick. Big, ugly tracks stretched from the crooks of his elbows all the way to his thick wrists, dark even in the dark.

"The drug, huh? Fucking pathetic," I said, peeling off my gloves, "but the fucking usual for a Benwayboy gangbanger. Shit." My right hand shot between his spread thighs, grabbed a big handful of balls, and tugged.

He squirmed, shifting his fucked-up little body. I pulled down harder. He moaned, pulled away, his sac even tighter. I was beginning to enjoy this.

He moaned something.

"What's that, fucker? Can't hear you."

"Fuck me," he said. I could see his breath.

My hand still grabbing his nuts, I angled my forearm upward, up between his meaty, sullied ass cheeks. His hole was hot and moist, a little sticky. He probably needed a bath. My cock was good and hard.

As I pressed into him, my gun jammed against his hot, starving butt. A searchlight, erratic but insistent, swept across the alley's mouth. The Mullah's patrol? Maybe. Probably. Fuck, I didn't want to be caught out. But like any good leader, the Mullah cared more about efficiency than morality. I'd capped the shit I'd been hired to kill, so didn't I deserve a little fun? I pulled off the little punk, grabbed, shoved him further into dark. His feet hit something with a soft *plouf.* He looked down. I did too. A body.

"I killed him," I said. I hadn't, had no fucking idea who he was, but I enjoyed the Benwayboy's resultant gasp. Those fucking moral hypocrites with their drug-soaked opposition to jihad. Fuck 'em, let 'em gasp. Let their meaty asses be fucked. Fucked.

The body in the alleyway stirred, sighed. I looked down again; a hypo was in one arm. Fuck. If I hadn't just killed somebody on the job, I'd have done away with the scum. Just because. Just because.

The Benwayboy was against the wall, slumping, sort of. "Fuck me, fuck," he drooled out. I looked down at his ass, all night-vision red. My gloves were in my right hand. I spun them out, brought them hard against his behind, metal studs against firm, shapely, Drugged-out flesh. He pushed his butt toward me, ready. It was too easy. A lot of the worst things in life are. Too easy.

I reached down and pulled out my cock, stroking at it hard. He was looking over his shoulder at me, smiling. A missing tooth. Two.

"Get down on all fours," I said.

"Facing east?" There was a drug-fuzzed smirk in his voice.

"Just do it, asshole. Leaving behind another dead boy won't make a shitload of difference to me." The pants around his ankles made it tough. But he managed. I dropped to my knees behind him, grabbed at his ass, spread the two cheeks, one with the rash, the other perfect. Half-perfect butt. Not bad. *If I could take a bite out of that ass, a big chunk...*

It was drizzling now and everything was slick. I got the dispenser from my pocket, shoved it up his hole, squirted out HyGel. I'd be damned if I was going to catch anything. Hell, I'll be damned anyway, to hear the fucking Mullah speak. But boys' assholes make damnation easier to bear. Easier.

"Uh!" I wasn't about to take my time—I'd shoved the head of my dick in semilubed hole, and then the rest of my I-hoped-brutal shaft followed, eeling right up the fuck's guts. Sudden hesitation: I should have reported back by now, let the Mullah know the deed was done, but the flesh is weak, right? And the hole is hot.

I reached around him, him on all fours like the little bitch we both knew he was. He had a bit of a belly, so maybe he hadn't been doing the drug long. Who the fuck cares, really? One damn gang-banger from Benway's troops is pretty much like another, all drugs and hungers and eventual stupor. I slammed in hard, and he gave a little shudder, then an "Oh, yeah." Whatever smell there was floated into the general stench of the alleyway, lost. I slapped a cheek, the one with the rash. Through the night visor, red got redder. I rocked back and forth, in and out. Sodomy for sure. Even with the uniform's knee pads, the asphalt hurt.

"Yeah, fuck that ass." Did he really have to say that? I felt like pulling out, leaving him there with his shithole gaping in the midnight breeze. But, hell, I was already in, might as well finish. I lifted the metal tube around my neck up to my nostrils. Inhale. A sudden rush into him, his hole, his stupid need.

Something. A hand grabbed at my ankle. The drugged-out not-corpse. I kicked it away, clipped its head with my boot, I think. Almost lost balance. Another noseful. With renewed ferocity I rammed my hard-on into the now-sloppy hole, gritting out "*This* is for Benway killing the only man I ever loved." In the stadium, after what passed for a trial. Nick. And when I thought of him, dead Nick, I came. Couldn't help myself, it was like a collision, car accident, angular crashes of sex, just sex. Breathe. Breathe. I pulled out from the punk's sunset of an ass, my slit still dripping. Reaching over for the shreds of the Benway boy's shirt, I wiped his traces off me. He was still whimpering and moaning, though if it was for me or for another dose of drug or just for the whole general disaster, who knows?

I stood up, rearranged my clothes, and walked out of the alley, not looking back, not like Lot's wife, not like Orpheus, not even a little. I did hear, though, as I strode out of the alley, back into the contested city, a shout above the roar of cold-late-night traffic, rumbles of hovertanks and maybe bombs. "I fucking hate you," the boy called. I kept going, boots on wet concrete. "We're going to fucking kill all of you." Then fainter: "Come back. Please." And finally, maybe plaintive in the distance, something that sounded like "I'm as much of a man as you."

Whatever. The Earth spun on its meaningless axis in the big, freezing void. The sun would rise again soon. There'd be, no doubt, another show trial in the stadium. More war. Even more war. And I'd probably get another job to do, another killing. Whatever the Mullah told me to do. Paid me to do. Oh well, fuck, I'd gotten me some ass. I looked down at my red right hand.

Payback

Dale Chase

The cowboy is the only one on the train to acknowledge me in any kind of positive way. Everyone else makes a point of keeping their distance, easily understood after the Senate hearings. Corporate thief, greedy bastard making millions while stockholders lost everything. Passengers avert their eyes when they see me, and some, when confronted with my presence in a narrow corridor, turn back in the other direction.

"Where you headed?" the cowboy asks when I keep looking at him. We're in the club car, standing opposite.

I have no answer. My ticket says Seattle, but that's only because it's as far from Washington, D.C., as you can get by train. The cowboy cocks his head to indicate he expects an answer.

"Do you know who I am?" I ask.

"Everybody knows who you are.'"

"My ticket says Seattle, but I have no real destination."

He nods. "Let me buy you a drink."

I watch him at the bar, savoring his ruggedness. Tanned from the outdoors, lean, handsome, he wears faded jeans, boots, and a plaid shirt. All he needs is the hat and maybe a six-shooter.

He turns and catches me staring, then hesitates as if to let me finish the thought. I can see an ample package in his jeans and allow for the first time since the hearings that what I need more than escape might be a good fuck.

"Ethan Cross," the cowboy says as he hands me my drink and sits down next to me.

"Walt Durrell, but then you know that."

"Good to meet you, Walt."

"Where are you going?" I ask.

"Billings, Mont. Home."

"A ranch?"

He chuckles but gives me nothing more. The mention of home seems to have sent some part of him on ahead, and I feel a pang of envy.

"I've been in a hotel for weeks," I tell him, "but New York is home. Co-op apartment. About as far from Montana as you can get."

He stares down into his drink, then slowly raises it and downs the last. "How about we get a couple more of these, have them in my room. I wouldn't mind some privacy."

"Fine but only if you let me buy."

As I follow him to his compartment, I note his every detail: broad shoulders that funnel down into narrow hips, firm ass, long legs. I'm no slouch in the workout department, yet near him I feel almost soft. He has a steel-like quality and a nearly overpowering masculinity. The fact that we're headed to his room leads me to believe he doesn't confine his sex life to the local schoolmarm.

In his compartment, we sit, and when he asks me about my all-too-public downfall, even though I want more than anything to get away from it, I tell him everything. "I'm at the lowest point of my life," I offer in conclusion. "It all seemed justified at the time simply because it was possible, a fortune there for the taking. Now I see how wrong it was. The irony is that I now feel quite poor."

He studies me as I unburden myself. He sits with his legs wide apart, drink resting on one thigh, and when I end my confession, he sets the drink aside, unzips his jeans, fishes out his cock, and says absolutely nothing.

I look at it, about halfway along, an impressive piece of meat, cut, flushed now with the rush of blood. And then I look at him. He is expressionless. There is no urging, no suggestion beyond the dick there for the taking. I finish my drink, get onto the floor, crawl over between his legs, and scoop the thing into my mouth. And for the first time in months feel pleasure.

I've never had a dick in my mouth, and I can't get enough. Gobbling its length, I feel the fat knob in my throat. I lick and pull, feeding madly until I finally ease back to concentrate on the head, sucking as I would a fat tit. This brings to mind my wife, who has no idea where I've gone. I release the prick, sit back, look up at Ethan Cross and ask him to fuck me.

"Undress," he says and he watches as I strip for him. His cock is hard now, but he takes his time, eyeing me up and down. My own dick is stiff, and I would love him to suck the come out of it, but I need him inside me far more. I want to be mounted and ridden in the worst way.

"Turn around," he says, and when I oblige, he commands, "Bend over and spread 'em."

As I do what he wants, I experience a surreal kind of moment, like I'm back on the Senate floor, only naked, spreading my cheeks for assembled body. I see them with their hands in their laps, discreetly massaging their pricks while issuing their condemnations. When Ethan's finger goes up me, the picture disappears and I thrill to the feel of penetration.

He's gotten down onto the floor and is giving me a good prodding, pressing my prostate as if playing doctor. And then his other hand reaches between my legs, cups my balls, rolls them in his palm while the finger keeps on inside me.

I can't help but squirm with pleasure. I've had nothing in me since college, when I allowed my freshman roommate to fuck me repeatedly over an entire semester. After much confusion, I made a choice to forgo such things. Now, as the last remnant of my life falls away, I bear down to receive and Ethan murmurs his approval.

When he withdraws his finger, I wait for the cock, and when it isn't immediately forthcoming, I turn. He's lowered his jeans, pulled off his boots and socks, but seems in no hurry. When he strips away the shirt I gasp. A dark pelt covers formidable pecs, nipples barely visible beneath the fur. It runs unchecked down his front, culminating in a thicket that engulfs the swollen prick.

"Hands and knees," he says. "On the floor."

I do as told, feel the squirt of lube in me, hear the condom packet rip open. And then he's behind me, going in. I let out a long moan, pleasure mixed with a good bit of pain.

"You're pretty tight," Ethan remarks.

"I haven't done this since college."

"Well, then, you're pretty damn well due."

I come almost immediately, as if all my turmoil has pooled in my balls and suddenly found an outlet. My dick squirts cream onto the floor, unaided, I might add—something that's never happened before. But I've also never had a cock this far up me. My muscles tense with the feel of that hose snaking up into my bowels, and my sphincter involuntarily clamps onto the big sausage.

"That's it," Ethan urges.

He doesn't stop thrusting, doesn't allow me any respite as I reel from the climax, he just keeps on, the slap of flesh filling the room. As I shudder, then nearly swoon, he holds me at the waist, riding my ass like he's out on the range. Galloping fuck.

Things then even out, and I begin to enjoy what he's doing to me, how a dick up my butt is all that matters any more. All the money in the world, all the striving—it's nothing. This is power. This is what I need.

It seems like hours go by. Twice Ethan adds lube. My knees are chafed, my back aches from the position, but he keeps on. And then I hear his breath quicken and feel his thrust become urgent. He begins to pump and pound and finally to grunt and groan, and I know he's doing what I want, coming up inside me, giving me my reward for serving up my ass to him. I picture his cock without the rubber, flushing come in great white streams. I squeeze my muscle to trap it there.

Ethan takes some time to finish, then withdraws. I collapse onto the floor while he goes into the bathroom. When he returns, he stands over me, prick substantial even at rest. I'm exhausted but still reach up to grab him. "Time enough for that," he assures me as he eludes my grasp. When I start to get up he tells me to stay put. "I'm not done with you."

He make me lie back, raise my legs high to reveal my tortured hole, and he just sits for a while looking at me down there. At that point I begin to wonder what's really going on.

Is he one of the unfortunates who lost money because of me?

He stands, leaves me like that, legs up, and he raises the window shade. Still naked and not seeming to care whether anyone sees, he strides about the compartment as the outer world whizzes by. I can't tell what's next, can't begin to read him, but know he's working toward something. He pulls on his cock almost absently, and when I start to lower my legs he tells me to keep them up.

Finally he picks up a half-empty wine bottle, upends it, drinks a good bit, then gets down beside me. He proceeds to lube me again and, with his prick rising, he guides the bottle's neck up my rectum.

"You like chardonnay?" he asks as he works the bottle in and out of me.

"Yeah," I manage, stunned by what he's doing. I've never had anything but cock up me and suffer momentary panic until I allow how good it feels. It's like some cool, very hard dick fucking me and the wine, for whatever law of physics might apply, stays in the bottle. Ethan watches my face, grins at what must have been a pleasurable expression.

"Good, isn't it," he says. "The bottle-cock never goes soft. It may not come, but it's the goddamn ultimate hard-on."

As he does me with the bottle, I descend into a kind of pleasure I've never before known. I also begin to picture myself as others would see me, not the big-shot CEO anymore, not the Senate's whipping boy, but a grown man lying on a floor with his legs spread, taking a bottle up the ass. It drives me wild.

Ethan watches the bottle go in and out, and I watch him until he looks up at me. I want a clue from him, some sign he's one of the wronged. How appropriate if he is, and if not, well, even more delectable. I pull my legs higher, squeeze my muscle against the glass.

Ethan's expression remains calm even as he screws the bottle into me and then he leans over and closes his mouth around my cock.

"Oh, God," I cry because in my whole life I'd never had a blow job. Ron, the roommate, refused when I asked him to suck me, saying it was faggy, and my wife won't let me put my prick anywhere but her pussy. Now I feel a tongue on me, sliding up the underside, mouth closing in.

"Oh, God, oh, God," I cry. I can't help myself. It's glory. Pure glory.

The bottle keeps on fucking me, as if there is someone attached to it and we've embarked on an odd kind of gang bang. Is that what I deserve? This takes me back to the hearings again, to the fat old southern senator who was unmerciful, and I see myself spread out before him, his gnarled hand on the bottle. He'd love this. He'd get it up, at least figuratively. I can see them all lined up to suck my dick while the old boy fucks my ass. I can see the cameras capturing it for the 6 o'clock news.

I come while visualizing the senatorial blow job. I shoot big gobs into Ethan's mouth, and he rumbles with pleasure as he swallows it all. And I think of him on his ranch, fucking everyone and everything: hired hands, horses, and finally the schoolmarm, who can't resist lifting her skirts to present him her little pink pussy.

Ethan sucks me dry and keeps on sucking. I'm soft, but he doesn't let that stop him. He seems to like rolling my limp piece of meat around in his mouth. He plays with it, pulling and slurping, and I bask in the feel of his tongue and the sight of him on me. When he finally relents, he withdraws the bottle as well, leaves my pucker gaping.

"Keep 'em up," he says when I start to lower my legs. They ache now, but he doesn't seem to care. He makes himself ready, gets down, and puts his prick into me. He takes my feet in hand and I let my arms fall to the side. Pushing my legs up around my ears, he bears down into me, going for maximum torque. I'm looser now, the bottle has helped, but his cock goes far beyond the chardonnay. He's back up in uncharted territory. My rectum is screaming, but I'm loving it.

"I thought you'd be good," Ethan says as he pumps my ass.

"Because of who I am?"

"Because you had that look, the same one you had during the hearings, like you needed things done to you." He pauses, thrusts for emphasis. "A good fuck solves everything, you know. You guys should do more of it—the real kind, I mean, like this."

I know what he would do on the Senate floor. He'd make them forget all about corporate crime, get their dicks hard and their asses squirming as he parades that big prick. They'd lower their pants and take their fucking like the gentlemen they imagine themselves to be. "Order, order," the chairman would call from his podium where he holds a gavel in one hand, his cock in the other.

Ethan rams into me as if to confirm he could take them all. Pumping harder now, grinding his big thing into me, he growls with pleasure even as his expression turns to grimace. I know another climax is imminent and can see that it's different this time. He growls and when it hits calls out, goes kind of crazy, dick in control now, body mere appendage. He pumps and moans, shakes his head from side to side, sweat flying off him. And when he's finally ridden me to a standstill, he pulls out, slips off the rubber, lowers my legs, crawls onto my chest, pulls my head up, and sticks his spent cock into my mouth. I know then: He is one of the victims. I'm sucking a cock that has just been up my ass. How much plainer can it get?

The amazing part is his staying power. Still hard, he pushes the dick into my throat until I gag, and when I try to pull back, he grabs my head, holds me, fucks my mouth. Sweat runs off him, drips from nose and chin. His face is flushed, his dark pelt glistens. I finally can't take it and let my mouth go slack. He withdraws.

He holds his prick, glares at me. "You'd like it if I'd come on you," he says, squeezing a drop of jizz from his cock head. I marvel that he has anything left. My prick lies limp, cowed.

"Whatever you want," I tell him, looking up into blazing eyes, then back down to the prick. "Use me," I offer, wishing he'd fuck my ass again.

He goes into the bathroom, splashes water on his face, mops

away the sweat, stiff cock pointed at the mirror the whole time. I stay on the floor, enjoying lying flat, legs finally at rest.

Ethan returns, rolls a fresh rubber down his shaft. "Come over here and sit on me," he commands.

The seat is at the window beside a small table. Fields are rushing by outside, cows, tractors. I stand, reeling more from what he's been doing to me than the drinks I've had. I climb onto him, back against his chest, lower myself, and feel the big prick slide up me. And there we sit, looking out the window, me anchored on this dick of a lifetime, him pushing up into me. He doesn't put his arms around me, keeps things impersonal. Neither of us is looking for intimacy.

I think about asking him if he lost money when my company's stock tanked and we declared bankruptcy. I watch Middle America rush by and wish I could say it, then allow that I don't deserve to know. It would skew things. If he wants me to know, he'll tell me. I wriggle on him, work the prick around in my rectum, and shudder with pleasure.

"You like that," he says. "Dick up your ass."

"Oh, yeah." I reach for my own, but he swats my hand away.

"You're not gonna handle yourself," he says. "This is pure fucking."

Dusk begins to settle over the outside world. "I have to pee," I say.

Ethan lets me climb off, makes me keep the bathroom door open. "No playing with it," he commands. "Piss, then get back out here for your fuck."

I can barely walk. My hole is chafed, tissues swollen, wet. As I pee, I savor the cool air against my tortured bottom, and when I linger too long Ethan calls me back out to him.

Exhaustion is setting in. I feel wonderfully used but tired as a result, and as much as I like Ethan inside me, I want more to lie down and sleep. When I hesitate, he tells me to get the hell back onto his prick.

It is night when he lets himself come. He makes a production of it. "They can see us," he says. Shade still up, compartment lights blazing, the outer world has a glimpse of us as we speed by, and when the tracks periodically run alongside the highway, drivers match our speed and take in the show.

"On the table," Ethan says, easing me off him. His cock is still up. I crawl onto the table and he stands, adjusts me until he has the angle he wants, then goes back in. I turn my head, look out into the night. It's pure black outside for a while, then a town and lights and barricades down at crossroads, cars waiting for us to pass. And when the highway comes back alongside, a pickup truck paces us, the driver's head snapping back and forth between us and the road as Ethan fucks my butt hole.

The amazing part is, I get stiff again. Ethan reaches around and gets hold of me, pulling like he would a cow's teat. He then he turns me so I'm pointed at the window. On my knees but upright now, him back inside me and my prick bared for all to see. The pickup truck starts honking and I wonder if the guy knows who I am or if he's just enjoying the unexpected show. My cock sways from the rear action, but Ethan won't let me touch it.

My balls begin to ache, draw tight in the sac. I think I might come but don't. And Ethan just keeps on fucking. Part of me wants him to stop, but a bigger part wants him to keep on because I've finally gotten to where I belong: splayed before the world, or at least before one lonely truck driver. Like a pig in his wallow, I'm finally in my element.

Wrought Iron Lace
Greg Herren

The guy who just moved in across the courtyard is gorgeous. I would guess that he's still in his early 30s, maybe still the late 20s. Since I turned 40 it's really hard for me to judge age. 20-year-olds look like babies, 50-year-olds look 40, and that group in between—I just have no fucking clue. I watched him move in the day after I came home from the hospital. I have three pins in my leg from the car accident, and I have to keep it elevated as much as possible. I can't stand on it yet, even with crutches, so I have a nice loaner wheelchair from the hospital. Friends are running errands for me when they can and checking in on me to make sure I'm not lying on the floor in the bathroom helpless. I don't think I've ever spent so much time at home by myself. It's amazing how little there is to watch on television, even with 80 cable channels. Is there anyone left on the planet who has not seen the movie *Sixteen Candles*? Why do they have to keep airing it?

It was Saturday, and if ever there was a day of television hell, it's Saturday. There's nothing on, at any time of the day. I don't really care that much about billiards, snowboarding, or timber sports, thank you very much. I knew that the vacant apartment on the other side of the courtyard—the lower one—had been rented, but I'd forgotten someone was moving in. My apartment is the second floor of a converted slave quarters, and my balcony has a view straight into the living room and bedroom windows of the lower in the back of the main house. I had seen the young lesbian couple who had lived there naked in the bedroom entirely too many times and had trained myself not to notice those windows.

What can I say? I was bored, bored, bored. It was 11 o'clock in the morning, I'd been up for three hours, and I wasn't expecting anyone to come by again until 2 o'clock. I put a Jewel CD on and pushed myself out onto the balcony. It was a beautiful October morning, the sky blue, the sun shining and warm, but none of the humidity that made New Orleans almost unlivable in the summer. There was a stack of books on the balcony table, and I figured this enforced captivity was a pretty good time to catch up on my reading. On top of the stack was a hardcover with two incredibly pretty young men giving each other the eye on the jacket. They were fully dressed, so I knew it was a romance rather than some porn. The sex would be soft-core, the characters fairly two-dimensional, and the problems they faced would be most likely vapid, but it would while away some time without requiring a vast degree of thought.

The door in the gate opened, and this guy came in. *Wow* was my instant reaction. I put the book down on the table. He was wearing a black tank top, tight black jean shorts that reached almost to his knees, with the bottom inch or so rolled up, and calfskin ankle boots with heavy socks pushed down on top of them. He was wearing a black baseball cap with the fleur-de-lis emblem of the Saints on the front. He had a key ring in his hand, and he walked right over to the door of the vacant apartment and unlocked it. When his back turned to me, my jaw dropped. He had without a doubt the most beautiful ass I have ever seen in my entire life. It was hard, round, and perfectly curved. It was an ass to make men weep, an ass that belonged on an underwear box, an ass that could launch a thousand hard-ons.

I lit a cigarette.

A couple of other guys—muscular, attractive enough, but nothing like the first—came back carrying boxes. Any other time I would probably have been attracted to either or both of them, but the incredible beauty of the first boy (I found myself thinking of him as a "boy," strangely) made them seem like the girls who don't make the finals at Miss America. I'm sure they were used to it—it probably happened to them in bars all the time. I sat there for several hours, watching them move boxes and furniture, occasionally breaking to have a beer or a smoke at one of the iron tables in the courtyard.

The also-rans eventually removed their shirts, displaying fairly nice torsos, one with some hair, the other completely smooth. Again, under ordinary circumstances I would have been fantasizing a pretty damn vivid three-way scene. If I could walk I'd be down there helping, flirting a little, feeling them out about trysting. I would watch the sweat glistening on their bare skin in the sun and wonder how it might taste, if their armpits were becoming a little smelly perhaps from the sweat, if their underwear was sticking to their asses. But my mind was solely on my new neighbor, hoping that he too would take his shirt off, give me a glimpse of his chest and back, maybe the waistband of his underwear showing above his shorts.

It never occurred to me that they might be aware of me, the aging man in the wheelchair up on the balcony watching them hungrily without even saying hello. I never saw them look up or give any indication they knew they were being watched. For all I knew, when they were out of sight on the street taking stuff out of the truck, they could be laughing their asses off at the perv on the balcony, thinking he's hidden behind the wrought iron lacework. But if that were the case, it wouldn't have mattered to me at all. I could not tear myself away from watching the boy in the black tank top.

They did talk loud enough for me to finally figure out their names: My neighbor was Mike, the tall redhead was (appropriately enough) Sandy, the shorter, Italian-looking guy's name was Axel. They were easy with each other, joking and teasing in that way longtime friends do. Every once in a while one of them would say something as incomprehensible to me as Sanksrit and they would all burst into hysterical laughter. They all knew the secret language of their friendship, which had been learned over too many drinks at the bar on Saturday night, from brunch on Sundays, from long, involved phone conversations. The rest of us were excluded from it.

I found myself wondering if Mike was dating either one of them, if there was more than friendship between them.

I also wondered if Mike slept with his curtains closed.

I watched until they were apparently finished, Mike's shirt remaining on the entire time, as though he were teasing me, knowing how desperate I was to see his bare torso. His shirt was wet with sweat, and it clung to him tantalizingly, just enough for me to see the outline of his round pecs, his flat stomach, to see the play of the muscles in his back. It was around 4 when Sandy and Axel took off, left Mike to deal with the boxes and the bags and the assorted debris of his life. I sat there on my balcony, watching the bedroom window, and sure enough, after a few moments Mike walked in carrying a can of Diet Pepsi. He stood in front of the dresser, reached down, and started pulling the shirt over his head. His skin was tanned, firm, supple, and smooth as silk. He wiped his face with the shirt before tossing it into a laundry basket and took a big drink from the can. The muscles in his arms moved under his skin, the afternoon sun glinting on the sweat. He then moved out of sight. I sat there for another few minutes, hoping that he would come back, remove the shorts and underwear, but the seconds ticked away maddeningly.

Reluctantly, I pushed myself back into the apartment.

Trailer Park Punk

Jay Starre

"Hey, you pricks! If you want to take my brother's car, you gotta wait for him to come home. And he won't be doin' that too fuckin' soon!" The slender young punk was jeering at us. Then, just to piss us off, he gave us the finger and slammed the door to his trailer in our faces.

Ted and I looked at each and shook our heads. "Dude's got a big mouth, but he was kind of hot, don't you think?" I laughed. We had been repossessing cars for a couple of years and had seen a lot in the course of our job. After a while you get pretty good at reading the signs. The trailer park we had entered that hot California afternoon had been pretty trashy. The dusky young Latino we had just confronted appeared to be as trashy as his surroundings—and I mean that as a compliment.

But then the twink surprised us again. "You two wanna come in and have a beer or somethin'? It's fuckin' hot today." He had the door open and was grinning in our faces. Also, he was practically naked. He had shed his tight little tank top and was bare from the waist up. And to top it off, he was nastily massaging an obvious hard-on through the flimsy material of his skimpy jogging shorts. I thrust my arm out just in time to prevent him from once more slamming the door on us. The stunned look on his face was priceless as we muscled our way through the aluminum doorway and pushed him onto the couch directly behind him.

"I doubt you even have any beer. You're just a fucking kid. You're probably still nursing on your momma's titties," Ted smirked as he stood over him menacingly.

"Fuck you too! I'm 18, you asshole!"

The kid had spunk. And he also had one big hard prick on him. I decided to rattle his chain. I'm quick when I want to be, so he was not prepared for the speed of my next move.

"OK punk, let's see if you can use that foul pussy-mouth of yours for more than swearing." I was straddling him on the couch with my own prick out and waving it in his face before he knew what hit him.

His smart-ass sneer faltered. His soft brown eyes were wide open and his cute little mouth was even wider open. He gasped and then gurgled loudly as I slid four inches of the fat thing between those lush, gaping lips. His eyes looked like they were going to bulge right out of his head.

"Good idea—let's drill the humpy little wiseass," Ted laughed beside me. He was quick too and had reached over and slammed the door shut behind us. Then he was whipping out his stiffening bone and climbing up on the couch to join me.

Smart-ass was slurping noisily over my growing dork as I fed him more of it. The moist, warm mouth was small, but it was busy. He was tonguing my fat prick head enthusiastically while sucking in and out with his cheeks at the same time. I looked down to see he had his hand jammed into his shorts and was whacking away at his own boner. I had read the punk right!

Ted and I are both big guys. It helps in our profession to be tall and muscular. We're both over six feet tall and built like brick shit houses. We dominated the slender young Latino, no question of it. But he was holding up surprisingly well. In fact, the little fucker was not only swallowing my fat prick like it was nothing more than a delicious salami, he had also reached up with his free hand and was working it up and down Ted's big ladle just as eagerly.

He was slobbering all over the shaft of my cock as I fed it to him, and drool was running down his dimpled chin. I scooped up some of the goo with my big fingers and reached down into his shorts. I rubbed the slick stuff all over the head of his big prick and laughed as he thrust upward with his hips and moaned around the meat in his mouth. I tugged down his shorts and lifted his ass to pull them off. He was now naked on the couch beneath us.

Slender and chocolate brown, without a hair in sight, the punk was sexy. He was also wriggling all over the couch under us with his legs up in the air and his prick humping up into his own hand as he sucked my cock and pulled on Ted's. We had a wild one on our hands.

"Let's fuck his ass! You first, while I keep his foul mouth busy," I nodded to Ted.

The tall blond was ruggedly handsome. The big features of his face were screwed up with lust. His big lips hung open as he groaned with pleasure while our little punk pulled on his tool. He grinned at me and nodded back. Then he was shoving two fat fingers in his mouth and slobbering all over them. Once he had them gooey with saliva, he pulled them out and immediately reached down to shove them up between the Latino's creamy brown butt cheeks. I lifted one of his ankles to open up his crack. Ted found the pulsing asshole with his fingers and began to rub the sticky spit all over the wrinkled rim.

Twink groaned and gulped over my meat. He sucked with increased vigor as Ted toyed with his puckered slot. Ted's fingers teased and tugged at the sphincter, dipping into the tight center with little jabs. Latino punk twitched and raised his ass to meet the probing fingertips.

We both laughed at that, and Ted removed his fingers to bring them back up to his mouth. He licked and slobbered on the digits, his big sexy lips grossly wet as he pulled the fingers back out and shoved them down into Twink's hot little butt crack again. This time he zeroed in on the hole and began to open it up with his digging fingers. I pulled one of the punk's ankles up high and watched as Ted twisted and shoved and finally managed to cram both fingers knuckle-deep up the twink's sweet little slot.

That was a very hot image. Ted's hairy knuckles protruded from the spasming butt hole, which glistened with spit as it clamped and twitched around them. Latino punk was groaning in his throat, which sent delicious shivers through my cock buried in his gurgling mouth. He even lifted his own leg and held it wide so that his hole was more easily penetrated. Ted laughed aloud at the punk's writhing antics, and once more pulled his big fingers out of the twitching asshole. The squishy plop was loud in the trailer's silence. Ted jammed those two big fingers back in his mouth and spit all over them, then he reached down and crammed them back up the twink's wide-open ass pucker. Both fingers sank deep. Ted twisted them and shoved in and out at the same time. His saliva oozed from the violated butt lips. He laughed and poked deeper, twisting his knuckles-deep fingers in circles to the twink's grunting squirms.

"I think that should open him up some," I chuckled, somewhat breathlessly. The rapid twirling of the punk's tongue around my sensitive prick head was beginning to get to me. And that hot sight of Ted's big fingers digging deep inside those creamy brown butt cheeks was getting me hotter.

"Let's strip and do him good!" Ted suggested.

It was hot in there. His suggestion met with my willing approval. With some reluctance, I slid my wet boner from the punk's mouth and began to take my clothes off. Ted was still fingering the punk's hot asshole, the gaping butt lips tight around the big knuckles.

"You two assholes can fuck me all you want, but you aren't getting my brother's car back!" the twink sneered the minute his mouth was no longer full of prick.

"We'll see about that," I muttered, busily discarding my T-shirt, shoes, and jeans. The little twink was staring at my big hard chest and licking his lips. Ted had pulled his fingers from the hot butt hole and was shucking his clothes as rapidly as I.

"What's your name, punk?" I asked as I hovered over him with my big hard prick thrusting toward his spit-slick mouth.

"Carlos, but I don't give a shit what you two fuckers are called. Fuck-face and Fuck-lips, that's what I'll call you!" Carlos spat out sarcastically just before I silenced him with my huge schlong. His sassy muttering was cut off as my prick slid deep into his hot mouth.

I shoved him down on his back and crawled up to straddle his face, my cock still buried in his wet mouth.

"Fuck his ass," I told Ted.

He was already working on it. He had scrambled up on the couch at the other end even as I had sat down on Carlos's gurgling face. I faced the husky blond as he began to probe between Carlos's spread legs with his hard prick. The purple mast looked brutally huge as Ted jabbed around Carlos's creamy brown butt crack in search of the wet hole. He found it and centered the plum head directly against the puckered opening. He was grinning as he spit down into the juncture, his gob landing directly on the head of his big bone.

Then Ted began to cram that fat thing up the twink's squirming asshole. I rode the punk's mouth, rising up and down and slapping my balls against his chin as Ted slowly shoved the big head between the glistening butt lips straining to accept it. Ted held Carlos by the ankles and knelt between his legs as he leaned into him. His big poker slowly disappeared, first the head, then inch after inch of the foot-long shaft. Carlos' quivering butt lips stretched and gaped as they clamped over the fat meat. Ted continued hawking spit down onto the glistening shaft as he buried it deeper and deeper up Carlos' shaking ass.

"Yeah, balls-deep in twink asshole," Ted grunted when his prick had finally hit bottom.

I was quite amazed. Ted's prick is long and fat. But the hot little dude had taken it with apparent ease. In fact, now that the big thing was stuffed all the way up his trembling butt hole, he began to squirm around it, as if he was trying to fuck himself with the big bat.

"What a little hole," I huffed. His mouth was heating me up as I rode it steadily and stared at Ted's big bone riding Carlos's other hole.

Ted was working his purple poker in and out in a squishy rhythm. He kept spitting down into the pistoning meat as he fed it to Carlos's steamy asshole. It was quite a sight. Hot, wet lips massaged my own hard shaft with increased enthusiasm. I noticed Carlos' own substantial boner was twitching and drooling precome. I grinned as I reached down and teased the jerking bone. Carlos moaned and mumbled something around the prick in his throat. I jerked his meat a few times and then moved upward on his torso. Two tight little nipples protruded from a compact yet nicely defined chest. I smiled as I took hold of the little nubs and began to tweak them.

Carlos went wild. He bucked and squirmed beneath us. His own hands were on my ass clenching the big hard mounds tightly. He squeezed forcefully as he thrust up with his chest and ass to meet my twisting fingers and Ted's ramming boner.

We had discovered his buttons, all right. Carlos practically knocked the two of us off the couch in his frenzy. He jerked and bucked and rammed his own ass back over Ted's pounding pud. We didn't touch his prick, instead concentrating on his tight little nipples, his slurping mouth, and his squishy, squirming asshole. His untouched meat drooled and twitched continually. He grew more frantic, bucking up into our two boners so hard he finally managed to get himself off.

It was amazing to watch. He was sucking on my meat with loud, slurping moans as I rode his face up and down. He was driving his butt up into Ted's drilling cock with his hard little can. He was lifting his torso up to meet my twisting fingertips. Then all of the sudden, his cock began to spurt. The stench of hot come filled the air.

We continued fucking him for a few more minutes until his body began to go limp and his cock's wild spurting began to die down. Then we both pulled out together. Stumbling to our feet to stand side by side, we stared down at the fucked twink.

"Now, where are those keys?" I growled.

Carlos was spent. His lean young body was bathed in sweat. He lay on the couch with jizz all over his belly and his mouth and ass glistening with spit. But he grinned up at us and laughed out loud.

"You can fuck 10 ten more times and I still won't give 'em to you!"

Ted and I looked at each other. Our pricks were stiff and wet. "I think we should oblige little Carlos. We should give him both cocks at once. Only this time let's see if we can stuff them up his hungry little butt hole at the same time," Ted smirked.

"Yeah, let's double-fuck the foul-mouthed punk," I agreed.

Carlos shuddered. But the look in his eyes was far from fearful. It was hungry.

I suddenly had an idea. I draped my arm around my big pal. "Let's get the hell out of here. I don't think Carlos is going to cooperate."

Ted blinked a few times, and then smiled. "OK," he nodded and bent over to gather up his clothes. I did the same.

Carlos had sat up on the couch and was staring at us speechless. I pulled my T-shirt over my head, my erection bobbing nastily in front of me. Ted was doing the same. When I glanced down at the punk, he was biting his lip and looking back and forth from one hard cock to the other.

"OK! The keys are under the cushions of the couch!" Carlos blurted out.

"Get them, punk!" I laughed.

Carlos was quick. He got up on his hands and knees and rummaged around under the cushions. His plump young can presented a tempting target.

He squealed as my big boner rammed straight up his tender slot. Then he was tossing the keys to his brother's car on the floor and waving his butt in our faces as he begged for more. Ted lifted the slim twink up and slid underneath him to lie back on the couch. I was banging him from behind, his slippery butt channel delightfully stretched and wet from Ted's earlier reaming.

"Fu-u-uck!" Carlos shouted as Ted crammed his fat boner in beside mine from underneath Carlos's squirming body.

Carlos's creamy can wriggled and squirmed in the air as we plunged in and out of his stretched asshole. I had never felt anything quite so good. The clamping hole burned my cock, and Ted's sliding pole only added to the pleasure. The twink's caterwauling was music to my ears.

"I'm coming!"

"Me too!"

We creamed the poor punk's battered butt hole to his moaning delight. And he too was spurting, his second load splattering Ted's heaving belly beneath.

We walked out of there on unsteady feet, but we had the car. Carlos stood in the doorway, dressed in his tight shorts, his chest dripping sweat and his prick still hard beneath those shorts. He waved to us with a satisfied smirk.

"I don't even like my brother!" he shouted as we drove off.

I was laughing. The smell of his sweet young body and the memory of his pussy-mouth and hungry butt hole still lingered. I didn't even give a shit about the car!

Friday Night at the Calvary Hotel

M. Christian

"Excuse me for saying this, but you're a freak." He smiled, almost shyly, but didn't say anything. He didn't need to. It was a given, the reason we were both there. Don't ask me why, I just had to say it—maybe to make sure he didn't really think he was in any way normal, or maybe because I just needed to say out loud what I'd been thinking all week.

He certainly didn't look like a freak. He was actually kind of handsome: tanned, lean, with curly dark hair and skin that was nearing, but not quite, leathery. *He works outside,* I thought. No button-pushing and fluorescent lights for him. Construction, maybe. Nothing heavy, though—he didn't have any serious heavy-lifting muscles.

Arabic? Swarthy Italian? A touch of the Hebrew brush? Hard to say. Definitely not from a place with snow-covered peaks. Hot sand, sweet wine, dates—that kind of place.

"Did Judith get the money to you?" he said, the smile staying on his face. His voice, though, was musical—a choir voice if ever there was one. If small talk was on the menu—and it wasn't—I would have asked whether he was a singer. He had that kind of voice.

I nodded, slipping the security chain on. The door probably

couldn't stand a good sneeze, but I needed something to do with my hands. My heart was hammering in my chest like it wanted out. "Spoke to the bank this morning. The wire transfer went through yesterday. Thirty thousand dollars. A lot of money." I almost thanked him, but didn't; it *was* a lot of money, money I'd definitely earn tonight.

"It's just money," he said, with a dismissive wave of an elegant hand. "Don't have much use for it myself. Root of evil and all. I like to indulge in a different sort of sin, if you know what I mean."

I certainly did, but I didn't say anything. I didn't need—or want—to hear anything more. Not that I wasn't curious. God knows I was dying of curiosity, but I was already in pretty damn deep. Sure, I'd gotten some fairly good assurances from the mysterious "Judith" that it was a straightforward, simple job—no responsibility, no liability, and all that—but, hell, it was just too damn freaky. Too freaky for me to want to find out if there was anything else. This guy and his trip were bad enough.

It started out simple enough, with an ad in the miscellaneous section of the local paper. Innocent enough. "High Pay, No Risk," and then something about an assistant needed for a gentleman with "special recreational needs." I don't have it anymore; after I called and spoke to Judith, I burned it to fluffy ash in my kitchen sink. And then took a long, hot shower.

But I called back. Freaky was freaky, but I was flat, busted broke. Out-on-the-street-at-the-end-of-the-week kind of broke. Watching-panhandlers-to-pick-up-moneymaking-tips kind of broke. Shoplifting-to-eat kind of broke.

I called back and I listened, trying not to fuck it all up by showing how much the whole thing freaked me out. The first thing was a shopping list, pretty specific—more than I would have expected for someone with "special recreational needs," but then what do I know? Before then all I could do to get off was watch TV and think about Ginger and Mary Ann doing each other.

"Is that it?" he said, nodding at my sheet-draped handiwork.

"That's it," I said, and damn if I didn't feel proud. I'd started out nervous as fuck, but then I'd started to really get into it. Kept thinking about my dad, about all the stuff we built when I was a boy. "Measure twice, cut once, kid." "Always go with the grain, son." "Accidents and screwups happen in a hurry, lad." Yeah, but there's a big difference between banging together a tree house or a bookshelf and what this guy wanted. Still, I couldn't help but think about dear old Dad as I hauled the lumber home and got to work.

"I made it in sections, held together with a couple of bolts. Strong as fuck but easy to haul around. The whole thing fits right into a big gym bag; no one noticed a thing."

He stepped up close to it but didn't touch the sheet. He was breathing real slow and deep, like he was going to run in a marathon. Psyching himself up, I thought—either that or trying real hard to keep his excitement bottled up.

"Not that anyone in this place would have cared," I added, prattling stupidly through my nervousness. The Calvary Hotel made other shitholes look like the Ritz. The morgue's body buggy could probably find its way there on its own, just out of habit. The atmosphere was hazy with pot and crack smoke, decades of B.O., and toilets never flushed. Hauling the stuff up the back stairs, I counted at least a dozen pitched sets of works and one—possibly two, I couldn't see if one guy was breathing—dead junkies. The bed was as soft as a boiled marshmallow, the walls looked like they'd been used for target practice, the TV was busted, the wood floor was white-hazy from too many chalk-outlined bodies, and the windows were nailed shut from the inside. It was perfect. Beg, scream, fire off a whole clip, the worst that could happen would be…fuck that, nothing would happen, that's what made it great.

It even had a couple of bonuses. The "bridal suite" I'd rented had a spare, windowless room—perfect for stowing my stuff—and the main room had a retaining wall. The studs were almost too easy to find—and no one would mind my quarter-inch bolt holes.

He was still standing there, still breathing slow and deep. My nerves were jangling so loud, I was surprised he didn't hear them. "Want to see it?" I finally croaked out.

In a real soft voice, he said, "Please."

So I pulled off the sheet, and there it was in all its glory. Freaky? Damn straight, but I'd done a good job, and a little burst of pride slowed my heart down a little, just enough for a question to leak out: "So tell me, you Catholic or something?"

There was a long—very long—minute, as he stared at what I'd made. "Something like that," he said, finally, turning his head slowly to look back over his shoulder at me, that wry little smile back on his lips.

"Ah," was all I could say, struck more stupid than usual.

"This is wonderful," he said, stepping up and running his hands over the smooth wood. "A perfect job."

I wanted to say, "Aw shucks," and start in about the hours of sanding, the three coats of lacquer, the buffing. But then I remembered why he'd had me build it and what he wanted to use it for.

He rubbed it a long time, like he was communing with it. Watching him stroke it, I noticed something about his hands. I asked, "Is this your—ahem—first time? I mean...doing this kind of thing?"

It took him a long minute to pull himself away. "Oh, no, not at all. It's just something I developed—well, I guess you could say 'a taste for'—a long time ago. Every once in a while I like to indulge myself, you know, when I can get away from the family business."

"Hmm...OK," I said, not wanting to know more. He'd done this before, he knew what he was getting into, and he wanted it: That was all that mattered. I was absolved of responsibility. Still, it didn't keep a sudden deep wave of nausea from surging up my throat.

"Can I see the rest?" he said, one hand still on the wood. "Good, I see you thought of the pegs—something to hold on to. Makes it much easier," he added, smiling. Smiling, damn it. He was actually smiling—an honest-to-goodness, "God's in his heaven and all's right with the world" kind of grin. The nausea bubbled in my throat.

I went into the side room, breathing deeply in the dark quiet. Dust, mildew, old wine, piss, butane. Still, I was away from him, so the air felt damn good wheezing in and out of my lungs.

Anyway, I'd been paid, and he wanted it, so I grabbed my toolbox. On the way out I remembered the stepladder, so I caught it with my free hand and pulled it behind me, the metal legs scraping thin lines in the wood floor.

He was almost dancing with excitement. I put down the toolbox, flipped open the latches, and handed him the stiff brown bag, then turned to open up the ladder.

"They're perfect," he said, his voice breaking with pleasure. I turned, catching sight of his deep brown eyes. Good eyes, kind and knowing—but they were also junkie eyes seeing a fix. "Just perfect."

It took me a while to find the perfect ones. Not too thick, but long and very sharp. He held first one, then the other three nails up to the dim yellow ceiling fixture, turning them slowly, entranced by the reflections coming off the steel.

He lowered them, a junkie gazing at my face, finally seeing me. "I want to do it. Now," he said, starting to unbuckle his belt.

"You're the man," I said, a serious quaver in my voice. "If you're ready, I'm ready."

"I've been waiting to do this for ages," he said, sitting on the bed, kicking off his running shoes. "Again, I mean," he added. The pants followed. Then the denim shirt. He had on a pair of faded yellow...well, it almost looked like a diaper, something wrapped around his waist and crotch. It didn't look comfortable, but then nothing about that Friday afternoon was even remotely comfortable—for either him or me.

There was something else. Something I noticed even though I didn't want to. He was hard. Very hard. I couldn't help but look, even stare. Hard as a fucking rock, his wrap-thing tented out by his cock. When he stepped toward me, I watched it, a big, stiff finger waving back and forth in his weird, loose underwear.

Before, what I'd made had been just a big wooden...thing, like something Dad and I would build in the garage, but watching him step up to it, climb up on it, I couldn't lie to myself. I'd built a cross. He'd paid me to build a real, honest-to-goodness cross. Life-size. Anchored to the wall of the Calvary Hotel with big fucking bolts. And that's not all he'd paid me to do.

"I know what you're thinking," he said. I'd spaced out, realizing that I was minutes—maybe just seconds—away from doing it. "I really do know, and it's all right. I want this. More than anything, I want it. It's going to be OK. Trust in me."

I was scared. No, fuck that, I was terrified. I wanted to puke, I wanted to run, I wanted to scream "No fucking way!" but I didn't. Yeah, part of it was that 30 grand in my bank account, but a lot more was…well, it was him. He wanted it. He wanted it bad, so it was all right to do it. He wanted it. He really did. Don't ask me how, but it was, really, all right.

After carefully, gingerly climbing the stepladder, he slowly turned around, balancing himself with one very tanned hand on the wood. When his back was up against it, he reached up, grabbed the right-hand peg, and pulled himself up onto the little step I'd attached, as per instructions, to the vertical beam. Then he was up there, hands spread wide, legs calmly crossed. He was up there, on the cross. He was on the cross. His eyes were closed and his breathing was slow and regular. And his cock…his cock was still very hard.

I needed to get away from the sight of him for just a moment, so I stepped into the side room. My own breathing was quick and shallow, and spots swam before my eyes. I wanted to pass out—just close my eyes and wake up someplace else.

"Are you OK?" his voice was calm, collected, with just a tiny vibration of excitement. Even though it came from the other room, it felt and sounded like he was standing right next to me.

"I'm…I'm fine," I said, taking a slow, deep breath. A bundle in one corner caught my eye. The tarp. Right, the tarp. "Just getting a few things."

"No problem. Take your time."

I grabbed the tarp and stepped back into the main room. The room was still dirty, broken, smelly. He was still on the cross, a beatific smile on his face. Stupidly, I showed him the tarp. "Just in case…you know…spillage."

"Sensible," he said. "I like that. You think ahead. Thank you."

He closed his eyes for a moment. "The right one. Always start with my right wrist. If you please."

"Right," I said, carefully—overly carefully—laying the tarp on the already stained floor. After I spent way too long getting the tarp positioned just right, I knew it was time. The moment of truth. Do it or don't do it. Walk or stay.

"It's OK," he said in that perfectly melodious voice again. "I want you to. The right one. Start with my right wrist, please."

Small sledge hammer from the toolbox. Nail from where he'd left it on the bed. Up the stepladder, slowly, carefully, bracing myself against the dirty wall. Absently, I noticed little piles of plaster dust on the floor from where I'd drilled the anchor bolts. Another step, then two, his groin at eye level, then below, his cock still very hard, very obvious. A little stain too—fresh. The smell of sweat and salty come in the air.

I put one hand on his arm, to balance. He was hot; the skin was slick with sweat, though not dripping. Just a light sheen. I felt his pulse, distantly, as I put the tip of the nail against his wrist, between two bones. What are they named again? Radius and something else? I'd have to look it up when I got home; got a copy of *Gray's Anatomy* around somewhere.

Then he said, "Please, do it now," and so I did.

The nail was sharp, very sharp, and the sledge was heavy, very heavy, and I put a lot of muscle into that first swing. I don't know what I was expecting—the nail not to go in at all, or the nail to go all the way through, biting into the wood with the first swing—but I didn't get either. The nail dented his flesh, breaking his skin, sinking deep into his wrist—but not all the way through.

He clenched his teeth but didn't scream. His breathing became fast but was still deep, and his eyes were squeezed tight shut. "Again," he hissed between his straight whites, "do it again." He groaned, deep and heavy—the kind of groan I thought came only from sex.

Again. This time the nail went through, but this time I'd swung at it with everything I had, trying to hit the dull gray head even though it gently rose and fell with his steady pulse. There was the bass sound of steel hitting wood, and for an instant it was Dad and me again, building a soapbox racer, a bookcase, a birdhouse, a tree house—anything but driving a nail through a man's wrist.

Blood welled up quickly around the nail, then started to slowly drip down onto the floor in heavy, steady drops. It was very thick—I remember that. Drip. Drip. Drip. It smelled of copper.

"The other one," he said. "Do the other one."

I walked down the ladder, surprisingly calm inside, and moved it. Back up, new nail in my hand. I knew how to do it now. I knew what it felt like to drive the nail. The surprise and shock was gone. Why does the murderer shoot back at the police? Because they can only execute him once. What's one more murder? What's one more swing of the hammer?

Still, it didn't go through with the first blow—again it stopped halfway through the muscle, the tendons, the veins, the arteries. Before he could ask, I swung again, this time driving the nail straight through, wrist to bone in one clean swing. I felt a flash of pride in a job well done—right before the bile rose in my throat and I had to swallow it down.

"Thank you, thank you, thank you..." he said, his voice distant, lost, but also joyous, ecstatic. His blood was a steady metronome drip, but not in time to his pulse—that was apparent in the hard, throbbing lift and sink of his cock. "Thank you—now, please, do the rest. My feet. Do my feet."

Planning. No one ever accused me of not being good at thinking things through. I might not be able to hold a job, keep a girlfriend, or do anything else worth a damn, but I do know how to look at something and know what's required. A cross that comes apart so you can haul it around easily. Big fucking bolts so you can attach it to the wall. A stud finder, to find where to attach it. A tarp, to catch some of the blood. A stepladder. Two long nails for the hands or wrists. A real long one for...for both feet.

I didn't have to climb the ladder. I did have to kneel down, though, get down on my hands and knees to be able to reach his feet.

I almost giggled, thinking of what I was doing, the position I was in.

He was mumbling, his words gone soft, lost in his perverted indulgence. Happy, so happy. I had to really listen to make out the words. Actually, it was only two of them, over and over again: "Thank you, thank you, thank you…"

I had the hammer in my right hand, the nail in my left. I could have put them both down on the bright blue tarp, turned and walked out. Craftsmanship, planning, maybe that was it. Maybe I just wanted to give him what he wanted—everything he wanted.

The skin over his ankle didn't dent as much as the wrists had. Stronger. More muscle. Bone. I pulled my arm back, putting everything I had into the first swing.

I'd never heard a bone break before. A wet snap, a gristly, moist kind of break—like a piece of fresh bamboo. My fingers were gripping the nail, so I felt it tear into his skin, hit the bone, which splintered under my sledge. I didn't let go fast enough, so I also felt the torn muscle jerk, spasm. Blood oozed around the metal, slid down the top of his foot, slipped between two toes, and drip, drip, dripped to the floor.

His breathing accelerated and a down-deep groan vibrated out of his narrow chest. His head was lifted back and his body arched out, pulling at the nails in his wrists and I feared for a second that he'd tear himself free.

Something wet dropped onto my forehead. I reached up, smeared it, then looked at my fingers. No red, so it wasn't blood. It smelled salty. Then I noticed the large, growing stain on the front of his diaper.

The words came again, a little more forced, heavy with panting ecstasy. "Thank you," but "more" was also there. Over and over again: "Thank you" and "more."

More. I swung the hammer again, as hard as I could, as hard as I ever could. I hit the nail right on the head, and with another crackle and pop of bone, cartilage—all the great red, wet stuff in our ankles—the nail went straight in and through.

He screamed. He screamed loud and long and hard. Not a

frightened or pained scream; he screamed like it was the best time of them all, the best time ever had by anyone. I was scared. Not because I thought anyone would come a-knockin'—after all ,this was the Calvary Hotel and a scream was just part of the general ambience— but because for a beat, a single moment, I was jealous. I wanted to feel what he was feeling, know the *bang, pop, wow* of the best time you could ever feel.

I watched him for what seemed like hours. His breathing slowed; his body sagged like it was melting from stone or he was falling asleep, emptied through that roaring voice, that soaking come. His eyes fluttered, then stilled, and his head gently fell onto his shoulder.

Then his breathing, without any kind of warning, just stopped. I stared for a second, maybe two, then my own heart started to race. A burning sweat covered me, and my brain slammed into *oh fuck oh fuck oh fuck oh fuck oh fuck oh fuck oh fuck* mode. Do something! But what? I didn't know CPR, it would take too long to get him down, and he'd already lost blood... Call for an ambulance? Explain to them, then the cops, then the D.A., then an attorney, then a jury, why I nailed him to a cross in a sleazy hotel?

So I watched him for another couple of hours, frozen. I watched him till the sun went down and the place got really dark. Finally, I got up and switched on the lights, knowing what I had to do.

It took me a long time; luckily, I'd booked the room for two days and nights. Getting him down was a bitch, but I managed. I wrapped him in a sheet, being careful what I touched, and locked him in the side room. I didn't think they'd be able to lift prints from the plastic tarp, but just to be safe, I bundled it up. Toolbox, tarp, and everything else I could think of went out the window and down the fire escape. And the cross. I'd burn it, I decided, when I got home, feed its carefully built pieces into my fireplace. Ashes to ashes.

Just to be safe, I took some regular nails and pounded a couple into the spare room's door, then I dragged the bed against it. No maid service in the Calvary Hotel, but I still wanted to keep any itchy fingers away from him, at least until I could think straight and figure out how to get rid of all the evidence,

Then I left. Went back out into the world, fear riding my back, thundering in my heart. I went out via the lobby, paying the pockmarked night clerk for another week, paying in cash.

I didn't think I'd ever go back. Funny how you sometimes do something you'd never, ever dream of doing. Like nailing a complete stranger to a cross. Or going back to check on his body.

Yeah. I did. Both of those things. It took three days before I decided to do it. Three days of feeding pieces of my carefully built cross into the fire, three days of trying to erase myself from what had happened. But then, on the third day, I started to think about him. Had it happened? Really? Maybe desperation had cooked my brain, maybe he wasn't dead, maybe he was in a coma or something—paralyzed, slowly dying of thirst and hunger, nailed into that dark, windowless room. I didn't know the guy. Sure, I'd crucified him, and I thought—no, knew—he was a real sick freak. But he still didn't deserve to just be left behind like that, tossed away like the wrapping from a cheap burger.

So three days later I climbed the fire escape and slipped inside. The bed was still pushed against the door, the door was still nailed shut, the room was still dark and windowless, and the sheet was there, in the middle of the floor. But he was gone.

No body. No crime. I left, hoping to leave that Friday night at the Calvary Hotel behind me. I tried to forget all about the guy, the cross, the nails, the hammer in my hand, the body. But sometimes I'll remember, everything coming back to me in one trembling recall.

Especially at Easter.

Just Looking

Michael Huxley

I was working at home recently, quick-reading newly submitted manuscripts, grading each one according to my "5-point scale"—2.5, 3.7, 0.5 (My God, this guy calls himself a writer...?), 3.0, etc.

I had just finished an excellent short story and was marking the top margin with a red-inked 4.8 when the phone, lying next to me on the bed, rang. It was my lover, Paul.

"Hey, babe, what's going on?" he inquired.

"I just finished reading a dynamite story from a new writer."

"Oh, yeah? You give him a 5.0?"

With bored braggadocio I quipped, "You know I reserve that grade exclusively for my own work."

"Did you get all worked up, reading it?"

"As per usual..." I replied, clutching my hard-on through the workout shorts I'd failed to change out of on returning from the gym earlier.

"You do anything about it?"

"No, but I *want* to."

"Good, hold that thought," he said. "I'm fuckin' horny as hell, saw the butchest motherfucker walkin' down the street just now, *whoa*: shirtless, torso to die for, long hair, tattoos, and what an ass... What a babe!"

171

"Sounds nice," I responded, ripping my Velcro fly asunder. "You... coming home for lunch?"

"I'm on my way. I want dessert first."

"No problem, I'm preparing it now." Hanging up, anticipating dessert, hauling my cock and balls through the Velcro partition, I milked my precome and savored it. *Yum...* I got up, gathered my paperwork into a pile and placed it on the dresser before stepping out of my shorts. My dick bobbing before me, I quickly snagged a porno film from our collection—*Biker Pigs From Hell,* perfect!—slammed it into the VCR, and, turning it on, reclaimed my place on the bed. Oh, yeah, there he was: a naked Bo Garrett, shot from behind, fucking the shit out of some sleazeball lying on his back, whose legs Mr. Garrett was holding high in the air.

The butchest motherfucker... torso to die for, long hair, tattoos, and what an ass! And how he was moving it! *You go for it, Bo. Dig it, man. Yeah.*

Luxuriantly, if cautiously, I played with my wet erection, but *man* did I feel like shooting a big one! *Get your ass home, Paul...* I thought, resisting the urge to just go for it. After maybe ten minutes, Bo and his bottom buddy disengaged and managed to walk to the Harley chopper in the background, where they fucked some more and finally shot their loads, jerking themselves off, snarling and cursing like the pigs they were depicting. *Holy shit,* I thought, *I want to do that.* Masochistically, I rewound the money shot and watched it again—and then again—before rewinding the film back to the beginning of the fucking scene. I hit play and settled into doing just that when I heard Paul's truck pull in.

The bedroom door was open, the door frame suddenly filled with my lover, who, grimy from his morning's house renovation and witness to my hedonic hand play, said: "Jesus, babe, look at you... Y'havin' a good time? Fuck, yeah, you are! Mmm... *Biker Pigs,* huh?" He stepped closer to the bed, where he stripped naked in a flash—a gorgeous man, if I do say so myself. The love of my life's wonderful dick was already hard, transecting his fist. Remaining standing, he began to watch the film, stroking himself, commenting, "Y'gotta admire the way that man fucks..."

"Babe…" I implored, drawing myself up a bit. "C'mere. Let's make out, suck dicks a little. Please…"

Giving sudden voice to concern, Paul said, "Oh, don't stop what you're doing; you look so beautiful! I don't wanna make love, Michael. I wanna get off watchin' the film, watchin' *you* watch it. Let's have a good wank, Babe. That OK with you?"

Nonplussed for about a half second, I readily complied, more than content to watch Bo Garrett's hot ass churning, his big dick slipping in and out of the other guy's slick anal grip. It was a stunning, extended fuck scene, nicely edited and shot mostly from mid range. Both actors were obviously enjoying themselves immensely, as were Paul and I, participating as both voyeurs and exhibitionists. Alternating my visual focus between the sizzling television screen and Paul jerking off, I gave myself completely over to pleasuring myself stereoscopically, every precome-y hand stroke rapturous.

Once again disengaged, Bo and his playmate were facing each other on the Harley, jerking off, talking dirty, getting close to orgasm. The other guy shoots off first, his face a twisted mask as copious spurts bolt from his piss slit in thick, white increments, spattering the bike's seat. Bo follows suit a few moments later, matching his costar's discharge shot for shot and then some. I noted for the umpteenth time the way Garrett's upper lip curls, sneers involuntarily, right before he lets loose with his first, dense man-blast of come. Paul, watching the scene intently, obviously on the brink himself, moved to my side of the bed, which afforded a closer study of his writhing, fist-fucking, shouting detonation of ecstasy. Watching him slam his wad so forcefully ushered my own crescendo at once, which spawned similarly self-induced arcs of mind-bending pleasure. Ascending, ascending, YEAH…

What man could ever forget the first time he brought himself to sexual climax? By the age of 12, I'd been playing with my dick for as many years before that momentous occasion as I could remember. But enjoyable as those hands of solitaire were, they never resulted in either "getting the white stuff" or the "supergood feeling" rumored to accompany that elusive phenomenon. Perhaps, suggested the more cocky representatives of the school-yard grapevine, I was still too young. But then again, I counterthought, perhaps not.

Suspecting that I just wasn't jacking off long enough, I stripped naked in my bedroom, home alone one evening. I sat on the edge of my bed, feet on the floor, my silky hard-on jutting straight up from my lap, and began moving the deliciously sensitive skin up and down my aching boner. I took my time, glancing at a magazine, whose cover featured a good-looking U.S. Army "grunt" in Vietnam. I remember the photo vividly: the G.I. was stripped to the sweaty waistband of his camouflage fatigue pants, wore a grimy bandanna on his head, and was badly in need of a shave. His dog tags bivouacked in a nest of dark chest hair, he was lighting a cigarette, cupping the match…

Time passed pleasurably enough, but nothing out of the ordinary was happening just yet. Determined, I quickened my pace somewhat, unconsciously allowing the Pfc. to lure me into a rhythm of hand-to-boner-involvement I had heretofore never experienced. I certainly didn't understand it at the time, but I felt myself becoming more involved with the image of the soldier, more caught up in the moment, as my enjoyment increased proportionately. It was taking forever, it seemed. But *what* was? What was the "it" I expected to happen? Whatever, I just kept that sweet skin a-movin' up and down my unsuspecting boner, having a grand ole time, just looking…

After a healthy, meat-beating while, I swallowed hard and thought, *Man, this is starting to feel pretty damn good, in a different kind of way.* I persevered, breathing faster and sweating a little. My heart was racing. *Damn,* I thought, fixating on the magazine cover, *this guy looks so cool…* My cock continued to feel better and better; I was fucking loving it! Suddenly I felt an intense wave of pleasure from deep within my cock. As I though, *Oh, this is startin' t'feel* really *good,* the wave subsided, but hot on its heels another, more potent one overtook it. Followed by another and another and *another,* each wave proved more intense than the one preceding it. I didn't think I could tolerate the pleasure growing any stronger, any *sharper,* but neither could I stop jerking off or exclaiming the word "Oh!" despite my joyous consternation. All at once my penis was gripped in an unrelenting frenzy of ecstasy. Unaware of why, I dropped the magazine, stood up, bent my knees a little, thrust my cock in the air, and let my first load fly sky high, screaming: "Oh, *shit...*"

I had no idea anything could feel so...*good* seems an inadequate word, but there you have it.

I was shocked by how quickly the mood went away, but it returned with a vengeance later that evening while I was lying in bed, thinking about what had transpired earlier. I jerked off again, with the same excellent result—only much, *much* quicker in the messing of my sheets. From that day forward, I became hooked something fierce to getting myself off, so much so that I began feeling guilty about how many times a day I felt compelled to do it.

For no logical reason, I had an impossible time picturing myself as a grown man jerking off, yet I couldn't fathom ever being able to stop. Hard as I tried, I could not keep my hands off my pud, indulging compulsively in orgasmic escape with my military hero and, God forbid, while looking at myself in the mirror! I was continually getting hard, oftentimes at the most inconvenient moments—staring at the crucifix during Mass, in the locker room before and after P.E., on a field trip with my classmates to the state correctional facility—and I knew of only one way to make those boners go away. Dashing to the nearest rest room, hands in my pockets, I increasingly viewed myself as a crazed sex junkie and resolved to end the cycle of guilt by confessing to my family's parish priest.

It took all the courage I possessed to utter the sin of masturbation in that confessional, whispering it shamefully through the screen.

"Say three Hail Marys, three Our Fathers, and never do it again" was the priest's fairly indifferent-sounding penance-prescription. It seemed I'd gotten off lucky! But would I ever get off again?

The prayers were easy enough to accomplish, and I actually lasted (get this, now) *six weeks* with the second half of my penance, but inevitably one afternoon, beyond desperate for an orgasm, I caved in. Standing before the bathroom mirror, wanking frantically,

I blew a load of such magnificent intensity into the sink that I fell to my knees, where—resisting the urge to rend my shirt and gnash my teeth—I flatly refused to beg God's forgiveness.

No, I resolved, I would never, *ever* confess the "sin" of masturbation again. Instead, I left the Catholic Church at 15, never to return to it or any other organized system of (what I have come to view as) moral indoctrination or mind control. In essence I concocted my own religion, set myself up as God, and elevated masturbation in status from sin to sacrament. Thus was my first major battle with self-loathing won. Dropping countless loads along the path to self-discovery, there have proven plenty more skirmishes, of course—far more intense waves of conflict (Note: That Vietnam grunt was definitely not a *PlayBOY* centerfold), but many, many more sacraments to hold sacred as well—Just Looking being but one.

The Long Haul
Karl Taggart

Sometimes it's everything—rush of emotion, an onslaught of desire—and sometimes it's nothing. Or close to nothing.

Tom kept both hands on the wheel, even when he came. Roaring along at 85 mph, headed north on Interstate 5 out of Los Angeles, he bucked up into my mouth as he let go but otherwise resembled any other motorist settling in for the long haul up central California.

We'd met just 10 hours before and fucked the night away. At dawn, after we'd reamed each other yet again, he said, "Come with me. Give yourself a couple days off. You writers can do that, can't you?"

There were all kinds of reason not to go—deadline on revisions to the novel, a meeting with my agent that afternoon, date that night—but I said, "Sure, why not?" and hopped into the car. We weren't even to the freeway when I got his dick out.

He shifted in his seat, spread his legs, and pushed up at me. I began an easy stroke, and when we hit the on-ramp I leaned over and took him into my mouth.

Tom had turned out to be a real wonder, a bit on the crazy side, but I'm attracted to those types, what with all my solitude. Where I spent words on the page, he threw them around without restraint, connecting with anyone and everyone, totally on every second. His

177

hard good looks only added to the mix, and when he asked me back to his place I knew I was in for some kind of ride.

We were a perfect fit in all sorts of ways—bodies well matched, neither locked into top or bottom roles. For every fuck I gave him, he gave me one back, and the more we did, the more we wanted. At one point we had a two-headed 18-inch dildo up both our asses, fucking back to back. By dawn we were sticky with come, the room reeking of sweat.

The car simply added a new dimension, and I wondered how long it would be before we had to pull to the side and fuck. As I gobbled Tom's cock, he kept me informed about where we were. "Westwood," he said at one point and just before he started coming, "Castaic. Grapevine's next."

I knew there were places to pull over at the summit, a rest area at the top of the long grade. When I sat up, mouth wet and tasting his salty cream, I told him, "I want to fuck you. Pull over."

"We do that, we'll never get to where we're going."

I had my dick out, smearing precome down the shaft. My balls were aching for release. "Well, you're not gonna do me much good concentrating on the road."

"I have to be in Stockton by 2."

"You should have thought of that before you asked me along."

He relented when I got his pants down, my fingers up his ass. Amazing how a good anal probe can shift a guy's priorities. In the rest stop bathroom I got him into a stall, got a rubber on, spread-eagled him against the wall, and shoved my cock up his ass. He moaned, opening to me as I kept up a steady stroke, fleshy slap echoing off the tile. Someone used the urinal while we were going at it. I heard the piss, the pause, pictured the guy listening, getting hard. Finally the flush and footsteps.

"Jeez," Tom cried, and I knew I was pumping the cream out of him. He hadn't touched his dick, and the idea of his cock shooting blindly made me do him all the harder. I rammed up into his bowels until I finally unleashed a torrent. Pounding his ass, I let out a long growl, the climax all the more intense because of the public venue.

"You drive," Tom said when he pulled up his pants. "I'm not sure I can even walk."

I put my arm around him, nuzzled his cheek, and bought him a Coke. When he handed me the keys I thought about getting his face into my lap and keeping it there until we hit Bakersfield. Before I started the car, I unzipped my jeans, made him do the same. "Get it out," I told him as we sped back onto the freeway. He had the seat back a notch, intending to relax, but he complied, pulling his soft cock out for me to enjoy. Once I had us headed north again, I reached over and played with him. He shut his eyes, feigned sleep. His cock, however, was wide awake.

Thank God for automatic transmissions. The only thing I wanted in my hand was his dick and at one point, after we'd descended the Grapevine and were on that barren stretch that is middle California, I tucked my knees up under the wheel, freed my cock, and began to jerk myself with my left hand.

Tom opened his eyes about this time and, stiff dick or no, freaked. "Holy shit!" he said when he saw I had no hands on the wheel.

"Relax. It's not like there are curves in the road."

He looked out the windshield as if he needed confirmation. "You could hit a bump and we'd be all over the place," he yelled.

"You could get over here and do this for me," I countered.

"I will if you'll put both hands on the wheel."

"One hand."

"Both," he said, pushing me away. I considered the situation, then lowered my knees and took the wheel, became the proper driver. Tom sighed with relief, his cock listing now.

"C'mon," I said. He reached over and took hold of me and then I told him what else I wanted. "Pull my pants down and get your finger up my ass."

"No way.'"

"Hey, I'm driving like you said. It's no problem to lift up and have you pull 'em down." I raised up off the seat and he retreated completely, then started laughing. "C'mon," I insisted, wiggling my butt. "This is crazy," he said but he did as asked, getting my pants down around my knees. "Wet your finger," I said and he gave me a smile, did as asked. And then he slid his hand under my butt, found my hole, and as he pushed his finger up into me I squirmed with pleasure. "Now my cock."

He took hold, began an easy stroke, then asked, "How long are we going to keep this up?"

"How far to Bakersfield?"

It was the longest masturbation session I'd ever had, mainly because very time I started toward a climax, I had him ease off. I rode that edge for miles, sitting on that finger, working it with my muscle, it working me back, prodding and pushing. I finally made him add a second digit, this near Bakersfield, and I started to bounce a little, to give myself a finger fuck. When I got ready to blow I told him to get his mouth on me, and he dove down and sucked out my load. Shortly after that, we stopped in Bakersfield to clean up, get gas, have a soft drink, and rest, but we got to eyeing each other there in the parking lot, and I wished we could get naked and do a full-body number. "You drive," I said when we got back into the car.

"Next stop Stockton," Tom said, and I laughed.

"Don't be so sure."

There is nothing between Bakersfield and Stockton. Farms give way to miles of desolate plain dotted with scrub. Monotony is the word, highway hypnosis if you don't keep yourself alert.

We hit the freeway, and for a while I did nothing, which threw Tom more than if I'd grabbed his cock. He knew I was going to get at him again, and I enjoyed the tease, saw he was getting hard with anticipation. I pulled open my pants, got them down around my knees, and started playing with myself, and it was all he could do to keep his eyes on the road. I wet my cock and did a total number, stroking, slapping, pulling, and when I thought he was going to go totally nuts from watching the show, I got a hand under my ass and played around my pucker. "God, I need something up there," I moaned, grinding my ass on the finger I was working into my hole. "I'm not gonna make it to Stockton without a fuck," I told Tom.

He checked his watch. "Shit," was all he said and he kept to the road, both hands on the wheel when I knew he wanted to get one on himself and the other on me. I was now writhing in the seat, cock dripping, really looking to get him into me. "Need some dick," I kept saying like a mantra.

Tom's eyes remained fixed ahead, so I decided to try another path. I began to search the glove compartment for something to help me out, but the only thing I found was a little flashlight, one of those miniature things about six inches long. Not all that hospitable, but what's a guy to do?

"What in hell?" Tom said when I began to spit on it. I then turned in the seat, butt toward him, and shoved the thing up my ass. Cold little fucker, flat-ended so it wasn't an easy fit, but once up there it felt good—the ultimate hard-on—and I could give myself a fairly good reaming. So there we were, hauling ass up I-5 in all kinds of ways.

Tom barely looked at the road now. As I gave myself a flashlight fuck, I kept looking back over my shoulder, and saw he had one hand on the wheel, the other in his pants. His head was whipping back and forth from the road to me as I kept working the flashlight in and out of myself, enjoying things until suddenly we turned, half skidding onto one of those long side roads to nowhere. Two lonesome lanes pointed toward mountains so distant they were barely visible. A few miles later, we went onto the shoulder and slid to a dusty stop.

"You want a goddamn fuck, you're gonna get one," Tom growled, and he grabbed the flashlight, threw it into the backseat, pulled his pants off, got a rubber on, and commanded, "Get on."

I shed my jeans, crawled into his lap, lowered myself onto him and felt his big piece of meat slide deep into my rectum. "Fuck yourself," Tom said, giving me a single thrust.

He sat with his hands at his sides while I bounced on his cock, getting just what I'd wanted for all those miles. The car rocked, and even though Tom made me do the work, he started bucking partway along, spewing at the mouth, letting go with cries of "Shit!" and "Fuck!" because he was headed for a big one, because I'd gotten him so worked up he was going to shoot a gusher. The idea of his dick squirting come up into my bowels pushed me over, and since we were halfway to hell and gone, not a soul around for miles, I let out a cry as my dick started firing long streams up onto the dashboard, the steering wheel, my stomach. We fucked and rode and bounced and yelled, did it all, then gradually quieted. Satisfied for the moment, I remained on the half-hard cock, reluctant to let it go, knowing we wouldn't get all that far up the road before I'd need it again. Tom checked his watch.

"Now I'm late."

"Why not blow it off? Let's fuck our way to Stockton and just keep going."

"Hey, I do have to make a living." Now he was soft. I slid off and we mopped up with a handkerchief, then sat awhile. He finally looked over at me. "When I asked you along I had no idea."

"You didn't really think I came along for the scenery."

"No, but I was thinking mainly of a motel in Stockton, you know, after my meeting. Spending the night."

"We can do that."

He laughed. "First you've got to let me get there. No more for now, OK?"

"Not easy."

He started the car. "Try."

I kept my hands off him as requested but told him about a bit of porn I'd been writing, knowing it would get him worked up. By the time we got to Stockton he had a major boner. "You fucking tease," he said as he got out of the car, adjusting himself. In the motel room he changed clothes while I got naked, lay on the bed stroking my cock. "Hurry back," I said as he slammed the door behind him.

I got some much-needed sleep while he was gone and had no idea of the time when he returned, only that he'd come in quietly, gotten undressed, pulled back the covers, and awakened me by sucking my cock. He licked and pulled until I was hard, then slid up next to me, his own stiff meat pressed against my thigh. "You all rested?" he asked.

"You bet. How was your meeting?"

"Closed the deal, so now we celebrate."

"How do you want to do that?"

He rolled me onto my back, got my legs up, and buried his face in my ass. He licked and poked like he was starving, and when he came up for air, mouth smeared and wet, he said, "This was what I had in the back of my mind the whole time I was at my meeting. I'm sitting at this big conference table with four other guys, and I'm thinking about eating out your ass, getting you sloppy wet, then fucking the shit out of you."

He sat back, fat knob oozing dribble juice, and just looked at me. "Keep 'em up," he said and I pulled my legs higher. He rolled a condom down his pole, greased himself, and then he was pushing in. "No more goddamn car," he said as he started thrusting in and out of me. "No hurry to get somewhere. I'm there now."

"Long haul," I offered.

"It's over now."

Reeling in the sensation of his steady stroke, his big cock deep in my gut, I argued the point. "I disagree. I think it's just begun."

The Story of O. Henry, or The Gifts of the Leathermen

Simon Sheppard

One hundred and eighty seven dollars. That was all the ready cash Jim and Del had between them, and Christmas was on its way. Since Master Jim's corporation had downsized and he'd had to take a demotion and pay cut, times for him and his slave, Del, had been tough. Now the holidays were coming, but all the cash in the house came to just $187, and the bills from the gym, the cable TV company, and their Internet service provider were yet to be paid.

Slave Del sat at home, naked and disconsolate. He'd finished cleaning the dungeon and polishing his master's boots, and now he had time to think. Christmas would be here in two days, and he hadn't yet bought a present for his master. He knew what he wanted to get him, of course: a black leather jacket. *The* black leather jacket, to replace the one that had been stolen.

They'd been at a play party in the fall when the theft occurred. Master Jim had arrived in full leathers, looking magnificent. Form-fitting chaps, gleaming studded harness, knee-high boots, and black leather motorcycle jacket, a matched outfit all made by The Leather-Man, the city's best purveyor of fine leather goods. They'd cost a pretty penny, all bought in the days when Master Jim was still a highly paid executive with his own custom-furnished office and impossibly cute office boy. The jacket had been stolen while Del, naked but for his broad leather collar, was firmly bound to a St, Andrew's cross. His master was working him over with a brutal single-tailed whip, raising welts and bringing forth cries of ecstasy. It was warm for October, and taking his boy to his limits was hard work for Jim, much harder than it had been back when they'd signed the contract and Del's limits had been much lower. Master Jim was working up a sweat. He laid the whip down for a moment and peeled off his shining leather jacket, folding it carefully and placing it in a corner near the cross. He picked up the whip again, stood just behind his slave, and pressed his bulging leather cock-pouch into his boy's butt. "Are you ready for more?" he whispered into Del's ear.

Del turned to look at his master. His eyes were filled with love, tears, and respect. "Oh, yes, sir. Please, sir."

Intently, raptly as an eagle, Master Jim aimed the whip's stinging tail at his slave's aching, bleeding flesh. The wounds, holy as stigmata, made his boy's broad, muscled back even more beautiful. Again and again he brought Del to a point where the slave thought, no, *knew* he couldn't take it any more. And Master Jim would back off, let the boy catch his breath, then start in again, taking them both to new peaks, higher plateaus, a mountain range of ecstasy. At last, when it was over and Master Jim had unshackled Del and gathered him into his embrace, he glanced over Del's shoulder at the corner where he'd laid his jacket. The corner was empty. The jacket was gone.

No one in the crowd had seen anything. They'd all been watching Jim and Del. The thief was never found. Jim had taken up wearing an older jacket, well broken in but nowhere near as fine as the one he had lost. And for months, Del had been longing to be able to buy his master a replacement.

And now Christmas, the time for gifts, was near. The slave boy knelt on the carpet, remembering the scene, the feel of the lash. His dick was hard, pulsing against his belly. Unable to afford a new jacket for his master, Slave Del was sad, and he did what he often did when he was sad, reaching down to his cock for consolation. Del felt fortunate; the terms of his contract with Master Jim permitted him to masturbate in his master's absence, as long as he thought only of Master Jim and as long as he was fully ready to service his master on his return. It was only 2 o'clock, and Master Jim wasn't due back till 5:30. He'd have no trouble getting it up again by then. He'd be more than ready.

Stroking his cock with his right hand, Del reached up to his nipple ring with his left, tugging at it, sending delicious jolts of sensation through his tit. It felt so good that he let go of his stiff, slightly curved dick and grabbed hold of his other nipple ring, working his nipple flesh against the thick gold rings. He thought of his master working his tits so hard they burned, slipping ropes through the rings, stretching his flesh, making him feel so very, very good. His hands let go of the precious rings, moved down over his lean belly, down to his warm, shaved crotch. His right hand grabbed his dick again, while his left wandered down over his big balls, the sweaty ridge between his legs, down to the comforting wet heat of his hole. Just the merest touch caused his well-trained ass to dilate.

He squeezed his dick head against the metal of his Prince Albert. The chunky ring through his dick head wasn't gold like his nipple rings; his master had been demoted before he'd had a chance to get him a pure gold replacement for the surgical steel ring, and now expensive gold was too much to hope for. Still, the piercing was fun to play with, to play with hard. A pearly drop of precome glistened where the ring entered his piss slit. Slave Del pressed his finger up into his butt, drew it out to cover it with spit, then slid two fingers all the way in. It was, of course, his master's hole, his master's to fuck, to fist, to own. But as his fingers plunged in and out, in and out, he was grateful for the loan.

He was working his dick with his whole hand now, his long foreskin almost engulfing cock head and ring, then peeling back again to reveal shiny, swollen flesh. It was something of an effort, when he was this close to spewing spunk, to keep his mind only on his master, not to think of those other men he'd seen, he'd desired, but was not permitted to touch. It was an effort, but he made the effort, and he succeeded, more or less, and he was glad he did. His fingers hooked back to give his prostate a jolt. He closed his eyes, murmured his master's name, and shot a creamy load from his stiff cock, from the slit where the silvery ring lazily glittered. He opened his eyes. On the little Christmas tree in the corner, multicolored lights twinkled happily.

After wiping up, Del went cheerfully to work, laying out his master's chaps, harness, and boots, gleaming black leather arrayed in anticipation of Master Jim's return. He felt a familiar tingle of happiness, knowing that the man who owned him would be back soon. If only he could afford to buy another jacket to match those beautiful chaps. What a surprise for his Master that would be! Just the thought made his still-damp dick stir a little bit.

The slave boy was in the kitchen, making crust for mincemeat pie, when he heard the car pull up the drive. He rushed to the door and knelt on the carpet, face downcast, hands clasped behind his back. The door opened. Master Jim stood before him. Wordlessly, he untied and pulled off his master's shoes, peeled off the dress socks, and kissed his master's warm, moist feet.

"Hello, boy," said Master Jim.

"Hello, sir."

"Undress me."

Del carefully removed his master's clothing, hanging up the suit, neatly folding the shirt. Master Jim's muscular, hairy body was completely naked,

"And now, sir?"

"My leathers, boy." The ritual was the same every night.

Del put the harness on his master's powerful torso, dressed his master in the formfitting chaps, put thick woolen socks and gleaming boots on his master's feet.

"Did I do well, sir?"

"Very well. I did a good job training you."

Jim looked down at the naked boy kneeling before him, and his heart was filled with affection. The smooth, young flesh that was his property. The broad, studded collar. The heavy gold rings hanging from the boy's pierced nipples. The chunky ring through the head of the boy's hard, quivering dick. Someday soon, when the household's finances improved, he would buy a solid gold ring to replace that steel Prince Albert. Gold: a sign of the esteem in which he held this boy whom he owned body and soul.

Master Jim's weighty cock jutted half-hard from the front of his chaps.

"Suck my dick, slave," he said.

The day before Christmas dawned cold and clear.

Del spent the morning putting the last touches on the house's decorations: a few silvery bells here, gossamer angels there, a sprig of mistletoe above the bondage table in the wreath-festooned dungeon. And all the while, he fretted over buying a Christmas gift for his master. The jacket. He wished with all his heart that he could buy the jacket. If only he had the money… But what did he, another man's property, have of his own to sell? Not even his body was his own, only the piercing rings his master had given him as a symbol of his servitude.

The rings!

An idea came to Del.

The contract permitted him a midday shopping trip while his master was at work. He dressed in jeans, a T-shirt, and work boots, pulled on a battered leather jacket, and headed out the door.

The shaved-headed boy behind the piercing shop's counter smiled at him, tongue-piercing winking in the fluorescent light.

"Well, it's not the kind of thing we usually do, but since it's the day before Christmas and all… Course, I can't give you as much as they were sold for, but… If they're not damaged or anything, I could resterilize 'em and re-sell 'em, maybe. And it *is* the day before Christmas…" He pulled at his distended earlobe. "OK, c'mon."

Once Del was lying on his back on the piercing table, it only took a few moments for the sales clerk—Chaos by name—to use his pliers to open the nipple rings and slip them from the piercings.

Del felt naked. Being stripped of these tokens of his master's ownership made him want to cry.

"OK, all done." Chaos smiled. He lay his hand on Del's upper thigh, just millimeters from his basket.

The piercing boy, with his tattooed scalp and face full of metal, was cute enough, but Del belonged to Master Jim. "Then I'll take the money, please." Del was in a hurry; he still had one place to go.

"OK," Chaos said. He stuck his tongue out slightly; the metal ball of his tongue piercing gleamed like a little Christmas tree ornament.

Once Del had set the sale-priced turkey to thaw in the refrigerator, he wrapped the gift he'd bought for his master and set it beneath the little tree. He grinned in anticipation of the happiness he'd see on Master Jim's face when the silvery wrapping paper was ripped away. He was glad they always opened their gifts on Christmas Eve; he'd have had a hard time waiting till the morning.

But a sudden thought ruffled his happiness. What if his master was angry at what he'd done? Master Jim was understanding, but he could also be stern. It might be wise not to let him know the nipple rings were gone until he'd had time to explain, until Master Jim had seen his elegant gift. He pulled on a T-shirt and spent the rest of the afternoon, naked from the waist down, tidying up the house.

At 4:30, dinner well under way, he went to his master's closet to fetch Master Jim's leathers. When he opened the closet door, a sudden jolt ran through his body. The chaps were gone—the hanger where he'd left them the night before dangling empty in the twilight's gloom. What could have happened? His master would never wear them to work. The bedroom window stood open. Had Del left it that way, or had a thief crept in while he was away?

The slave boy's throat tightened as he thought of how angry his master would be at finding another piece of his leathers missing *and* the rings gone from his slave boy's nipples. His master would feel betrayed. Del knew with sickening certainty that he was unworthy of servitude. He wouldn't blame Master Jim if he threw him out on the streets.

With trepidation, Del laid out the harness and boots and knelt, his mind racing, to wait for his master's return.

At last, after what seemed like hours, the front door opened. Del could already feel the pain of his master's disappointment, a punishment harsher than the heaviest blows. He could take anything—he'd been trained to take anything—anything except the loss of his master's loving power.

Master Jim strode to his kneeling slave.

"Hello, boy."

"Hello, sir."

"Undress me." Master Jim hadn't said a word about the missing chaps; he must not have noticed yet. "But first take off that T-shirt. Did I tell you you could wear a T-shirt?"

"Yes, sir. No, sir." Del shuddered as he drew the shirt over his head.

Jim stared down at his slave's naked chest. "What happened to your nipple rings, boy?" His voice sounded cruel, baffled, and hurt, all at once.

Del winced. Tears came to his eyes. "Please don't be angry, sir. I did it for you, Master. Please let me explain."

"I'm waiting."

"May I rise, sir? And get your gift?"

"Do it." Jim's voice was stern.

Del walked to the tree, fetched the heavy, foil-wrapped package, and took it back to his waiting master.

"Merry Christmas, sir."

Master Jim took the gift.

"May I look at your face, sir?" He'd not yet looked into his master's eyes.

"You may, boy," Jim said as he unwrapped the package. Inside was a new leather jacket, a perfect match for the one that he'd lost.

"Thank you, boy," he said simply, but the happiness on his face made Del's heart leap with joy.

"I sold my nipple rings so that I'd be able to afford it, sir."

"I understand."

Del, in his happiness, had forgotten about the missing chaps. He held his breath: How could he tell his master?

"Sir…"

"Yes?"

"Your chaps, sir…" he stammered.

"Ah yes, perhaps I should have told you, so you wouldn't be concerned. Like you, boy, I couldn't afford the gift I wanted to give you. So I sold the chaps and used the money to buy you this." He reached into his jacket pocket and pulled out a small, gaily wrapped box.

Del tore away the red-and-green paper. A jewelry box. He flipped open the lid. Inside lay a thick gold ring, beautifully wrought. A ring for his dick. A precious ring that perfectly matched the nipple rings that were no longer his.

"Merry Christmas, boy."

"Oh, thank you, sir, thank you." Not waiting for permission, he threw his arms around his master and kissed him hard on the lips.

"You're welcome, boy," Master Jim smiled. "But you've disobeyed me by selling the rings without my permission, and for that you'll have to be flogged."

A broad grin lit up Del's face. "Oh, yes, sir. Thank you, sir!"

For hours, Del had been hanging suspended in the dungeon, leather wrist restraints chained to a hook in the ceiling. His master had threaded twine through the empty piercings on his chest and tied it off to the overhead hook, so that every time Del's body jerked in response to a blow, a painful tug at his chest reminded him of his disobedience and of their mutual love.

Master Jim had started slowly with a suede flogger, warming up his slave boy's back and butt. But in time he switched to a heavier bull-skin flogger, then to a braided cat-o'-nine-tails that raised searing red welts on Del's naked flesh. The escalation of pain sent the slave deeper and deeper into an ecstasy of submission, till his dick was aching with come and he had to strain to keep from babbling out a litany of love and praise. At last, Master Jim put down the whip, grabbed his own cock, and pissed all over his boy's bruised and bleeding back. The hot sting made Del scream from between clenched teeth. Master Jim shook the last few drops of piss from his dick and tenderly stroked Del's hair.

"I'll be right back," he said, and left the dungeon.

Within a minute, the electronic music that had for hours throbbed over the dungeon's speakers was replaced by the chanting of nuns, singing hymns of praise written by a 12th-century French abbess. Del had thought he couldn't go any higher, any deeper, but the ineffably gorgeous music made his spirits soar, rise on the wings of angels to a paradise of devotion and bliss.

It was late on the night before Christmas now, time for Santa to come and deliver his gifts. But Del, the good little slave boy, knew that, for him, Santa Claus had already arrived.

Limo Scene

Dale Chase

He jumped out of a limo in the middle of California Street at 2 in the afternoon, lurching slightly, then recovering. Later I found out he'd been pushed.

He made his way to the sidewalk, where I stood transfixed like some tourist gawking at a cable car. He wore a dinner jacket and was barefoot. How could I not stare?

Gorgeous, of course. Dark-haired, olive-kinned, smooth, trim in his evening wear. In the few seconds it took for him to reach the curb I crafted a scenario onto him: abandoned by his lover, told en route the affair was over. By the time he reached me, I was caught in a mix of curiosity and desire.

He stubbed his toe as he moved past. "Shit!" he cried, reaching down to rub the injured digit. It was then he saw I was watching, and he glared for a second, then laughed. "My shoes are still in the car." He looked out into the street as if the limo might still be there. "Shit," he said again.

"Can I help?" I asked.

"Like how?"

"I have no idea, you just seem to be in some kind of…circumstance."

He laughed again. "That's a good way to put it. How about buying me breakfast?"

He evidently had no idea of the time. I'd already eaten lunch,

193

but I took him to a café on Battery Street and listened as he replayed his night.

"I'm at this Nob Hill party, it's like 4 A.M., and this guy comes on to me. He's a mogul or something, richer than shit, and he spends hours telling me about his fabulous life, the hotels, the jets, the parties. Then he sucks my dick in the bathroom and starts making all these promises: fly us to New York, go everywhere together, you know, the scene, all the best clubs. You name it, we'd do it."

He stopped, shook his head, paused so long I asked, "So what happened?"

"It was all a line. The limo was a rental, and he was nobody. We fucked in the car, and that was the end. He had to be somewhere—probably turn in the car, the shithead. He told me to get out, and when I called him an asshole, he opened the door and pushed me. I'm lucky I've got my pants on."

"Tough break."

"Tell me about it. He was everything I wanted, and he was built, incredible body, big dick." He stopped and stared at his half-eaten eggs. "Now all I have is a cold Saturday morning and no shoes."

"Afternoon, actually," I said.

He glared as if I'd offered the final insult. "Sorry," I said. Then, "So what now?"

He shook his head. Whatever life he had, he didn't seem anxious to get back to it. "Would you like to come to my place?" I asked. "Maybe get a shower. I can lend you some jeans."

He looked at me like he'd just awakened to what we had here. I watched his expression change from rejection to anticipation. "I could use a shower," he said with a tentative smile.

"Let's go."

We walked to my place, and he told me his name was Marty and that he'd never had sex in a limo before. "It's really plush, and there's all this room. Not like a regular car. God, I hate that, sucking cock with a gearshift in your ear."

He spoke so matter-of-factly about his sexual exploits that I began to think he was a hustler. I didn't let this interfere with my plans, however. I just took note and kept walking. "Where do you live anyway?" he finally asked as we climbed toward Russian Hill.

"Up there." I pointed to my high-rise.

"Holy shit." He looked at me with new eyes, realizing I might have the substance his earlier encounter lacked. "So why are you walking?" he asked, suddenly skeptical.

"It's good for you," I said.

"Not barefoot," he shot back.

"True. We'll have to give those feet a rest, then."

He was like a little kid when we reached my apartment, rushing around, trying each piece of furniture, looking out at my spectacular view. True, the place was impressive. I counted on that with these young things.

I let him wind down, then led him to the bathroom, turned on the shower. "Let me help you," I said as he took off his jacket. I hung it up and when he undid his pants, I took charge, pulled them off. He was bare underneath, and his little cock was stiff. *Amusing,* I thought as I knelt and got it into my mouth. He was probably hard as much for where he was as who he was with but I didn't care. I was going to enjoy this little urchin, take him for a real ride.

When he began to buck and squirm, I knew he was going to come. I held fast, kept working him, and he let go. I gobbled every drop of his wonderful elixir.

When I'd sucked him dry, I stripped and got him into the shower. He was willing, pliable, just as he'd undoubtedly been with his previous partner, but this time it was real and he knew it.

I soaped him thoroughly. He had a slight build, smooth chest, tiny tit nubs, meager little black bush where his stubby cock nested. I lathered every inch, then turned him around and worked my way down to his round little bottom.

He spread his legs to let me soap his crack and moaned softly when I slid a finger up him. Riding the digit, he begged for more, and I added a second, began to work him. The soap was discarded as my other hand reached around and grabbed his prick.

He was hard again and began to thrust as soon as I took hold, the finger fuck driving him wild. I kept at it until he cried out. I looked over his shoulder and was treated to the sight of jizz squirting out of him.

My cock, hard and flailing blindly against his butt, was more than ready. When Marty quieted, I turned off the water and got him out of the shower.

My bathroom is spacious, full of mirrors. I watched us as I dried him, thick blue towels rubbing every inch, my stiff cock attending patiently. When I had him dry, I got condom and lube from the vanity, suited up, greased myself, and set him on the counter. With his legs high, spread wide, I pushed my cock into his rectum and began to fuck, watching myself in the mirror. It was like starring in a porn film, me and my beautiful supporting player. He held his legs apart. All I had to do was stand there and shove my meat in and out of his juicy hole.

"This makes up for everything," he said as I rode his sweet ass.

"Everything?"

"Well, last night, I mean. Or this morning. The shitheel."

"Begone, shitheel," I said and thrust for emphasis.

"You're watching us fuck," he offered after a while.

"Yes, it's a wonderful sight."

"Can I see?"

I pulled out, got him off the counter, turned him around, bent him forward, and shoved back in. He winced with pleasure as I plowed him, then started grinding back onto me. He was playing to the mirror, and I loved it, natural actor. I slid my hands up to his pecs and fingered his hard little tits and he reached for his cock, began to stroke, our fuck-slap echoing off the tile.

We kept at it for long minutes, both basking in our mirrored playlet. Every time I got close to coming, I eased off, rode the edge. He, on the other hand, had no such control and began to wiggle, bounce and beg. And then he was squirting jizz into the counter, recoiling onto my pole with each pulse, ass muscles clenching, grabbing me until I thought I'd unload, but I managed to hold back.

He slumped when he was empty, but I took hold of his hips,

held him in place while I continued the fuck. I wanted to do him until he couldn't stand, ride his ass until it was sloppy wet, flushed, and swollen. And then I wanted to get my face down there to lick that sweet, tortured hole.

I did exactly that. He grew pliable in my hands, and when I added more lube, he became absolutely juicy, my dick going in and out of his hole with a squishy thwack. Liquefied lube ran down onto his balls, and I added still more because it cushioned the ride, helped me hold back the climax churning in my sac.

"Oh, man," he finally said, and I knew he wasn't used to this. Fucking around, sure, but not a marathon. I pulled out, got him down onto the floor, rolled towels under him to get his ass high, and then I pulled open his cheeks and savored the sight. He glistened now, and I ran a finger around his rim, heard him moan. I pushed it into him and felt the ooze, played in it, tickled his prostate, which made him flinch. I thought about getting my tongue into him but decided it would be better after I'd come in him. I slid my cock back up his chute and he moaned again, softer now. Occupied, home.

I was going to let myself come this time, and I told him so. "I've been saving this since I saw you get pushed out of that limo," I said. "Freshly fucked. How I like that. Ass tingling, hole still wet, open, ready for more. I wanted to get into you in the restaurant. I was thinking about you in my lap, sitting on my dick while you ate your eggs. But now I have you and I'm going to fill you with come. Rubber be damned, you're going to feel it flush up into you like an enema. I am so ready."

I was pounding him now, prone atop his body, arms circling him, thrusting madly as I felt the rise, as I talked myself over the edge. And then it hit, balls drawing up tight as the pulse sent waves through me and my cock shot long streams into the sweetest of bottoms. I let myself go verbally as well, taking the narrative down inside him, down where it was steamy and dark.

I used every foul word I knew for what I was doing, and when the climax subsided I relented to a mere whisper. "Fuck your hole," I said over and over, then finally went silent.

I lay atop him, feeling the tension drain from my body. My extremities tingled as if they'd been asleep, as if the climax had awakened me. Marty squeezed his ass muscles, which sent another pleasurable wave through me. I groaned my approval, then slid out, sat back, and looked at where I'd been. I thought about all that cream I'd shot up inside Marty. His bunghole was red and swollen, and I ran my fingers over it, lovingly now, then leaned down and nuzzled it, licking gently, poking in where my dick had gone.

When I finally retreated and let Marty sit up, I saw he'd made a little puddle on the towel. "You fucked it outta me," he said, holding his cock. It was all I could do not to get him into my mouth and start over again.

Instead, we washed up and moved to the kitchen, where I opened a bottle of chardonnay. I poured two glasses and we drank to our mutual happiness, and then I lay him on the table, got his legs up, and stuck the bottle's long green neck up his ass.

Sipping wine with one hand while giving him a bottle-fuck with the other was a whole new kind of high. Marty squirmed and giggled, and I knew we were going to keep at this for hours, that there was so much I could do to him besides stick my cock in his hole. He moaned as if to agree.

He turned out to be the most resilient creature. After I'd used the bottle on him, I fucked his sweet bottom until I was beyond empty, then amused myself with a dildo, a banana, shoving all manner of things up him while I sucked his cock. I relented periodically for food and drink, the occasional pee, but for much of the night I had him. Truly had him.

He drank just a single glass of wine, yet took on the characteristics of a pliable drunk, which let me believe he was intoxicated by what I'd done to him. The constant presence of my cock and the assorted pseudo-cocks had broken him down the way alcohol breaks down even the most resilient men.

I also thought of how it must be from his viewpoint. As I pushed the fat pink dildo up him, burying it to its fat pink balls, I considered what it was doing to him up there, how it felt to have his rectum used this way, how much pleasure it gave him. I've never allowed anything up my own ass—God forbid—but I do appreciate what it is to receive the dick or implement of the moment. And I think this appreciation heightens the experience for me, makes me want to get even more into him, to stay inside him, to watch him sleep with my dick lodged in his backside and find my morning hard-on already accommodated.

I told Marty none of this. He need not know my inner thoughts. Time enough to reveal the depth of need. For now, I basked in his beautiful body, his delectable bottom.

At one point he asked to pee. I had the dildo up him, and I made him keep it there, stood behind him while he pissed an urgent stream and savored the sight of lube all down his thighs. When he was done, I made him kneel over the bowl, and I slowly withdrew the dildo and stuck in my prick. I'd already pulled on a rubber, and God knows he needed no more lube. I felt my cock head slide back up the familiar chute and settle where it belonged, thrilling to the sight of Marty bent over the toilet, dirty little fucker. It didn't matter that the bathroom was spotless, porcelain gleaming white; it still felt wonderfully nasty to be doing what we were doing where we were doing it.

I had little juice left in me, but my prick never concerns itself with such things. People like Marty keep it stiff, and a dry climax is sometimes every bit as good as a wet one. It's all a matter of orchestration. So when I came this time, I did not fill the reservoir. I just reeled to my dick firing blanks inside Marty's tortured hole. And when I withdrew, discarded the empty rubber, I took a moment to enjoy the view, then leaned down and began to feed at the sacred hole.

Again it was heightened by the setting. I'd done a lot of fucking in this bathroom but for some reason never at the toilet. Such an omission. Hands on the porcelain sides, I buried my face in Marty's crack and drove my tongue up his hole, giving him a spirited tongue fuck. I worked him until he squirmed, then said almost tentatively, "Lick me?"

I retreated. "You like your hole licked?"

"Oh, yeah, man, that does it for me, especially when I've had a dick up there."

I leaned in, ran my tongue down to his balls, gave them a swipe, then slid back up to the glistening hole. And I began to play with his swollen pucker, diddling the rim with just the tip of my tongue until I had him begging, then progressing to a full-out lick, like some dog at his own genitals. Marty wriggled and moaned, grabbed his little prick, and shot drops of come onto the bowl. I relented then, put him on the floor, got my mouth on his softening cock, and licked his residue.

After this, we collapsed onto the little bathroom rug for a quiet interlude. His breathing was soft, which gave the illusion of innocent slumber, and this stirred me. I rearranged myself, climbed over him, got my crotch up at his face, and hovered there, balls tickling his chin. He smiled, then opened his mouth like a baby bird, and I dropped my soft prick into him.

He sucked it like a tit, and I watched his cheeks work, felt the suction pull at me, drawing blood to the shaft. When I was hard, I pulled a towel down, rolled it, slid it under his head so he need not strain his neck as he took me. And then I fucked his mouth until he finally could hold me no longer. Exhaustion was approaching for both of us, a mixed bag at this point. Part of me wanted to slide into bed with him, curl around him, and sleep for hours, days; part of me wanted to roll him over and make use of the renewed erection. I pulled out of his mouth and he worked his jaw, chuckled. I took him to bed. We slept.

I kept him close all night, my dick parked at his ass, arms around his little body. The sun was high when I awakened, cock hard against the round little bottom. I reached for lube and a rubber, suited up, greased myself, all without Marty stirring. Then I parted his cheeks and eased my dick into that well-used hole.

He groaned but did not fully wake, and I loved the idea of fucking him in a half-asleep state, working myself into his sex dreams. We lay for some time, me with an easy thrust, him issuing a murmur now and then. Finally he squeezed his sphincter to announce he was fully awake. "You're gonna make me come," he said as he took hold of his cock and began to stroke. He then grew frantic, wriggling and squirming until he let out a cry and shot a stream into the already soiled sheets. I picked up my pace, slapping against his tight little butt as I felt the rise.

"Now you're going to make me come," I told him, and I pounded him as long squirts pulsed into his juicy rectum. When I was done I eased out, discarded the rubber, then got back behind him, parked my spent cock at his ass. We slept several hours more.

I was alone in the bed when I woke again. I recalled the fuck, tried to determine whether it had been a dream, then saw the used condom, which hadn't quite made it to the floor. It clung to the far corner of the bed, hard evidence. I rubbed my cock in acknowledgement, then got up.

When I went to find Marty I stayed naked. He was in the kitchen, also naked, making toast, coffee brewing. He'd set the table with my best china and linens, obviously savoring the luxury and reminding me that his failed encounter had surely been a deep disappointment. I decided then and there that he belonged here with me. He was too striking, too beautiful, and too willing to be wasted on the larger and infinitely more insensitive world.

As I watched him butter the toast, I reminded myself how much I didn't know about him, but I quickly rationalized life would begin here, with me. I would give him to a new life, mold him to my every need. "Can you stay?" I asked as he poured coffee.

He beamed. "Sure. I'd love to. Could we maybe go for a drive later? It's a gorgeous day."

I glanced out at the city, saw bright blue among the high-rises. "Good idea," I said.

"What kind of car do you have?" he asked.

"Porsche."

He smiled, nodded, bit into his toast and said no more. As I sipped my coffee, I considered the day ahead. Part of me wanted to get him into my lap, get my cock up him while we had our break-fast. I could almost feel my arms around him, pushing into that sweet little tunnel. My cock began to fill, and I did battle with myself because another idea had come to mind. Something even better.

"I have some calls to make," I told Marty. "Why don't you catch a shower, put on whatever you want of mine, and we'll take that drive. Over to Marin, through the redwoods, then on up the coast if we're so inclined. Maybe dinner in Mendocino."

He lit up at this, finished his toast and coffee, and was off down the hall, singing some tune I didn't recognize. I made the single call to arrange our afternoon, then exercised enormous restraint in not fucking him in the shower, not fucking him when he stood naked before my closet, pondering what to wear. I hurried through a shower, then dressed quickly. In the elevator he could hardly stand still, such was his excitement, and I could hardly refrain from doing him right there.

He was surprised when we didn't descend into the subter-ranean garage. "Where do you keep the car?" he asked.

"Just follow me." I led him out to the curb, where awaited the limousine I'd ordered. "I thought this might be more to our liking," I added as the driver held the door for us. Marty stopped in his tracks, obviously moved by the gesture, then suddenly kissed me. "I love it!" he cried as he got inside.

The driver already had his instructions: Marin, the redwoods, and if not told otherwise, on up the coast to Mendocino. Do not disturb the occupants.

I raised the dark glass barrier, then turned to Marty. He'd chosen a pair of Dockers. I eased down the zipper, fished out his cock, lowered myself, and took him into my mouth. I could feel the car's motion as I fed, gliding up and down San Francisco's hills, then onto the Golden Gate Bridge.

When Marty came he got vocal, shoving up into me as cream squirted out of him in an impressive stream. I gobbled every drop, and when I sat up I lowered the window, looked out. We were deep in the redwoods: the air was cool and damp, everything a pungent green. Marty got his face to the window and drew a long breath while I pulled off his Dockers, pulled off my own as well.

He wiggled his ass in anticipation as I pulled on a condom, opened a packet of lube and greased myself, ran a dollop into him. He murmured, squirmed on my finger, and I knew he was more than ready. I got behind him, pushed in, and there we remained, fucking our way along, creating our own little limo scene.

Box Boy

Scott Whittier

Yeah. That's me up there. You've seen me. I'm that guy. That boy. The one who defies gravity. The one who braves the chill of the empty room and sober gazes. I do it first. I do it shirtless. I am the boy dancing on the box.

Box boy—like a fixture. Always there. You wonder whether I work here. I'm not a stripper, a performer, a show. But I am.

I sway slowly, my feet in place, my hands hooked in belt loops. My hips dance alone to the early songs, the ones you don't really like. I close my eyes, lick my lips. I can feel you looking at me now, with your coat still on, wondering whether you should stay. Should you have another drink?

You've seen me before. Right now you don't like me any better than this song. Maybe later. I can feel you thinking beyond the lights. And I think to myself. I think about the box, the empty dance floor, the tank top dangling from my back pocket.

I give you a reason to stand around with your coat on. I give you something to sneer at and leer at as you order your second drink. So they let me in early, let me stay late, let me through the back room and the back door. They laugh about my tight new pants in a way that sounds like a compliment. They call me by name, even if you'll never know it.

It's still cold, before the throbbing sweat of dancing masses.

Before the fat boys take off their shirts. But people are beginning to trickle in. Things are heating up. This song is faster. This drink tastes better. It's almost worth the price. Tip the bartender well now. Maybe he'll remember you later.

As you take off your coat, I let go of my hips. My hands move up my body like a lover. You watch as my fingers touch flesh for the first time tonight.

From the button of my jeans to my navel, the first finger finds its way along the slight, dark trail. Hair by hair, onto the bare skin above. It's smooth and hard. The sway moves up my body with my hand. My torso bends. A tight ripple of muscle shivers through my stomach, and I define each one with a touch. This is how I would feel.

I swivel and turn my back to you, arms behind my head, my body stretched and taut. You can see my silhouette against the light. It's almost orange, gold and black, a glowing outline of shoulders and biceps, the smooth lines of muscle that wrap around my back and twist as I dance.

Beyond my sloppy spot of light, I can almost see you. I can almost pick you out of the crowd, out of the dark. Coat off. Drink in hand.

You've decided to stay. You haven't joined the ambitious dancers. You haven't returned initial glances. You play it cool. Maybe you light a cigarette. But if you do, that glowing moment is lost in the smoke and the voices and the music.

Focus is lost in movement. I roll and flex and forget my loss. I fall completely into that movement, that moment. Focus and freedom swirl into motion.

My drink is waiting on the bar.

"Thanks, Doug."

"Gotta keep that sweat pumping."

Doug just had to be a bartender. Everyone wants to see him lifting bottles, sliding glasses. Muscle and charm mix well with a little stubble and attitude. Tip him because he's cute or because you're not sure he'll remember you when it gets busy. Tip him because he's kind of a jerk and that's kind of sexy.

I see eyes across the bar. I almost feel them. It's not the man who just walked by too close too soon. It's not the leering gaze to my right. It's someone watching, just looking at me.

It's you. So I raise my head and smile. I look right back.

You may have seen me, but I've never seen you. Because, as cheesy pickup lines can attest, I would have remembered you. I can see the line of your jaw from across the room, strong and square, smudged with tomorrow's beard. The gray hinting at your temples says you might be a little older than most of the crowd.

You look straightforward like your gaze. Your shirt stretches across the width of your shoulders, pulls at your chest. Your jeans fit, but you could wear them to work if you weren't in a tie all day. It's refreshing to see less glitter and polish. It's refreshing to see the way your jeans hold the curve of your thigh, the way your forearms spread thick as you lean on the bar. It's even better to see you watching.

I feel that flicker of challenge somewhere in my gut, next to my drink. It warms and seeps down into my crotch. It pulses. My cock jumps against my thigh. I feel its heat and weight as it bounces there, skin against skin. I lean into the bar, press my hardening bulge into the rail. I can't help but smile a little wider, grind my hips. It's the dancer in me, the exhibitionist.

So I dance, return to the box, and go with the flow.

The night has momentum. It seethes and pulses with every drunken step and shout. It moves to a hundred different beats, a hundred different bodies. Every boy who approaches my box—who stares or hoots—adds to the rhythm. This is my favorite song. This is the night music I dance to. I dance for the smell of sweat and the flickering touch of lights across my skin. I dance to a chorus of glances.

I dance till I'm soaking, until my breath is hard and rhythmic. The music stops. The lights come up. Dancing colors vanish.

Darkness evaporates in the harsh buzz of fluorescent bulbs. This is the precursor of tomorrow's headache. It hurries them along, out the door. They stagger to escape the promise of sobriety, to find refuge in the night, in slices of pizza and the backseats of taxicabs. They rush toward darkness and the slurring urgings of lovers and strangers before they fall asleep, before the light of day washes away the moment.

I swab my stomach and give consideration to the receding masses. I look at them in the light and know that they won't look the same to me out there in the darkness as they did moments before on the dance floor. I look, and I don't see you there.

It's just a thought, one quick possibility that flashes through my mind and my cock like a pulse. But it's gone in a heartbeat. You're gone. So I turn, less dramatically and less gracefully than I've turned all night, and I leave the night through the back door.

"Hey, wanna give me a hand over here?" Doug's voice is as jarring as broken glass. The back room is full of bustle and sweeping. And there's going to be more glass breaking if I don't pitch in.

Doug's arms bulge and strain. The vein that runs along the top of each bicep throbs with effort. For some reason he has piled five racks of glasses in those solid arms. A chime of warning ripples through glassware. He is a bull in a china shop. More veins strain across forearms.

I save the first three trays from toppling. Doug relaxes.

"Thanks, tough guy," Doug slaps my back, slides down my spine, squeezes the back pocket of my jeans. "Just throw them in the back office."

There's a push broom standing at the office door. It's holding up a man. Nick is propped there, smiling, waiting for things to shatter. He doesn't lift a finger until the aftermath. He doesn't lift a finger to turn on the office light for a guy carrying a load.

As I walk past him, he lifts the corners of his smile, smirks through his grin. Nick is shorter, darker—a pair of rough hands, a swatch of chest hair sprouting from a V-neck. I smile back and carry the racks into the dim office. He winks. He nods.

He slams the door behind me. It's dark, but I've spent the entire night in darkness, punctuated by strobes and bass. I'm not about to lose my footing now. I'm not about to jump for a janitor's joke. So I walk to the far end and set the pile on the desk.

"They said you wouldn't freak out."

I jump. I turn to look in darkness. There's nothing but the remnants of the glowing message seared across my eyes. But I recognize your voice. It's like your gaze, solid and straightforward. The bright blindness seeps from my vision. It melts into a cool pool of electric blue. It fills the room and illuminates the scene.

You're watching me again, from across the room, sitting shirtless, jeans gathered tight around your thighs. You see my sight return. You recognize the moment I see you, when our eyes meet and lock. It's stronger than the door. It alone would keep me here.

"So did you fall for the same trick?" I ask.

"I think I am the trick."

My hand traces curves of my triceps and shoulder. I caress my chest and run fingertips in circles around my nipple. I squeeze and pull. I imagine your mouth and teeth and breath. I exhale as you unzip your pants.

I've been putting on a solo act all night. Now I need a partner. If you want a private show, you'd better be willing to perform too.

"Ready for the encore?"

I stroke my cock through my pants as I straddle your spread legs. You can see it throb and jump under the material as your knees press the inside of my thighs.

Through the two layers of our jeans I feel the heat I've felt all night, the heat of your gaze from across the room, the heat of my cock dancing against my leg, the heat of your body against mine.

I begin to move, my body slower, more subtle than any music. I sway against the weight of your legs that hold me open in a wide, vulnerable pose. My hips rock and thrust.

I feel your hand a moment before your mouth. You grip the back of my thigh, cup the curve of my ass, pull me closer. Your tongue finds the dark line sprouting from my jeans, flicks at the flat hole of my stomach and soaks the hair with warmth. I hold your head to me, knuckles in hair, feel the rough line of my jaw and scratch of your chin surrounding the soft, hot circle of your mouth.

Buttons and zipper fall away. I nearly collapse as your mouth grips my cock. Instead of falling, I rise and arch into you. You don't hesitate. The dripping kiss is like one long, slow swallow.

I pull free and fall onto you, sliding down your body.

I grind myself into that narrow space of fur and hardness between chest muscles. I drag my cock down your torso, through the coarse path of hair. Our mouths open and meet. I can taste my cock on you, inside you. It's hot and wet where it left the shadow of its warmth on your tongue. My scent is on your face, and I lick it from the stubbled divot of your upper lip. My fingers grasp your jaw, pry your mouth. I open you wide and dive into our kiss.

You pull free and leave me gasping for the taste of you. For one moment we half-smile at each other. It's almost a smirk, the kind you catch from across the club.

The expression changes quickly as you grab me and flip me, onto my stomach. I feel spit and precome drip onto the floor at the same time I feel the cold dripping of lube oozing down my crack. I raise my hips, spread my ass. Your fingers find my hole, preparing that tight place for you. I exhale, relax, and let your fingers slide and open me. I hear the distinct crinkle of the condom package tearing between teeth.

The pressure of your firm head against my greasy hole seems like impossible anticipation. The suspense doesn't last. Slow, gentle urgency makes me give. And as you take me, sliding hot and thick, the deep groan from your throat drowns out the murmur of pain that quivers through me.

I breathe and bend. I feel your jeans pulled down tight around your thick thighs. I feel the cold teeth of the zipper bite into my ass. I feel you fill me.

"Nice rhythm, boy." I lift my head and see them standing there. They smile down at us as you thrust into me. You never miss a beat. Your hands pull me closer, push you deeper.

Doug and Nick share a look of smug pleasure. This was their idea.

Nick reaches to his crotch, rubbing hard as if he's still cleaning. His eyes never move from the sight of you fucking me, of my groaning submission. I watch Doug reach over, reach inside Nick's shirt, stroking where his chest hair sprouts from his dingy work clothes. It's an unexpected sight, one that only turns me on more as you pound me harder. Anything would be hot with you inside me.

Doug's tall, muscled form towers above Nick by half a foot. The two make an odd pairing. But the pretty bar boy seems more than pleased with the situation as he peels off Nick's shirt and sets to work on the man's large, soft nipples. He devours each one as the smaller man squeezes and kneads himself, watching me moan, my cock jerking with pleasure as yours stretches me.

"You look like you're enjoying yourself." Nick approaches us, shirtless, rubbing. Doug follows, shedding clothes along the way. He is hard and thick, ready for whatever comes next. "I've got something else you'll enjoy."

You slam into me hard, make we wince with pleasure. Nick unzips, and I discover one reason Doug is so willing. Nick's cock thrusts huge and full in front of my face, precome spilling from his fist pumping its base. He can barely wrap his own hand around its width. He settles onto his knees, mirroring your stance behind me.

You pump and fuck as he works his giant hard-on. Each of your thrusts pushes me closer to him. Doug joins the scene from behind. He falls to a crawl, reaches for the floor. He presses his hard cock against the carpet as his face meets Nick's ass. The shorter man lets a vulgar groan escape as Doug's tongue works its way into his hairy hole. Nick jabs his fat cock at my face.

There's no question what I'm supposed to do as your hand pushes my head from behind, urging me to tackle the huge task in front of me. I open my mouth and taste the strong scent of work and sweat. I strain my lips around the massive shaft.

"You can take it," you say. You coax and drive me with your words. You drive me even harder with your cock.

You press me on from behind, from inside. Nick's big dick pushes farther down my throat. He pushes from the front; you shove from behind. I am so full of man I can hardly breathe or move. You two move for me, rocking me back and forth between you.

Doug joins the motion, crawls among legs and limbs. He is under me, between hands and knees. He licks and bites at my hard nipples, grasps my even harder cock.

"Feed it to him," you instruct the little man with the huge cock as you pound long and hard at my hole. "I'm going to blow inside his tight little ass."

Nick forces himself all the way into my throat. He slides in and out, buries my nose in his thick bush. I feel the head of his cock swell more. I ready myself for the coming flood.

Your fingers dig into my sides. I have opened to you completely, and I welcome the insistent pounding. You shove rough, hold yourself as deep as you can, and pause.

Connected by skin and sweat, we all feel you shudder inside me. Over and over, I feel your cock surge, filling the condom, filling me.

Nick answers your groan with several thrusting jabs. From beneath, Doug grabs the head of my cock in his mouth, savors it as it fills painfully with pulsing pleasure. Nick tenses and suddenly pulls his huge tip from beyond my tonsils and out of my mouth. I watch the thick, hot liquid pour from Nick's wide spout as it spatters my cheeks, drips down my chin.

"Come on, boy," your voice is deep. I still feel you inside me, subsiding. "Give that bartender something to drink."

Doug is slurping under me, teasing my primed cock. Nick brushes away my hair, admiring his handiwork. Your hands are on my back, bracing—you slip out of me.

I feel hollow. Vacant. I fall exhausted and empty onto Doug, into his mouth. He takes my weight and the last of my energy pent up tight and hard in the end of my cock. I come in a sudden release. All that hot pounding and sucking streams from me like a loud, molten sigh.

"Splendid performance," Doug wipes his mouth. He puts the attitude back on before his pants.

"Yes, great show." Nick is buttoning and tucking. He winks. He nods.

I share a laugh with them as they leave, weak and satisfied, barely audible. I could just be breathing. But I'm breathing through a smile, a glib grin. It's almost the same sound as laughter. I guess that's the punch line they've been waiting for.

I run a hand through moist hair, lift limp bangs. It's almost a dance move. It's almost rhythm without music. You stand in front of me, shirt unbuttoned, watching my performance. It's not my best. But you know that. You squat to my level, reach out and touch my jaw. You kiss me, soft and slow. Our lips make the slightest sound, but it seems like a chorus.

"I'm glad I decided to stay for that second drink," you leave with a smile. You leave me with one too, a smile on just-kissed lips.

I gather myself and my clothes. I wonder whether the sun is up somewhere out there. I wonder how long until it sets, how long until it goes down and the lights come up. I wonder what the crowd will be like and whether their favorite song will sound any different. I wonder whether it will all look the same from up on that box. Most of all, I wonder whether I will ever repeat the steps that danced me into a night like tonight.

Sex Piggy in the Middle

Bob Condron

Darkroom etiquette, German-style: One moment he is standing next to me at the counter up front. Close. Real close. Almost brushing up against me. Almost, but not quite. Then, as quickly as he appears, he disappears toward the darkroom at the back of the bar. He's cute—a real hunk, in fact. But if he wants a fuck, I tell myself, he's going to have to signal his interest better than that. A simple "Hi!" might have been the place to start.

A short time later, I enter the toilets. Need a piss. I *really* need a piss. And he's standing there against the back wall. Waiting for me? I turn my back, open my fly and let the stream of piss loose. Golden. Cascading over porcelain like Niagara Falls. A torrent. A fleeting memory of a guy in a barrel. Riding the waves. Into the gutter and away. A tragic loss.

I feel his eyes bore into me. I turn my head and check him out. Yep, *real* cute. I smile. Next thing I know he slams up behind me. I turn my head to meet his. Next thing, he's crushing his lips up against mine. Feeding on my face. His need is urgent, palpable. The need for man-to-man sex. His hand grips my chin, his lips suck on my tongue, drawing me ever deeper into him. And this strikes me as a pretty clear signal of what he's after. No dialogue required.

I button up quickly. Turn around. Wrestle and kiss. Slam him back against the mirror. Watch myself kissing him. Over his shoulder. Glancing in the mirror. What a beautiful picture. Two hot, hairy, masculine guys hard at each other. I fumble for his zipper. He grabs my wrist, takes hold and leads me through to the darkroom without further ado.

I feel his cock long before I see it. Rock-hard against the thin veneer of his faded Levi's. Straining for release. I do the honors. His cock springs free from his zipper. Huge. Distended. I trace the veins with my fingers. Run them over his shaved balls. Connect with the thick, hard metal of his cock ring. Peel back his foreskin and feel the velvety skin of his mammoth cock head. Dripping with desire. I flip him around. Finger his tight asshole. Next thing I know, he's lubed up, welcoming my fingers. First one, then two, then three, then four… Grinding his buttocks back to meet my greased-up knuckles. His moist, vacant hole is ready to be stuffed. That is only too apparent. But not yet. I make him wait.

On my knees, I suck him. I chow down on his meat. Abandoned. That gorgeous, bulbous cock head clamped between my lips. Pumping hard. Backward and forward. Sucking the life out of him. He thrusts to meet me head-on. Bucking his hips, working himself into a lather. And suddenly the come flows. Ropes of come, spraying my face, hanging from my goatee. Dangling as I grip and squeeze his powerful thighs. Hear his chest heave in the exquisite aftermath of orgasm.

Moments pass in silence. He reaches down. Rubs my shaved head.

"Can I buy you a beer?"

His accent is rough-edged, sexy. And unmistakably German. He hands me a tissue. I take it thankfully. And wipe his desire from my chin.

Sitting at the bar now, beer in hand.

"How did you know I spoke English?"

"Didn't." He smiles. "But you do have TEXAS written on your T-shirt!"

I laugh. "Yeah, I guess that could have given you some idea!"

He runs his tongue around the lip of his bottle. "So. You a tourist?"

"Yep."

"How you like Germany?"

I lean forward and kiss his full, succulent lips. "It's getting better every minute."

He returns the kiss. "Sweet."

"And you?" I ask. "You from Cologne?"

"From Karlsruhe."

"Never heard of it…"

"Believe me, it exists."

I look into his eyes. Slightly slanted. Clear blue. Beautiful. Piercing. The pupils dilated like two dark moons. "I don't doubt it."

"I have a friend. He comes later. He must meet you…"

I grin. Suck the froth from the neck of my beer bottle. "Looking forward to it already."

"And your name?"

"Troy," I lie.

"My name is Wolf," he replies, and holds out his hand for a firm, meaty handshake.

For the next half an hour he tells me his life story. Condensed version. I always ask the difficult questions. He tells me how he had lived too long in some small backwater. How he has no contact with his family, how he had been alone until he met his partner eight years ago…and all the time I am drinking in his salt-and-pepper, close-cropped hair, his trim goatee. And a mirror ball spins above our heads, sprinkling the darkness with stars.

Suddenly, his partner is there, leaning over Wolf's shoulder. Equally handsome. Full beard, six feet tall. Shaved bald. Liquid brown eyes.

"Say hello to Troy."

"Hi, Troy. I'm Kai."

I take his hand. His grip is firm and meaty too. Huge hands. Calluses on the palm. Manual work?

Kai whispers into Wolf's ear. A brief exchange.

Wolf leans over the bar and orders another round. Kai launches himself at me.

"You want to come home with us?" Kai asks when we finally prize our lips apart and come up for air.

"Ready when you are!" seems like the only reasonable response in the circumstances.

Hand in hand in hand we exit through the swinging doors. Me as sex piggy in the middle. The fresh air hits me like a wave. Filling my head and my lungs. Out of the smoky atmosphere and into the freshness of the night. Only a short walk, they assure me. Crashing at a friend's pad. She is away for the weekend. I take it one step at a time.

We burst through the door of the apartment and, with a quick flick of a switch, into the fluorescent light.

"For God's sake, Kai, light some candles." Wolf is insistent.

Hunger overtakes me. "I'm hungry, boys. Need to eat."

Wolf bends to untie his boot. "Got some salami and bread in the fridge." He points in the direction of the kitchenette. "Help yourself."

I do the business as the boys do theirs. Kai lights candles, Wolf selects a CD and presses play, then yanks the first boot free of his foot. Mellow music to compliment the golden glow cast over the studio flat. The room dominated by one big double bed. Metal frame. Jailhouse fuck.

I watch them begin to strip naked…turn back to the work surface and food. Set to work. But even as I ram the hastily made sandwich into my mouth, Kai is working my jeans down over my hairy thighs, down to my ankles. Boots, socks, and pants discarded, Kai parts my buttocks, and he buries his mouth in my hairy crack. His hunger equally ravenous as mine was just a short time before, or so it seems to me as I pull my T-shirt over my head.

I reach back, grip his head, and force him to drink deeply of my butt crack. I cast an eye at the now stark-naked Wolf. Out of the darkroom and in the candlelight, his cock is truly magnificent in all its full-blooded glory. He holds the swollen shaft between thumb and forefinger. Stiff as rock. I glance from dick to face. See the evil gleam in his eye as he directs his cock with precision and lets free a spurt of piss. Stop, start. A steady pulse. Stop,s tart. An impressive display of bladder control. Splashing over Kai's head and shoulders, over my ass cheeks, running down my legs, rivulets running between my toes, forming a pool on the tiled floor.

I look down. My dick so hard. Veins raised on the shaft of my thick penis. Throbbing. So swollen it is sore. The moist, cherry head of my ripe cock bursts with lifeblood. Pulsing. Twitching.

I'm laughing now. "You bastard!"

I grab Wolf by the hand and lead him to the shower cubicle. Push him through the door. Press him down, my palm on the top of his head. Bidding him kneel. His mouth opens wide. His tongue lolls out the corner of his mouth. With a grunt, I let flow my own golden shower. It sprays against his lips. Lips that yawn to receive. I watch his Adam's apple rise and fall, gulp and swallow. A shimmering stream springs from the depths of my full bladder, blasting his throat. He welcomes every drop. Spitting some. Swallowing most. Even as I let fly, I feel Kai crawl up behind me on all fours, bury his face in my ass crack once again. Feasting on my hairy asshole. Hungry like the Wolf. Snuffling. Baying. Howling at my moon. My two hard, firm, rosy cheeks encasing his own. My buttocks grip and squeeze his face like a vise as he feasts on my hot and tender manhole.

I look down. Watch Wolf suck my meat. Admire the rhythmic action of his head. Bobbing forward and back with the precision of a milking machine. Working overtime.

"Give me your come," Wolf splutters. "Give it to me!"

"Beg."

"I'm begging you! Give me all your come!"

My dick is slick with his saliva. I pump in and out of his mouth. "You want my hot load!"

He gulps reflexively. "I want it all!"

I watch my dick disappear into the depths of his throat…and slide out reluctantly. Almost free. The ripe head embraced by the firm grip of Wolf's tight, pumping lips. Unwilling to let me go. "I'm going to come loads, Wolf. My balls are so full of come, just for you."

"Oh, yeah!" His mouth is rampant. Suction to the nth degree. "Give it to me, big man."

I spread my legs wider, feel Kai's hot, wet tongue flick over my shaved balls, and shudder as he grabs my nuts from behind, stuffing both swollen orbs into his mouth. Suckling like a hog.

"You want it bad?" I ask Wolf. "My load."

"Oh, yeah!"

Kai so hungry. Feasting on my big low-hangers. Wolf so hungry munching on my bone.

"How much do you want it, Wolf?"

"Want it real bad!"

Kai traces the line between balls and anus with his talented tongue.

"Beg me, Wolf."

"I beg you."

"Beg me!"

He redoubles his efforts. Huffing and puffing on my cock like he's going to blow the house down. Actions speaking so much louder than words. He plunges forward, swallowing me up to the hilt. Gobbling me all up.

Kai grips my buttocks with his big, rough hands. His fingers digging into the taut flesh. Spreading my cheeks. His talented tongue lapping my hole, probing, and tickling. I feel my balls rise. Tighten. Ready to spray, to spurt, to empty their steaming, fertile load.

"Oh, yeah, Wolf. Oh, yeah, man. Suck!"

Bizarre. I suddenly become aware of the environment. Gray tiles. A white fleck running through them. A marble effect. The shower door with its pattern of blue dolphins swimming across the frosted glass. Need to lose focus. Need to keep focus. Need to hold off the moment. Prolong the pleasure. Sensations deeply felt. The tremor down to the very tips of my toes. Trembling knees. Making me quake. Aching. I look down and see Wolf's hands grip my pumped, hairy thighs. See Kai's fingers wrapped around my calves. Watch those same calves flex against his fingers.

Kai's tongue is now so far up my ass it feels as if it is tickling my tonsils.

"Come, for me. Come on fuckin' give it to me." Wolf's mouth is pleading.

"No. Wait!"

"Can wait no longer. Come."

"Please…"

"Come now, you fucker."

"Please…"

"Come."

How can I resist? "Get ready."

"I'm ready, big guy." He opens his throat to receive.

"Get ready."

Gulping. "I'm ready, stud."

"I'm gonna come." And the sap starts to rise.

"Oh, yeah!"

"Oh, fuck! Oh, fu-u-uck!" And the dam begins to burst.

Such a hot mouth. Such a thirst. Pumping like crazy. "Oh, yeah…"

And, suddenly, that irresistible sensation. The unstoppable force of nature. Come pulsing through my tubes. Traveling toward its inevitable, copious discharge. Feeling each potent, aching pulse. Blasting out of my piss slit. Squirting. Up and out of my piss slit. Spurting forth. A torrent. Flooding his mouth as he gulps and swallows. Threatening to overwhelm him. He struggles manfully to consume the full load. Pulsing again and again and again… Come slut. Swooning under the weight and the wealth of my masculine juices. Wanting more. Always more. Begging for it. Loving it. Needing it. Every drop.

"Come on, man, come on…" His chest is heaving; his throat is wide open. Kai still working his tongue so deep up my ass now I swear by this point I can feel it in my nostrils. Feel my ring pulse against his tongue with every spurt. Wolf savoring each drop, smacking his lips. Jerking his cock. Jerking his big, hard uncut cock.

Kai grunts against my ring, lips up close, tongue working furiously, as his come begins to flow, blasting a heavy stream over my ankles.

"Oh, ja! Geil! Sau geil..."

Up front, Wolf begins to shoot in unison. Working his dick like a power tool. Over my hairy toes. Sperm spraying over my toes... His face a silent howl... Humping and heaving. Head buried in my crotch. Then growling and yelping...

Stillness. Moments pass in stillness. Then Wolf reaches up. Toys with my tits. Suckles on the last few drops from my softening tool. His tongue dipping into the eye of the storm. Savoring the taste. Kai rests his cheek against my butt cheeks. I hear him sigh. Satisfied.

With one hand, I reach down in front to stroke the stubble on Wolf's number 2 crop and, with the other, I reach behind to stoke Kai's smooth pate. "That was some sandwich," I say.

"Some filling," Kai replies.

"Heavy on the mayo?" Wolf adds with a grin.

"You complaining, buddy?" I ask.

He smacks his lips. Rubs his hairy belly. "As if," he replies. "I have a good appetite."

"I noticed."

"I'm still hungry," Kai pipes up.

"Want me to feed you a length?" I ask.

He nods enthusiastically.

I feel my cock begin to swell. "So...part those buns and get ready to be filled..."

Sticks and Balls

Kyle Warner

The stranger dropped more change in the jukebox and the sounds of AC/DC poured out. Tommy sighed. Wouldn't this guy ever leave? The man looked over his shoulder at Tommy and chalked his cue.

It wasn't as if there was anything to do after midnight on a Friday night at the ass-end of summer in the wide spot in the road that Tommy called home between semesters. The air held layers of smoke, chalk, and sweat. His eyes were tired, and he wanted nothing more than to suck down a cold one, and maybe jerk off.

"Wanna take me on?" the stranger asked. "If I lose, I'll clear out." Tommy tried to decide who had the advantage. He'd seen the guy playing all night, losing a little bit, then reeling in his marks and emptying their wallets. Tommy had seen hustlers before and didn't mind turning the tables on them. He'd been hanging around his uncle's pool hall since he was 6 and sometimes doubled his weekly wages by playing the wide-eyed, slightly drunk college boy who didn't know his stick from his balls.

"Gee, mister," he replied uncertainly, coming out from behind the counter. "I don't know if I'm good enough for you."

The stranger cracked a broad grin and ran his fingers through his short hair, displaying a heavy, well-defined arm that looked as though it could do some damage. His skin was the shade of a guy who spends all his waking hours outdoors, stripped to the waist, and Tommy could see a set of well formed pecs etched under his sleeveless shirt. Worn jeans clung to his legs, and the stranger wiped off the extra chalk on his thighs.

"I think you'll do, sonny," he said. "I expect I can teach you a thing or two, if you're willing to learn. My name's Press Watson."

"Tommy Flynn." He held out his hand. Press took it and Tommy felt his fingers squeezed tight in a strong grip. "Hey, careful there!" he said. "I have to shoot some pool with that hand." He was several inches shorter and much skinnier than Press, and he knew he looked younger than a college senior. He could play the part of the bumpkin ready to be suckered.

"Are we playing for anything else?" Press asked, and Tommy pretended to think.

"Well," he finally said. "I just got paid, and I wouldn't object to a little bet..." He pulled his billfold out.

"It's not your money I want," Press said, and for the first time, Tommy felt uncertain. "If you win, I clear out."

"And if you win?" Tommy asked.

"You'll have to do something for me," Press said, with a wink. He grabbed Tommy's upper arm, and seemed to be testing his muscle. "Do you want to break?"

"Sure..." Tommy said. He went behind the counter and got his cue case.

"Hey...you know what you're doing!" Press said, surprised. Tommy screwed his stick together and nervously ran his hands up and down it. He racked the balls and bent low for the break. Press stood just behind him, and Tommy could feel his warm breath.

"Do you mind?" he asked, irritably.

"Yes," said Press, not moving.

Tommy took his frustration out on the cue ball, and his break scattered the balls all over the table. The two ball went in, and he said "I've got solids...you've got stripes." Press nodded, and moved even closer. His thigh brushed Tommy's as he worked out his next shot.

His hand found the small of Tommy's back as he leaned over

the table for the right angle. Instead of bothering him, Press's touch seemed to focus Tommy, and he played a ruthless game, sinking his shots with a finesse and spin he normally would have saved until there was big money riding on the outcome. He knew something was riding on it, but he waited for Press to let him know what it was.

"Well, Tommy," Press whispered into his ear. "It looks like you have some experience at this game."

"Do you feel conned?" Tommy asked. He felt Press corner him from behind.

"No," replied the other player. "I feel hot." His hand darted around to the front of Tommy's jeans. "Someone else has a pretty big cue."

Tommy rubbed his ass against Press's crotch and felt the hard-on. Press started to unzip Tommy's fly.

"Oh, no," Tommy reminded him. "If I beat you, you have to clear out. If you beat me, then…I do what you want me to do."

"Well, boy," said Press, "you have about one more shot to make and I have to leave. And I get the feeling you could make it with your eyes shut."

"Actually, I like to keep my eyes open," Tommy said. He sank his final shot, but pocketed the cue ball as well. "Oops, I scratched. Looks like you have a chance."

"That's all I need," Press said, and proceeded to run the table. When he sank his last shot, he turned to Tommy and said, "What do I win?"

Tommy dropped his jeans and kicked them aside. Press pulled off Tommy's shirt, then reached into his pants. Tommy's cock grew harder at the touch. Press drew Tommy to him, and kissed him roughly, biting Tommy's lips and shoving his tongue deep into his mouth. Tommy ground against Press, reaching into his jeans to squeeze his ass and grind closer to Press's hard bulge. Press wasn't wearing underwear, Tommy realized the instant the other man dropped his pants. He took Press's cock in his hands and fell to his knees, opening his mouth to take in the prick. He rode up and down it with his lips and tongue, grazing the edge of his teeth along the shaft. Press moaned and grunted, pushing Tommy's head farther and farther down. Tommy stroked his own cock as he felt Press getting closer and closer to release.

Suddenly Press stepped back, grabbed Tommy under both arms, and heaved him onto the pool table. The felt was smooth against his naked back as Press pushed up Tommy's shirt, squeezing his nipples, touching his dick with Tommy's.

"I wanna go in you," he said. "I have to fuck that ass of yours. You want me to?" Tommy pulled his briefs out of the way, and threw his legs over Press's shoulders. "I guess that's a yes," Press said. He teased Tommy's ass with his fingers first, then leaned in and licked his asshole until Tommy was choking back sobs of pleasure. Then, his ass dripping with Press's spit, Tommy felt the other man's cock circling his hole. He ached to have it inside him.

"I can take it all," he told Press. "I want it." Press guided himself into Tommy's ass, and began to thrust, first slowly, then hard, pumping into Tommy like a piston, slamming his body into Tommy's with every thrust. He dripped sweat onto Tommy's cock, which made Tommy's hand slide up and down faster as he felt himself being penetrated by the biggest dick he'd ever taken. Press pulled out and held his cock to Tommy's, and they rubbed them together, and Tommy couldn't tell who began to come first, but whoever it was, the other followed in the next instant, and their come mixed and landed everywhere—on chests, crotches, legs. Press rubbed his come into Tommy's chest, and Tommy reached up and squeezed both of Press's wet nipples.

Press put his hand to Tommy's cheek.

"I know you let me win," he said. "So if you want, I'll still clear out."

"Well," said Tommy. "I'm willing to go again, double or nothing."

"All right, boy," Press said. "Rack 'em up."

Arkansas Heat
Jack Whitestone

I'm not sure what it is about the summer in Arkansas that awakens carnal appetites. Perhaps it is the seemingly endless days when the atmosphere mimics the human body, turning the air to 98.6 degrees and 60% water. But if the torridness of these days awakens emotions, it also prevents them from stirring. When the heat of the day is so heavy even the breezes refuse to move, general lethargy sets in upon all living creatures. Hence, it is the sultry evenings that, freed from the sun's clutches, the breezes gently cool the sweat-drenched skin of the day's survivors and passions quicken in the coolness of the evening shade.

"It gets in your veins," my dad used to say about the Arkansas heat, recalling his childhood years and extolling our family's pilgrimages to his birthplace. Nearly every July my parents took me 1,500 miles by car to Arkansas to visit my dad's father and stepmother in a small town called Searcy that lay sleeping in the foothills of the Ozarks. The summer visits were adventures of exposure to a slew of aunts, uncles, and cousins whom I recognized from the Kodak pictures they dutifully enclosed with their Christmas cards.

In my preschool years I was especially drawn to my Uncle Buck, my dad's younger half brother, whose trek to Searcy from a neighboring state would often coincide with our own family visit. When I was small Uncle Buck would lift me high above his head and swing me round and round. In his strong hands I felt like I was riding a carousel in the sky.

Early one evening Uncle Buck was cooling off in my grandparents' backyard after a humid Searcy day and a hearty Southern supper. As I watched from the back porch, Uncle Buck took off his shirt to capture the evening breeze against his skin. When I saw the glistening sweat on his bare chest and muscular arms, a flame of desire ignited in my 5-year-old mind. I too impulsively peeled off my shirt and ran out onto the lawn to be caught up in the arms of my favorite uncle. He hoisted me high off the ground and twirled me above his head, much to my glee.

It was innocent behavior, of course, although the bare-chested spin would be indelibly etched in my mind.

I came across many "Uncle Bucks" on my path to puberty: the neighbor boy I idolized because he was a star on the high school football team and took me swimming; the Woolworth's soda jerk who added an extra scoop of ice cream to my milkshakes; the serviceman who lived across the street and took me on short rides on the back of his motorcycle and who let me read his book of ribald limericks. Then there was Gardner McKay, who played the itinerant Captain Adam Troy in the *Adventures in Paradise* TV series. The sometimes-shirtless Captain Troy weekly sailed his schooner, the Tiki, from tropical island to island in the South Seas—and dropped anchor right into my boyish heart.

At first I thought nothing was unusual about the parade of men I lionized. Whether they were young men who befriended me or were beamed in from Hollywood studios, my longing to be close to them seemed natural. They were my heroes. I didn't realize until many years later that I had been infatuated. These handsome men were not mere role models; they were my first crushes. I longed for intimate contact with a man long before I ever knew that the wiggly thing between my legs had a use beyond that of a spigot for expelling pee.

It was several summers later when the Arkansas heat once again raced through my veins. I was barely 16 and proud of my teenage status. In a couple of months I would enter my sophomore year of high school. By this age I had begun to wonder why I did not feel the same curiosity or enthusiasm for girl classmates that my buddies were professing to feel, so I learned to be wary of talking about the magnetism I felt toward men. Otherwise, I did not give sexual matters much thought, pushing aside the occasional temptations that crept into my mind—especially in the showers after gym class. I had already begun to explore and develop beliefs of my own, quite apart from my parents' conservative views. Soon during this hot summer, I was destined to begin exploring my sexual orientation as well; although, unlike today's streetwise and sex-savvy youth, I had no idea what the words *homosexual* or *gay* meant.

It was 1963, and gay people were not portrayed as likable, funny characters on TV sitcoms as they are now. In fact, they were not portrayed at all. I did not read about gay men in books or hear about them in school, except to learn that being called "fag" or "queer" was a terrible thing. The words were associated with wimpy, girlish behavior rather than with sexual attraction and affection for members of the same sex. If gay people were portrayed at all in motion pictures, the roles only vaguely hinted at their sexuality, and they were generally written out of the scripts by way of sudden and premature deaths. No one had ever heard of the phrase "gay pride," let alone had a clue of what it would come to mean. Fortunately, for a man coming of age like myself, this was also a time before people feared the menace of herpes or were stalked by the specter of AIDS.

Searcy in 1963 was a close-knit community where people did not lock their front doors, even when they went away on vacation, so my parents felt secure in allowing me to wander about the town's streets—even after dark.

The people of Searcy were God-fearing folk, and the ratio of churches to movie theaters was roughly 20 to 1. But I was, after all, a teenager and more interested in seeing a movie than hearing a sermon. With only one movie theater in town, picking a motion picture was an easy decision. I don't recall the movie's title—it might have been *Parrish* or *Palm Springs Weekend,* starring my new secret idol, Troy Donahue—but I do remember standing outside the theater in the fading light when I met him, the retreating Arkansas sun preparing to bring my passions to a boil.

He was an engaging young man, a few months older than I was, and genuinely glad to make a new friend. We walked around the small town square and park, discussing our teenage lives and interests. I instantly liked him. And I liked how he began calling me "buddy" right away, especially in his entrancing Southern drawl. I couldn't help but notice how much more hair he had on his arms than I had grown and how the muscles in his arms pushed up the veins under his skin. An exciting thought crept into my head: I wanted to be naked with this young man. My parents had set strict rules about not ever touching girls' "private parts," as they called them, and I supposed their admonition applied to boys too. Yet I felt an overpowering yearning to be close to this guy and touch him in ways my parents would surely disapprove.

As we talked, he told me he was not living with his parents but boarding with another couple. *Boarding? How exciting,* I thought. I had no idea how he might have paid for boarding; I suspected he had actually been taken in by his grandparents or a kindly aunt and uncle. Nevertheless, I was impressed by this man of the world—a man who boarded in his very own place.

His very own place turned out to be an attic bedroom on what would have been the third floor of a clapboard house, typical of houses in the community. Whoever his landlords were, they were away or fast asleep when he ushered me into his tiny room.

The house was still, save for our hushed talk and quickened breathing. Soon our conversation drifted into silence. He didn't need to tell me why he had invited him to his room. I didn't need to say why I felt compelled to be there. We understood without words why we were together. Yet we were both afraid of making the first over-ture, so we sat in awkward silence for what seemed an eternity.

I looked over at his makeshift bookshelves, built of wood planks and painted cinder blocks. "You've got lots of books," I commented.

He pulled out a worn magazine from a place tucked behind books. Handing it to me, he said, "You might like this one, buddy."

The magazine was about the page size of a *Reader's Digest* but not nearly as thick. Beginning to leaf through the pages, I saw it was filled with black-and-white photos of a male model I took to be in his early 20s. Each page revealed the man with fewer ad fewer articles of clothing. I could feel my heart starting to pound by the time I reached the page where the model had taken off his shirt. Although I had stared at the Charles Atlas and Joe Weider muscle-building ads in the backs of comic books, I had never seen anything as stimulating as the magazine I held in my hands. I hastily flipped to the back pages, where the model looked provocative in what seemed like an abbreviated jockstrap with the tiniest bit of string in place of the elastic waistband.

"What's he wearing?" I asked.

"I'm not sure. I think it's called a posing strap. I saw one in a catalog once."

I could feel my cheeks burning. Even my eyes felt like they were on fire. The photo on the last page emphasized a huge bulge beneath the man's posing strap—looking as though it would break through the flimsy garment the next minute if there had been another photo. "I hope I look like this when I'm older," I ventured.

"Hey, buddy, I think you look plenty good right now." He stepped closer to me and unbuttoned the top button of my shirt.

We didn't say the words of lovemaking because we didn't know the words to say. Neither one of us knew that two men together could enjoy kissing, hand-holding, necking, and the things we had seen Troy Donahue and Connie Stevens do in movies. I didn't know about man-to-man sex at all, and I barely understood the mechanics of masturbation. Yet we both understood the swellings inside our trousers were summoning us to action.

I began to quiver. I wanted to press him close to me and entwine my body with his. It was a mutual attraction, to be sure, and our youthful, hardening members could not be corralled by our pants much longer. Wordlessly, breathlessly, we began pulling off each other's clothes, probing and reveling in the beauty of our budding puberty with each freshly shed piece of clothing. We marveled at comparing our nipples: Mine were flat, wide, apple-red welts, while his were erect, tan cones. When at last we were stripped down to our boxer shorts, we maneuvered whatever ways we could to touch and rub against each other's flesh, even as our insistent dicks tugged to break free of our underwear. Our eyes and our hands raced across each other in a rising frenzy. The hair carpeting his legs and arms excited me. When he saw me admiring the trickle of hair starting to sprout in the cleft between his pecs, he said slyly, "I plan to grow lots more hair there."

We enshrined each new view of our young manhood in our minds as if we were inspecting a masterpiece of art. I didn't know if I would ever have an opportunity to do this again, and I wanted to capture every image in my memory.

The air was heavy and hot in his seemingly unventilated attic room, but the Arkansas temperature only intensified the fire that we felt inside our bodies. We tussled about his bed, stroking any manly crevice or appendage we could discover on each other. We pressed our bodies so close that we seemed to be melded into one. We wrestled in tight, intimate ways we had not been taught in gym class, feeling a rising ecstasy course through our bodies. Eventually, we could not hold back any longer and yanked off each other's undershorts, exposing our hard muscles of manhood. I had never seen a hardened dick other than my own, and the thrill of touching another man's drove me to new heights of arousal.

While my dick was lean, straight, long, and capped with a large, swollen, rosy head, his was bulbous, thick, and shaped in a gentle arc. Like those in his arms, the veins in his dick stood out against his flesh, and his dick was rooted in a dense mat of pubic hair. Although we were clumsy, we instinctively trusted the demands of our male members and let them guide us on this newfound road to joy. Now completely nude, we returned to our playful grappling, which was more intense than ever. Each contact between our bodies was more electrifying than the last.

We paused in our frenzy when we had our legs clenched around each other's skull in mutual headlocks. He relaxed his legs a bit, and I moved my face into his crotch. I liked the faint, musky odor around his dick and balls. So this is what a man smells like.

When a drop of precome emerged on the head of his dick, I impulsively licked it. "Don't stop, buddy," he moaned.

I timidly extended my tongue and started lapping around the head of his stiff one. Then the wet heat of his mouth engulfed my hard rod, descending until his nose was in my pubic hair. I tried swallowing his too, gagged a little, withdrew, and then let his cock fill my mouth again. His mouth moved up and down on the shaft of my dick, pausing just long enough to encourage me.

"That's it, buddy. Stroke my dick with your mouth."

I had noticed a jar of Vaseline by his bed, so when I heard the sound of a lid unscrewing, I thought he intended to grease up my dick. (Once I had foamed up my dick with my dad's shaving cream while I was experimenting with masturbation.) Instead, his lubed-up finger probed my butt. I spread my legs a little because I didn't want to miss a single sensation in this adventure. Suddenly he thrust his finger inside my hole. I stiffened and jerked my head away from his dick.

"You OK, buddy?" he whispered.

"I dunno. It feels kind of odd. Have you ever done this before?"

"Nah, but a cousin told me how. Just relax." With his assurance, I loosened my sphincter a bit. He wiggled his finger a little inside my hole. I couldn't see what he was doing, but in my mind I pictured his hairy, veined arm I had admired in the park just a couple of hours ago. Now it was working over my most private of parts. I nestled my face deep into his crotch with a sense of utter pleasure.

"Now I want you to put your finger in my hole," he said, pushing the jar of Vaseline toward me.

I globed up a massive amount of the petroleum jelly and quickly found his man hole. I slid in my index finger. His hole felt warm and moist. We went on tonguing each other's dicks while we toyed with our holes. It seemed to become hotter and hotter in his small room. My pulse raced as I imagined how we must have looked: two virile young men docked together by their dicks and fingers in each other's mouths and butts.

Abruptly he said, "I want you to ride me."

"Ride you?"

"Yeah, I want you to stick your dick in my hole and ride me. Would you like that?" He dug his hand into the jar and began greasing my dick with a wad of Vaseline.

I could barely contain my burning excitement. "I would."

He rolled onto his belly, spread his legs a bit, and offered up his butt. I planted my greased-up dick at his hole, admiring the sight for a moment. He had just a few hairs sprouting around a tight, puckered opening.

He spread his legs a little wider. "Let me have it, buddy."

I drove my dick in. His hole was tight, so I barely got my large head in when he clenched. I was determined and pushed a little harder, pinning him down in a full nelson. He seemed to relax a little and spread his legs still wider. "Go for it," he panted.

I did. Feeling the warmth of his tight man butt enveloping my dick was making me crazy. I began thrusting my dick up and down, feeling ecstasy in every stroke, driving faster and driving deeper inside him.

"Now I want to ride you," he said, taking me by surprise. I didn't want to stop, but I also thought that what's fair is fair. Moreover, I had already made up my mind to experience all I could.

I pulled out, and we traded places. He was slathering his dick with Vaseline with one hand, while he ran his finger back in my hole with the other. "You've got to loosen up, buddy," he said. "Do you want it?"

"Yeah," I said.

"Let me hear you say it, then."

"I want you to ride me. I want you to ride my hole." A feeling of eager anticipation, with a twinge of dread, came over me.

He jammed his rod inside me. Pain rocked my body. I gasped and clenched my teeth down on the pillow. *I can buck up and take this like a man,* I told myself.

He took it easy at first, but he was solidly plowed into me, with no intention of withdrawing. The pain quickly gave way to pleasure as he gently drove his man rod fully inside me until I could feel his pubic hair and balls at my opening. Although I was facedown on the pillow, I could imagine how it must look to be mounted and impaled on his hard dick. My body shook with pleasure and yielded. I spread my legs a little more and elevated my butt to him. As he began riding me in strong, even stokes, he reached under me and began stroking my dick in the same rhythm.

"You like me fucking you?" he breathed into my ear.

Fucking. Just hearing the word, thinking the thought, excited me. I was being fucked by a man. "Yeah, I like you fucking me. Fuck me good."

He rode me like I was a wild bronco. Our fevered panting grew more furious.

Suddenly he withdrew. "Turn over," he ordered. I rolled over on my back, and he grasped my ankles and spread my legs wide apart, pinning them down so my tender hole was wide open to him. I watched the sweat drip off his face, down his chest, and over his hardened nipples, then onto my belly. He peered at my open, unprotected hole. "Whose hole is it?" he asked in a hoarse whisper.

"It's yours, man," I said. "It's your hole. Take it. Fuck it."

With a mighty plunge he sent his rod back inside me, riding, humping, yes, fucking me hard. The sweat poured off him as he claimed my ass in an unrelenting fury.

I felt like we were one person tethered together by his dick. I couldn't keep my hands off my dick while I was being fucked. I stroked it, remembering the passion of being in him and lost in the euphoria of him fucking me now. As soon as I began giving the telltale signs of erupting, he pulled out of my hole, clenched our dicks together in his fist, and ran his hand up and down them like a jackhammer. Suddenly, we exploded across each other's bellies in a raging torrent of man juice.

Afterward we lay on his bed, panting and marveling at what we had done. We said nothing for a long while, as we were both lost in relishing how we had unlocked a new and forbidden door in our lives. The feeling of a pent-up release was breathtaking. The thrill of discovering someone like myself, who shared a secret passion to be with another man, left me in awe.

We didn't disguise our feelings by saying insincere things like "It would've been better if we had girls," which I would hear in future encounters with men. Instead, we exchanged addresses and promised to write each other. I would later discover that the ritual exchange of contact information after sex, without the remotest intention of using it, is a secondary sexual characteristic of being a gay man.

A few years ago and many sexual encounters later, a good friend introduced me to stock car races. I was exhilarated by the din of the car engines and mesmerized by the ballet of the flagman. I soon figured out the two primary purposes of stock car races. People do not hang around in the afternoon sun to see if one car goes faster than another one; everyone instinctively knows that. The first purpose is to witness firsthand the shock of a spectacular crash, when one car is sent careening into a block wall or hurled into a bank of other cars amid the screech and sparks of scraping metal. The second purpose is to drink vast amounts of draft beer. I happily embraced both purposes.

In the row behind us I noticed a handsome, husky man, whose age had advanced just as mine had—totally without my permission—to about 45. He seemed intent on the crash-watching and beer-drinking rites of the day under the sun. The man had a rugged, weathered look to him, although my attention was riveted to his snow-white T-shirt, which was riding atop a thick crop of chest hair. The thin layer of cotton, I imagined, might easily have drifted off his sea of hair had it not been anchored by his nipples, which were protruding like two small buoys beneath the cloth. When he caught my eyes glancing his way, he grinned broadly.

At these races, people spend about half of the day in the grandstands. The balance of the time is spent in two lines—one to buy beer and another to take a leak to make way for more beer. By a wonderful stroke of chance, this handsome, hairy man appeared immediately behind me in line at the men's room.

The beer not only loosened my kidneys but my tongue as well. "Some race?"

"Yeah," he said. "We don't have 'em like these back home."

"Back home? Where's that?"

"Arkansas," he answered.

Arkansas. I was enchanted with his Southern drawl and hoped I could coax him into saying "y'all." "Arkansas, huh," I said. "Pretty country. What part do you live in?"

"We're right in the foothills of the Ozarks, buddy."

My heart skipped a beat. Memories were beginning to boil. "Searcy, by any chance?" I ventured. "My dad was born there."

"Nah. Me and the wife live outside Fort Smith."

It was not the answer I would like to have heard, but faster than any of the racing cars that afternoon, my mind sped back to an evening in an attic room when my coming-of-age fermented into an intoxicating ecstasy.

For a moment the torrid Arkansas heat surged through my veins once again.

The Sea Where It's Shallow

Todd Gregory

They weren't happy. I could tell. The couple were sitting on beach towels a few feet beyond where the lapping of the waves at the sand turned it a darker hue than where it was dry. One was blond, the other brunet. The blond was older—maybe by as few as five years, maybe as many as 10. The brunette was taller by about four inches, but the blond was stockier, with thicker muscles.

I crossed the line where the depth of the water changes, where it switches from blue to green. I'd been swimming a long time, and perhaps it was time to come out. This couple definitely needed me, my intervention. Their auras were all wrong. They loved each other, but something was going on with them, something that was making them forget how much they loved, how much they cared, how deep the feelings actually ran. The brunet was scowling. They weren't talking—they were merely sitting side by side on their individual blankets on the powdery white sand. Not even looking at each other, not even stealing the occasional sidelong glance.

My feet brushed against the bottom and I smiled. I'd been in the water long enough it seemed to forget how to walk. OK, maybe that was an exaggeration. I hoped not, at any rate. My feet sank a fraction of an inch into the sand, and the small waves lifted the weight off my feet momentarily as each one passed, moving me a little closer to the water's edge.

I kept my eyes on the brunet as more of me emerged from the water. He tried to make it look like he wasn't looking at me. I was getting the sidelong glances as his eyes scanned the horizon, but they always came back to me. He seemed afraid to look me in the eyes, for our gazes to lock, but his eyes, I could see them moving, drinking in every inch of my dripping body as it emerged from the green sea. The white, sugary sand of the Florida panhandle scrunched under my feet as I walked at last out of the water. I smiled at the brunet. The blond lay back, sunglasses on, his eyes unreadable. The brunet was more susceptible to my charms, I decided, sitting down on the sand a few feet from where he sat.

I would wait a few minutes, letting the sun dry my skin, I decided, giving him the opportunity to speak first. Unless I missed my guess, he would.

The sun's rays were warm, and my skin dried quickly in its glare. I sensed him there, wanting to speak, to open a dialogue, but afraid of how the blond would react.

Fair enough.

I turned my head and looked right into his brown eyes. He looked away quickly, his tanned face coloring slightly, embarrassed at being caught looking. "Hello." I said, rearranging my facial muscles into a smile. It felt awkward. Surely it hadn't been that long since I'd smiled? For a brief moment, I tried to recall the last time I'd smiled.

"Um, hi." He looked back at me. He really had a pretty face, the skin still soft and supple with the last fading glow of youth. Late 20s, I decided. His eyes were beautiful in their brownness, golden flecks lightening them just enough to make them different from the many others with the same coloring. His lashes were long, thick, black, curling up and away from the lids. Deep dimples appeared in his cheeks as his red lips spread across his face in a slightly shy smile. Large, white, straight, even teeth appeared over the cleft in his chin.

His skin was olive, the kind that tans deeply and easily. Black curly hair framed his face, and below it a graceful neck reached down into powerful shoulders. Between widely set pectorals there was a patch of curly hair that trailed down over a flat stomach before disappearing into the white Lycra of his bikini. "My name's Matt."

I inclined my head down a bit, closing my eyes. "Alexandros." I could sense the blond's eyes on us behind his sunglasses. There was no expression on his face, but the muscles in his neck tightened.

Matt made a gesture at him. "This is my partner, Chris."

Who feels threatened, I thought. Matt was still smiling at me. "A pleasure, Chris." I said, inclining my head at him. Chris pulled himself up till he was reclining on his elbows. His torso was hairless, thickly muscled.

"Alexander, did you say?" He lifted his sunglasses to look at me in the bright glare. His eyes were gray. He glanced up and down my body.

"Alexandros." I corrected him softly. "Call me Sandy."

"You swim a lot?" His skin gleamed in the sunlight, a mixture of suntan oil and sweat shining in the bright sun.

"Yes."

His eyes flickered down again before meeting mine. "It shows." He got to his feet. His legs were thick with muscle. He wasn't as tall as I originally had thought, maybe five eight or nine. His black bikini had ridden up a bit in the back, revealing pale skin on his round hard ass. "I think I'll go for a swim myself."

\ Matt and I watched him as he walked down to the waterline, then waded out. Once he was in deep enough water, he dove under the surface and started swimming out. I turned back to Matt. "He's quite beautiful." I said.

"Yes." A shadow passed over Matt's face, then lifted as he smiled at me. "So are you."

"Thank you." I replied. "You are as well. You make quite a striking couple."

Matt looked away from me, up the beach. "Thanks."

"How long have you been together?"

"Three years."

Three years—that could explain some of it, I thought. The bloom is now off the rose. The first year is all giddy with love and sexual exploration of each other. In the second year the passion starts to die, just a little bit. The third year is the tricky one, when eyes start to wander, when the sex becomes a little stale and boring. Little things that used to be dismissed now begin to rankle just a little, simmering beneath the surface. "And it's going well?"

"Well—" Matt made a gesture with his hands. "Things are changing a bit. I don't know if it's a good or a bad thing. I mean, I still love him, and I think he still loves me, but things just aren't the way they used to be."

"Ah."

"We met in a bar, of all places," Matt went on. "I was out with some friends, celebrating my birthday. I saw him standing in a corner, by himself. He really took my breath away when I looked at him." He closed his eyes. "He was so gorgeous and sexy—the kind of guy I'd always wanted but could never get."

"Really?"

He looked at me, his eyes sad. "I was different then, Sandy. I didn't work out—I hadn't set foot in a gym since high school. I was pretty overweight, kind of dumpy. One of my friends noticed me staring at him, and he went over to Chris." He laughed. "He told Chris that it was my birthday and he wanted Chris to be my birthday present. Chris went along with it and came over. We started talking, and I went home with him." He sighed. "It was pretty amazing, and then he actually called me and asked me out again. I was crazy about him, and after a few months I moved in with him. He got me to join his gym, and he put me on a program." He gestured to his body. "And this is the result."

"You look great."

"Yeah." He stared out at the water. Chris was a small dot out in the distance. "I look great. So why doesn't Chris want me anymore?"

There it was—the root of the problem. "He doesn't?"

"No." A tall, lean young man of about 20 with deeply bronzed skin wearing long, baggy yellow shorts walked by at the water line. We both watched him for a moment, and then Matt looked back at me. "I mean, when I was fat we had sex all the time. Every day. He couldn't get enough of me—but the better shape I got in, the less sex we had. Now I look better than I ever have, good enough for total strangers to hit on me, and Chris can't be bothered with me unless we have someone else with us, a three-way. And even then, Chris is more into the other guy than he is me." He shrugged. "I mean, he was the one who wanted me to work out. Why would he do that if he liked me better when I was fat?"

"It doesn't make sense to me," I shrugged back at him. "Have you talked to him about it?"

"No."

"Ah."

Matt looked out at the water. "You see, he took the swim so we could talk. When he gets back, the first thing he'll do is ask me what I think, and if I nod, he'll ask you back to our room for a drink. At some point during the walk back, he'll say to you, 'I can't wait to watch Matt fuck you.' If you're open to it—" He shrugged again.

"Is that what you want, Matt?"

He smiled then, a big smile that lit up his entire face. "You're pretty hot, Sandy. Yeah, I would really like to fuck you."

"But you'd rather fuck Chris."

The smile faded. "Yeah."

We sat in silence as Chris became bigger and bigger as he swam to shore. He emerged from the sea, salty water streaming off his body. He shook his head, sending water droplets flying in all directions from his hair. He walked toward us. He looked at Matt. "What do you think?"

I saw the pain briefly flash across Matt's face. Then he lowered his head and nodded. An odd look went across his face as he turned to me and smiled. "Would you like to come back to our room for a drink?"

I looked him square in those murky gray eyes. "Only if the drink is a preliminary to fucking."

He was startled, but only for a moment, and then he smiled. "Whatever you want, Sandy."

It took them a few moments to fold their towels, pack up their stuff, and then we were walking across the hot sand. Matt walked faster than Chris and I. Chris reached over and stroked my back. "You really have a great body," he whispered. "I can't wait to see Matt fuck you."

I smiled back at him. "But you'll be joining us, won't you?"

His face lit up with a smile that told me everything I needed to know. It was so clear, so obvious, but of course Matt, wrapped up in his insecurities, couldn't know, couldn't notice, didn't see it. To him, Chris was perfect, the perfect man, the perfect lover, everything he had ever wanted. How could Chris be insecure? Chris draped his arm around my shoulders. I looked deep into his eyes and saw things that had never occurred to Matt. Chris was older. The age difference was even greater than I originally thought. Chris was 40, Matt only 27. He looked at Matt and saw an incredibly beautiful younger man with his whole life in front of him. Matt had been fat and shy when they met.

Chris was expecting Matt to find someone younger and prettier and leave him.

He had no idea how much Matt loved him.

Neither one of them could really see.

Their hotel room was actually a suite on one of the upper floors of their hotel. One wall was all glass and faced the sea. Once we were inside, Matt took a shower to wash the oil and sweat off. Chris poured himself a gin and tonic and me a water. He walked over to the glass and stared out at the sea.

"You think he's going to leave you."

He turned back to me, and I could see the pain in his eyes. He shrugged. "He's young and he's beautiful. I'm getting old. You do the math."

As though 40 was the end.

"You think he loves you as little as that?"

The sound of the shower stopped. He smiled at me. "My turn."

Matt came out, wearing a large white towel wrapped around his waist. Chris passed him without a word, without a touch. Matt looked after him and then at me. He smiled at me and shrugged. He walked over to where I was sitting in a wingback chair and pulled me to my feet. He touched my chest with one hand and his other came around the back, squeezing my ass. His erection loosened the towel, and it fell off. His cock was long, hard, and thick, springing out from a small patch of trimmed black pubic hair. He slipped a hand into my bikini, fingers exploring the gully in the center. I reached down and slid it down and off of me. "Wow," he said, looking down momentarily.

"Let's wait for Chris."

He nodded and pulled me over to the bed. We climbed on top of it, side by side, and started kissing. He was a wonderful kisser. Our tongues explored the inside of each other's mouths. I was getting aroused—how could I not? I wanted to feel that big thick cock inside of me. I heard the shower turn off and we kept kissing, softly, gently. Out of the corner of my eye I saw Chris walk back into the room, naked, toweling off his back. He looked at us, his eyes somewhat downcast, and sat down in the wingback chair I had vacated.

I pulled my head away from the kissing and looked at Chris. His eyes were full of pain. I could see it. *Is Sandy the one,* he was asking himself, *the elusive one out there Matt will leave me for?*

Such amazing stupidity.

I held out my hand toward him, and beckoned him to join us.

He smiled almost gratefully and walked over to the bed. He took my hand and climbed up with us, his own cock springing to life. He was almost as big as Matt, but where Matt's had a huge head and stayed thick all the way down, Chris's cock had a small head at the top, growing thicker and longer as it reached back into his magnificent body. He brought his head down to my right nipple and began teasing it with his tongue.

My body immediately responded, a moan escaping my lips and my back arching slightly. When Matt saw what stimulated this response, he lowered his head to my left nipple and began doing the same.

My entire body went rigid, my breath coming in gasps.

I reached down with both hands, taking a thick cock in each hand, and began to massage them, my hands moving up and down.

Moans escaped each of them.

Their mouths then began exploring my body, lips and tongues moving down and about my torso.

Chris reached into a bag and pulled out a bottle of lube. He squirted some onto his cock, then onto Matt's, then onto mine. I continued rubbing their cocks, only now my hands were more slippery, gliding along the skin, sliding over the heads.

"I want to fuck you," Matt whispered.

I looked up at Chris. Lust blazed in his eyes, and he nodded. I turned myself over onto my stomach, arching my back, lifting my ass up into the air. Matt moved down behind me. Chris opened a condom and handed it to Matt. Chris positioned himself in front of me, my head between his legs. That big tapering cock was right in front of me. He wiped the lube off with a towel. I felt exploratory fingers probing me. I shuddered. I flicked my tongue over the head of Chris's beautiful cock.

I gasped and flinched as Matt moved inside of me.

"Slow down, honey," Chris said. To me he whispered, "He forgets how big he is."

I smiled up at him, and then began licking his cock again. Chris moaned as Matt began to slide gently inside of me. I opened up for him, relaxing the necessary muscles so that he could get there.

He needed to be completely inside of me for this to work.

I moaned as I felt his cock slide all the way in.

But before I could do what I needed to do, he slid back out.

I took Chris into my mouth, swirling my tongue around. I took him down, opening my throat, tilting my head back slightly to open the passage. I reached the root and stayed there, waiting, waiting, waiting...

Matt slammed into me from behind.

I opened the portal in my mind.

No matter how many times I have done this, I am never prepared for it, and there certainly is no way to prepare them for it.

The purity of their love for each other flowed through my body, Matt's emotion passing through my mouth into Chris's body, Chris's passing through the other side.

All three of our bodies went completely rigid, every muscle tightening up.

"Oh, my God," Chris breathed.

My body was trembling as the love passed through. Visions of the two of them together—fucking each other, loving each other— flashed through my brain like a kaleidoscope. As did their fears, their doubts, and their insecurities. I focused on stopping them from passing through. That wasn't the idea. But it was so difficult—the love was so pure, so powerful, so strong. Wave after wave of pleasure was passing through me, pleasure from the big cock in my ass, the big cock in my mouth. But I had to focus, I had to take the bad away from the two of them, I couldn't fail them. I focused on grabbing the impure with my mind: I visualized a suitcase and started shoving those bad emotions into the suitcase. When there were none left—when all that was passing through was purity—I shut the suitcase and closed the portal.

Both Chris and Matt were shuddering.

I pulled my head back from Chris in time, as he released a stream of come into my face and hair.

Matt's entire body erupted, convulsed, as his orgasm exploded into the condom.

My own pumped out into the sheets.

Matt withdrew from me, and collapsed onto the bed beside me.

I sat up, my chest and stomach covered with my own orgasm.

Chris slid down onto the bed and smiled. "My God."

I stood up. "Mind if I shower?"

They both shook their heads no.

The water was hot as I scrubbed my skin clean, washing come out of my hair, off my face, off my chest. I dried myself and walked back into the bedroom, picking up my bikini off the floor, sliding it up my legs, tucking myself back into it.

Matt and Chris were in each other's arms, kissing gently, staring into each other's eyes.

When I reached the door, Chris said, "You don't have to leave."

I turned back to them. "No, I think I do."

"Will we see you again?" Matt asked.

I smiled at them—one dark, one light. So beautiful together. "Perhaps." I shut the door behind me.

The sand was hot on my feet as I walked back down to the water's edge. My skin was getting dry. I turned and looked back at the hotel, finding their windows. I raised my hand in a salute, although I doubted they were watching. I walked into the water, the warm, welcoming green water of the gulf. When I reached waist level, I started to swim. At the line where the water turns blue, I dived to the bottom. No need for the crowd of sunbathers to see what was going to happen. I thrust through the water, and felt the gills starting to open again on the side of my throat. My legs came together, the skin meeting in the center and starting to knit. I pointed my toes and the fin began to form.

I swam out to sea.

Special Delivery

Jay Starre

Kenny shoved his cock deep past Brad's lubed ass lips. The tall blond's lean arms tensed as he clamped his hands over Brad's shoulders, holding him in place over the arm of the living room couch as he fucked him with deep rhythmic strokes.

"Sweet ass," Kenny murmured, reveling in the feel of Brad's lush, hairless ass cheeks against his thighs.

"Nice big cock, Kenny. It feels like magic up there. Shove it deeper," Brad gasped lewdly.

Brad was a stocky soccer jock, while Kenny was a tall basketball player. Both were graduate students at the local university and had bumped into each other outside class that morning. After they met each other's eyes and then exchanged smiles, it was the bolder Kenny who'd asked Brad to come to his place for that afternoon fuck.

Stripping as soon as they passed the front door, the two jocks were all over each other. They quickly calculated each other's most pressing needs with a few murmured questions. Soon enough the sandy-haired Brad was bent over the side of the couch with first Kenny's well-lubed fingers up his asshole, then Kenny's fat poker ramming into the stretched hole.

Brad was feeling that big meat inside him. He grunted and hissed, and when the head of Kenny's bone hit hard against his prostate, he shouted out loud, "Yeah, fuck my ass!"

Kenny laughed as he obliged the stocky stud by shoving his hips into Brad's ass and slamming his cock all the way to the balls.

Just then the doorbell rang. Brad seemed not to have even heard it, writhing around a fat beer-can cock stretching his fuck tunnel nicely. Kenny was tempted to ignore it too, then suddenly recalled the delivery he was expecting.

"Just a minute, Brad. I've got a package coming. Don't move! I'll be back for more of that ass in a minute or two." Kenny said as he slipped his lubed cock from Brad's warm asshole.

Kenny grabbed his discarded shorts and quickly pulled them on over his hard cock. Brad was laughing as he told Kenny to hurry back.

"This wet slot is waiting for your big boner," Brad leered.

Kenny glanced back at Brad and had to laugh too. Brad had one of his thighs up on the arm of the couch and was digging a pair of fingers into his own slippery asshole, a raunchy grin on his face.

Kenny turned away toward the door but then on his way noticed the living room window was wide open due to the summer heat. Whoever was at the door had to have passed directly under that open window a moment earlier. They would have heard Brad shout, "Fuck my ass!"

Kenny was wondering how the delivery worker was dealing with that when he opened the door and found himself facing a smiling stud. Thick black hair framed a handsome face. The dude was of medium height, with bare arms that were packed with muscle. He wore khaki uniform shorts that revealed hairy, powerful calves and thighs. Kenny immediately noticed the huge swell in the guy's crotch. The dude had a boner!

"Special delivery for Kenny Star."

The voice was even, but the smile was bold. Kenny was dumbfounded for a moment, then smiled back as took the package and clipboard to sign with a sweaty hand. He was acutely aware of the deliveryman's eyes on him, and conscious of his own half-naked body and sweaty fuck stench. As he finished signing, he looked up to see the stud still grinning, and one of his hands on his crotch massaging that big lump there.

Kenny had to ask, "Do you have another package for me, maybe?"

The dark-haired stud laughed out loud. He hadn't missed the innuendo. But then his sparkling amber eyes veered to the right, obviously looking at something as he replied.

"If you need a real special delivery, I might be able to oblige. But it's hot out here. Should I maybe come in?"

Kenny glanced over to where the deliveryman's eyes were riveted. Kenny's mouth dropped open as he realized what the dude was staring at. In the wall mirror, Brad's naked butt was spread-eagled over the couch in the living room, and Brad was still exploring his own asshole with a pair of eager fingers.

Kenny burst out in startled laughter, but then turned back to the newcomer and grabbed his arm. He was dragging the handsome dude inside and still laughing.

"I'm John, and I wouldn't mind a crack at that sweet butt," the delivery dude chuckled. He was stripping off his uniform as soon as the door shut behind him.

Kenny nodded with a grin and then called out to Brad as they came into the living room. "The package is for you. And looks like it's a big one."

John had shed his shirt and shorts and was now wearing only his shoes and underwear. The white skivvies clung to a jutting pole that looked to be a good 10 inches in length. He was staring at Brad's naked body with raw lust and smiling while licking his big lips.

Brad's eyes had been closed—he was intent on exploring the depths of his asshole as he recalled the fat cock that had just been reaming it out. His eyes snapped open just in time to see the good-looking hunk approaching beside Kenny. The dark-haired dude was tearing off his underwear as he came forward, revealing a drooling purple fuck-stick.

Brad flushed with momentary embarrassment, his fingers up his butt and his crack wide open with one knee up on the couch. But then Kenny reached him and dug a pair of his fingers up into Brad's slick asshole. Brad gasped at the invasion, pulling out his own fingers and immediately arching his back and leaning forward with a moaning sigh. He was all asshole for the time being, hot and ready to get fucked. Another cock riding his butt sounded only more exciting.

"Go for it! Fuck me with both those cocks!"

Brad's slutty response had John so excited he lunged forward to cram his hand into that slippery ass crack beside Kenny's. Their eyes met as they began to take turns digging fingers into Brad's stretched hole. The feel of that slippery ass heat had them both shaking.

"Who's first?" John grinned in Kenny's face.

"Put yours in for a minute, then I'll take a turn."

"Sounds hot," John replied in a shaky voice.

The delivery dude moved in behind Brad and shoved his lengthy pole up against the soccer player's butt hole. Kenny pulled out his fingers just as John lunged upward with his cock.

"How's that feel? Nice and hot?" Kenny whispered in John's ear.

"Sweet! Wet and wide open for a big cock," John answered as he drove deep.

Brad cried out. "Uhhngg...oh, yeah...shove it way up there!" Brad had both hands on his own ass, pulling it open for John's long cock as he grunted around it. Brad leaned farther over the couch in an effort to take all that meat riding up his asshole.

John leaned forward too, enough to clamp his lush lips over Kenny's and suck the blond's tongue into his mouth. Then he lunged upward with his cock, burying all 10 inches up Brad's fluttering asshole. All three men grunted simultaneously. John sucked Kenny's tongue and rammed his cock in and out of Brad's lubed hole. Brad groaned encouragement as he lay his head on the couch and pulled his knee up against his chest to completely open up his steaming asshole to the length of John's pummeling meat.

Kenny had his fingers around John's driving cock, feeling the slick rod riding in and out of Brad's asshole. The pole was hard as rock. Kenny stabbed his tongue into John's mouth for a hot moment or two, then pulled away to gasp out loud.

"I gotta take a turn! Let me shove my cock up that asshole!"

John grinned and nodded. His face was beaded with sweat already, and his naked chest heaved with excitement. He pulled his cock from Brad's asshole and moved to the side. Kenny immediately moved in and rammed his cock balls deep into Brad's upended butt. The fat meat stretched Brad wide open, and he screamed out his pleasure.

"Give me all that fat cock! Fuck my wet hole!"

Kenny slammed deep then pulled all the way out. Both men stared down at Brad's pulsing asshole. The lips were swollen and pouted outward. Lube dribbled from the quivering rim. Their eyes met again, and they nodded in understanding. Kenny placed his fingers on either side of the gaping hole and pulled it apart. John moved in and shoved his long shaft between the trembling lips.

"Oh, my God! Fuck my asshole!" Brad shouted.

John thrust into the steamy hole a few times and then pulled out. The slot drooled and twitched. Kenny immediately moved in to slam his fat meat up the distended asshole. Brad shouted out again while John and Kenny shared a lewd smirk.

"The college jock is quite a hole, isn't he?" Kenny laughed in John's face.

"That's for sure. He's a bottomless pit," John answered in a gasp.

"Fuck me hard! I want your dicks inside me," Brad put in, his face on the cushions of the couch, his tongue lolling from wet lips.

"We'll do that, you little pussy," Kenny laughed as he slapped one of Brad's plump butt cheeks for good measure.

"I wonder if he can take both our cocks at once?" John grinned at Kenny as he pulled out his bone and let the tall blond take over.

Kenny was sliding his fat shaft up Brad's asshole at the time. His eyes glittered at the raunchy suggestion. For a moment he contemplated how to go about it, then he smiled and nodded.

"Let's have him sit on yours and then I'll come in from behind."

They both guffawed at the exciting proposition while Brad moaned and begged for more cock up his hungry ass. He hadn't really heard them, and he was taken by surprise when both men gripped his body and lifted him off the couch.

The next moment he was standing over John's prone body. The naked delivery worker was on his back on the carpet and grinning up at Brad. John's body was about midway between taller Kenny's and stockier Brad's. His dark hair was in tousled disarray. His thick lips were wet with spittle. His arms and legs were muscular, and his chest swelled with power. John's long rod jutted up from his hips, slippery with lube and throbbing.

"Sit on that big cock," Kenny whispered in Brad's ear as he pushed down on Brad's shoulders.

Brad was shaking as he complied. He squatted over John's hairy hips and then took the shaft in hand and fed it to his own palpitating asshole. Brad let out a deep moan as he sat down on the stiff poker, inhaling it with his asshole.

With a squishy slurp, Brad took the whole thing inside, moaning louder. Kenny immediately squatted down behind Brad on John's hairy thighs. In his hand he held a bottle of lube. As Brad began to fuck himself over John's 10-incher, moaning steadily, Kenny squirted a handful of lube over his fingers. He stared down at the juncture of cock and asshole, pulling apart Brad's lush, hairless butt cheeks to reveal the distended lips of Brad's hole. John's purple poker appeared and disappeared as Brad rode it with bucking pleasure.

Kenny grinned as he shoved a pair of fingers up against the stretched butt lips. He worked them around the slamming asshole before sliding one in beside John's cock.

"Oh! Oh, yeah! Open me up!" Brad gasped at the extra invasion.

Kenny planted a hand between Brad's shoulder blades and pushed him forward so that he was bent over John and his face was nearly on the carpet. Brad's ass opened up.

Kenny panted with excitement as he stared at that lush butt spread open. John's cock filled the drooling slot. Kenny had one finger up beside the pole and was working another lubed finger in beside it.

"Open up that fuck tunnel," Kenny growled.

Brad was shaking, his thighs wide apart and his ass full of cock and fingers. It was amazing. He suddenly felt his asshole gape open.

"Stick your cock up there! I can take it!"

Kenny felt Brad's hole yawn open. He scooted up and yanked

his fingers out just as he rammed his cock forward. The hole resisted a moment, then yielded. Kenny was feeding his fat meat into the quivering orifice!

"Oh, my God! My poor asshole! Fuck it. Stick your fat rod all the way up there!" Brad moaned as he slobbered all over the carpet.

John was sucking on Brad's nipple in his face. He could feel Kenny's fat meat slithering up beside his. Brad's steamy fuck hole was quivering and clamping over his cock. He sucked harder on the nipple in his mouth and groaned.

Kenny stared down at Brad's flushed butt cheeks as he fed inch after inch of his cock between the lubed butt rim. Brad was on his stomach, his big ass cheeks shaking and his asshole slowly yielding to the fat invader. Kenny groaned as his entire shaft disappeared up that fuck cavern.

"What a hole," Kenny muttered. As he began to fuck, his whole body grew hot and sweaty with crazed lust.

Brad shivered and panted. He flung his legs wide apart and his asshole felt stuffed to the limit. When Kenny began to ram in and out, Brad felt his lubed hole gape wide open. Brad surrendered to the total sensation of two cocks up his ass at the same time. His own cock lurched against John's flat belly as he felt the constant pressure against his prostate build up in his guts. As Kenny shoved cock up Brad's asshole with faster strokes, Brad's stretched butt lips burned with rising pleasure. His orgasm came like a sudden tidal wave, breaching his defenses and rocketing up his cock shaft and out the slit. Brad's sticky cream gushed all over John's belly.

Kenny felt the convulsing of Brad's asshole over his cock as Brad orgasmed. Kenny rammed to the balls and held his cock inside the quivering hole. The massaging lips pulled the jizz right out of his nuts.

"I'm shooting up your ass," he shouted.

John felt the two college jocks shaking and coming over him. He could feel Brad's asshole going wild over his own buried poker, and Kenny's scummy cock jerking and emptying beside his. Brad's sweaty body slithered over John's, spraying jizz on their bellies. John sucked on Brad's nipple fervidly as he bucked upward into Brad's quivering hole. Two quick thrusts were enough. He was coming too.

The moans and shouts slowly subsided as all three men's balls drained dry. Kenny was lying over Brad as he slid his cock from Brad's battered asshole. Brad moaned and rose up to relinquish John's slick rod.

The three lay together on the carpet in a tangle of sweaty limbs and come-coated cocks. It was John who finally spoke.

"I've got a few more deliveries to make today. But I'll come back later if you like—with another package."

They all laughed together, rolling around on the floor as Kenny and John groped Brad's mushy asshole for one last time. John left them like that, naked on the floor with Brad's rounded ass in the air and Kenny's fat cock rising up for a second time.

6 Inches of Separation

M. Christian

William Swartz was determinedly fucking Todd Brewster on the big, thick-legged table in the main room of the Men's Club. His thick cock slid in and out of Todd Brewster's greased asshole like the cylinder on some thunderous, powerful locomotive: chug, chug, chug, in, out, in, out.

Thick drops of grease plopped down onto the raw cement floor with every pull back, and a slithering, smacking, suction echoed through the tiled bathhouse with every thrust in.

William Swartz's body was doing the determined fucking, but his mind was back at the office: still burning, still blistered from Old Man McAllister's chewing him out. His boss's face—slack-jowls and eyes like thumbprints in fresh dough—hung in front of him. He wished he were hammering his iron dick into that saggy face. It wasn't his fault that the shipment of medium-size inlaid Japanese puzzle boxes was late. The rest were coming in, for chrissake— maybe not in time for the scheduled delivery to Pier 1, but it wasn't like they were going to lose them as clients or anything. Hell, they'd accepted partial orders before without bitching.

It was just like McAllister to notice that one fucking glitch in

Bill's otherwise well-run department and use it as an excuse to question his entire job performance. One little fucking problem and 12 years of good work out the fucking window.

It made him feel small, like a boy, to be treated like that. He didn't like that. Didn't like it at all. It had taken him 40 years of hard work to become a man, and a man he wanted to stay for the rest of his life.

He worked out to build up manly muscles, he fucked and didn't get fucked, he got sucked but never sucked, he ate steak, he never cried—even when he wanted to, when he ached to. Sure, he wanted to punch McAllister in the face, but he also wanted to take his boss's loose, flabby face in his hands, lift his head, and stare into his eyes. *Why can't I ever be good enough for you?* he wanted to ask. Crying, he wanted to say it.

William Swartz's orgasm came around his blind side, his rage and frustration like static on the channel of his fucking the slick, tight grip of Todd Brewster's asshole around his cock. When Bill came, it was a dull jolt of pleasure: more a thudding kick to his balls than a high-voltage scream of joy. Rather than screaming, he simply grunted out the thick stream of come into Brewster's ass. As he came he felt good, but he knew it could have felt even better—for a man like himself, though, that was as good as it was going to get.

Todd Brewster was getting energetically fucked by William Swartz on the big, thick-legged table in the main room of the Men's Club. As the stranger's dick plopped and slurped into his asshole, Todd sucked the cock of Steven Reineer. Todd was sucking exactly the way he loved to suck, as if his whole being was doing the sucking, not just lips and tongue, but rather a soul suck, a deep self suck. Sucking like this, Todd's mind faded, skipped somewhere close to a dream. Impressions and images danced through him as he worked Steven's big cock: half thoughts and wildly associated memories.

Standing on the street corner. Standing on the street corner near the Castro. Sunlight, like a big, warm hand cradling his face. A good day. A day of birdsong and smiles, of sweet words and held hands. A day for picnics—a day for barefoot walks through the grass.

A day to look at the world, to admire it: to see the everyday beauty that so often gets pushed aside in the rush from point A to point B.

A day to fall in love. Just like that—with the snap of fingers. Standing on the street corner, waiting for love to come, he saw the young man: tight jeans, black boots, tight white T-shirt. He fell in love. He fell immediately in love, absolutely in love. He wanted to kiss this young man. He wanted to hold his hand. He wanted to take barefoot walks with him. He wanted to suck his cock. He wanted to bake a cake for him.

But then his love turned, looked at Todd looking at him, and said, "What you looking at, faggot?" The young man made fists, moved toward Todd with intent. Todd had turned, run off—all the way down the street, away from the Castro, back to his apartment. His cold, dark little basement in the Mission.

Being fucked by William Swartz on the big, thick-legged table in the main room of the Men's Club, sucking Steven Reineer's dick, Todd just wanted someone to look at him, smile, and take his hand.

As Todd Brewster was being rhythmically fucked by William Swartz, Todd sucked the cock of Steven Reineer. Steven was into the suck, as deep and soulfully into a suck as a man could get, in fact. It was a great suck, a spiritual suck—more so for Steven than perhaps any other man in the main room of the Men's Club that night. It was a suck and a night he'd waited just about his whole life for.

He was getting his dick sucked in a room full of men getting their dicks sucked. The air smelled of sweat, come, and wet leather. Of steaming piss, the earthy musk of shit, the metal tang of poppers, the heavily sweet smell of pot, the vacation smell of hot rubber, and latex softening from the heat of friction. It even smelled of pennies and of spilled blood somewhere. It smelled the way he'd always hoped it would smell—a thousand olfactory surprises with every fresh, deep breath.

And the sights—the sights were images he'd take with him the rest of his life: getting sucked by an alabaster young man, who in turn was being determinedly, energetically, rhythmically fucked by a great hulking, muscular brute of a man—a flesh-and-bone fucking engine. In one corner, a bald boy—a punk with polished skin and too many silver rings in his ears to count—was kneeling and sucking an elegant, silver-haired black man. In the other corner, a couple were holding each other, an exhausted pietà—no marble, but shimmering sweat made them looked carved from smooth stone. There were others—too many to see except for quick glances, half-impressions: sections of a mosaic of a Saturday night at the baths. Put together all around him to make a beautiful, wonderful, picture.

"May I?" Toby Jillian said, reaching around from behind Steven Reineer, thumbs and forefingers rubbing inches in front of Steven's tight nipples.

"You may," Steven Reineer said to Toby Jillian. And so Toby Jillian started to play with Steven Reineer's nipples as he was cosmically sucked by Todd Brewster, who in turn was being determinedly, energetically, rhythmically fucked by William Swartz.

His life had brought him to this night and this place. Ever since Steven had first looked at a boy and hoped, by the looking and by the hard-on that prompted the thoughts and the looking, that these places would exist: places where men could be naked and hard together. A place of men and men's sex.

Getting older, doing more than just looking at other boys, he read, he asked, he looked and discovered that they did exist, these places where men, naked men, were hard together. With that confirmation his home of cornfields and tractors, of fertilizer and the seasons as gods became so much smaller.

It had taken him years of cornfields and tractors, of fertilizer and worshiping the gods of winter, summer, spring, and fall before he'd had enough to escape. Years before leaving it all behind to hitch a ride with a truck driver heading west—all the way west.

Years before coming with that one truck driver to this town, to this place, this night—the night when he could finally walk in and be a part of a room full of naked men, doing naked things together. That other place was where Steven Reineer had been born, where he went to school, where he kissed his first boy, but the instant he walked into the Men's Club, he knew that in this place, and doing these things, he was finally home.

Playing with Steven Reineer's nipples as Steven Reineer was being cosmically sucked by Todd Brewster, who in turn was being determinedly, energetically, rhythmically fucked by William Swartz, Toby Jillian smiled sweetly to himself. This was good, this was very good—this was just about as good as it could get. He was playing with a handsome little guy's nipples.

Not that he was gay or anything. He just liked nipples. Guy nipples. He really didn't know where it started. But it was there nonetheless: Some men cruised for tits, others for asses, still others for legs—but Toby looked for a good flat chest, a plane of tight muscles. Flat was too busty for him. He liked toughness, muscles and bones, not soft skin.

Not that he was gay—he just liked them firm, hard, tough, and strong. Women came close…sometimes, but it was never enough. And so Toby went out, hunting down the best nipples and chests he could. He went to places like the Men's Club, where he'd ask—politely, mind you—to touch, to fondle, to kiss, to lick, to nibble. Like tonight, standing behind Steven Reineer while he got sucked by Todd Brewster, who got fucked by William Swartz.

Nipples—any nipples—in his hands were great. Nipples like these, right then, were even better. Down there he felt his cock swell and strain against his briefs, tenting the fabric with his good time. It felt good, it felt damn good: The nipples between his thumb and forefinger were tight and hard, with just the right ring of fine hairs around the areolae. Twirling them, tugging at the nipples was like a cord, a rope between fingers and nipples and his hardening cock. Each pull, each tug, each caress of the rubbery flesh was like a stroke of his dick. The connection was base, primal, and powerful.

If he stopped to think about it, which he did only when his cock was full and hard and beaded with a pearl of liquid, salty, bitter excitement, he might be able to trace it out: beginning with today, then playing with Steven Reineer's tight, rubbery nipples. The feeling of warm sunlight on his bare shoulders. A Saturday kind of day—which is when it was—a summer Saturday when the only thing anyone, anywhere was supposed to do was go swimming. At the huge public swimming pool—old enough to have feelings, too young to know just what those feelings were—he watched the young lifeguard walk down the rough concrete edge of the pool.

The lifeguard's chest was a solid geometry of muscles, and there—aggressive, tempting, strong, and certain—were his nipples: the nipples to end all nipples, the nipples that were the start of his pursuit, the founders of his quest. But he really wasn't thinking about those two nipples on that hot Saturday summer day. No, he was too much into Steven Reineer's nipples and the thudding, hammering horniness they conjured up.

Despite himself, Toby groaned, deep and operatic, as his cock swelled and pushed away from him like an arrow pulled by the bow, straining to launch itself toward anything and anyone but more importantly in the direction of a wonderful, definitive, thudding orgasm.

Then something deep inside him, something coiled around his balls and snaking all the way up his spine into the dim parts of his hidden mind, let go of the bow. With a shake, a quake, a shudder, and a small scream he did, right then, in his shorts, come. It was good, so good, so damn good. Not that he was gay or anything.

Watching Toby Jillian play with Steven Reineer's nipples as Steven Reineer was being profoundly sucked by Todd Brewster, who in turn was being relentlessly screwed by William Swartz, Jack Sawtell had one, just one thought: *Here I go again.* He was in love.

To be honest, Jack fell in love quite easily. Checkout boys, cab drivers, salesmen, strangers on the street, inappropriate relatives, total strangers without even the barest of social contexts. Jack looked, and he fell fast and hard.

Standing just off to the side of the groaning, heaving, working, sweating, steaming tableau of queer bliss, he looked at Toby Jillian and felt himself fall down the long, slippery slope. Looking at Toby, he wanted to kiss him—for the two of them to touch lip to lip, dance tongues, breathe one another's breath. He wanted to touch him. He wanted to slide his hands down his taut chest and have the other man do the same to him, and he wanted to fuck him. Slide his cock deep, in and out, in and out, and he wanted to be fucked by him—to have him fuck his asshole until he cried and begged and screamed for him to stop but always hoped he wouldn't.

Jack was in love, and it felt good. He watched Toby Jillian play with Steven Reineer's nipples as Steven Reineer was being wonderfully sucked by Todd Brewster, who was being dynamically screwed by William Swartz. Jack felt the same way he always felt when he fell in love: All was right with the world and it would all work out well.

But then, as it always happened when Jack Sawtell fell in love, he woke up: He was in another bathhouse, watching other men have all the fun, while he stood there with his cock in his hand. As with every time he fell in love, he remembered the beauty and perfection of his first boyfriend, who had left him—a long time ago in a place far away. It had been more than good, it had been wonderful, but then it had ended. It wasn't the ending so much as the barbed words that were spoken—a curse that shadowed Jack Sawtell every day, because every day he fell in love.

Walking out, leaving, his boyfriend had turned and said, "Yeah, you might fall for someone else, but you'll always think of me because I'm your first."

Standing there, sadness lying heavily on him, wilting dick in his hand, Jack Sawtell watched Toby Jillian play with Steven Reineer's nipples as Steven Reineer was being glorious sucked by Todd Brewster, who in turn was being poundingly fucked by William Swartz. Jack felt the same way he always felt when he realized that no matter how much, how often, he fell in love, he'd always think of the beautiful bastard who walked away, saying those cruel words that still haunted him.

Peter Lowell stood by the door, watching Jack Sawtell look longingly at Toby Jillian playing with Steven Reineer's nipples as Steven Reineer was being miraculously sucked by Todd Brewster, who in turn was being beautifully fucked by William Swartz. Peter watched Jack. There was something beautiful in the way Jack

Sawtell stood there, watching Toby Jillian tweak Steven Reineer's nipples as Steven Reiner was in turn blown by Todd Brewster, who in turn was being fucked by William Swartz. In the whole room, in the whole of the Men's Club, there was nothing quite so lovely as that handsome young man standing there, entranced.

There was something about him. Something in the way he stood, in the exact way he watched the men suck, fuck, and all the rest. He was excited—his semihard cock was proof of that. And what a handsome cock! There was something else, though. Something lost, like a little boy who was the last to get picked for playing ball, like the kid who never got a valentine. He was standing right there in the room, but he also seemed to be miles away.

Looking at Jack Sawtell, Peter Lowell remembered another young man, standing lost and alone in a place like this one. He remembered the way he wanted to join in, wanted just to step up and become one with the group. But for some reason he felt lost and alone. Too much old baggage dragging him down, holding him in place.

He remembered how someone, completely out of the blue, had walked up to him, taken him by the hand, and brought him in—made him feel welcome. The memory was as fresh as yesterday morning: the heat but also the chill of standing outside of it all, the way the older man had walked up, put his rough hand on his, and said five brief words. After that Peter had been inside, part of it all.

He owed that older man a lot, a debt he was still repaying. Taking a slow, deep breath, he walked across the floor toward where Jack Sawtell gazed at Toby Jillian playing with Steven Reineer's nipples as Steven Reineer was being elegantly blown by Todd Brewster, who in turn was being brutally fucked by William Swartz.

He didn't know exactly what he'd say to the slightly sad young man, but he knew it would be very similar to what he'd been asked so long ago. If he was lucky, then they'd have a good time, and if they were very lucky, who knows where it could lead? Love, Peter Lowell, had discovered, is found in all kinds of places.

Into the rest of the night and into the very late morning they all played: Peter Lowell, Jack Sawtell, Toby Jillian, Steven Reineer,

Todd Brewster, William Swartz, and many others. Some of them had good times, some of them had great times, some of them had OK times, some of them had bad times—as many times as there were men in the club that night.

In more than one way they were connected. With cock, mouth, hand, asshole, fist, and all the rest to be sure, but in other ways as well: a structure of happenstance and coincidence, luck and synchronicity. A web as complex as the men themselves.

The older man who had helped Peter Lowell become part of the party rather than just a spectator was the same lover who had hurt Jack Sawtell so long ago. He'd also been a lifeguard back in the small town where Toby Jillian had grown up, who'd given Steven Reineer a ride to the big city, who'd made a clumsy pass at the little skinhead creep who'd insulted Todd Brewster, and who'd been late making William Swartz's delivery.

Six men in that club that night, joined in bliss in many ways, and as men through one other.

The Downward Spiral

Simon Sheppard

Call me Jeremy. It's not my real name, but I like it. A few years back I was working at the mall, keeping the burbs well-supplied with CDs and videos. And I was just coming to accept that I was less turned on by Madonna than by whatever hunk she was currently fucking.

It must have been around the time R.E.M. did "Losing My Religion." I loved that video. It was January, time for the annual clearance sale, really busy at the store. I was going crazy. Thank God it was nearing the end of the day.

This dude came up to the counter with a handful of CDs: Nine Inch Nails, Nick Cave, stuff like that. Bleached blond, dorky black glasses, lots of earrings, and a shiny stud right through his lower lip. Really, really cute. And let's face it, I was really horny and had been for weeks. There's just so much fun you can have downloading dirty pictures from the Web.

I rang up the dude's purchase, and he dropped a Platinum American Express Card on the counter. Not the kind of card you'd expect a Nine Inch Nails fan to be carrying, not one whose T-shirt read DIE YUPPIE SCUM. He must have caught my glance. "It's my parents' account," he explained.

After I'd bagged his CDs, I looked straight into his four eyes and asked, "Anything else I can do for you?"

"What? You a fag?" he asked.

I was speechless. As a stupid blush hit my cheeks, the boy turned and clomped out of the store in his Docs.

I'd been clocked—was I really that fucking obvious? My heart was racing a mile a minute. I was sure my blush was so bright you could see it all the way from the Athlete's Foot to Hickory Farms. I had to get out of the store and calm down.

"Listen," I said to my coworker Alara, a poser with a nose ring and blue hair, "I gotta pee real bad. Cover for me, OK?"

"Now? Look at that line. Can't you..." But before she could finish whining her objections, I'd booked. The bathroom was a little ways off, just past the food court. As I turned the corner by Toys R Us, I noticed the bleached-blond guy there, kind of hanging around the Piercing Hut. Whatever on him hadn't been pierced yet, I was sure it was beyond the scope of the Piercing Hut.

The damn mall was so crowded that there was even a line at the men's room, so it's lucky I wasn't really in need of a piss. One of the three urinals was taped over with duct tape and an OUT OF ORDER sign. A fat guy in a Tommy Hilfiger jacket flushed and cleared out and I stepped right up, next urinal over from a father holding his little boy up to take a wee-wee. I was still so upset that I was pee shy. Little Johnny finished his business and Daddy helped him zip up. I was about to give up when the bleached-blond homophobe stepped up next to me.

"Awesome dick, dude," he said.

Was he kidding? If I reacted positively, would he take a swing at me? I looked at his face. A smile split his goatee, and it seemed for real. My piece began to swell. I looked down. He was stroking a big fat dick with a silvery ring though its head. A snake tattoo curled around his forearm.

"My parents are out of town," he said. "What time do you get off?"

"Huh?" I said, all buzzed with lust.

"What time do you get off work?"

"Seven." We were standing there side by side in a crowded men's room at the mall. With hard-ons. I couldn't fucking believe it.

"I'll come pick you up at the store." He stuffed his half-hard dick inside his shorts, flushed, and split, leaving me there with a hard-on and a stupid grin.

For the rest of my shift, I was so preoccupied with the prospect of finally getting laid that not even Alara's mega-attitude got me down.

Time crawled by while I drowned in a sea of cut-price CDs and videos. I figured that chances were good the guy wouldn't show up. But when 7 o'clock finally rolled around, I looked out the window and there he was, kind of leaning up against a bench. I cashed out as quickly as I could and hurried out the door before Alara could complain or the boss could stop me.

As we made our way to the parking lot, he told me his name was Kevyn, with a *y*. We got into his parents' shiny green Land Rover and drove through the perfectly boring flatness of central Florida.

"You know," I made myself say, "this is the first time I've ever been with a guy."

"Really?" Kevyn-with-a-y asked. "How old are you?"

"Twenty-three, but I'm a slow starter. How old are you?"

"Eighteen."

I was surprised; I'd figured he was older. "You sure?" I asked.

"Don't worry. I'm legal," he grinned.

His family had a nice house, and Kevyn had a nice room in it, with an expensive stereo setup, a drum kit in one corner, and posters of Primus and Trent Reznor on the walls.

"So what do we do now?" I said, trying not to look at the unmade bed.

Kevyn replied, "We take off our clothes and fuck."

I felt a little shy about stripping down. Actually, I stood awkwardly, still in my briefs, until Kevyn pulled down my underwear. My naked dick stood straight out. So did Kevyn's. In fact, our cocks looked a lot alike, except for the silvery ring through his.

"You're nervous," he said. "Do you wanna smoke some dope?"

"Uh, no thanks," I said. Things were confusing enough.

"OK," Kevyn said. "I'll put on some music."

He went over to the stereo and tore open the wrapping of *The Downward Spiral,* the Nine Inch Nails album he'd just bought. The opening chords rang out like a buzz saw; it wouldn't have been my choice for the soundtrack to a first date.

Kevyn stood right in front of me, and our dicks touched in a little slam dance. With a weird smile, he pushed me, and I fell backward onto his bed. He threw himself on top of me. The shock of our naked bodies touching made me want to shout. He slithered himself down between my legs until his head was in my crotch. He looked up at me, opened his mouth wide, and stuck his tongue out, and that was pierced too. With a move like a lizard catching a fly, he darted for my cock and gulped it down. The music throbbed on.

Jacking off had never felt as good as Kevyn's mouth did. He used the stud through his tongue to play with the underside of my shaft, then gulped my whole cock into his wet, wet mouth. It was fucking amazing, and it felt sweet.

I started bucking upward in time with the music, instinctively plowing his throat. Shit, if this what gay sex was like, I wanted more. I looked down at the top of his head, blond with black roots, and wanted to reached down and grab his ears, shove my cock ever deeper into his mouth. But I was new to this, so I wasn't sure whether that would be the right thing to do.

Little by little, he pulled his mouth off my cock, sucking at every millimeter. "Nice meat," he said. That was all. Then he reached down for my ankles and pushed up at my legs until they were up the air, my ass wide open. He wasn't going to screw me, was he? Jesus, I'd only been having queer sex for five minutes—I wasn't ready.

But he didn't screw me. He buried his head between my thighs and started licking at my ass while Trent Reznor sang about fucking like an animal and getting closer to God. I'd heard about the rimming thing, but I never imagined it would happen to me. Unbelievable. Some stranger with a pierced tongue was eating my butt, and it felt fucking great. The tip of his tongue pressed at my hole, working its wet way up inside me. How could he do something like that? Whatever the answer might have been, I wanted him never, ever to stop. Nothing could ever have prepared me for the sensation of being rimmed, nothing.

He used his hands to spread my cheeks apart, grinding his tongue even deeper into me. Nine Inch Nails was still pounding away, and I was finally getting laid. Then Kevyn started pushing his fingertips inside me, and I started to freak.

He pulled his mouth away from my ass. "Just relax," he said. "It won't hurt."

But it did hurt, his finger going into my ass did hurt, and it felt funny. But he didn't stop, and it stopped hurting, and then he touched something inside me, and it felt just fine.

"Is this safe?" I managed to ask above the music.

"Don't fucking worry," Kevyn said. So I didn't worry.

I didn't worry as Kevyn reached into his bedside table and pulled out a condom. I didn't worry as he unrolled the rubber over his stiff, pierced boner. It wasn't till the head of his cock was pressing against my hole that I began to worry. Would it hurt too much? Was it going to get messy? "I don't know how clean I am in there," I blurted out.

"Shut up," Kevyn growled. "Just shut fucking up." Suddenly, he was less reassuring than scary, and I discovered I liked being scared.

And then he was inside me, the first cock inside me ever, and it felt a little weird but mostly good, better than his finger had, and I closed my eyes and just let him pound away into me, as hard and overwhelming as Nine Inch Nails. The guy had wanted to fuck me, actually wanted to fuck me, and I'd let him and he was inside me, his dick was inside me. Like an animal.

"Yeah, fuck, take me, you fuck. Fuck my fucking ass." Where had *that* come from? Having his cock inside me had started to hurt a little, but I didn't care. I gritted my teeth, and I wanted him to screw me even harder. And then I couldn't help it. I reached down for my cock, started pulling at it, and I was ready to come—so ready that I went quickly over the brink, like a car crash on a mountain road. Suddenly I was shooting, spraying come all over my belly and chest. One gob even hit me in the eye. It stung. I was afraid that maybe Kevyn would be angry, since I hadn't waited for him to come, I'd just gone right ahead like some selfish punk. But Kevyn was smiling.

"Dude, that was one nice load," Kevyn said, sliding his hard dick out of my retightening ass and peeling off the rubber. I snuck a look; it wasn't even dirty, just shiny. "Now you want to try sucking *my* cock?"

"Uh…" I said like a stoned dunce, "I don't think so, thanks. Not this time."

"OK. Whatever," Kevyn-with-a-y said. He rose and, standing between my outstretched legs, stroked on his pierced dick until it pumped out a big load of come, squirt after squirt landing on my already spew-covered bod.

I was blown away and exhausted, still catching my breath. Kevyn walked off into his bathroom and returned with a damp towel. He tossed the towel at me and started gathering up his clothes. I wanted to hug him, maybe spend the night with him, maybe even kiss him. But he said, "I'll drive you back to your car. Get dressed, OK? My parents should be home soon."

"I thought they were away for the night."

"Get dressed," he repeated. The music had stopped.

Back at the mall, I got into my old Toyota and drove home. My roommate was still awake, but I wordlessly went to my room, where I lay awake in bed for hours until I finally drifted off to sleep. And the next morning when I awoke, I could still hear the throb of Nine Inch Nails in my no-longer-virgin brain.

I thought of getting Kevyn's phone number from his credit card slip, but I never did. I thought of driving to his house, but I never did. I thought about having sex with somebody else, but I never did that either. I guess I was kind of pathetic.

I didn't see Kevyn again for months, till finally he came back into the store just before Easter. He smiled at me and nodded, that was all, and tossed his platinum card on the counter. He bought a CD of Nine Inch Nails remixes, said "Thanks," and split. But at the door, he stopped, looked back over his shoulder and smiled at me. He stuck his tongue out and waggled it, the little silver tongue-stud winking a secret wink. And then he was gone.

It only took a second to decide. I'm not sure I even thought about it at all. I walked out from behind the counter and followed him out the door. The burbs would just have to get their fucking music without my help.

Tail Spin

J. D. Roman

The lovers fish him out of the frigid sea. The drowned man is as heavy and stiff as a granite statue. The two men hoist him onto the deck. Their hands go numb from holding his frozen body. They lay him down carefully, afraid he'll shatter like an ice sculpture.

Dewey kneels and listens at his mouth. "He's breathing."

"Too bad. No mouth to mouth." Eddie wisecracks because he's relieved—he's not sure they know how to rescue a human ice cube.

Dewey surveys their larger-than-life catch. The drowned man's skin is blue-tinged. His frost-covered hair and beard twinkle in the sunset, as if he wears the constellations in his shaggy black locks. He trails seaweed, his body festooned with slimy ribbons. Slick algae coats his fingernails.

"Jesus, there's nothing around for miles. How'd he get here?" Eddie scans the bobbing, dusk-blue horizon in all directions. The ocean is calm, and the boat rocks gently under his feet.

"Dunno. Shipwreck, I guess."

"Shipwrecks take storms." Eddie jams his fists in his parka. "Hasn't been wind or a cloud in days."

Dewey knows this. They have drifted in the doldrums, unconcerned, their lovemaking as slow and languorous as the unhurried, directionless tide. Below deck, they generate their own heat. Their bodies slap together like the gentle smacks of the waves on the hull,

270

a dull knocking that startles them in the absolute quiet. Dewey mistakes the low creaking of swollen timbers for a voice. Eddie berates him as he goes above to put his lover's mind at rest,but adores him for the fertile imagination that nourishes bedroom fantasy. Good thing Eddie humors him, or else he would never have spied this shipwrecked soul floating past the *Poseidon II.*

A fresh breeze now teases Dewey's coat and the lashed sails. "He's a crusty old salt, that's for sure. Looks like he could steer a pirate ship through a hurricane."

"Yeah, Christ, what a getup. Like someone needs to tell him it's a new century."

"Come on, fashion queen, better dry him off."

They strip him. The ill-fitting outfit falls apart in their hands.

They stand and gawk, their mortal minds struggling to explain a creature this magnificent. The man is chiseled marble, fallen off his pedestal. He is a temple shrine. He has risen from an ancient, treasure-laden shipwreck, a divinity that sank on his travels to another continent. Humans have been sacrificed at his ivory feet. This dredged cargo should not be prone before them. They should be prostrate before him in lustful homage, a pair of supplicants beseeching fulfillment of their desires. But they are not God-fearing. They worship the male body, and they have hooked this icon of their religion. He is not a primeval carving but frozen flesh. Alive.

His cock is as stiff, blue, and impressive as the rest of him. They stare, touching hands. Eddie whistles low. "Jesus. We found the fucking *Titanic.*"

"You'd think it'd shrivel in the cold," Dewey whispers in reverent awe.

"It's bigger than our damn anchor."

"Just don't bump it. It might chip off. Like those castrated statues."

"Some memento of our trip that would be. Maybe they could surgically attach it to me." Eddie's dick is big enough to feature heavily in local mythology as well as a few porn flicks, but he feels puny in comparison to this mighty godhead. "It's frozen. It'll stay preserved, right?"

Dewey shakes his head, snaps out of this idolatrous stupor. "Let's get him inside."

They towel him down, Eddie taking great care to dry the man's awesome cock. Scales cover the towel. Eddie grimaces. "Yuck. What's that stuff?"

"Must have been in an oil slick when his boat went down."

"Smells funny, that's for damn sure."

"There something strange about all this. I'm not sure I like it."

"You and your superstitions. What's there not to like about snagging a nuclear submarine? Our friends'll never believe us." Eddie stretches his arms wide. "It was *this* big."

They lift the rescued colossus. He is a slick totem pole and slips in their grip. His rigid body will not bend. They wedge him into the cabin, like sliding a frozen pizza into an oven.

They lay him on the V-berth. The head of the bed is a mere point at the prow of the ship, but the bed widens as the ship does, so that the foot of the bed is expansive. The boat is small, but the mattress is big. Recreation is limited at open sea, and the lovers don't want their style cramped. They sail for privacy. They rock and cry out with abandon. They don't yet know what their wails have summoned.

The man's arms cross over his chest; he is a stern, disapproving deity. His forearms lift his pecs, and his fingers brush opposite, alert, inky nipples. He seems to be offering his breasts. Eddie appraises him. "Man, he's got big titties."

"He's got big everything."

"Yeah, but he spends more time on his upper body."

Dewey agrees that the man's legs do look underdeveloped in comparison. His hips are slender, but his upper body is massive, with slabbed abs and mammoth biceps.

They jump back, startled, and embrace. He is thawing. His expression relaxes into contentment. The blue cast of his skin fades. His skin is milky, his thighs creamy white. "How come he's not tan?" Dewey asks.

Eddie ignores him. "Come on. He needs our body heat."

Dewey rolls his eyes. "Aren't you suddenly the practical one." But he doesn't argue.

Simultaneously, they strip and climb onto the bed, one on either side of him, pressed up tight. They spear his thighs with their aroused worship. Against their sun-dark bodies, his skin is snowy, white-white from top to bottom, no tan lines. His long hair dries into wiry curls, resembling his thatch of seaweedy pubic hair and full beard. His black eyelashes lie dark and long against his alabaster cheeks. Like a wax figure, the rest of his body is smooth.

They roll him onto his side. Eddie is immediately at his tits, gulping them in. He drinks nectar, mead, the golden waterfalls of Olympus. His body crooks around the thrust of that godly cock.

In back, without thinking, Dewey raises the titan's marble cheek. His hand is a magnet compelled by an exotic force. Normally hypercautious, he doesn't pause to consider protection. He maneuvers his cock, then yelps. He has plunged his dick into a bucket of ice water. And something else. He glimpses centuries of stored-up pleasure. But he's gone soft from the frigid shock. He cannot penetrate this glacial soul. He whimpers a small noise of frustration.

Eddie releases the man's breast, feeling drugged. He is surprised at the boldness of his lover, the wallflower he has to peel onto the dance floor and into back rooms. His eyes meet Dewey's over the man's shoulder. The morality of what they are doing is slippery. This could be called a dirty word, a crime. But something drives them, pounding at them with the insistence of centaur hooves, beating with the drums of an ancient race. They know the man wants it, even in his unconsciousness. He emits a beckoning aura, pulsing. He sweeps across their senses like a lighthouse beacon, leaving them intermittently blinded. He lures them even in glassy stillness.

"Let me." They switch places, climbing over the bewitching body, caressing each other as they pass. Eddie aims his cock into this live flotsam, grimacing as frozen tongues lap at his dick. As slick inside as it is outside, the body closes around him. Eddie bucks, frantic—it will freeze shut, lock his cock in its shark jaws, abutting icebergs grinding him into pulp.

But then Eddie moans. He's never felt anything like this, though he's slept with half the nearest continent. This cavity undulates, murmurs, ripples with waves of seaweed in a current. A swarm of jellyfish pulses, gelatinous, against him. Silken eels weave melodies around his cock. Eddie rides a seahorse through a watery realm. He digs in with his heels, bruising ivory flesh.

In front, the noises of his partner warm Dewey's arousal. He takes that supernatural cock into his mouth whole. The slippery cock creeps down his throat, leaking sea foam and whitecaps. It thrums and hums inside him. Dewey takes in this trident of cock and balls. Color shoots behind his eyes. He drifts in an underwater cavern. Vivid-hued coral dissolves in his mouth. He buries his nose in seaweed. He pumps through the ocean depths, swimming down, the cock is down, farther down his throat, in his lungs, in his intestines, raping his asshole from the inside out. Dewey swallows the tides. He feeds on godly ambrosia. He nurses octopus ink. It stains his insides so that every nerve and synapse and bone and shred of tissue glows through his skin. He will light up from the inside and explode.

The lovers both explode, simultaneously. They swim in their own slippery juices.

The titan's body relaxes. He is pliant. He fits into Eddie's curve behind him. His plywood plank–resistance eases. His body's frozen clutch thaws, releases Eddie's cock from inside him. Dewey eases his mouth off that divine cock, gulps in air.

This singular part of him, a Corinthian column—its base nestled in curlicues of wiry hair—remains an ice statue, stubborn in its thrust. The man makes a gurgling noise of agitation. He presses back against the one, presses forward against the other, an undulating fish movement on the bed, a flap of demand and desire.

The lovers need him again. They can't explain themselves, can't rationalize their actions. They can only obey a siren call that beats at them with the insistence of whales slamming their bodies against the ocean surface. They surge with a tide. They are caught in a flood. They have rammed up against the dam of this creature's body. They don't yet know whether this temptation will be their salvation or destruction.

They trade places. Dewey, now behind the man, opens him, eases in cautiously, remembering the biting frost of that ass. No frigid jolt this time, only water lilies blooming across his buried cock. Phosphorescent plankton torture him with invisible, whispered caresses. Bubbles burble secrets along his shaft. Passing phantasmal fish torment him with transparent fins. Dewey gasps, takes in a mouthful of the man's kelp-forest hair, and moans. He rolls onto his back, pulling this sleeping lover on top of him, still embedded in this dreamscape grotto.

Eddie props the joined pair up against pillows so they are half-reclined, both facing him, though Dewey is mostly hidden behind the big man. Eddie straddles them, legs stretched wide, and lowers himself onto the sovereign cock that coaxes, commands, compels. He is frightened. He understands this union will bless him with pain. It is a pillar that holds up the roof of the world. He cannot possibly encompass it. But he cannot resist its pull. It guides his open body, harpoons him, and climbs up inside him. Once connected, Eddie cannot pull back. The man's pubic hair ententacles him, and he must sink down, down. Eddie yells, his arms spread wide. The cock is a steel rod through his body, holding him up straight. He is a trembling building in an earthquake, and this cock girds him up.

And the man is moving now, though not awake. He is a swimming fish, his body fluid movement as he pushes through water. A continual reversing *S,* he swims through them, steers them. They cling to him, one cleaving him, one cleaved by him. He is so far inside Eddie's body on top of him that his cock is Eddie's tongue. His hips are forward, now back. Each pulse of his body shoots pleasure through all three. They surf cresting tidal waves. They invade Atlantis. The pair grip his hair to remain astride. They penetrate icebergs, the Great Barrier Reef, the earth's core. They drink hot lava at the base of submerged volcanoes.

His cavernous yell roars out of him like the frothing sea. He bucks and fills the body of the one on top of him, a raging river that breaks its banks. His icy sap flows and flows until Eddie thinks he will drown from the inside out. A vast ice floe melts inside him.

Eddie's back goes numb from the cold oozing through him. He is saturated. Paralyzed. He'll crack into pieces in a breath of arctic wind.

The drowned man's eyes flutter open. They are ocean-depth blue. His square fist comes up. It will connect with Eddie's jaw. But as a drowning man reaches for a driftwood log, it instead closes on the swollen cock thrust towards his face.

His grip is hard, but his palm is bathwater-soft. He squeezes but keeps his hand still, as if he will wring the life juices out of the one whose body he still possesses, his cock still solid and expansive within the rider on top of him though he has come in torrents. Eddie bounces in his hand, mad for relief. He swirls inside a whirlpool, banging against its sides, desperate for release. He struggles to swim upward, toward air, but he is caught in a riptide that pushes him under. He can't escape this anchored cock. It has grown within him, pierced his innards.

Eddie shouts, bucks, and that cock still buried deep inside him, still spilling a waterfall, still an unthawed icicle, hard and cold, seems to emerge from his throat. It splays his body wide open. He is impaled upon this Greek column that holds up temples, too much for a mortal man.

Eddie sprays the face of the drowned man. He shudders. He would fall over if the man didn't buoy him up, the cock inside him forging a new spine, Eddie's shrinking cock still locked in his grip.

The man licks the life-creating substance, tastes it, touches his free hand to it and rubs his fingers together. He holds his fingers to Eddie's mouth, feeds him a taste of himself. He grabs the back of Eddie's neck, brings him down into a kiss. Eddie drinks in the salt water that covers planet Earth. The titan's beard tendrils hiss and tangle in Eddie's hair, binding him close. The man's tongue flickers deep, touches the tip of his own cock inside Eddie's guts.

Dewey, still lodged behind them, hears the titan's thunderbolt shout, hears Eddie's mortal echo a minute later, feels the vibration of their seismic heaving, cries out with the pulsing grip of the body he trespasses into. Juices flow out of his lover's body onto his legs, onto the bed, flooding the cabin floor. Dewey cannot move, his body pinned by the stab of his own cock in that holy passageway. He is one of those tiny creatures attached to the body of a whale.

Dewey flails, drowning, trapped in a swirling eddy. He reaches around, grabs those two inky nipples.

The frozen man gasps and murmurs. He throws the one on top of him off. Eddie lands with a splash and a yelp on the floor, his body a gaping hole, still trickling brine.

The titan rolls off the one behind him. Dewey cries out. His cock thrusts, seeking connection.

The man turns over, takes Dewey's suddenly abandoned cock into his mouth. He swallows it, ingests it, digests it. He eats in the nuts, chews on them. His tongue reaches back to the asshole, violates the barren tunnel of this body's exit. The tentacled tongue snakes through the mortal passageways, explores its inner fjords down to the fingertips, laps at the inner ear and tickles the scalp insides, flicks at the inner nipples.

Dewey thrashes. The frozen man feeds him his fist, corks his cries. The stuffed man suckles.

The titan retracts his tongue. He stuffs his fist up the asshole instead. He stuffs his other hand down that mortal throat until his paired knuckles touch under the navel, tectonic plates shifting under tender skin. Dewey's cock is still down his throat. His tongue parts the cock slit, creeps inside, penetrating its length. He will swallow the entire man gulp by gulp.

Eddie scrambles behind him, sneaks his puny cock inside that infinite cave. He is a tiny pearl locked in an immense oyster. He clings tight. The trio bathes at the base of rainbows, circles the equator, tours ice castles. The man shoots liquid silver in their wake.

The man motions to the morning sunlight pouring in through the hold. He half-walks and the lovers half-carry him up to the deck, splashing through the knee-deep, iridescent water, the flood of his eternal arousal. Each step seems to cause him pain. They too walk gingerly. They are raw and chafed to their cores. He has possessed and baptized every bodily crevice. They are disintegrating shrapnel in the wake of his unquenchable lust. His cock still rises, threatens. They are wary of it, crave it. They quiver like jellyfish, exhausted. He has wrung them out like sponges, milked them dry. They are empty of human fluid. They are cleansed and purified. He has filled them with his own piscine juices.

He blinks into the sunrise, inhales, tosses his hair in the crisp breeze. The rigging strains in the rising wind, smacking the yard with a discordant *ping, ping*. He stretches and rubs his chest. He looks up at the ship's sky-reaching masthead, touches his own, clamps it in the jaws of his fist, and roars. He fills the ocean with his salt spray. On their knees beside him, the lovers paw at his clenching haunches. They are two babbling brooks.

He dives overboard with a quiet splash, his body parting the water, legs transforming into scales and fins before he disappears beneath the sea. He bobs up close to the boat and beckons.

The lovers look at each other, deciding. They touch hands.

He impatiently slaps his green tail on the surface of the water.

His lovers slip in after him into the frigid depths, their new tails unfurling and glistening under the red sky.

Cornered
in the Closet

Christopher Pierce

Pedro didn't tell me what was going on until after he had me tied up and gagged in the electrical closet.

I should've seen it coming, so I guess I got what I deserved. It had all started a few weeks before when the circuit breakers in the building I work in started acting up. We had to call in a team of electricians to deal with the problem.

The office is very open and gay-friendly, so I didn't think anything about wearing T-shirts to work that said things like GAY FREE-DOM, SAFER SEX NOW, and SOUTHWEST LEATHER ASSOCIATION on them.

The electrical crews arrived the next day and started their work. Before long, wires were ripped out of the wall and left trailing on the floor like guts from an animal's kill. Everywhere you looked there were guys with tool belts kneeling on the floor, standing on ladders, messing with the circuit breakers trying to find out what was going on. I didn't think much of it.

But there was this one guy.

His name was Pedro. Hispanic and muscular with a full mustache, he was always there in the corner of my eye. I'd linger a few minutes when I saw him, getting as much of him as I could. Whenever I saw him he was doing something unconsciously sexy, like slinging coils of cable over his shoulder or stroking his mustache while deep in thought. Little things like that would just stick in my mind, and I found myself thinking about him more and more.

I hadn't actually spoken to Pedro at all. How could I? He was dealing directly with the superintendent of the building, and I wasn't even management. What use did he have for a skinny little white boy like me?

A lot more than I thought, as it turns out. He was just so fucking hot, I was stuck on him. I tried to say hello a few times, but I would get embarrassed and turn away. His look was so intense, his eyes dark and steamy under heavy black brows. He always seemed so serious, so stern. I was so meaningless in his world—he probably didn't even know my name.

But that didn't stop me from thinking about him all the time. And I began to wonder, as the days went by, whether there wasn't a change in him. It seemed like more and more he would return my looks, if only for a few seconds. When I'd walk by, he'd look up from his work. I even thought I caught him staring at me when he thought I didn't know. As unthinkable as it was, I even thought I caught him rubbing a sizable bulge in his jeans one time late in the day.

That couldn't have been true, though, could it? It was just my overactive imagination, making subtle shifts in my perception to make me think that somehow this big Mexican stud was returning my attention.

At the end of two weeks I vowed to stop brooding about Pedro. I wasn't getting any work done, and my supervisor wanted to know what the hell was going on. What could I say? "I'm sorry, sir, I can't keep my mind on my work because I keep imagining what it would be like to suck on that big electrician's cock." That'd go over real well at my next employee review.

So I had to quit it because it was pointless. The guy was straight anyway—the band of gold on his finger was proof enough of that. And even if he was bi-curious or gay and closeted, I could hardly work up the nerve to even look at the man, much less talk to him. What was I thinking?

So I just cut it off. When I saw Pedro coming, I'd find another way around. If he was working in a hallway, I pretended my pager was going off and head back the way I came. I had convinced myself so well that his responsiveness to me was all in my head, it didn't even occur to me to see whether my change in attitude affected him.

Bad mistake. The few times I accidentally caught Pedro's eyes, they had a weird look in them. It was a look of hurt pride. Soon enough those looks of hurt became looks of resentment and anger. Then the looks became glares.

But I had so successfully convinced myself that Pedro's responses to me were all imaginary, I ignored them. I should've known better.

One Saturday I decided to go in to work. I knew no one would be there, I figured it'd be a great time to catch up on all the work I'd been slacking off on. Maybe I could get everything done and save my reputation in my supervisor's eyes before I got reported. That was my plan anyway. I never expected anyone else to be working on the weekend.

And I certainly didn't expect Pedro to be there.

But he was, looking hotter than ever. With so few people at the building and the summer sun heating up, he had taken his shirt off and hung it from his tool belt.

My knees almost gave out at the sight of him, kneeling at the far end of the hallway, working on a panel through an exposed section of the wall. As soon as I turned the corner he looked up and saw me. No turning away this time.

Both of us frozen in place, we stared at each other, my pale blue eyes locked onto his smoldering brown ones. I felt like a mouse who'd stumbled onto a cobra's nest.

I didn't know what was going to happen next, but I knew I'd face it alone. The whole building was quiet, totally different from the noisy confusion of the week. There was no one else there and we both knew it.

"Hey, man, how you doing?" I said before I could stop myself.

It sounded so lame in the gravity of the moment. So ordinary, so normal.

But the smile I hoped would spread on Pedro's face never came. Instead, he stopped what he was doing and started walking toward me, his eyes never leaving mine.

"Uh..." I started, frightened. The closer he got, the more I realized just how big this man really was. The sour, musky smell of his sweat was getting stronger and stronger in my nostrils.

"I was hoping you'd come today," he said. It was the first time I'd heard his voice, with its heavy Hispanic accent. "I have a question for you."

"A question for me?" I repeated dumbly.

"Yeah," Pedro said as he reached me, standing a full two inches taller than me. "What's the matter, don't you speak English?" He laughed without humor.

"But...I don't know anything about this electrical stuff. You're the expert..."

"Oh," he said as he took me by the arm. "You know the answer to this question, I'm sure."

"Hey!" I said as I twisted in his grip. But he was moving me now, pushing my body toward the open door of one of the many electrical closets that dotted the corridors. Then he shoved me into the brightly lit interior of the tiny room. Every inch of wall was covered with exposed wire. Pedro walked in behind me and closed the door, locking it.

"What the hell do you think you're doing?" I yelled at him. Without warning he punched me, his fist flying out faster than my eyes could follow. I stumbled backward, landing on my butt on the hard floor.

"You're going to answer my question," he said. I rubbed my chin and glared up at him.

"What's the question?" I asked. He looked down at me, and for the first time, he smiled. I had to admit it made him look hotter than ever, but this situation had gotten way too weird way too fast for my taste.

"The question is, Why shouldn't I fuck the shit out of you right here and now?"

I was so shocked my bladder almost let go. But at the same time my dick got hard, poking up into my underwear as if it could get out of my pants on its own.

"You're out of your fucking mind!" I said angrily as I stood up. I don't know what I was thinking—I never could've taken him in a fight.

Pedro just grabbed me by the front of my shirt and yanked me to him. The smell of beer on his breath was strong, but his eyes were clear as hard gems. He knew exactly what he was doing. Pedro leaned down, and with his other hand he picked up one end of a coil of wire that was piled on the floor next to us.

"Now," he said as he started wrapping the wire around my wrists, "are you going to behave, or do I have to take another poke at you?" I started to struggle and he slapped my face, hard. I was so stunned by the blow that he finished tying up my hands with little trouble. Then he took the other end of the wire and tossed it over an overhead beam, catching it as it fell and tying it off to one of the poles that held up the corners of the room.

"Please, man," I said. "What do you want? I'll give you anything…"

Pedro shook his head and pulled his shirt out from his tool belt. "I'm real tired of your mouth, boy," he said as he stuffed a fistful of the sweat-stained fabric in my mouth. The rest of it hung down from my lips like drool.

"What do I want?" he echoed me. "Nothing you can give me, what I want is what I'm going to take." Gagged as I was, I tried to communicate with the brute with my facial expressions. He looked at me and laughed again.

"It's you that I want, punk, and that's what I'm taking. Right here and right now, there's no getting out of this. There's no one else in the building, I made sure of that."

The surprise in my face must have been obvious.

"Yes, I planned this, boy," Pedro said as he unbuckled his jeans and let them fall. His belt buckle made a loud clank as it struck the floor. He wasn't wearing any underwear. His cock was jutting out, full and large with precome dripping from the foreskin. The fear was raging in me, but somehow it was mixing with desire, together forming a fire that blazed inside me, making my own dick strain for release.

"You might think I'm just some dumb laborer," he continued as he stepped forward and put his hands on my sides. Shaking my head wildly, I tried to let him know I'd never thought that. "But I'm a lot smarter than you think. I'm smart enough to know the answer to my question. The answer is, there's no reason why I shouldn't fuck the shit out of you."

I was terrified, but there was nothing I could do. I was bound and gagged in a closet with a man who was determined to use me— what could I do?

"There's all kinds of reasons why I should take you, punk. Want to hear them?" He flipped me around so I was facing away from him. Then he reached and opened my pants, pulling them and my briefs down to my ankles. I whimpered a little as my naked flesh was revealed. Now there was nothing to protect me, nothing standing between his dick and my ass. I didn't answer his question, so he started telling me anyway.

"I love my wife, but she's been real sick lately, she can't put out for me. I love her too much to get a whore or even a girl on the side, but I'm a man and need to get my rocks off or I'll lose my mind."

I heard him work up some spit and hock it into his hand, then the slippery whispery sound of him slicking his cock up with it.

"I've seen you around; I know what you are. I know you're a little gay boy…I know you like getting reamed by big dicks…so you're going to take care of me…"

I started struggling again, yanking on the wire that bound my hands, and trying to dislodge the tight knot that held it in place. He laughed again and slapped my naked ass. A little thrill of excitement shot through me despite my fear.

"And I've asked around about you, I know the score. You don't have a boyfriend, nobody that's gonna come lookin' for me if I screw your little whore hole. I know you know all about AIDS and safer sex from those shirts you always wear...you're a clean boy."

Pedro came up behind me and started rubbing his club up and down my ass crack, getting it slimy with his spit. Against my will I found myself pushing back against him, pulling against the wire in an effort to get him inside me.

"You're the perfect little boy for me. Because I've heard what else you're into...leather." My cock sprung up even harder at the sound of those words spoken in that thick Hispanic accent. "I know you like masters and slaves, you're probably really gettin' off on bein' tied up right now...so guess what? From now on, you're my slave."

He rammed his dick into me and I screamed into the gag, the sound instantly muffled. There was no delicacy here, none of the tenderness of a lover. It was the pure artless fucking of a man with full nuts who needed to get off. He was using me for his pleasure, just like the slave he said I was. It was fucking hot, far beyond any of the daydreams I had had about him. I was being made into the fuck hole of this big Hispanic stud.

He was pumping me harder than I'd ever been pumped before. Hard and fast and raw. Pedro's heavy breathing was loud in my ears. He slipped his arms around me and squeezed me tight to him, crushing my back against his chest.

"Yeah, that's it, white boy..." he whispered. "I'm gonna shoot off in you, shoot my hot come into your tight little ass..."

All of a sudden he reached down and grabbed hold of my leaking cock. It squirmed in his grip, electric in its tension. This was totally unexpected—I figured he'd use me and throw me away without a thought for my pleasure. But no, he was jerking off my meat in his fist as expertly as he was plowing my butt.

Then it was happening. Pedro's chest heaved against me and I felt his cock piston inside me, shooting off like a machine gun. That same instant he squeezed my dick tight in his hand and I felt my dick explode and come squirted out, splattering all over the wall of wires. I groaned into the gag in animal release. He held me tight in his arms, silently expelling the rest of his load into me.

"Yeah…" he whispered. "You're gonna be a perfect little slave for me, aren't you, boy?"

"Yes, sir," I said through the gag. It had come out without thinking, but there it was. All resistance was gone.

"I'm gonna keep you on the side to take care of me," Pedro said as he slowly pulled himself out of me. My asshole felt empty and yearning without him. He leaned over and pulled my pants up, fastening them back around my waist before he yanked his shirt out of my mouth.

He came around to look at me. My knees almost melted again as I saw the huge man standing in front of me, a light sheen of sweat on his dark skin.

"Now tell me the phone number for your pager, boy." Without a thought of disobeying, I told him and he scribbled it down on the pad of paper attached to his tool belt.

"We're going to be working in this building for a long time," he said. "Every time you get a page that says '911' that's me calling you, and you're to report to this closet as soon as you get it. It's 911 because nothing's more important than serving your master. You got that, boy?"

"Yes, sir!" I said.

"And maybe when we're done here, I'll take you with me."

I nodded vigorously, and he laughed.

"Good slave. I know you're not going to tell no one, you get off on it too much." Pedro reached up to untie me, and I moved forward and rubbed my crotch against his leg.

"Master…" I whispered.

"Yeah, slave?"

"Please let me serve you again, sir…"

Pedro grinned, and again I heard the clink of his belt buckle as his pants dropped and hit the floor.

Artful Fur

Jay Neal

The woman tilted her head critically and sipped her champagne through pursed lips. She peered at the gallery card announcing the painting's title: *Big Bear Dick IX*. She tilted her head the other way. "Oh, I don't know." She gestured vaguely at the painting in front of her with her champagne flute.

"I don't know, but in the brutal slathering of paint and the, oh, I don't know, sensual voluptuousness of the hirsute male figure, I imagine, I don't know, that I see a definite post–Lucian Freud influence on your work."

When John Marrin looked at the piece he had painted, he saw his friend Bill spread naked and hairy across 48 square feet of canvas. He had employed a sensuous palette of burnt sienna, cadmium red, and vermilion, with a touch of viridian. When he looked at the piece of work talking to him, he saw a tiresome woman with much more money than artistic understanding. He decided to flatter the money.

"I see that madam has a keen sensitivity to trends in modern portraiture."

"I do try to keep up, of course." Her lips unpursed. "But I'm not sure that the colors would complement my sitting room decor, and your subjects are, oh, I don't know, rather aggressively hairy."

Oh, dear. Getting this philistine to buy the painting would probably take more work than painting the damn thing had. Marrin stroked his beard and was trying to work out a strategy when he felt a hand on his arm.

"I'm so sorry to interrupt your fascinating conversation, Mrs. Pristina, but could I steal John away just for a moment?"

Mrs. Pristina quietly assented. Mr. Marrin silently rejoiced. His savior was Gene Westwood, gallery owner, longtime friend, and host of the evening's festive opening. An altogether agreeable polar bear of diminutive stature, Gene was a prime subject for Marrin to paint, but they had never quite gotten around to it.

However, at that moment, Gene had business on his mind, and that meant selling more of John's paintings. He steered Marrin across the gallery, whispering as he went. "I have someone I want you to meet. He looks like a very good prospect. Be nice to him."

Marrin looked aggrieved. "Am I not always perfectly behaved with the customers? Besides, don't they prefer eccentric artists?"

Gene didn't bother to look long-suffering. "Just be nice. Anyway, he's your type."

They approached the short, stout figure who was admiring a large painting titled *Wayne's Hairy Butt VI*. As he moved his head side to side, one hand stroked his beard, the other hand maneuvered discreetly in the pocket of his trousers.

"Robert, may I present John Marrin." As Gene began the introductions, the viewer turned to face them. "John, this is Robert Bentley."

Marrin was transfixed and didn't notice that Bentley pulled his hand from his pocket, ready to shake. Being nice to Robert would be easy; not jumping his bear bones right there would be the challenge. When Marrin painted Bentley, as he surely would, he would use gallons of titanium white to re-create Bentley's luminous white hair and beard. Rendering his mischievous blue-gray eyes would tax Marrin's skill. Robert's round belly was a compositional element certain to demand an entire series of paintings. Perhaps something allegorical—Bentley as Neptune.

"Mr. Marrin, it's a pleasure. Your paintings are quite stimulating."

Marrin was slow to realize that his Neptune had spoken. Belatedly, he shook the offered hand. "Please, call me John. I'm pleased that you like them, but I am myself only a pitiful conduit through which the raw, bear sexuality of my models pours itself onto the canvas."

"Of course you are. And how do you go about finding this raw, bear sexuality?"

"Serendipity. It finds me. Maybe at the bar, maybe at the super-market, maybe even at an art gallery where it's looking at one of my paintings."

"And how do you proceed when you've found it, or rather, when it has found you?"

"I seize the moment—and the bear, if I'm lucky. Perhaps..."

Marrin was nearly engulfed in the artistic and erotic rapture induced by this bear Bentley, but it was not to last. As if by a whirlpool, he was sucked away by a group of fawning but unen-lightened fans to drown in more banal conversation. Not even his Neptune, receding into the distance, could intercede.

And so the evening wore on and wound down. The remaining canapés were consumed, all the champagne was imbibed, and many of the paintings were sold. It was altogether a very successful open-ing, but Marrin was not satisfied. Although he had caught further glimpses of his Neptune, may even have caught a wink, he never again was allowed close enough to speak or touch.

The crowd thinned. A few small groups of people remained, their conversations sputtering to an end. Gene was doing his best to make one last sale before closing. Marrin finally found himself by himself. He had hoped for one last chance to net his catch, but scan-ning the gallery, he didn't spot his Neptune anywhere. Certainly Gene could put him in touch with Mr. Bentley tomorrow, but Mar-rin wanted to touch him now.

He admitted defeat. He would say good night to the remaining patrons, thank Gene for all his hard work, and go home to sleep off the champagne. First, though, he'd better take a piss or he wouldn't make it home. He slouched through the archway at the rear of the gallery and moped down the long hallway toward the bathroom.

Inside, he stood at the urinal and pissed out a long, strong stream. He didn't notice that the stall next to him was occupied until its occupant spoke to him, just as he shook the last drops off the end of his dick.

"Is that you?" asked the next stall.

Merciful heavens, bathroom ontology was not one of his favorite topics, and he was tired.

"Yes," he answered. "It certainly is I. I believe this because I can certainly feel what is certainly my right hand shaking piss off what is certainly my own dick."

"It was a rhetorical, not a metaphysical question. This is Robert." His Neptune! "I was thinking that we might continue the thoroughly stimulating interaction we were having earlier, that is, if you'd like to."

Like to! But here? Now?

"Of course I would, most decidedly and immediately, but please not here. I couldn't possibly. Once when I was much younger, I was in a bathroom stall when a man in the next stall signaled that he wanted sex. I mistakenly thought he was asking for more toilet paper. When I discovered otherwise I was so embarrassed that I've never been able to get hard within six feet of anything porcelain."

"Well, then, perhaps…"

The bathroom door swung open, and Gene stepped to the urinals. He unzipped his trousers and pulled out his dick. Robert flushed the toilet and made a quick and unobtrusive exit from the bathroom. Marrin was momentarily indecisive.

Gene started pissing. "Oh, that's a relief. I'm glad I caught you, John. I was hoping…"

"I'd like to stay and share this male-bonding ritual with you, Gene, but I have something urgent I simply must attend to." Marrin stuffed his dick back into his pants and zipped up before Gene could finish and follow him. He made his own quick exit, yanking open the bathroom door and stumbling into the welcoming arms of the waiting Bentley.

"Mr. Marrin, I'm glad I caught you."

Held in Robert's arms, John looked into Robert's encouraging eyes from his unexpectedly intimate vantage point. Their lips slowly drew closer together. Marrin shifted his weight and lifted a hand to touch the white-bearded cheek before him. His other hand slid around Bentley's waist. Their lips parted slightly, tongues at the ready, preparing for approaching ecstasy.

They heard the flushing sound in the bathroom.

"Shit!" Marrin nearly bit Bentley's tongue. "Come on."

He grabbed Robert's hand and dragged him down the hallway. Headed for the office, they passed the gallery archway and reached a janitor's closet when they heard the bathroom door open. Marrin hastily grabbed the doorknob, propelled Bentley into the closet, and pulled the door shut behind them. They stood breathlessly still in the dark, listening to Gene's exit from the bathroom and his return to the gallery. Face to face, their noses were inches apart, their bellies touching.

"At last." Robert's breath warmed John's lips. "A bit of privacy. And I note that the sink pressing against my ass is stainless steel, not porcelain. Why don't you feel it?"

"The sink?"

"No, you dolt. Feel my ass."

Bentley took Marrin's hands, pulled them around his own waist, and planted them firmly on his haunches. Acquiescing, Marrin felt. *Surprisingly full and firm,* he thought, *for a man as splendidly mature as Robert.* The texture of Bentley's suit was very fine; John could feel the nape of the hair on Robert's ass through the fabric. His hands circled lower on Robert's ass and down onto the thighs. He realized something.

"You're not wearing underwear," he said.

"Quite so. Are you scandalized?"

"Not scandalized," Marrin said. "Surprised but delighted."

"I find briefs too confining and boxers altogether too ridiculous."

"Don't you ever worry about getting…"

"An erection? I never worry about getting an erection." Robert pulled John's hands around to his crotch. "It's a shame to waste one, don't you think?"

John's appreciative "mmm" upon feeling Robert's stiffening

dick was swallowed when Robert kissed him. And kissed him again. And again. And again. Increasingly fervent kissing helped to release the evening's frustrations through their tongues.

With the dexterous hands of an artist, and without interrupting the rhythm of their kissing, John loosened Robert's tie. Ruffling Robert's chest fur as he went, he unbuttoned Robert's shirt. Button after taunting button challenged his fumbling fingers. The last button succumbed to John's rising impatience and popped off onto the floor. The shirt open, John steered his hands across Robert's chest, navigating the nipples. After overcoming all obstacles, he finally had his hands on Robert's body!

But hands alone proved inadequate to curb his appetite. Pulling Robert's shirt further open, John pressed Robert against the closet sink and bent over to taste his nipples. John felt left, tongued right, then pinched right and bit left, keeping Robert's nipples on full alert and his dick straining against his trousers.

John couldn't avoid noticing the effect he was having on Robert's dick, pressing as it was into John's belly, since his own dick was just as hard and pressing against Robert's leg. Continuing his oral ministrations at Robert's nipples, John resumed fumbling with his hands, this time loosening Robert's belt and dealing with the trouser buttons, hooks, and zipper.

The trousers fell. For a few moments John stroked the hair on Robert's thick thighs, feeling their accent on the curving muscle. Then he weighed Robert's heavy balls in his hands, feeling which hung lower. Balls in one hand, John curled the fingers of his other hand around the upward curve of Robert's dick, squeezing and stroking with regained dexterity. Robert recognized the work of a true artist with appropriately critical moans and groans of his own.

John ached to have Robert's dick in his mouth, to trace its curve with his tongue, to feel its throbbing head on the inside of his cheek. The confines of the closet demanded a coordinated effort from both of them, but persistent wiggling and rearranging got John wedged into a teetering squat in front of Robert's contorted body.

As they settled into position, Robert's dick landed in John's beard. It was a pleasant enough sensation for both, bristly beard rubbing against sensitive skin. Arching his neck and twisting his head, John managed to place his tongue so that he could slide it along the bottom the dick at his lips. It was just possible for the tip of his tongue to tickle the end.

Emboldened by this success, John opened his mouth wider and got his lips around the middle of the shaft. He used his tongue to pull it closer. Keenly determined, John inched his mouth upwards, his lips crawling along as his tongue struggled to keep its grip. Lips, tongue, lips, tongue moved in a steady march to the summit. One more maneuver and he would have pulled Robert's dick completely into his mouth.

Would have, except for the crashing noise in the gallery. There were sounds of metal hitting the floor and glass breaking, indicating a general upset of the refreshment table. Fortunately, given the delicate situation in the closet, neither man flinched, and permanent tooth marks were avoided. However, their attention was distracted. They hastily assessed their situation and realized just how tight a spot they were in, shortly before they heard Gene announce that he'd get something from the closet to clean up. Their response was immediate.

"Fuck!" from John.

"One hoped so," from Robert.

The next move was awkward. Wriggling John up from his wedged-in squat took considerably more effort yet significantly less time than getting him into it. John grabbed Robert's hand; Robert grabbed onto his trousers, yanking them back up over his ass. Despite John's aching knees and Robert's dishabille, they escaped from the closet and ran down the hallway into Gene's office without being noticed. John pulled the disheveled Robert through the door and slammed it shut, locking it with little pretense of stealth. It was no time for finesse.

With single-minded intent, John raced to Gene's desk and began rifling through the drawers. Robert stood by the door and watched the antics. John's mumbled, "I know they're in here somewhere," was quickly followed by his exclamation of discovery. He displayed the condom package in victory, then tossed it to Robert. Robert caught it. Consequently, his trousers slipped to the floor.

John started pulling off his own suit as fast as he could, snarling at his tie when it got tangled. "Well," he said with some impatience, "take those off and put that on." Robert proceeded to do that with his trousers, then the condom, in that order.

John's shirt followed his tie to the floor. Not bothering to remove his shoes, John got his trousers and boxer shorts off without entirely losing his balance. He brushed aside the paraphernalia covering a corner of Gene's desk, planted his naked butt on it, and rolled back onto the desk with legs held expectantly in the air.

He waved his hand at Robert. "Come on, come on, hurry up and fuck me before something else happens." Needing no further encouragement, Robert moved with alacrity to the naked man lying on the desk.

John's legs went up around Robert's shoulders. Robert stood with the tip of his sheathed dick at the brink of John's asshole. "Do all your prospective models get to fuck the artist?"

John was in no mood for badinage. "They do if their luck holds and they quit talking. Now shove it in."

Robert shoved it in and got on with it. The groan that dissipated John's evening of frustration was most gratifying. Savoring the situation, Robert fucked at a gracious pace. This satisfied John only briefly.

"I so hate to ruin the moment with trite expressions and words like 'harder' and 'deeper,' but perhaps you get the idea." Maintaining his good humor, Robert got the idea and increased the pace of his fucking, making it both harder and deeper. His full-body pounding of John's ass was evidently hitting the right spot, judging by John's gasping and moaning. Doing his best to keep from sliding off the desk beneath Robert's onslaught, John was about to come. Would have come, except for the sound of the key turning the lock in the office door.

Robert slowed his thrusting.

John yelled "Fuck!"

Robert shoved his dick back into John's ass and stopped his fucking, waiting to see what would happen this time.

"Fuck!" John almost growled. He pounded the desk to regain Robert's attention. "I mean, keep fucking me. No way you're stopping now!"

This tactic suited Robert. He immediately resumed his previous pace. John resumed his synchronous groaning. The door opened and Gene entered, showing little surprise at the primal scene being enacted on his desktop. He closed the door.

John turned his oscillating head in Gene's direction. "Well, don't just stand there. Drop your pants and get over here so I can suck your dick." Gene honored the artistic imperative.

Moments later the tableau resembled an allegory of lust. Robert was holding onto John's feet and fucking him vigorously. John's back squeaked against the desktop with each of Robert's weighty thrusts, while he gripped the edges of the desk in a bid to stay on the ride. Gene was holding on to John's beard, thrusting his dick into John's mouth with abandon. The arrangement displayed little artistic merit, but no one cared.

Their climax arrived soon enough. John shot his load in a thick stream up his belly. Robert barked once to announce his orgasm, then collapsed into the sticky pool on John's belly. Gene pulled his dick out of John's mouth, jerked it twice with his right hand, and came in John's beard, a small rivulet running across John's Adam's apple and down the side of his neck.

Gene leaned forward onto the desk and breathed heavily, his dick reclining against John's neck. "I see you didn't need any more encouragement to be nice to Robert."

John waved his hand languorously. "It was fate, undeniable destiny."

"I don't know about destiny, but it's undeniable that he bought three of your paintings."

John would have sat up but he was pinned to the desk. "Three! Why didn't you tell me?"

"I've been trying to catch up with you two all night, but you made it unusually difficult."

Robert mumbled, his mouth obscured by John's hairy belly. "I did what I could, Gene, but I think John wanted to be alone."

"Alone? No, I just didn't want Gene to think I was running off with his customers."

"Too late," Gene said. "Robert's already signed the check."

"Too late," Robert said. "I've already fucked the artist. Now you have to paint me and give Gene something to sell. Have you thought of an approach yet?"

"No idea. But it's bound to be a long series, and it could take quite some time for you to fuck the muse into submission."

Robert sighed. "How I must suffer for your art."

Dear Bobby

Greg Herren

Dear Bobby,

I'm not really sure why I am writing this letter to you. I've been thinking about you a lot lately and, frankly, wishing I could see you more often. It's such a pity that we don't live in the same town.

I used to think that was a good thing. In the very beginning my attraction to you was so overpowering I was glad you lived five hours away. How on earth could I keep my relationship with my boyfriend going if you were a 10-minute drive away? I'd have wanted to be over at your place all of the time, naked, wrestling, seeing who could come out on top.

That first time we met, at that hotel out on Causeway Boulevard, I had no idea what to expect. Yes, you had sent me a hot pic over the Internet, but I've gotten plenty of those that have turned out to be six or seven years old, or belonged to someone else. There was just something about that picture, though, and the confident attitude you had. You were absolutely convinced you were going to kick my ass wrestling.

Of course, you did, and have many times since that first time. I was only sorry we had so few hours to enjoy each other. There's always an element of nervousness when you meet someone for the first time in that situation, isn't there? I am always afraid that I am going to like the person and they aren't going to like me, or vice versa. When, despite all the wrestling and the afterplay, you couldn't get hard, that really had me nervous. Oh, God, am I that unattractive that lots of physical contact won't get him hard? Seems funny to remember that now, three years later, considering everything that has happened since then.

I was especially nervous when you never seemed interested in scheduling another time. I know now that I was overreacting; it's not like I have tons of free time either. But when there was time after time that nothing seemed to work out and it always seemed like it was me suggesting it, I slowly came to the conclusion that it was never going to happen again.

I was disappointed because I felt we hadn't had as much fun as we could have that first time, but I was happy enough with the memory of the afternoon we had spent together. So imagine my surprise when you agreed to have me drive over from New Orleans and spend the night! I was so excited…literally. I would think about what was coming and would get hard and have to beat off. I would pull up your picture online and beat off to it. I would watch wrestling videos and fantasize that it was you and me wrestling and beat off. I really was starting to worry about myself. This was bordering on a sexual obsession, and in my writer's mind I started thinking about how this could play out as a thriller novel. Sexually obsessed wrestler becomes stalker. Kills off his competition. Or how easy it would be to have this sexual obsession used against me—the subject of the obsession could start manipulating me into doing things I wouldn't ordinarily do. Like in that movie *Body Heat* or the novels of James M. Cain and Patricia Highsmith. Had anything like that ever been written with a gay theme? That's when I knew that I wasn't dangerously obsessed. My mind wouldn't go off in that direction if I were.

I still remember driving to Pensacola that day. It was a bright day, and all the way I kept wondering if I was wasting my time, if I would get to Pensacola and call your cell phone only to find out "something's come up" or something, and I would have wasted the drive. I decided that if that were the case, I would just go to the beach and think for a few hours. My mother always said to prepare for the worst.

But that didn't happen. I called your cell phone and met you at your apartment. You opened the door wearing a red Speedo, just like you promised. It was so good to see you again. Your dark olive skin, your black hair, your green eyes, your muscular body. It had been years since a man with body hair had attracted me, but I just wanted to run my tongue over your hard pecs. You just grinned and said, "Hey, boy" and let me in.

Once the door closed behind me your arms were around me and we were kissing. I love that I have to stand on tiptoe to kiss you. You started running your hands all over my body and started to undress me. I had my Speedo on under my pants, and we got the mattresses out and put them on the floor. We warmed up by making out for about an hour, and then started wrestling.

That second time you beat me every time, just like the first. At first it annoyed me that you kept beating me, and beating me so easily, or so it seemed to me. But I found myself enjoying being trapped in your submission holds, in your headlocks, your camel clutches, your head scissors. I enjoyed struggling against your strength, listening to you say, "Give it up boy," in that rural Florida accent, fighting against the inevitable moment when the hold became too painful for me to hold out any longer.

After you got about five submissions out of me I stripped you out of your Speedo and you peeled mine off of me. We lay down together on the mattresses, with you on top of me, and this time you had no trouble with a hard-on. I sucked your cock between working over your mouth, your neck, your ears, and your nipples with my tongue and teeth. You sucked mine and teased me about being able to take all of mine in your mouth when I couldn't with yours. Well, Bobby, you know damn well you have a huge cock, long and thick, and I doubt very seriously that there are many men who could deep-throat you. At least out of porn movies.

We went out to dinner, which was nice, and I got to know you a little better. Much to my pleasure, I discovered that you were a really nice guy, with a good sense of humor. We went back to your apartment, watched a videotape you had made of one of your matches with another guy, and before long we both were so aroused that we were soon naked and back on the mattresses, wrestling and making out. This time, when we were finally finished, we went to bed. We spent the night in each other's arms, taking turns holding one another. It was very nice sleeping up against your warm muscular body, feeling your big strong arms wrapped around me, curled up against your long muscular legs, or turning so that I had my arms wrapped around you, and one of my legs nestled inside of yours. It felt right somehow.

It still bothered me that you could beat me so easily whenever we wrestled, and it really stirred up a competitive streak inside of me that I always knew was there. I had moderate success wrestling before, but never really took it seriously or tried to get better at it. You inspired me to start wrestling more, trying to learn from my defeats, to sharpen my mental focus during the match instead of just relying on instinct to carry me through, to start thinking, planning and staying sharp. I found myself winning matches more frequently, but whenever we got together again it was always the same thing: beaten again, feeling your strength overpowering me, holding me down, that sweet Southern accent saying, "What do you say, boy?"

I burned to beat you, to hear you say those words to me. But not in an angry way, not out of frustration or humiliation, but to finally reach the point where I could hold you down, crank the hold until you couldn't bear it anymore, to hear you say, "OK, I give," and look at me with a renewed respect. Not that you didn't respect me—I know that you do, always did. One of the reasons you always wrestled me so hard was from respect, knowing that unless you gave it your all I might beat you. And I knew that when the day came that I did finally win a fall from you, I would have earned it. You aren't the kind of man who would just let someone win.

Remember that first time I won a fall from you? It was a surprise, wasn't it? Even though it has been two years since that first time, remembering it still makes me smile a little bit. You went for the headlock, as always—one of your best moves and holds. I was able to counter it by wrapping my legs around one of yours and grabbing the other with both hands and flipping you backward. You still held on to the headlock, but your leverage was gone, and my dick was getting hard as I moved over on top of you. You were squeezing and moving, but I was able to get on top.

Instead of fighting the strength of your arms I started working on a hold of my own, grabbing onto both of your pecs right where they join the deltoids at the shoulder, hooking my fingers into the muscle and squeezing. The tighter you squeezed, the harder I dug my hands in, until you finally let go of my head and went after my hands. Then I was able to get my own arms around your head and put on my own headlock, only I had the necessary leverage to put the pressure on that made you, after so long, after so many matches, after so many wins, concede the fall.

It was one of the best moments of my life.

I have won falls from you since then but have never won the majority of them…giving you the match every time. But my confidence grew from winning falls from you, and I began beating other people regularly.

I guess the reason I have been thinking about you so much lately is that now I have found someone like I was in the beginning, someone totally into wrestling with a hot body, who burns with the desire to beat me, which he hasn't been able to do yet. He learns faster than I did, and the sex the two of us have is incredible, almost as incredible as the sex we have always had.

I guess I always thought, Bobby, we would always wrestle each other. I never really thought—which was stupid, I guess—that you would find someone and fall in love, especially with someone who doesn't wrestle, doesn't understand it, and doesn't want you to do it anymore. I thought we would still wrestle every few months or so and have the incredible sex that always went with it afterward. I don't resent your new boyfriend, and I am happy for you. Nobody deserves to be in love and happy more so than you do.

What I am really saying is thank you. Thank you for being a

part of my life for so long, for making it that much richer for being a part of it. Thank you for teaching me the joy of wrestling, for taking something that was a hobby and showing me what a truly magnificent way of physical expression it is. Thank you for being with me and holding me while we slept and always, always being so kind and caring when we weren't on the mats.

I'll never send this letter to you. I knew that I wouldn't when I started writing it. We never really had that kind of relationship, did we? I used to wonder sometimes what it would be like for you and me to be in love, to be a couple. Could we get along, could we make each other happy? Or would we, in the comfort and familiarity that comes with coupling, lose the joy of wrestling, the joy of struggling together on the mats? That would have been the greater loss. So, no—it was better that our relationship was what it was: two guys getting together every couple of months to wrestle and have a good time.

I'll always cherish it.

Muscling In

Bob Condron

"**M**an, you've been making some excellent progress." We were sitting opposite each other in the Jacuzzi. I had never talked to this guy before, but there was no doubt that I had been aware of him. I had often seen him around, but other than exchanging a friendly smile and a wave, we had never spoken. The fitness studio was a place to work, and my program was intense. It wasn't a place to socialize but a place to do the business. Now, resting back in the Jacuzzi, muscles battered by bubbles, I allowed my focus to shift.

"Thanks," I said. "Good of you to notice."

"Are you kidding?" he replied. "All of your hard work? You've been a real inspiration to me." A firm, meaty paw appeared out of the water and was held out toward me as he leaned forward. "My name's Michael. My friends call me Micha."

I took hold and felt his iron grip. "Pleased to meet you, Micha. Mine's Joseph—Joe."

It was late morning, a time I loved to train, just missing the lunchtime rush. Only me and handsome in the Jacuzzi—which could contain a maximum of seven bodies, albeit uncomfortably. With just the two of us, there was plenty of room to stretch out and relax. His hand disappeared once more under the foam and brushed my foot as I raised it to rest on the shelf beside his butt. His fingers lingered just a moment too long, then moved away.

He grinned. "Sorry."

I smiled. "No problem."

The Jacuzzi stopped, the bubbles disappearing. He stood up and stretched his taut, bull-like muscularity while reaching over to press the restart button. As the pump kicked in, he returned to a seated position but this time slid alongside me. Closing his eyes, he rested his neck back against the rim of the pool. Seconds later he spread his knees wide so that his thick, muscular thigh rested against mine.

He let out a sigh. "Think I overdid it today. My muscles are so stiff." He opened his eyes, raised his head, and turned it toward me. "You wouldn't believe how stiff I am." And then came the almost imperceptible increase in pressure of his leg against mine.

I turned my head to face him, saw the unmistakable twinkle in his clear blue eyes. So much for this being a straight fitness studio, one I had chosen for its potential lack of distractions. I let my eyes linger on his face—a brutish, patently masculine face. Golden hair cropped to no more than stubble, a full, neat beard. Slowly, I reached out a hand under the swirling waves.

My fingertips brushed the erect column between his spreading thighs. His dick was colossal. He trembled slightly as I took hold. My fingers strained to wrap around the circumference as he again closed his eyes and leaned his head back. I turned to check the wall of glass that looked directly out onto the passageway. One man wandered back from the fitness studio, casually wiping a towel over his brow; a second passed the first on his way toward the sauna, towel wrapped around his waist. Both were oblivious; neither looked our way. What would they have seen? Only two heads peeking out above the water—the real action was hidden beneath the foam.

Micha reached out a hand to stroke my hairy inner thigh, brushing against my own erect member. His touch was surprisingly tender, kneading the muscle like a masseur. My fist tightened around his rock-hard penis, felt it swell to bursting.

"Better not to come in the Jacuzzi," he groaned. "Care to take me home, Big Man?"

Toweled dry, dressed in a pair of light gray briefs, he looked like a professional wrestler. No tattoos, no piercings, shaved smooth. Unadorned. His body was a statement on its own: Don't fuck with me! A statement I had every intention of ignoring. Finally, dressed in jeans and work boots, a white T-shirt stretched tightly across his V-shaped chest, he led the way to the parking lot.

His battered green VW Beetle had clearly seen better days. As we climbed aboard, he assured me with a chuckle that it was in fact still roadworthy.

"That's OK," I replied. "I live only a few minutes' drive. If it comes to the worst, we could always get out and push! Take a right onto Schloss Strasse, straight ahead through Steglitz. I'll tell you when to turn left."

The key turned in the ignition and off we went.

The back of the vehicle was strewn with work tools and luggage. "You're not from Berlin, are you?" Not a question so much as a statement. His accent was pure Bavarian.

"Munich, originally. Moved a couple of months ago. Been living with a buddy and his girlfriend in Mitte. Last night she decided that three's a crowd. Moved out this morning."

"*Schade.*" I focused on the road ahead. Thought it best to change the subject. "Got a trade?"

"Well, I'm good with my hands..." he grinned.

"Don't doubt it."

"Carpenter, by trade. But can turn my hand to anything. And you?"

"I own a local bar. *Straight* bar." A silence fell. "How old are you?" I asked.

"Me? I'm 23."

"Oh, you look a little older."

"Must be the beard. And you?"

"Forty," I replied, somewhat ruefully.

"You look younger."

"Must be the goatee. Thanks."

"I prefer older guys, as a matter of fact. Anyway, the way I look at it, if you're hot, you're hot."

"Yeah? Take a left here."

He swung the wheel. "Yeah." Again he grinned as he pulled up to stop. "Older guys have that little something extra."

"Oh, yeah? And what might that be?"

He placed a hand on my bulging basket. "If I'm lucky...the experience to know how to use that big thing!"

We walked down the side alley and entered the building through the back, directly into the kitchen. I closed the door behind us and indicated the stairwell that led to upstairs.

"You live above the bar?"

"Makes sense. I keep late hours."

At the top of the stairs I pointed to the master bedroom. "In there. Would you like a drink?"

"Beer?"

"Coming right up."

When I entered the bedroom he had already lain back on crisp, black cotton sheets, his head resting on the pillow. One hand was stuffed down the front of his gray briefs, playing with the barely contained erection, while the other toyed with a bullet-like nipple standing out from his hairless chest. I held out the beer toward him. His hand left his chest and took hold. He tipped the neck toward his mouth and sucked on the tip. He looked up at me with a new intensity in his pale blue eyes.

"Taste good?" I asked.

His knuckles brushed up against my chest fur. "Don't mean to sound ungrateful, Joe. But I'd rather have my lips around your dick."

I sat on the bed beside him and took his beer bottle—placing it on the bedside cabinet. I ran my palm over the flat of his belly and watched as his abdominals reflexively tensed, accentuating the eggbox musculature. Tracing the grooves with my fingers, I worked my way up to the two slabs of beefsteak that formed his mountainous pecs. They were rock-solid and smooth as a baby's bottom. I took hold of one nipple and tugged on it gently.

He slipped an arm behind his head, flexing an impressive

biceps. "Are you just gonna play?" he teased. "Or are we gonna get naked and party!"

I stood and crossed to the end of the bed, yanking my sweatshirt over my head and kicking off my trainers. I bent to pull the white sports socks from my feet and turned my head to see him hook his thumbs under the high-cut waist of his briefs. He spread his thighs and kept his eyes focused on mine as he hoisted his legs and peeled his underwear over his ass cheeks. Low-slung balls came into view, followed by his cock and butt hole, revealed in all of their naked glory. He hiked his briefs over his calves, then, flinging them aside, he knelt, palms on either thigh and held the pose.

"You like what you see?"

At that moment, the zipper on my jeans split wide open to reveal my monster erection.

"I take it that's a yes?"

Dropping my jeans to the floor, I kicked them aside, then clambered onto the bed to face him. We paused a moment, sizing each other up. I felt his hot breath on my cheek, and in an instant he threw his arms around me, smothering me with a mighty hug. His grip was so strong, I thought he'd squeeze the air out of my lungs. And then my mouth found his—grinding down against it, sucking the life force out of his body, demanding his complete surrender.

His stiff dick was poking into my thigh, and mine against his. I grabbed a handful of firm pec and squeezed hard. He whimpered, clutched my hairy buttocks, thrust his groin against mine. He began to sweat. Moist, salty droplets running down his brow, flavoring our kisses. I let my tongue roam over his face—his cheeks, his forehead. He began to tremble.

"Suck me, Big Daddy."

I manhandled him down onto the bed and pounced on his awesome, uncut dick. Consuming it in one fell swoop and filling my throat with his maleness, I let my nose nuzzle into his blond pubic curls. He gasped, ground his balls against my chin, and fucked my throat. Slow, measured thrusts deliberate in their intensity, stuffing my face, stretching my cavity till it was fit to burst. Reluctantly, I felt

I had to pull back. My fingers played along the length of his slick, rock-hard cock, right up to the tip. I gripped his heavy foreskin and pulled it forward to fully cover the bulbous crimson helmet. Holding it in place, I forced my tongue under the light fold of skin, poking and swirling my tongue beneath his silken coverlet. He pressed his lips together, breathing out in short, sharp bursts. Wrapping his powerful thighs around my chest, he hooked his feet at the ankle, resting them over my broad back, and began to squeeze.

Letting my tongue play over his smooth, hairless ball sac, I worked my way to his inner thighs, running the tip over prominent veins pushed to the surface by the surfeit of muscle. He spread his thighs wider to accommodate my explorations and finally unhooked his ankles, lifting them high and wide to present his shaved butt crack and his hot little hole for my inspection. I pried his solid buttocks wide and buried my face in the crevice, licking and sucking and feasting on his manhole. His response was vocal and physical; even as he started to growl he was pressing the back of my head deeper into him. There was no real need for him to pile on the pressure, though—my tongue was already one jump ahead of him.

I finally came up for air, and he flipped over onto his belly, grinding his erection against the bedsheet, his ass rising and falling.

"You want me to fuck you?"

He looked over his shoulder, nonplussed. "You want it in writing? Yeah, Big Daddy, I want you to fuck me. And how."

I greased up his ass with lube. His tight ring-piece dilated at the touch of my fingertips, welcoming first one slick finger, then a second, then a third. Actively passive, he pushed back to consume all that I offered and then some. Finally he was holding his buttocks wide.

"Stick it in, Big Daddy. Just fuckin' stick it in!"

I positioned the tip of my cock up against his hole and pushed, watched as his ring opened to welcome the fat mushroom head of my dick. Swallowing it in one gulp. Then slowly, inch by inch by inch, I eased the fullness of my stiff, throbbing pole into the depths of him. Taking my time, watching it slowly disappear, right up to my come-filled nuts. Stretching him wide. I slid out equally slowly, then plunged my cock back in up to the hilt.

Fucking him hard—in and out—setting up a rhythm. Each time I pulled out, he let out a long moan; as I thrust into him, he buried his face into the pillow and gasped. Becoming more vocal with each thrust.

"Oh, yeah, Big Man. Fill me up. Fill me right up. All the way. All the…"

I began to increase my pace. Sweat dripped from my brow and splashed onto his magnificent ass. Forward and back, forward and back. He struggled up onto his knees, his face still buried in the pillow, and began to rock backward, his beefy buttocks matching my every thrust. I let my hands glide over his taut ass cheeks, squeezing them, cupping them. Two solid hunks of muscle under a velvet coating. Warm to the touch, burning with desire. I slammed into him, my balls slapping against him. Big balls swinging, heavy with come, swollen with desire.

He spit on his hand, then began to jerk on his own length. Beating his meat in rhythm with mine. His groans grew ever louder, building inexorably with the increasing force of his backward thrusts. His triceps flexing as he hammered on his power tool. "I'm gonna come, Big Daddy. Oh, yeah. Fuck, yeah!"

His back arched as the first blast of his warm, pungent man juice splattered onto the sheets beneath him. Then a second. Then a third… And with each pulse his sphincter tightened around my shaft, urging me to shoot my load too. To shoot my big, creamy load. To fill him up with my Big Daddy jizz. There was to be no argument from me. The unmistakable rumbling deep in my balls drove the point home. I knew that I was about to erupt too. And as my balls reached boiling point, ropes of steaming come exploded deep in his asshole. Deep into the muscular heart of him. Bucking my hips. Slamming into him. Bucking and slamming and coming.

I slept on the wet patch he had so generously deposited on the mattress. It seemed like no sacrifice under the circumstances. Micha snuggled up to me, his head on my chest, snoring gently. Sweet dreams. I woke to find him dressed, perched on the edge of my bed, lost in contemplation. He swung around when I reached out to touch his arm and planted a sloppy kiss on my forehead.

"My instincts were good."

I raised my eyebrows, puzzled. "Sorry?"

"You do know how to use that big thing." Micha reached out and gave my dick an affectionate tug. Then with a hint of regret he stood up. "Oh, well. Guess I better be going."

"Go where?"

"Find a place to stay. Got to check on a couple of possibilities…"

Time for me to follow my instincts. "I've got a spare room."

"I wouldn't want to put you out…" he said.

"You wouldn't. Stay until you find a place. Of course, I would expect you to earn your keep."

He grinned. "And just how would I go about doing that?"

"Well, for one thing, I could do with a training partner."

"And for another?"

"I could use a pair of good strong hands to help out in the bar."

"And for another?"

"You are one fabulous fuck."

Micha shrugged. Smiled. "So…where do I put my bags?"

CU @ 1

Thom Wolf

Sticky summer heat had invaded my bones; my mind and my body were in a restless place. Working from home in the summer is real pain. Winters are effortless. When the days are murky and wet I can board myself up in the study and pound my keyboard from 9 till 6. But it's hard to be so disciplined when the sun is glaring against the monitor and, even with the windows wide open, there's not the smallest breath of air stirring my workplace.

Libido is a great inhibitor of productivity too, and on a hot afternoon all I want to do is strip naked and allow my cock to throb. I'd got into the habit of jerking off first thing in the morning—beating off a speedy load before switching on the PC gave my mind a respite from sex. I could usually manage a few pages before the sap started to rise again around lunchtime. As the day really starts to warm up it gets harder to concentrate on the job.

Some days another session with my hand is all it takes to quiet the ache and get me back to work. But often that's not enough. On the days that my cock won't let me concentrate I have to give in to it and try to make up that lost time in the evening. It's a good thing I'm self-employed. I can't see another boss being so understanding when I announce, "I'm taking the afternoon off. I'm too horny to work."

In all honesty, I hate those days. I'll grasp at anything that will take my mind off sex: letter writing, e-mails, phone messages, research. Anything.

It was one of those balmy mornings, just as my cock was starting to rise again, that I noticed the envelope icon on my cell phone. I had a text message. I clicked into the menu and accessed the message. The number was unfamiliar. The content of the message was even more unusual.

"Hi," it read. "One o'clock at Saints. I'm looking forward to it. I could use an active boy's cock up my ass. Rico."

I laughed. Rico had the wrong number. Saints was a bar down by the river. I'd been in there only a couple of times. It was pretty nice—modern, trendy, a place for the beautiful. It sounded like someone was planning the kind of afternoon I could do with myself. I set about composing an answer to Rico's message, a cheeky reply to let him know he'd made a mistake. I'd hate for the poor guy to miss out on a good shafting on account of one wrong number.

I'd got no further than hitting "answer" when my cock put a stop to my honorable intention. Rico wanted a cock up his ass, and I wanted to empty my balls into something other than my fist. He might have sent his message to the wrong cell phone, but it didn't have to spell disappointment.

I should have called him back and pointed out the mistake. I should have asked him whether he wanted to meet me instead. But I didn't. The anonymity of turning up blind and surprising him excited me. Besides, it gave me a getaway. If Rico was a dog, I could slip away unseen. Cruel and selfish, but so what? He should have been more careful with his numbers.

Saints wasn't far from my apartment—two stops on the bus and a five-minute walk. I got there before 1. The bar was incorporated into what had originally been the vaults of an old indoor market, long since redeveloped. The red brickwork and high arches had been restored, and the large two-story bar was full of inlays and cozy corners. Floor-to-ceiling windows filled the interior with natural light and granted an amazing view of the river.

The place was two-thirds full—mainly businesspeople in

suits. A handful of guys, like myself, were looking casual.

I took a slow wander to the bar, straying through the tables, looking for the man who wanted fucking so badly. All I knew was his name. I trusted my instincts; gay men are adept at locating each other in crowded rooms. If he was there, I would find him.

Nothing worth the effort. A couple of admiring glances from the suits—not my type. I don't do married men, however good they look. It was early. I went to the bar and got a beer while I waited. I remained standing, one elbow on the counter, turned toward the door to see who came in.

An abstract dance track was blaring over the room. I drank my beer, wallowing in the synthesized beats. Waiting. Starting to feel stupid. What the hell possessed me? This was like the plot of a Hollywood comedy: Julia Roberts would mistakenly receive a text message from the man of her dreams and after 90 minutes of screwball comedy she'd live happily ever after. I didn't want twee romance; I wanted porno. It wasn't going to happen.

I was finishing off my beer, resigned to a session with my fist, when a guy walked through the door. He stood for a moment, looking around uncertainly, before sitting down at empty table.

I was thinking with my cock again, praying that this was my careless messenger. The sight of him made my heart stop beating for a second; when it recommenced my pulse was rapid. From where he sat I could see him in profile. He looked at his watch, gazed around the room. Back at his watch.

He was young—maybe 19 or 20—and pretty, with Latino features. His hair was dark and glossy, hanging heavily across his brow, the fringe just a centimeter or so above his eyebrows. His nose was small and straight, and from the other side of the room I could see that his lips were large and juicy. I was already imaging that mouth stretching around my cock, desperate to please me. He was wearing red jeans and a blue sleeveless T-shirt with white piping that displayed his perfect, muscular arms. There was a retro '80s look to his appearance that reminded me of the old Jeff Stryker films I used to watch. He was wearing white socks too.

When I fuck him, I thought, *I'm going to make him leave the T-shirt and socks on.*

I took out my cell phone and hit redial.

His telephone rang at the same time.

Jackpot.

"Hello," he answered in an accented voice.

"Rico?"

"Yes. Who is this?"

"I have to tell you that there's been some mistake. I received a text message from you this morning that may have been intended for somebody else."

There was a beat before he said, "Oh." I saw his brown cheeks darken.

"I should have called you earlier," the words tumbled out, "but I wanted to see you. I wanted to see what you looked like. I wanted to see the boy who needed a cock up his ass so badly. I'm not the man you thought I was. But Rico, I've got a cock that would love to get inside that cute ass of yours."

If he hangs up, I thought, *I'm leaving without looking back.*

"Where are you?" he asked.

"Standing at the bar. Brown hair, blue shirt."

Rico turned. After a beat, he smiled. "Do you have a place to go?"

"It's not far."

Less than an hour later we were back at my apartment. The afternoon heat had not relented. I opened the living room windows and put on some music. Rico stood awkwardly in the middle of the room. His arms hung loosely at his sides as though he did not know what to do with them.

"Are you free for the afternoon?" I asked him.

"I have to be home by 7."

Fantastic. Not only was I going to fuck this young beauty, but I could take my time doing it. "How old are you?" I asked.

"Twenty," he said, now caressing his abdomen through his T-shirt.

"Gotta get home to Mommy and Daddy?"

Steady eyes. A twitch of the lips. "Just Daddy," he said.

So he was somebody else's boy. I liked it.

"Who were you supposed to meeting today?"

He smiled, a mischievous glint in his dark eyes. "Just a guy I met on the Internet. We exchanged numbers and photographs, but I haven't met him before."

"He must be pissed off at missing you."

He licked his juicy lips. "He'll get his chance another time."

"Does Daddy know his little boy is a whore for other men?"

A shrug. "Daddy doesn't know everything."

"Take off your jeans," I told him.

Smiling, maintaining eye contact, Rico unfastened his jeans. As the zipper loosened I caught a glimpse of hair; he wasn't wearing any underwear. My cock leaped.

"Wait," I said, before he could shuffle his jeans down. "Turn around."

"What for?"

"Just do it."

I moved closer, putting a hand in the middle of his back and forcing him over. He knew what I wanted, putting his hands on the arm of the chair and supporting himself. I glanced down his back, catching an eyeful of crack through the loose waist of his jeans. There was a two-inch swath of brown skin at the base of his spine before his ass began. The skin down his back to his buttocks was a uniform color; there was no tan line. I slid a hand into his jeans, feeling hot ass flesh against my palm. His skin was moist with perspiration. He gave a little moan and pressed his hips back, lifting his ass onto my hand. I cupped a cheek. The flesh was firm. Soft hair, getting denser near the crack. Hotter. Wetter.

"You like it?" he asked. I murmured assent, giving his ass a squeeze.

I hitched his jeans down his thighs, wanting an eyeful of ass. My God, it was perfect. A creamy brown bubble butt split right down the center by a lush spread of glossy black hair. I gasped. It was divine, shimmering in the afternoon sun with a mist of sweat. He wiggled his hips in my face. I kissed the skin on the back of his thigh, just below his ass, teasing him, making him wait for what we both wanted. He tasted fresh and salty, better than a chicken dinner. He bent right over on the chair, thrusting his bubble butt into my face. I spread him with both hands, watching. I found his rosebud, small and brown, in a soft bed of fur. It stretched, speaking to me, as I pulled his cheeks apart. He groaned when I licked him, skirting right over the pouting lips. I circled it, swirling the hair around with my tongue before moving in for a taste of his cherry. My mouth was right over it, and my tongue pressed against its surface, feeling it twitch, promising greatness. I licked, kissed, sucked, and finally penetrated, pushing deep, as if my tongue were a little cock. My nose was right up against his crack, inhaling his moist bouquet.

I pulled back a little, sucked a finger, and plunged it into him, smoothly, up to the knuckle. It made him gasp. I watched my finger move past the brown rim into the rose colored interior. I wriggled it a little, twisting, feeling the confident response of his warm rectum. Rico moaned, moving his ass in rhythm with my hand.

I withdrew and pulled his jeans all the way off. His shoes too. The socks and T-shirt remained. After a moment of uncertainty he warmed to the idea. Probably fancied himself a porn star, I imagine. I stood up, unzipped, tugged out my cock. I told him to kneel and slapped him across the face with it. The dripping head left a slivery trail across his beautiful, unblemished cheek.

"Suck," I said, hitching my shirt up around my abs.

His full mouth glistened as he moved close, licking his lips. He wrapped a hand around the shaft—firm but not too tight—and put his mouth straight over the head. His tongue swirled, licking up the precome that covered the head. I felt myself swell, oozing more. His lips bulged around my meat. He moved down the shaft, swallowing. His nostrils flaring. I'm a big boy, but he was full of experience, sliding his tongue down the throbbing underside.

"Nice boy," I murmured. "Very nice."

Encouraged, he stretched his jaw wider, managing to swallow more of me. He hitched my jeans and underwear lower, greedy fingers grabbing at my hairy balls. He tugged my nuts, giving a little twist, feeding more of my cock into his mouth. I brushed the silky hair away from his forehead. Chocolate-brown eyes looked upward as he sucked. He was a total submissive. I felt the veins pumping in my cock; I held his head still and humped his mouth. He let go of my balls and steadied himself against my thighs, head tilted to take me deep.

I knew that I was going to come and wondered about letting up a little. *What the hell,* I thought, *I can afford to blow a load.* With this little pup around I was unlikely to lose any hardness afterward. I let him suck me right up to the final instant before pulling out. I blasted straight into his face. Rico closed his eyes as the first surge splattered his forehead. A second landed high up on his left cheek. Brilliant white fluid dribbled over creamy brown skin. A third spurt went broad across his nose. My knees shuddered as I took in the sublime image of his angelic face dripping with my ball juice. I got down beside him, catching him off-guard when I held his head in both hands and slowly licked the cream off his face. He broke into a broad smile while I washed him clean.

I lifted the young guy up onto a chair and pulled him to the edge. I drew his T-shirt back a little to reveal a flat abdomen. A trail of silky hair began below his navel and trickled down, widened to a dense, curly bush in his groin. His cock was bigger than I expected—generous and fleshy. The foreskin opened over a dark pink head, tiny little lips glistening with sticky sap. I put my mouth over it, feeling it pulse, tasting his savory freshness. Rico groaned. Going down to the fleshy root was easy. I drew back and forth, sucking him top to bottom. I jiggled his hairy balls in my palm, squeezing, not too tight, just enough to make his cock twitch and slather more precome into my mouth. His balls grew heavy and tight. Waiting right until the end before moving back. I jerked him to finish.

He hitched his T-shirt up around his nipples before unleashing a furious volley of come across his tight little belly. His face tensed, full lips drawn back from white teeth. He spermed all over his taut skin. Milky liquid pooled in the hollows of muscle and in his navel. The tension edged out of his pretty features and he closed his eyes, smiling now. There was a robust blush to his brown cheeks.

"Oh, God," he sighed heavily. "I needed that."

His come started to lose its white brilliance, becoming translucent. I kissed his sweaty thighs, softly on either side, before rubbing his come into his skin. I massaged it into the flesh like an expensive beauty cream. He lay back in the chair, legs open, watching me through lidded eyes. "You don't like wasting that stuff, do you?" he grinned.

"Never if I can help it."

My cock was still hard, just as I'd hoped it would be. Rico's too, jutting up from its bed of thick curls. That's what I love most about young guys: stamina. "I'm gonna sort out that problem you were having with your asshole now," I said.

Rico grinned. "It's a major problem. It could take some work."

I lifted him off the chair and set him down on the floor. He was on his knees, elbows resting on the seat of the chair, his muscled ass cheeks spreading naturally. Rico reached behind, one hand on his butt, spreading it wider. "There it is," he said. "Fuck me."

I pulled a condom over my throbbing dick and fisted a handful of lube over the shaft. Rico lifted his ass higher, and I squeezed the tube over his tiny hole, juicing him up. I shoved the lube into him with fingers, twisting, pushing it deep into the passage. He started moaning when I rubbed my cock up and down his crack, pressing against the opening. "Tell me that you want it."

"I want it. Fuck me, man. Put that cock in my ass and fuck me senseless."

I pushed in, past the resistance of his ass muscles, feeling the sphincter give up and let me in there. I was all the way inside, slipping down his passage. I held his tiny waist and rooted my cock in his ass. His back arched beneath the tight blue T-shirt, and he shoved his butt back against me. I exhaled, savoring the press of warm buns against my hips. "Does my cock feel nice in your ass? Is that what you wanted?"

"It's all I've ever wanted."

I fucked him with long, controlled strokes, strokes that grazed the warm, juicy lining of his insides. One hand on his hip, the other buried in his hair, pulling his head right back. He was nice and sweaty; clear beads formed on his face and on his ass, rolling down his coffee skin. It would be easy to love a boy like this, a boy who wants nothing more than to be ridden hard and deep.

"Do you like fucking me?" he asked, his voice going higher with each thrust. "Is my ass good enough for you?"

"I love fucking you," I assured him, leaning forward to whisper right into his ear. "Are you gonna tell your daddy how much I love fucking you?"

"Daddy doesn't have to know."

He smiled. I turned his head so I could kiss him. His tongue came out of his mouth and into mine. I sucked it. I ran my hands around his body, pinching his nipples through his T-shirt, feeling the tight lines of his stomach. We were burning up.

I pulled out of him to change position. As I sat in the chair, he climbed up on top of me, facing away, and sat down, swallowing my cock with his ass. He rode the full length of me, digging his heels into the soft cushions and bouncing up and down my shaft. His T-shirt was stained with sweat all down the back. I could have sat there all day just watching my cock coming in and out of his bubble ass. The hair around his opening fascinated me.

He climbed off and we got down on the floor. Rico lay on his back and I moved on top of him, sliding back inside. I could feel his heart beating solidly against my chest. His eyes were opening, looking into my face, full of bliss. I was pumping faster, rabbit-fucking him with short, sharp jabs. He was moaning, licking the sweat from his lips. His cock was a pole between our bellies, precome forming a slick amalgam with our sweat. He was responding with the whole of his body, lifting his hips from the floor, humping back, wanting every brutal inch of me. Hands clawed into my ass, drawing us tighter together. I covered his mouth with mine. This could go on forever.

"Shh," I said when I could feel myself coming, not yet ready. We froze, suspended in time, waiting for the profound sense of pleasure to pass. When it was safe I started thrusting again, building back up to the rabbit-fuck pace. Rico's face was screwed up tight, except for his mouth, which was open wide, gasping. Once again I rode him to a hair-width of orgasm before stopping, waiting for the moment to subside. He had wanted a solid fuck, and that's what I was determined to give him. There's nothing a bottom hates more than a top who comes too soon.

I rode him deeper and savored the tension of his legs wrapped tight around my back. "I'm gonna come," he cried, squeezing his thighs like a man possessed. He was rubbing his cock off against my stomach. I buried my hard-on far into his ass; sweat poured off my face and onto his. He shuddered and bucked. I felt the wet heat of his come on my stomach. I relaxed and let my own orgasm surge out of my cock and into him. Intense. My body trembled. My heart felt like it was coming through my rib cage.

Within an hour we were doing it again. A frenzied, passionate fuck that made my bedsprings squeal like a slaughtered pig. More sweat. More positions. More come. So much come that my dick felt raw when I withdrew it from his gaping red hole. Earlier, when we started, it had been a tight, perfect rosebud. Now, after an afternoon of heart-stopping sex, it was more like a mushy piece of fruit.

He crawled into my arms, resting his wet head on my chest. He was still wearing the T-shirt and socks. Later he took them off to shower. I gave him one of my own shirts to wear on the way home.

"Thanks," he said, running his fingers through his damp hair.

"Wanna do this again?" I asked from the bed.

Rico was standing in the doorway, ready to leave. "I've got your number," he smiled, closing the door on his way out.

Piggy

Van Scott

OK. I'm going to start over, just to refresh your memories. What are we dealing with here? Fucked-up people, right? And me? I'm 19, fucked-up, and I've got my head up my ass as well. It's a who-screws-who party with me doing everyone and getting done by everyone.

How long have I been doing this? I know America isn't Eastern Europe, but it comes pretty close sometimes. I was young when I started.

I had a dream last night. Some people wanted me to teach a scuba-diving class. I've never scuba-dived before so I thought they were crazy. The people seemed pretty convinced I could do it. I wasn't so sure.

It's too bad that the most unattractive men are usually the smartest. It doesn't say much about me, but it's true: The piggiest-looking ones usually act like pigs. I always thought that the way a person looked corresponded to some kind of order in the universe. Like if you were perfect-looking, then you had to be sort of perfect inside. And those who are less than perfect on the outside must also be less than perfect on the inside. Are you with me so far?

Maybe that explains why I treat piggy men like pigs. Of course, you know that even real pigs aren't so bad in comparison to certain human beings. Sure, it's the pot calling the kettle black, but that's me.

About one particular pig I have the following description: He was of average height, but one could see he was far too intelligent for his own good. How could I tell? By the way he couldn't look anyone directly in the eye—particularly me—while he was trying to get me to consider. A shrewd and essentially fucked-up character, this piggy was. At first I didn't want anything to do with him.

"You take Porky Pig," I said to a richly endowed friend of mine.

"No, he's yours," he said. It depended ,of course, on who Porky wanted: Super 10-inch or me.

He was balding and had a small, upturned nose (what else), plus small, beady eyes and short, stubby fingers. He didn't dress too piggishly, though; Piggy was rather turned out. The tweed suit fit him even though the collar was too tight and his round belly was bursting a few buttons here and there.

He was dawdling at the bar. Any hustler worth his salt can identify his mark.

He'd take a quick sip of his drink, his little eyes darting to and fro. He was going to take my ass and treat it like a truffle—I could see that. I imagined him rooting away in it. No innocence there, I can't help but see them for what they are (porkers).

Intelligent people aren't always that patient, and Piggy was no exception. Again my friend left me to the wolves.

When it came down to him and me, Piggy would not look me in the eye.

I stood stock-still with a corner of my mouth turned up.

What next? A trite dialogue followed. His name was Fredrick, which somehow fit him. I gave him the standard bullshit, and he took it in and kept glancing over his shoulder like he was waiting for someone to join him. He wanted to drink and talk, said he was "nerv- ous." Looked like he had just come from somewhere where he'd done something naughty. *Naughty Mr. Piggy, what are you doing out so late at night chasing boys?* I thought. I pegged him as a cheating-on- the-wife type. A pillar of society, except when he was coyly eyeing illegal rough trade; I was sure he could easily be found sticking knives into unsuspecting hustlers' insides—a specialty fetish, you might say.

I have too much imagination, and I know it. Well, shit, standing around and looking at these faces can set a guy's mind tripping. Imagination makes up more than three quarters of reality anyway.

I tried the old trick of getting him to light my cigarette; then looked at his watch. "Is that a Rolex?" I asked.

"A Rolex?" He asked sounding perplexed. "Don't be ridiculous," he said. "It's just a Longines."

Just a Longines. But a nice Longines. "What time does it say?" I asked.

"It says 11:25," he said. *What a waste of a night this is going to be,* I thought.

You could see he wasn't taking the bait. He needed to get sloshed first. Then his greedy little mouth was going to open and sleazy propositions would fall out. But I made it easy for the prick—I propositioned him.

He was no virgin, just hung up with psychological complexes that fags sometimes have. (Remember the phrase "closets kill"?) He spoke in low, furtive tones, as if I might have a tape recorder hidden on me and might be in the blackmail business, which I'm not, in case you're wondering. "What's your figure?" He asked.

I did the routine. Stating that I was not a urinal or a place to ejaculate into. Perhaps the crudeness of my language shocked him, but he said OK.

"We're going to my place," he said. My friend Robbie was busy making faces at me off in the distance. I grinned and left.

It was nice him having his own place; I could curl up in a ball and go to sleep, maybe. I wouldn't turn down a penthouse there if it were offered to me. He had no wife, just a cat. He could very well be a fag, I realized. He seemed nervous. Guess he couldn't believe he was getting what he wanted, finally.

These kinds of situations often freak me out. When there are no glitches you wonder whether something's up. He was a quiet, polite pig. I was waiting for the nasty stuff to appear.

He wasn't exactly butch. He gave me something to wear: a bright yellow pair of bathing trunks with a white line down the sides.

"Try these on," he said. They fit. He looked pleased. We'd talked cash, and he'd paid without a whimper. I was looking for a diversion, and he pulled out a little spoon and fed my nose with white powder. We were bonding.

He didn't change in his private sphere, still the furtiveness and that inability to catch one's eye. You could see he was up to something. I couldn't help but feel like a piece of flesh picked out at the local butcher.

"So, my boy, what's next?"

"It's up to you," I answered.

"Well, what does one ordinarily do in these situations?" he asked. I found a station I liked on the stereo and he poured me a drink. Then I danced for him in his living room. It was just me dancing, not the romantic kind where two people cling to each other while sappy music plays. I wanted to show him that I didn't care one way or another.

He came over and reached out his hand, like Adam in the Garden of Eden to touch the forbidden fruit.

He caressed my cock through the swimsuit. A soft, tentative caress. He couldn't seem to move his hand elsewhere. And I wasn't about to make it easier for him.

I could take off the suit and watch an SHO movie. That was his suggestion. Cornball, but so what.

"What's on?" I asked. He threw me the TV guide.

"Have a look." I did another line of coke and perused the movie listings.

"You must work out," he said. "You have quite a physique."

"I scuba-dive once in a while," I said.

"Oh, really?"

"Yep."

"I like to swim," he said.

How romantic. It was all fitting into his fantasy. "What exactly do you do?" I asked.

"Well, it's rather complicated," he said. "It has to do with the stock market." Oh. Only an asshole would think otherwise. It was clear that he'd been looking at a computer screen for the last 15 years. Porn.

"You're not married, are you?" I asked. I was in the bedroom. The trunks were still on. The remote was in my hand. He was in the kitchen.

"Oh, no," he called out. "Why would you say that?" He stood in the doorway and I could see that he'd removed his pants.

His ridiculous little legs were crossed at the ankles; one hand was on a hip.

"Well I don't know," I said. "You just don't seem—gay." But all of a sudden he seemed gay. I turned my eyes to the TV screen. *The Texas Chainsaw Massacre* was on IFC. I changed the channel.

I don't think I was being paid to watch cable. *Guilty as Sin* was on channel 55.

I found him in the kitchen dancing next to the refrigerator. He had a glass in his hand and short gray socks on his feet. A tight pair of white boxers did a poor job of containing his bulging stomach and equipment. I needed a refill and reached for the icebox.

"You're a prince!" he sang out. "Did anybody ever tell you that?"

"Once in awhile," I said. "Do you mind if I get some ice cubes?"

"Not at all, help yourself." I was getting the ice cube tray when he suddenly started touching my shoulders.

"You must show me how you swim, someday."

"Sure," I said.

"Perhaps we could go to the shore together."

"There's a good movie on," I said. "It's about this guy who marries rich women and then murders them."

"Really?" he said, doubtfully.

"It's got Don Johnson in it."

"Oh, that queen," he said. "Would you care for a little more coke?"

"Sure," I said. I'd fallen into some kind of role with Piggy. It was too easy. He wasn't all that bad, but he acted a little like an asshole. I'd taken him for someone a little more serious. He was a little plucked, over-the-hill peacock who stood in front of mirrors, and there wasn't much to coo about.

"Do you think we could rent a car and drive to the shore one of these days?" he asked.

Summer was months away.

"Sure," I said.

"Selwyn," he said suddenly. "You know, we are not here just to talk." I was on the bed watching the movie. Rebecca DeMornay had Don Johnson hanging by his fingers.

"Well, you suggested it," I said.

"I know," he said. "But I'm feeling a little...neglected."

I could hang here, I thought, *if he'd only leave.*

"Come here," I said, patting my side of the bed. He sat down next to me and ran a hand tentatively down my leg.

"Let's take these off," he said. The trunks came off.

Suddenly he switched into overdrive. I don't know what his problem was—something must have broken the restraints in him, drink probably. Or the prospect of dick being so near. Whatever the case, once he caught a glimpse of my pecker he was like an escaped convict in a whorehouse.

I practically had to beat him off me with my fists. He was a priapic pig intent upon sticking it in and telling me how good it was going to be.

I grabbed his hands and told him I didn't deserve to be treated this way. He acted surprised and hurt. "Well, you have to do what I say," he said.

"Says who?" He pulled some string out of a drawer. "What's that for?"

"It's for bad boys who don't know any better," he said.

I had my face down in the pillows. My ass was in the air, and he was...well, doing what pigs do.

Whoa. I almost laughed. He huffed and he puffed, and he snuffed his way in. Then he yelled, "I'm coming!" That stupid string was around my wrists, decorating them.

I thanked God when it was over. But I was hard for some reason, and he smiled when he saw that.

"Don't worry," he said, "I have just the solution."

He didn't seem to know how to give head, so I pushed him off me. "Let me do it," I said. "Take these fucking strings off me."

I did one of my lightning-fast hand jobs, then said, "Now, if you'll excuse me, I think I'll take a shower."

"There's food in the fridge," he said as I headed for the bathroom.

Did Piggy make me feel good about myself? Not really. Being looked at and admired by a john was tantamount to looking in a mirror all the time. You get tired of seeing the same old thing. Besides, he was ugly as a car wreck.

When I came out of the bathroom he wanted to graduate into something more hard-core. He was swigging alcohol from a bottle and talking about videotaping me "for his personal records."

"I'm no porn star," I told him.

"But you could be," he said. Just like he could be a jackass. Watching TV suited me better.

He kept indiscreetly grabbing my pecker, and I thought it would serve him right if I bashed his head in. Maybe every john deserves his head bashed in. But that was his bag, anyway. I mean— pushing someone to the limit.

We were on the bed, getting sloshed. Another movie was on— *Midnight in the Garden of Good and Evil*—though I didn't catch most of it because he had me tied and wanted to stick things in my ass. I was OK with that as long as he didn't try to go for a hard-core anal fuck. But of course he tried. When I cursed him he seemed to hold his breath and wait for more. Then he was the one who was tied up and I was sticking things up his ass.

Pretty humdrum.

Suddenly, out of nowhere, I felt this urge to hurt him for real.

I knocked him on the side of the head with a see-through glass unicorn paperweight he had lying around. He gasped, looked at me in disbelief, then fell back on the bed. That was easy. It wasn't like I did it all the time, but it was damn easy nonetheless.

I took a look around, now that I was alone all of a sudden. I wanted to see what I might pocket. His watch, of course. He was moaning on the bed. Apparently he'd live. I managed to get the watch off and decided to go through his wallet as well; it was in his jacket. Why, not? There were some $50 bills and a picture of him with a woman in there. Looked like a wife. He had a 1,000 lire note in among the bills and I took this as well. It seemed like a lot of money.

I walked out and left him like that. The lire bill came out to a measly 45 cents when I looked it up on the exchange. I got pissed off and gave it to a bleary-eyed bum sitting on the sidewalk examining two packages of bologna. The guy must've thought he'd hit it big. I laughed mercilessly as I imagined him trying to buy a bottle of hooch with it.

I didn't head for the hills, though I knew I might be in a pack of trouble. I took a three-week vacation. Went out to the country, where I got some peace and quiet, finally.

Pigs are hard to kill. I was to run into him some two months later. It was early summer and I was back in action, hanging in my usual haunt after having avoided the place for over a month. It seems he'd come around looking for me, but people told him I was no longer around.

He seemed altogether different when I saw him again. Still very much a pig but now happy.

"Well, look who's here," he said. I was in the middle of a conversation with someone.

"I'm sorry to butt in," he said, "but the lad and me need to have a word."

He grabbed hold of my arm and pulled me off to a corner. "You've got some nerve!" He said. "Hitting me on the head like that—you nearly killed me, you know. And taking my wallet. Don't you have anything to say for yourself?"

"No," I said.

"It's not too late for an apology," he said.

"Well, I'm sorry."

"You should say it more like you mean it."

"I'm sorry for almost bashing your head in," I said.

"That's better. Have you thought about professional counseling?"

"No," I said.

"What's the matter? he asked. "The Longines didn't pull in as much as you thought it would?

"On the contrary," I lied. "I traveled in style for quite some time on that little object alone." He was obviously not from New York and thus played by a different set of rules.

But it was a thief's game and there was no honor. So now where were we?

"You wouldn't happen to be in debt to an old man, would you?" he asked.

I stared back uncomprehendingly. Stupid me—at the time I didn't know that in a way I was in the process of being robbed. Of my innocence. A thief's comeuppance, someone would say.

"I don't know what you're talking about," I answered.

"Yes, you do," he said. His piggy face was practically in mine.

"You ungrateful little fuck!" he said. "What was the purpose of that?"

"Of what?" I asked.

"I treated you well," he said, "and what did I get?"

"You were acting like an idiot," I said.

"Don't talk back to me," he said. "As far as I can see you don't have a leg to stand on."

And neither did he, crazy queer.

"But you know what?" he said. His expression changed. Now he was smiling. "I'm going to let it slide...because you're my special boy."

"Fine," I said. "Why don't we have a drink. We have a lot of catching up to do." I humored the bastard, then gave him the slip, as he probably knew I would (if he didn't, then he *really* was hopeless). Sure I enjoyed sex once in a while, but I couldn't get off unless money was involved. It might sound sick to a lot of people. You could look it up in the DSM under the heading: "Can't come unless remuneration involved."

Contributor Biographies

A native Californian, **Bearmuffin** lives in San Diego with two leatherbears in a stimulating ménage à trois. He has written gay erotica for *Mandate, Honcho, Torso, Manscape,* and *Hot Shots.*

Dale Chase has been writing erotica for six years and has had nearly 100 stories published in *Freshmen, In Touch,* and *Indulge.* His work has appeared in a dozen anthologies, including a translation into German. One story has been acquired by Cinema Bravo and may some day reach the big screen. Chase lives near San Francisco.

M. Christian's work can be seen in *The Best American Erotica, Best Gay Erotica, Best Lesbian Erotica, Best Fetish Erotica, Best of Friction, Of the Flesh,* and more than 150 other books, magazines, and Web sites. He's the editor of over a dozen anthologies, including *The Burning Pen, Love Under Foot* (with Greg Wharton), *Rough Stuff* (with Simon Sheppard), *Roughed Up* (also with Simon Sheppard), and *Best S/M Erotica.* He's the author of three collections, including *Dirty Words* (gay erotica) and *Speaking Parts* (lesbian erotica). For more info, check out www.mchristian.com.

Bob Condron is the author of two erotic novels, *Easy Money* and *Sweating It Out.* His short stories have appeared in the likes of *Bear* magazine and numerous anthologies, including Alyson's *Sex Bud-*

dies and *Bearotica*. He lives in Germany with Tommy, his Irish huzbear.

Landon Dixon's writing has appeared online at Three Pillows.com, Thermoerotic.com, and elsewhere. He also has a story in the Alyson Books anthology *Straight? Volume 2*. He's a big guy with a sense of humor.

Todd Gregory is a New Orleans-based writer and unabashed slut who can frequently be found in the seedier bars of the French Quarter, wearing no shirt with a beer in one hand and a cigarette dangling from his lip while he looks for his next bit of erotic research. He considers erotica the most subversive form of writing being published today. He is currently working on an erotic thriller called *Sunburn* and coediting (with M. Christian) a volume of erotic vampire tales called *Bloodlust*.

Greg Herren is the author of *Murder in the Rue Dauphine* and *Bourbon Street Blues* and the editor of the anthologies *Full Body Contact, Shadows of the Night,* and the forthcoming *FratSex*. His work has been frequently anthologized, and his literary criticism has appeared in numerous publications. A former personal trainer, he currently works as the program coordinator for the Lesbian and Gay Community Center of New Orleans. He lives quietly with his partner of eight years in a delightful carriage house in the lower Garden District of New Orleans.

Michael Huxley, editorial director of STAR Books Press since April 2002, has assembled three anthologies of male literotica thus far: *Fantasies Made Flesh, Saints and Sinners,* and *Men, Amplified*—with a fourth, *Wet Nightmares, Wet Dreams,* well under way. Please feel free to contact Michael, for any reason whatsoever, at mikeh@starbooks-press.com.

Roddy Martin's work has appeared in volumes 1, 2, and 4 of *Friction, Best Gay Erotica 1998, Advocate Classifieds, Freshmen, In Touch, Indulge, Playguy, Blackmale,* and in magazines for teens and children.

Jim McDonough lives and writes smut in a house on a cul-de-sac in suburban South Florida. His fiction can be found online, in dozens of dirty magazines, and in anthologies such as *Quickies, Nature in the Raw, Saints & Sinners, Latin Boys,* and *Men, Amplified.* E-mail him at jim@queerwriters.com.

Attracted to husky, hairy men since birth, **Jay Neal** has been writing about them since late in the last century. His stories regularly appear in *American Bear* and *American Grizzly* magazines and have been published in the anthologies *Bearotica, Best Gay Erotica 2002* and *2003,* and others. He lives in suburban Washington, D.C.

The erotic fiction of **Christopher Pierce** has been published in *Three the Hard Way, Saints and Sinners, Sex Buddies, Latin Boys,* and *Friction 6.* He is currently coediting *Men on the Edge* with Michael Huxley for STARBooks Press. Write to him at chris@christopherpierceerotica.com and visit his Web site at www.ChristopherPierceErotica.com.

Scott D. Pomfret has published stories in many volumes of *Friction* as well as in *Genre* magazine, *Post Road, New Delta Review, Gertrude,* and many others. He and his boyfriend, Scott Whittier (also in this volume of *Friction*), have a line of hot new gay romance novels available at GreatScottsRomances.com.

"Life in upstate New York is proof that the erotic life flourishes in the most unlikely places," says **CB Potts.** A freelance writer for many years, Potts has done a great deal of investigation into what really happens during cold Adirondack nights. The results can be seen in *Options, Indulge, BlackFire,* and the recent Alyson anthology *Just the Sex.*

J.D. Roman is an inept but enthusiastic juggler living in Seattle with a mutt named Gumbo and a penchant for dark beer, dark chocolate, and dark, um, fantasies. Contact J.D. at ginproductions@hotmail.com.

Van Scott has a master's degree in philosophy from New York University. He has had short stories published in *Modern Words 7,* Spoon-FedAmerika.com (fall 2002), *Harrington Gay Men's Fiction Quarterly* (issue 3), and VelvetMafia.com (several issues). He is a native of New York and of Irish/Italian extraction. The piece featured here ("Piggy") is from part of a longer work titled *Curb's Eye View.*

Simon Sheppard is the author of *Kinkorama: Dispatches From the Front Lines of Desire* and the award-winning *Hotter Than Hell and Other Stories.* His next collection, *In Deep,* is coming soon from Alyson Books. Simon's work has been published in nearly 100 anthologies, including *The Best American Erotica 2004, Best Gay Erotica 2004,* and four previous volumes in the *Friction* series. He's also the coeditor, with M. Christian, of *Rough Stuff* and *Roughed Up.* He lives in San Francisco, and loiters quite shamelessly at www.simonsheppard.com.

Doug Smith writes short gay erotica in his spare time. His first story met with success and he has been hard at work since trying to sell more. You can find him on the beach or in the park in beautiful Vancouver, Canada, where he lives.

Also from Vancouver, Canada, **Jay Starre** has written for gay magazines including *Men, Honcho, Torso, American Bear,* and *Indulge,* and for anthologies including the *Friction* series, *Full Body Contact,* and *Twink* from Alyson. Regular exercise and plenty of sexual adventures allow him to keep working hard on all the hot stories he writes.

Karl Taggart started writing erotica several years ago and has had a few stories published in magazines and in *Friction 5* and *Friction 6.* He works for a suburban San Francisco insurance company. They have no idea a porn writer lurks in their midst.

Kyle Walker's "Sticks and Balls" originally appeared on Michael Broderick's Hottlead Web site (gay male erotic art) as winner of the fiction contest. It was inspired by one of the illustrations on the site (which involved a pool table).

Arizonan **Jack Whitestone** likes to weave tales from true stories. "I haven't much imagination," he freely admits."But life itself is imaginative enough." In "Arkansas Heat," he recounts his first sexual adventure with another man. The story was first published in *My First Time: Volume Three* from Alyson Books. When he is not spinning tales, Jack puts positive spins on news stories as part of his public relations work with a human services organization.

Scott Whittier is an advertising copywriter in Boston. He has published fiction in *Children Churches and Daddies, Playguy, In Touch,* and Alyson's anthology *Just the Sex.* Scott and his boyfriend (also named Scott, also in *Friction 7*) are the authors of a line of gay romances, available soon at GreatScottsRomances.com.

Thom Wolf is the author of *Words Made Flesh* and *The Chain.* He lives in the north of England with his boyfriend, Liam, and is working on his third erotic novel. Find out more or contact Thom at his Web page, http://hometown.aol.co.uk/twolfne.

Publication Information

Magazines

American Bear magazine ("Army Green," "Artful Fur") can be contacted at (216) 251-3330.

Boy Next Door ("All Soaped Up") can be contacted at Sportomatic Ltd., P.O. Box 392, White Plains, NY 10602 USA.

Indulge ("Limo Scene," "Payback," "Politically Incorrect," "Over the Moon," "Where the Buffalo Roam") can be contacted at (818) 764-2288.

In Touch ("Box Boy," "CU@1," "The Help") can be contacted at (800) 637-0101.

Mandate ("Special Delivery") can be contacted at (888) 664-7827.

Men ("Long Haul," "Shrinks") can be contacted at (800) 664-7827.

Playguy ("Trailer Park Punk," "Vulnerable Youth") can be contacted at (888) 664-7827.

Online

Dirty Boys Club ("The Downward Spiral") is available at www.dirtyboysclub.com

Hottlead ("Sticks and Balls") is available at www.home.earthlink.net/~hottlead/page1.html

Velvetmafia.com ("Piggy," "The Sea Where It's Shallow") is available at www.velvetmafia.com.